"My favorite part is when Hilo travels through galaxies. If I had to describe it in three words, I'd say it's **'SUCH A BLAST!'** D.J. is my favorite because he's a really good friend!"
—Matt A., age 10, Bloomfield, N.J.

"I love the Hilo books. Thank you so much! I really, **REALLY LOVE** the Hilo books."
—Angel O., age 10, Brooklyn

"**GINA WAS MY FAVORITE** character because she's into science and soccer like me! I also liked D.J.'s family because it looks like mine!"
—Kiran M., age 7, Carlsbad, Calif.

"*Hilo* is really cool and funny. It's **FUNNY** that he likes mangoes. You should read it because it's actually just **REALLY FUNNY!**"
—Gerard A., age 8, Bloomfield, N.J.

"**HIGH ENERGY** and **HILARIOUS**!"
—Gene Luen Yang, National Ambassador for Young People's Literature

"**FANTASTIC. EVERY SINGLE THING ABOUT THIS . . . IS TERRIFIC.**"
—Boingboing.net

"My students are obsessed with this series. **OBSESSED!**"
—Colby Sharp, teacher, blogger, and co-founder of the Nerdy Book Club

"More **GIANT ROBOTIC ANTS** . . . than in the complete works of Jane Austen."
—Neil Gaiman, author of *Coraline*

"Anyone who loves to laugh should read *Hilo*. It is **ACTION-PACKED** with a robotic touch."
—Breslin S., age 10, Jackson, Mich.

"*Hilo* is loads of **SLAPSTICK FUN!**"
—Dan Santat, winner of the Caldecott Medal

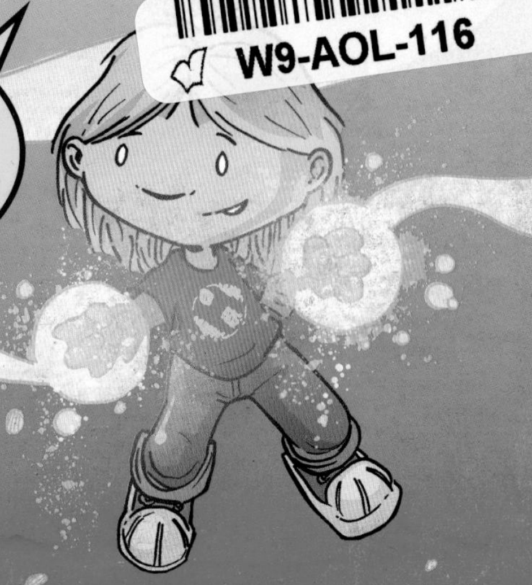

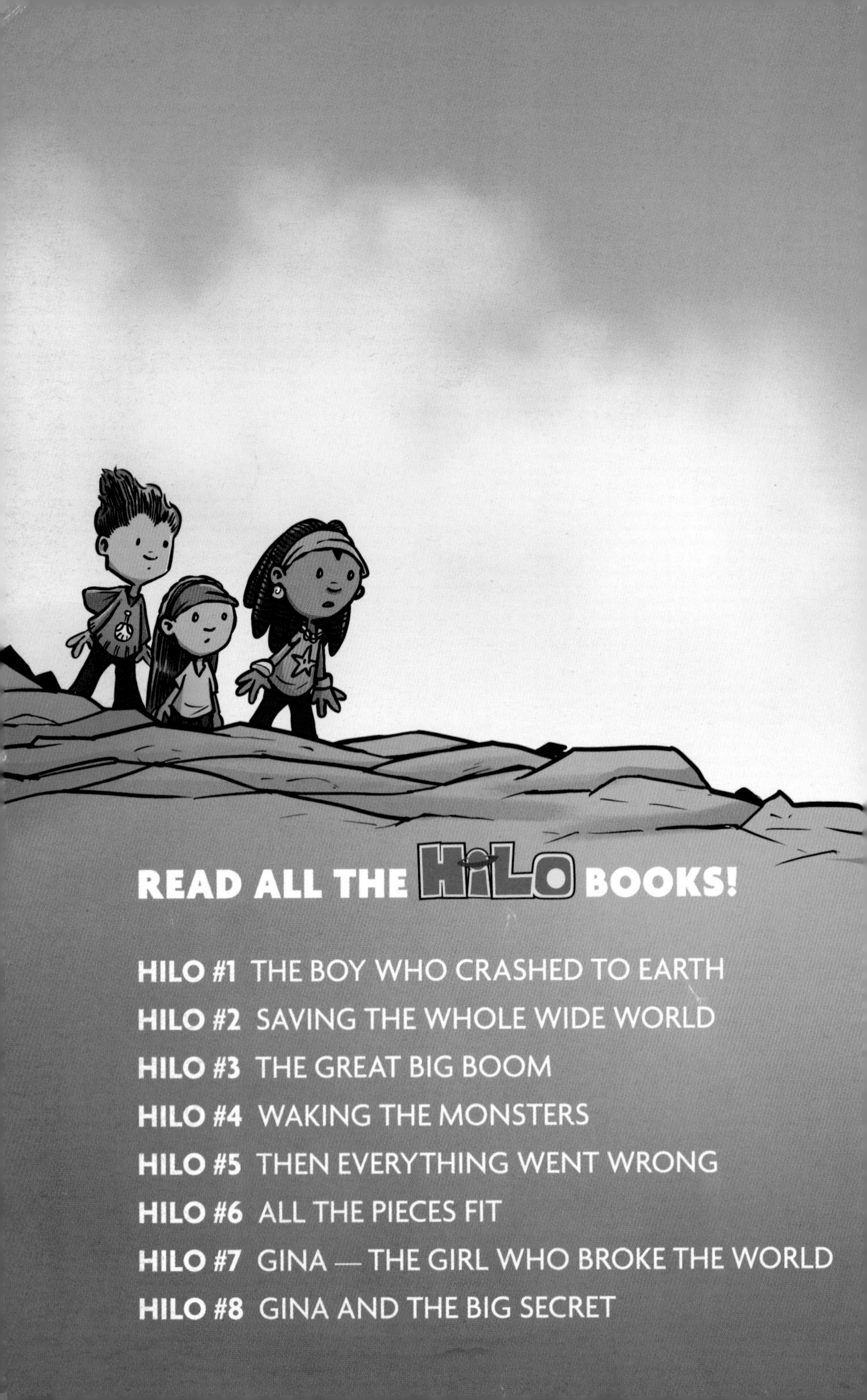

READ ALL THE HILO BOOKS!

HILO #1 THE BOY WHO CRASHED TO EARTH

HILO #2 SAVING THE WHOLE WIDE WORLD

HILO #3 THE GREAT BIG BOOM

HILO #4 WAKING THE MONSTERS

HILO #5 THEN EVERYTHING WENT WRONG

HILO #6 ALL THE PIECES FIT

HILO #7 GINA — THE GIRL WHO BROKE THE WORLD

HILO #8 GINA AND THE BIG SECRET

BOOK 8

HiLO

GiNA AND THE BIG SECRET

BY JUDD WINICK

COLOR BY
MAARTA LAIHO

RANDOM HOUSE 🏠 NEW YORK

With thanks to Shasta Clinch,
for her thoughtful feedback, insights,
and perspective

Copyright © 2022 by Judd Winick

All rights reserved. Published in the United States by Random House Children's Books, a division of Penguin Random House LLC, New York.

Random House and the colophon are registered trademarks of Penguin Random House LLC.

RH Graphic with the book design is a trademark of Penguin Random House, LLC.

Visit us on the Web! rhcbooks.com

Educators and librarians, for a variety of teaching tools, visit us at RHTeachersLibrarians.com

Library of Congress Cataloging-in-Publication Data
Names: Winick, Judd, author, illustrator. | Laiho, Maarta, colorist.
Title: Hilo. Book 8, Gina and the big secret / Judd Winick; color by Maarta Laiho.
Description: First edition. | New York: Random House Children's Books, [2022] | Series: Hilo; book 8
Summary: "The earth has been remade and magical creatures are everywhere—now Gina, DJ, and Hilo have to find the key to turn the world back to what it was" —Provided by publisher.
Identifiers: LCCN 2021016040 | ISBN 978-0-593-37966-0 (hardcover)
ISBN 978-0-593-37967-7 (library binding) | ISBN 978-0-593-37968-4 (ebook)
Subjects: LCSH: Graphic novels. | CYAC: Graphic novels. | Magic—Fiction.
Imaginary creatures—Fiction. | Science fiction.
Classification: LCC PZ7.7.W57 Hp 2022 | DDC 741.5/973—dc23

Book design by Bob Bianchini

MANUFACTURED IN CHINA

10 9 8 7 6 5 4 3 2 1

First Edition

Dedicated to all the
frontline health-care
workers

You are
our heroes.

CHAPTER 1

HANG ON

MY NAME IS REGINA LEE COOPER.
BUT EVERYONE CALLS ME GINA.
AND MY LIFE IS WEIRD.
HOW WEIRD?

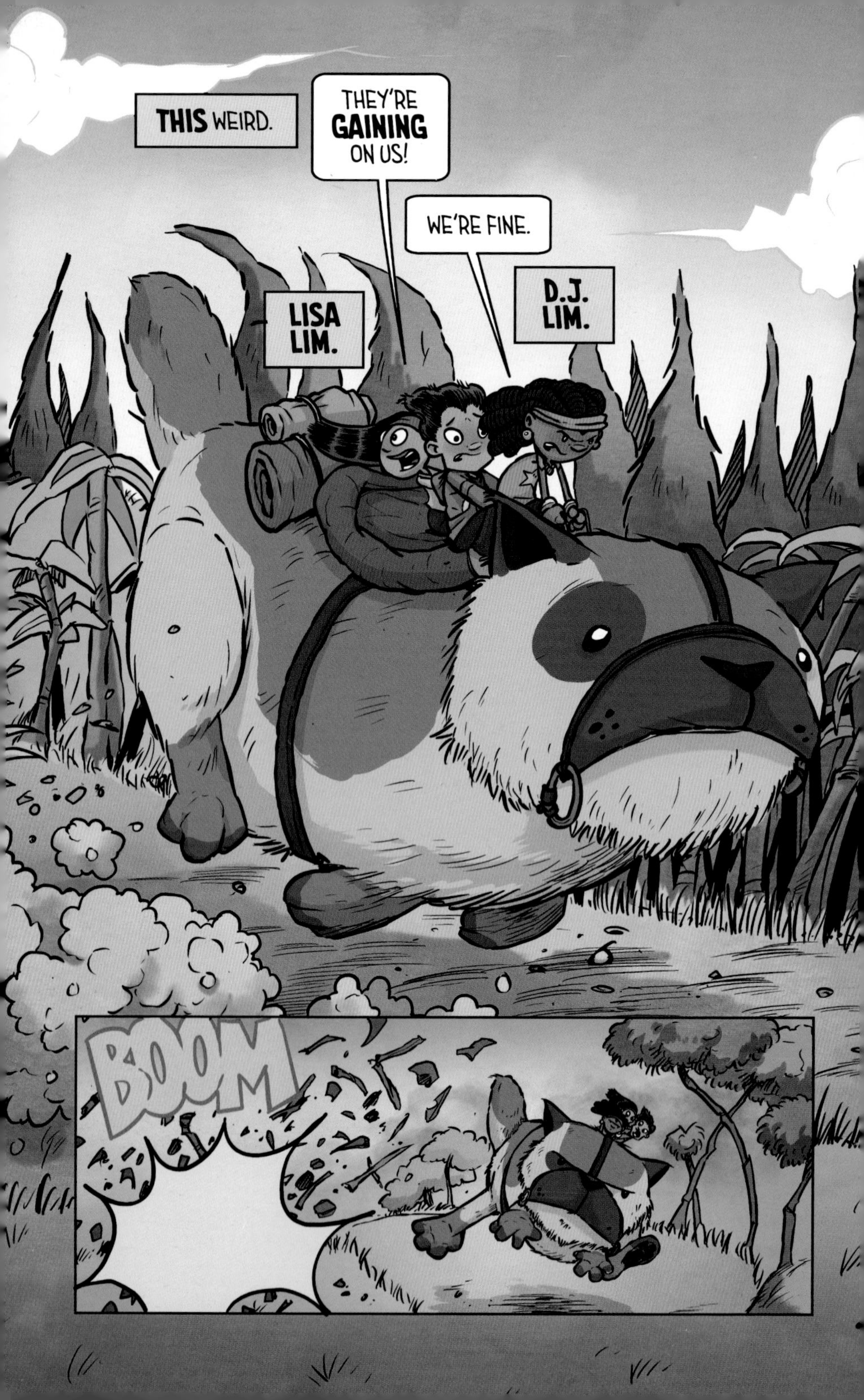
THIS WEIRD.
THEY'RE GAINING ON US!
WE'RE FINE.
LISA LIM.
D.J. LIM.
BOOM

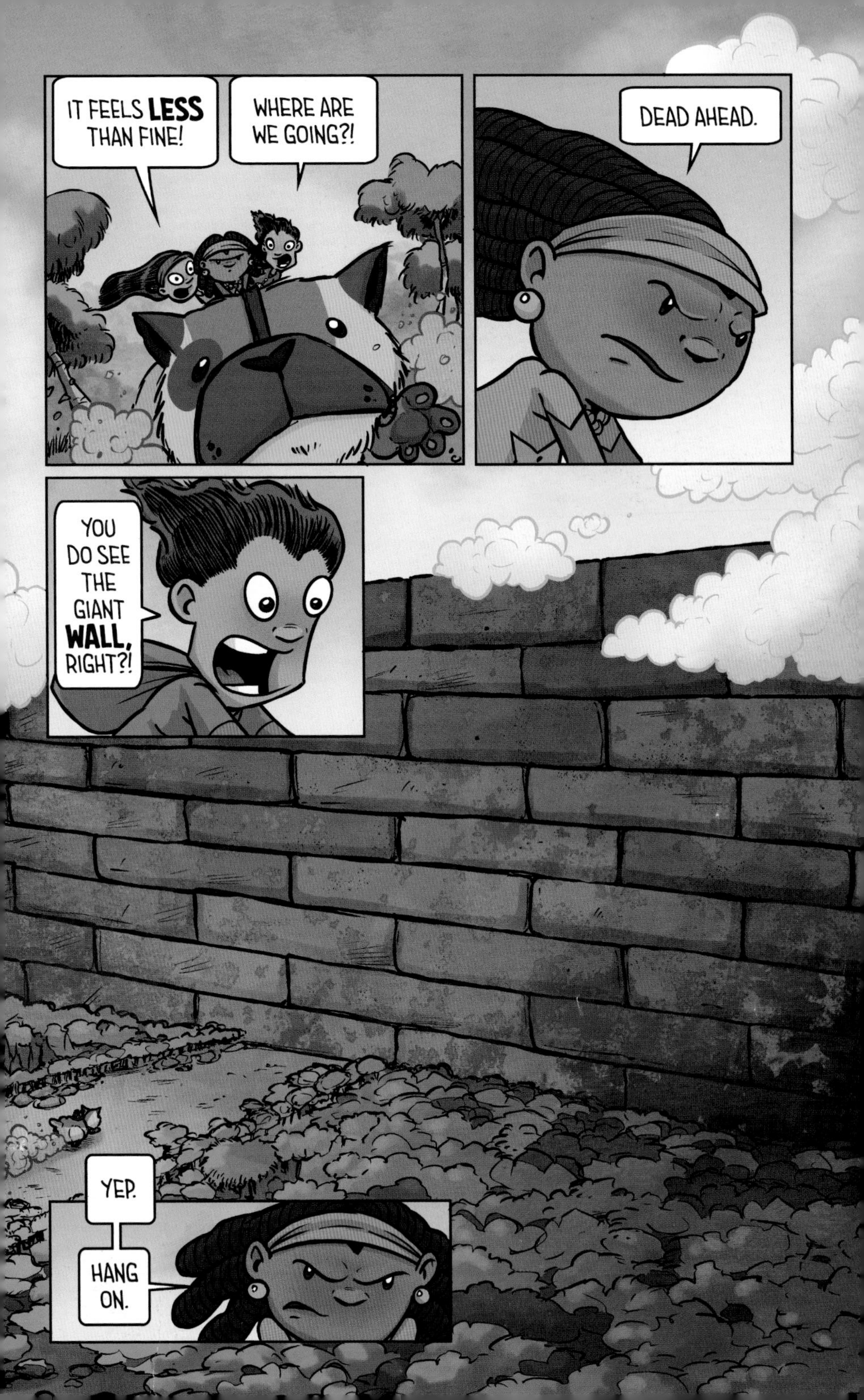
IT FEELS LESS THAN FINE!
WHERE ARE WE GOING?!
DEAD AHEAD.
YOU DO SEE THE GIANT WALL, RIGHT?!
YEP.
HANG ON.

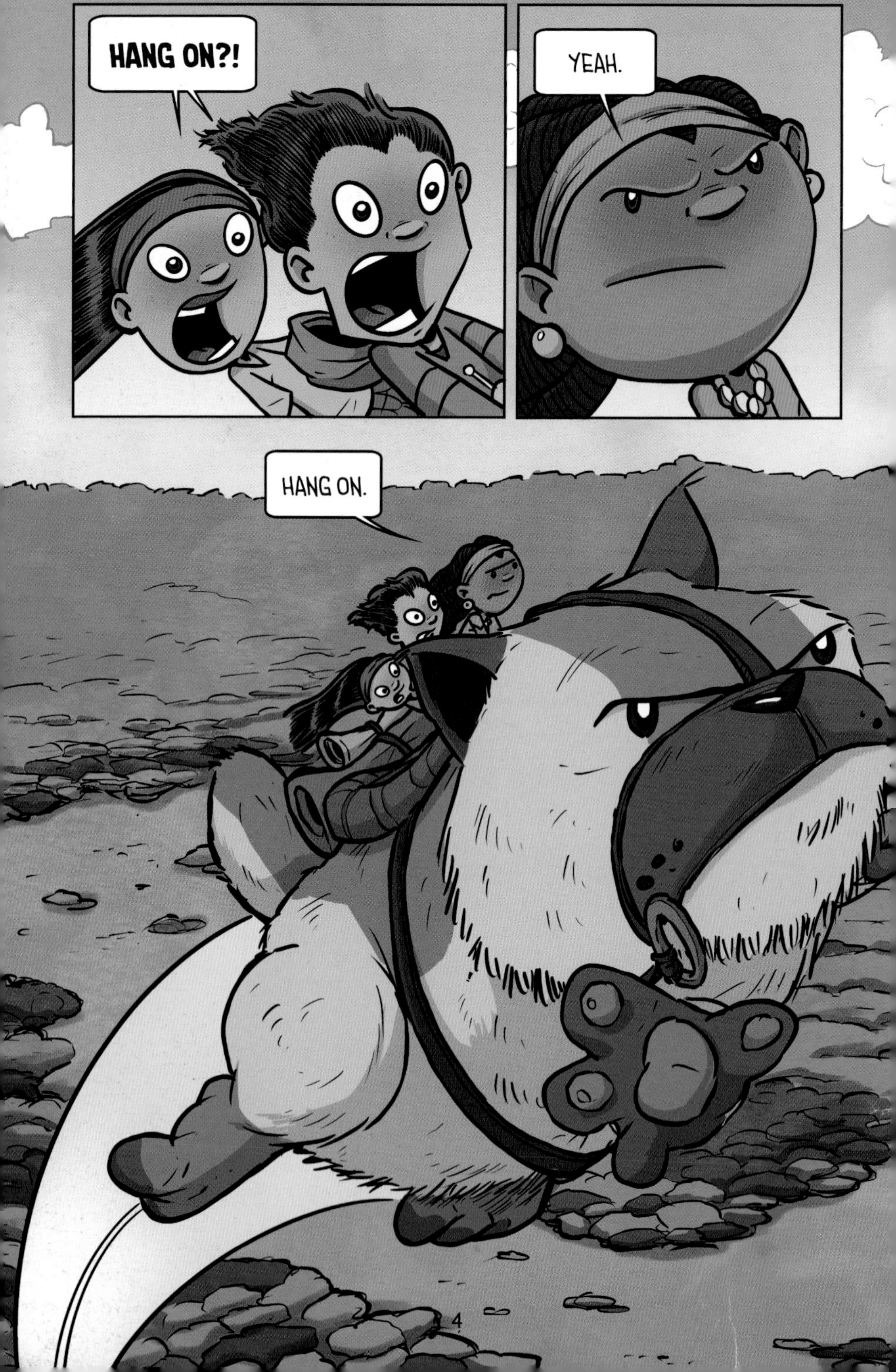
HANG ON?!
YEAH.
HANG ON.

CHAPTER 2

HOWDY DO, BUCKAROOS!

ONE DAY AGO.
OKAY.
WE'RE GOING TO FIX **EVERYTHING.**
YEAH?

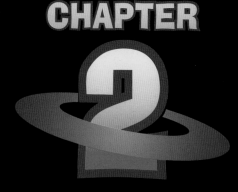

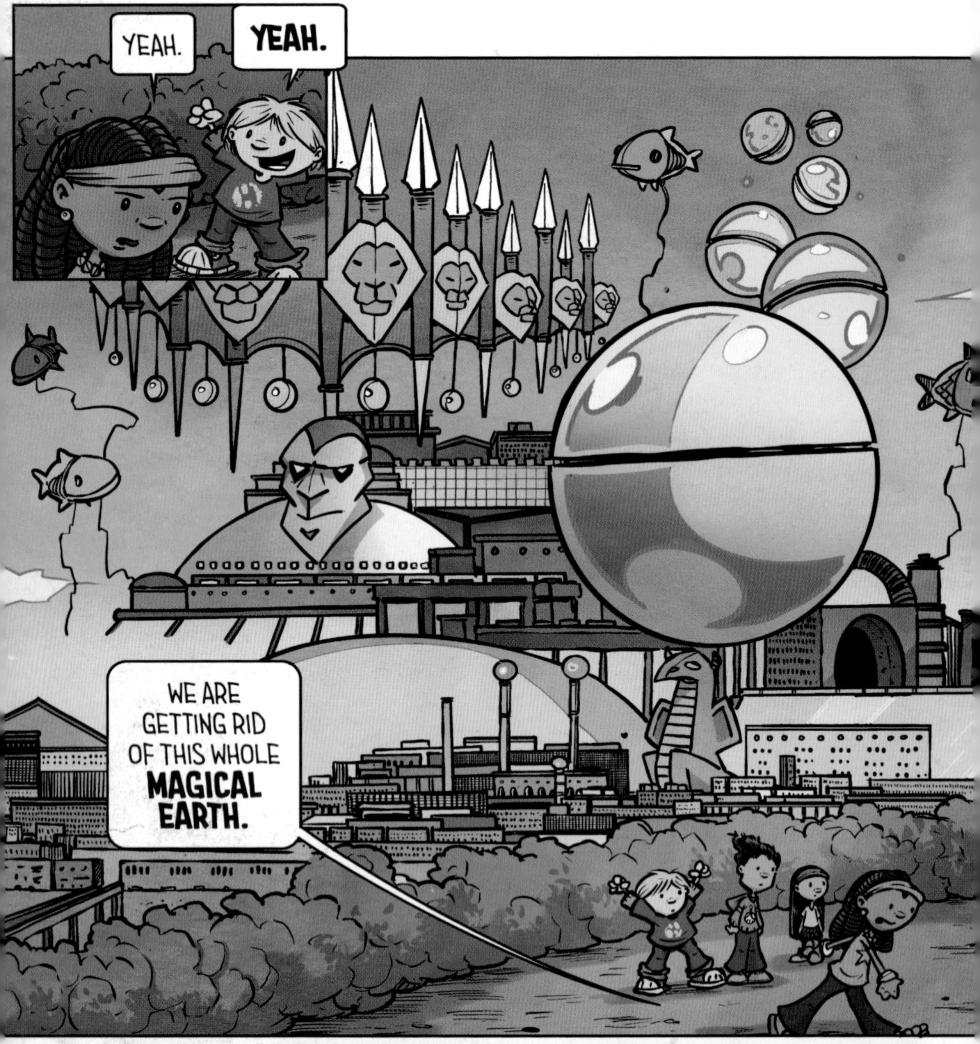
YEAH.
YEAH.
WE ARE GETTING RID OF THIS WHOLE **MAGICAL EARTH.**
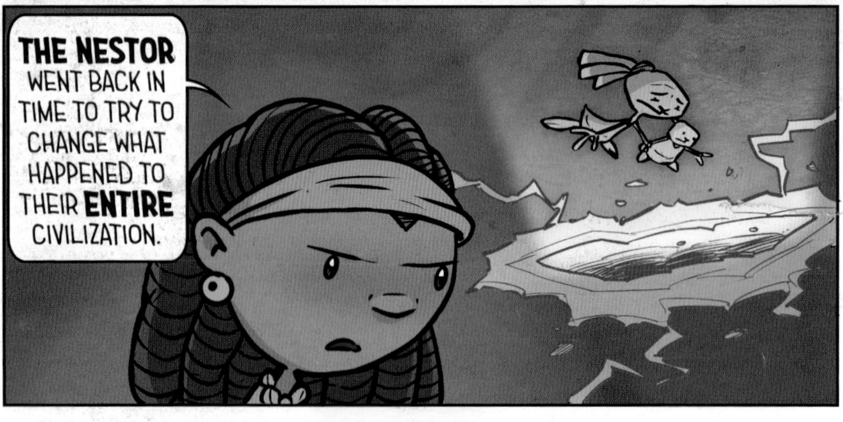
THE NESTOR WENT BACK IN TIME TO TRY TO CHANGE WHAT HAPPENED TO THEIR **ENTIRE** CIVILIZATION.

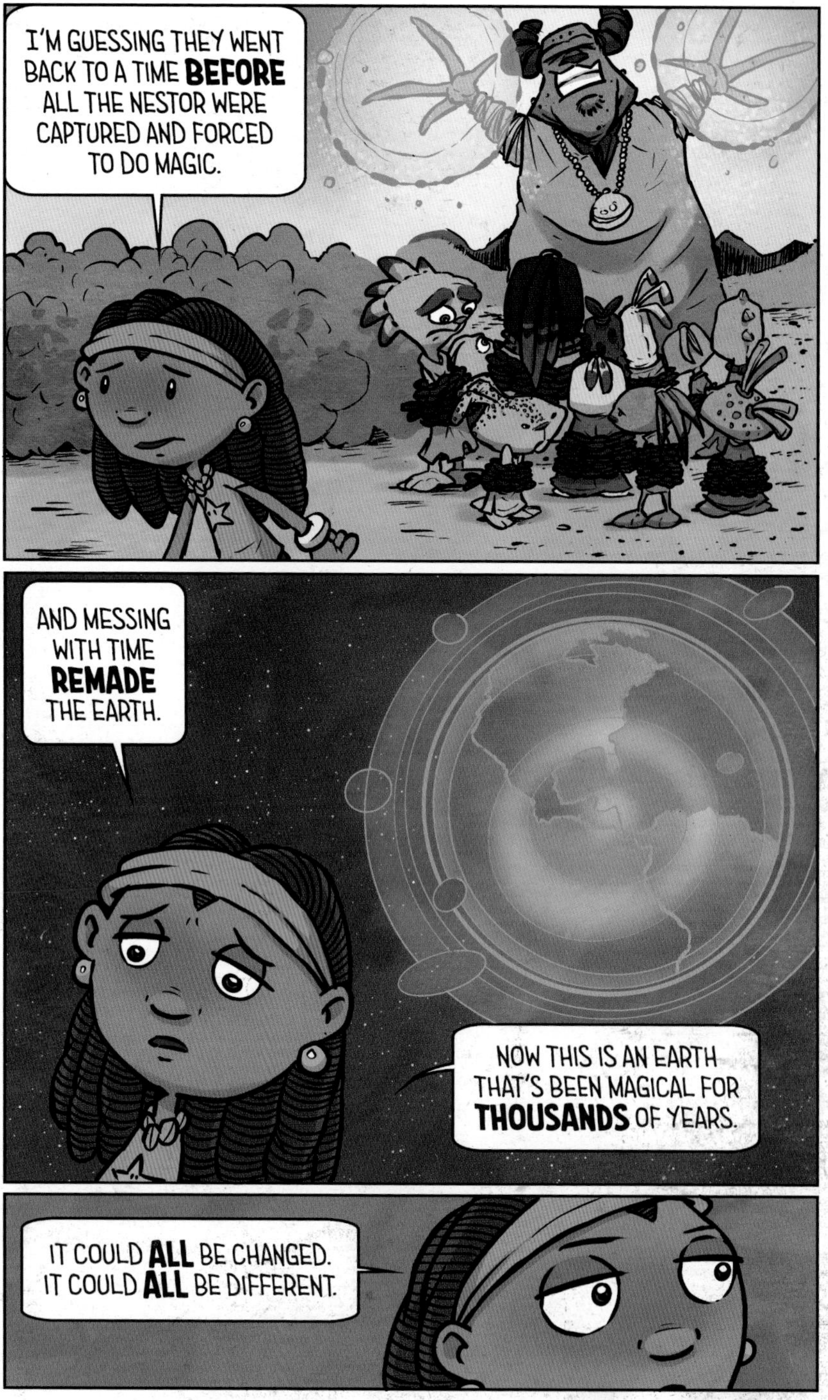
I'M GUESSING THEY WENT BACK TO A TIME BEFORE ALL THE NESTOR WERE CAPTURED AND FORCED TO DO MAGIC.
AND MESSING WITH TIME REMADE THE EARTH.
NOW THIS IS AN EARTH THAT'S BEEN MAGICAL FOR THOUSANDS OF YEARS.
IT COULD ALL BE CHANGED. IT COULD ALL BE DIFFERENT.

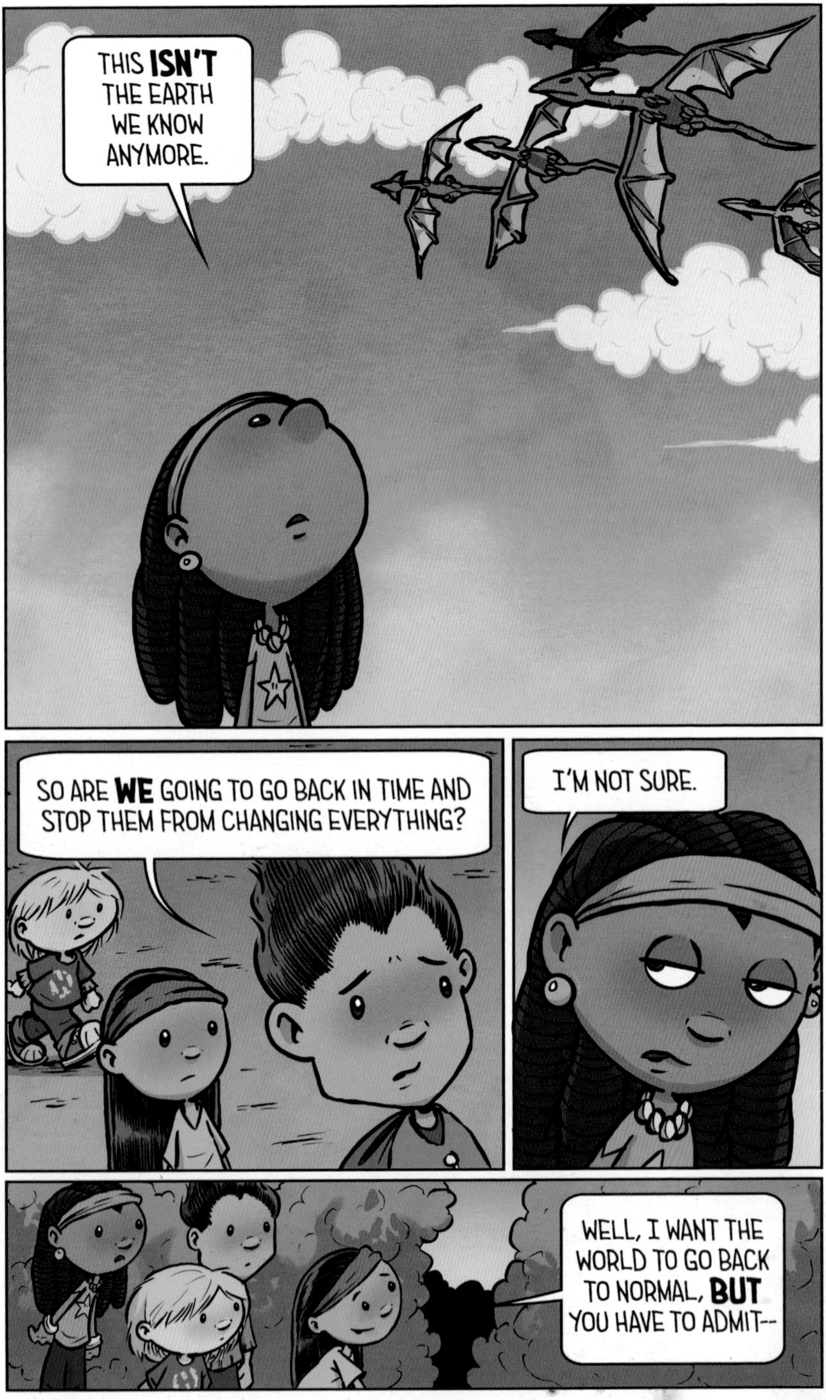
THIS **ISN'T** THE EARTH WE KNOW ANYMORE.
SO ARE **WE** GOING TO GO BACK IN TIME AND STOP THEM FROM CHANGING EVERYTHING?
I'M NOT SURE.
WELL, I WANT THE WORLD TO GO BACK TO NORMAL, **BUT** YOU HAVE TO ADMIT--

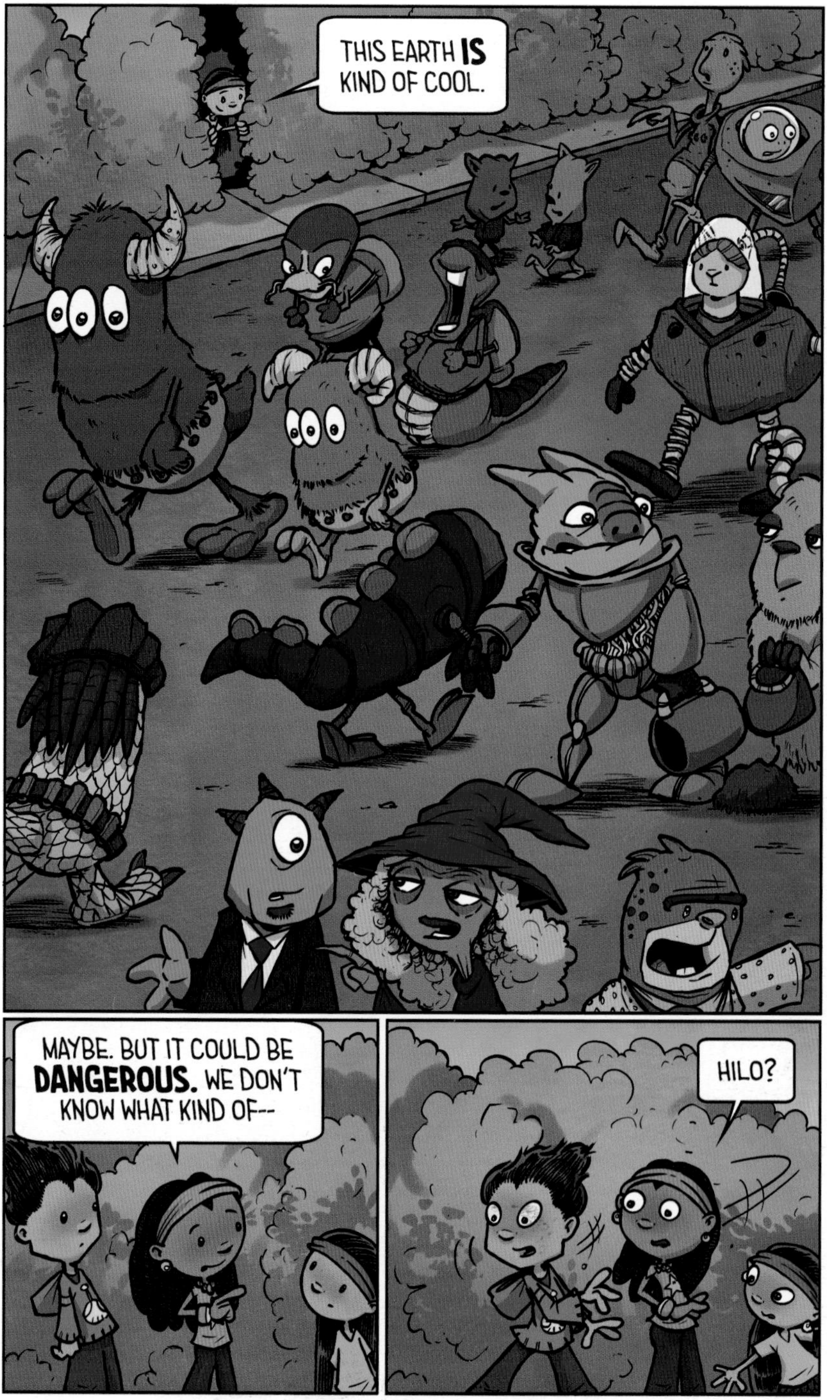
THIS EARTH **IS** KIND OF COOL.
MAYBE. BUT IT COULD BE **DANGEROUS.** WE DON'T KNOW WHAT KIND OF--
HILO?

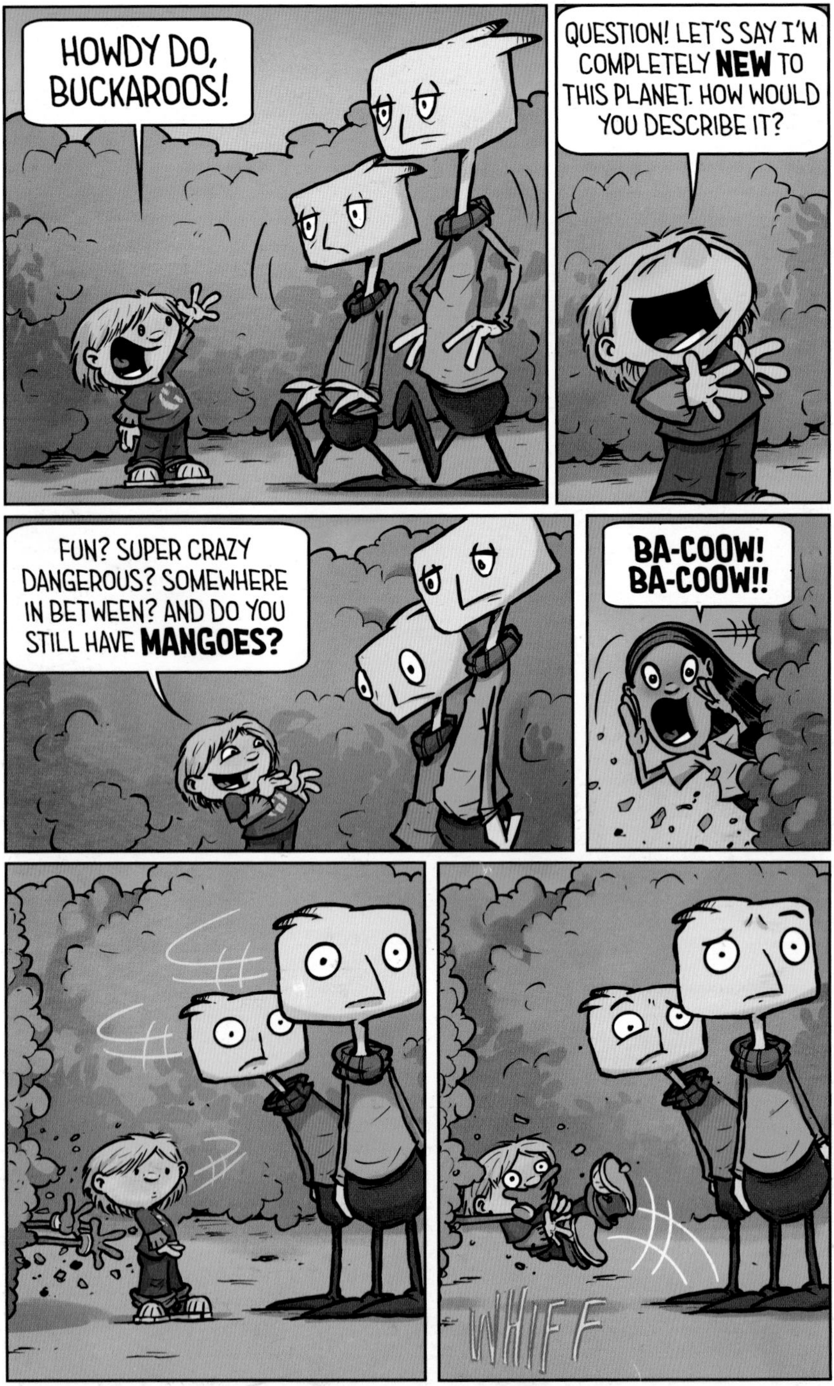
HOWDY DO, BUCKAROOS!
QUESTION! LET'S SAY I'M COMPLETELY **NEW** TO THIS PLANET. HOW WOULD YOU DESCRIBE IT?
FUN? SUPER CRAZY DANGEROUS? SOMEWHERE IN BETWEEN? AND DO YOU STILL HAVE **MANGOES?**
BA-COOW! BA-COOW!!
WHIFF

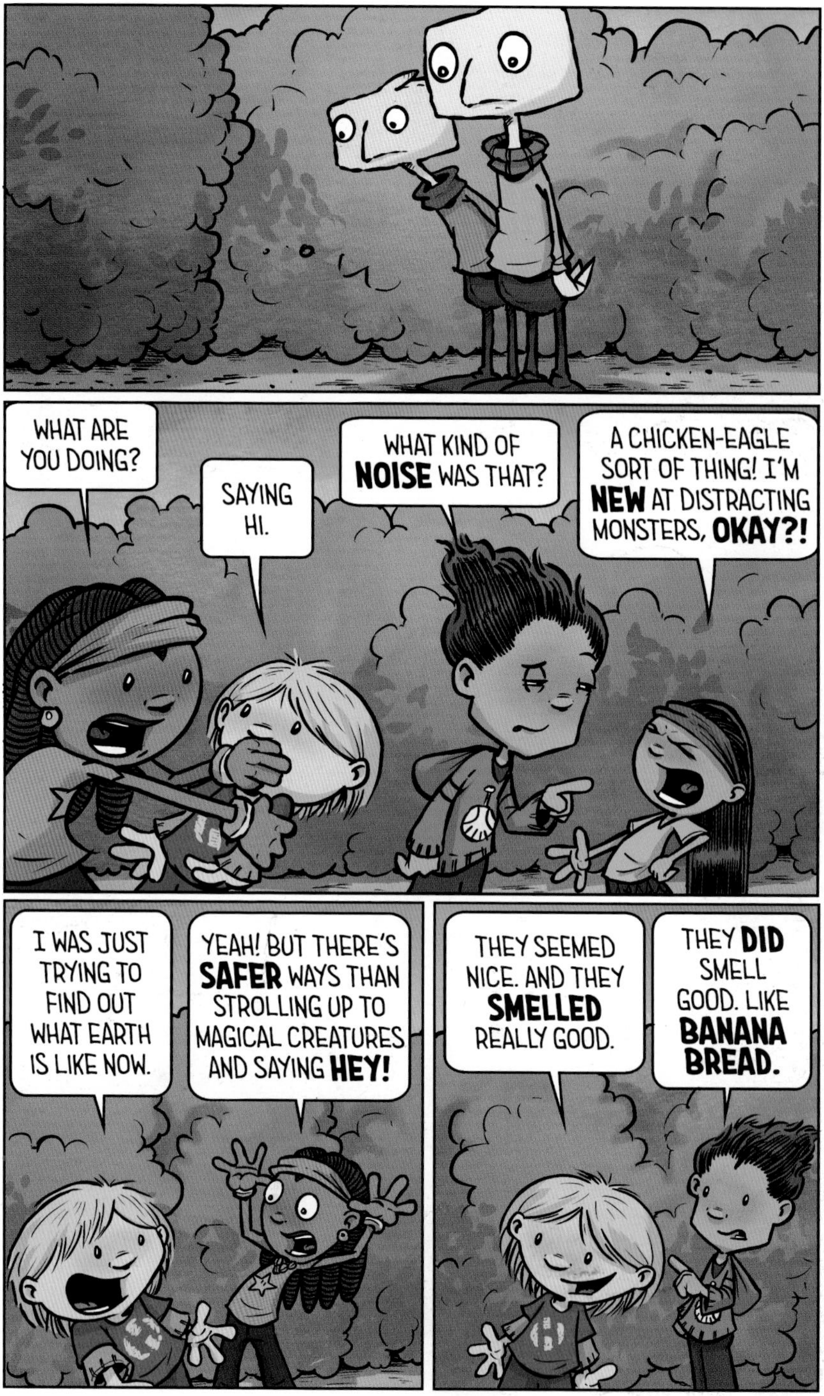
WHAT ARE YOU DOING?
SAYING HI.
WHAT KIND OF **NOISE** WAS THAT?
A CHICKEN-EAGLE SORT OF THING! I'M **NEW** AT DISTRACTING MONSTERS, **OKAY?!**
I WAS JUST TRYING TO FIND OUT WHAT EARTH IS LIKE NOW.
YEAH! BUT THERE'S **SAFER** WAYS THAN STROLLING UP TO MAGICAL CREATURES AND SAYING **HEY!**
THEY SEEMED NICE. AND THEY **SMELLED** REALLY GOOD.
THEY **DID** SMELL GOOD. LIKE **BANANA BREAD.**

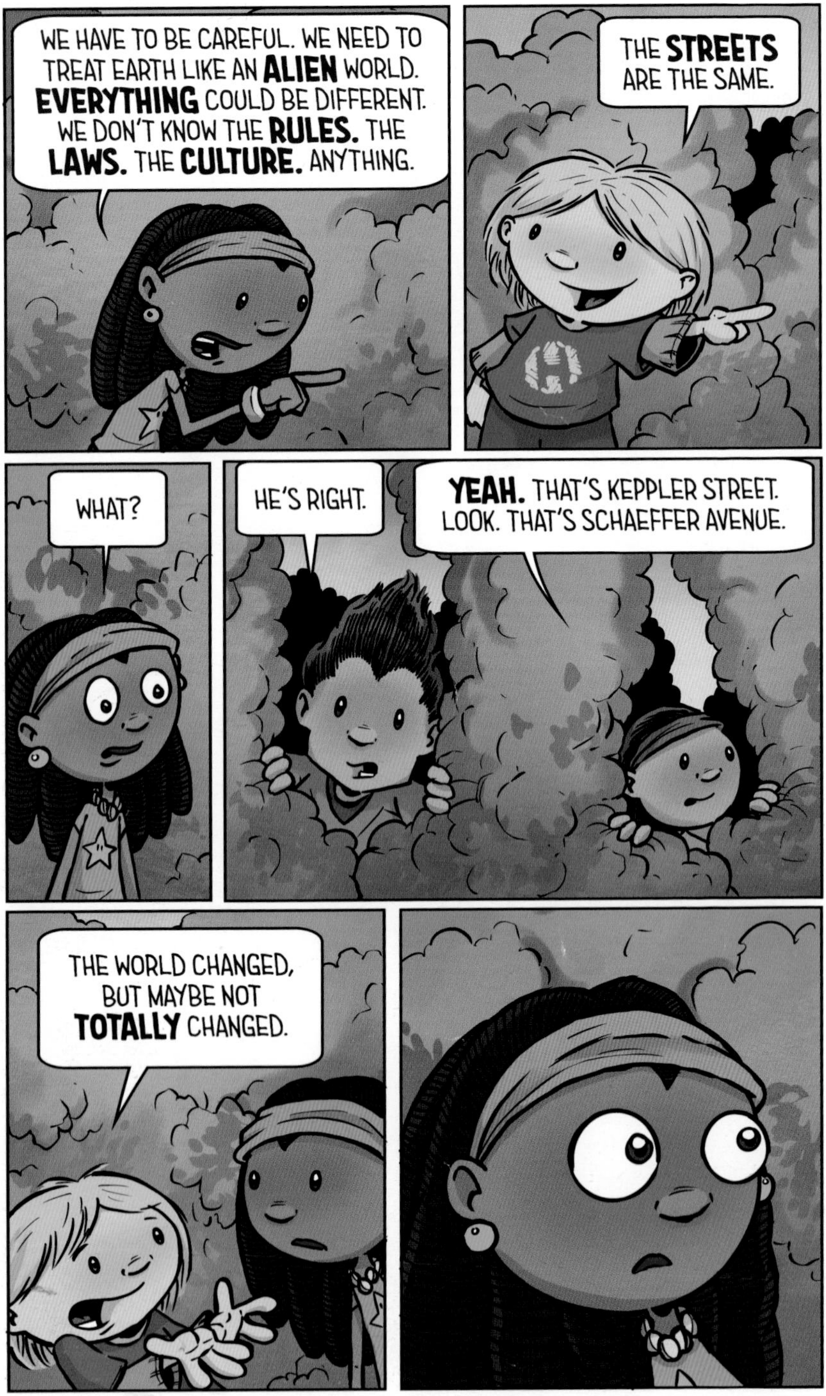
WE HAVE TO BE CAREFUL. WE NEED TO TREAT EARTH LIKE AN **ALIEN** WORLD. **EVERYTHING** COULD BE DIFFERENT. WE DON'T KNOW THE **RULES.** THE **LAWS.** THE **CULTURE.** ANYTHING.
THE **STREETS** ARE THE SAME.
WHAT?
HE'S RIGHT.
YEAH. THAT'S KEPPLER STREET. LOOK. THAT'S SCHAEFFER AVENUE.
THE WORLD CHANGED, BUT MAYBE NOT **TOTALLY** CHANGED.

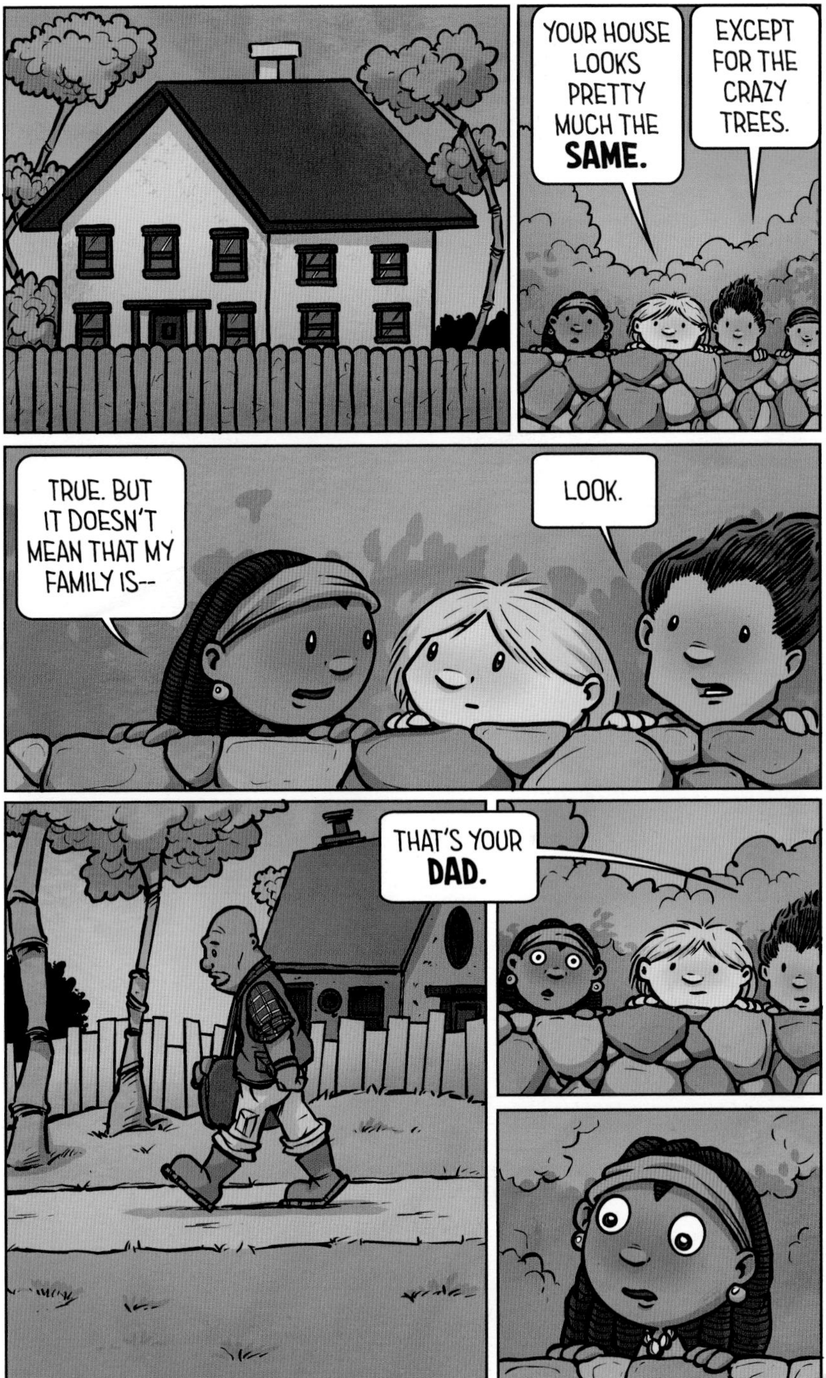
YOUR HOUSE LOOKS PRETTY MUCH THE **SAME.**
EXCEPT FOR THE CRAZY TREES.
TRUE. BUT IT DOESN'T MEAN THAT MY FAMILY IS--
LOOK.
THAT'S YOUR **DAD.**

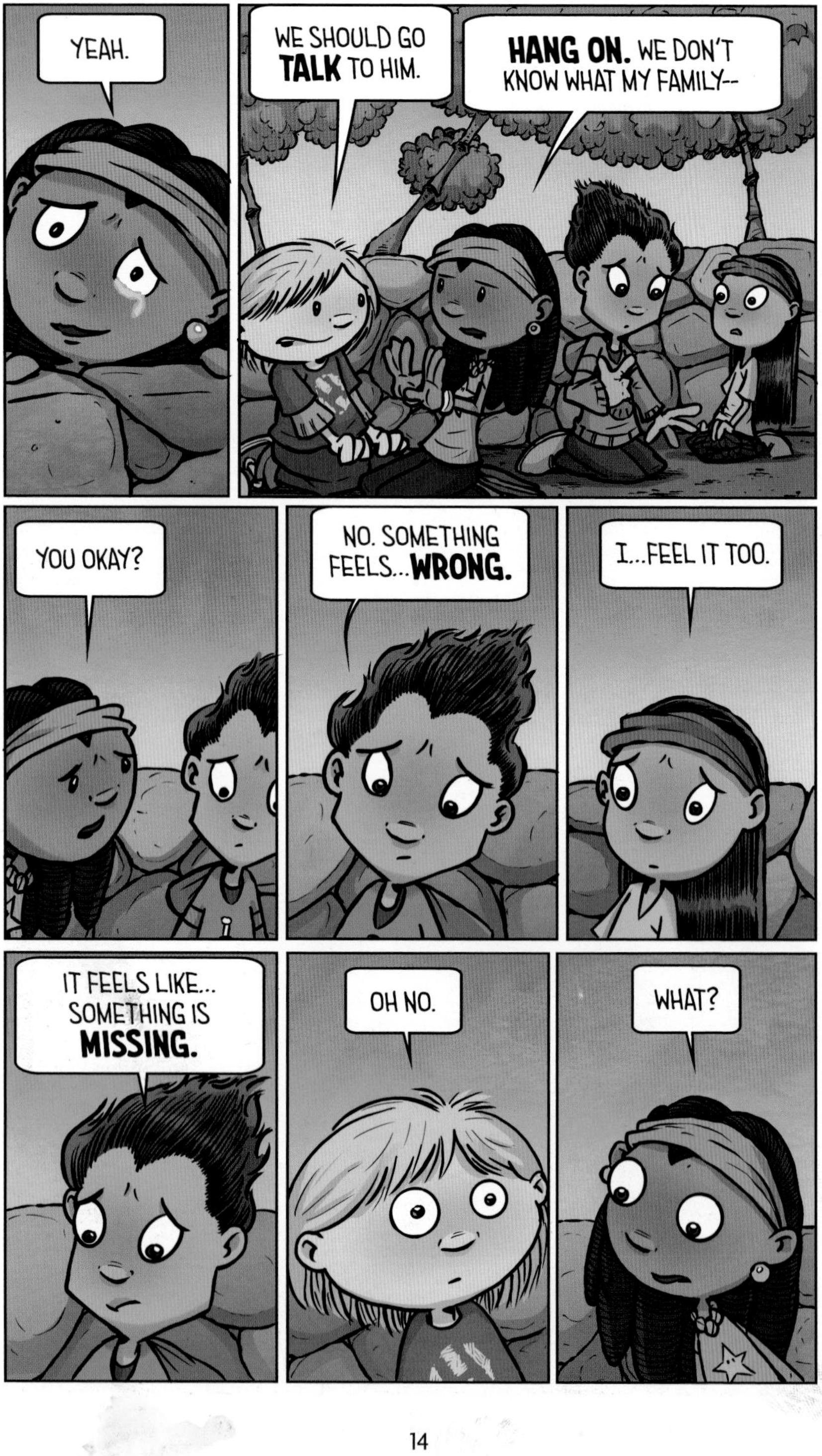
YEAH.
WE SHOULD GO TALK TO HIM.
HANG ON. WE DON'T KNOW WHAT MY FAMILY--
YOU OKAY?
NO. SOMETHING FEELS...WRONG.
I...FEEL IT TOO.
IT FEELS LIKE... SOMETHING IS MISSING.
OH NO.
WHAT?

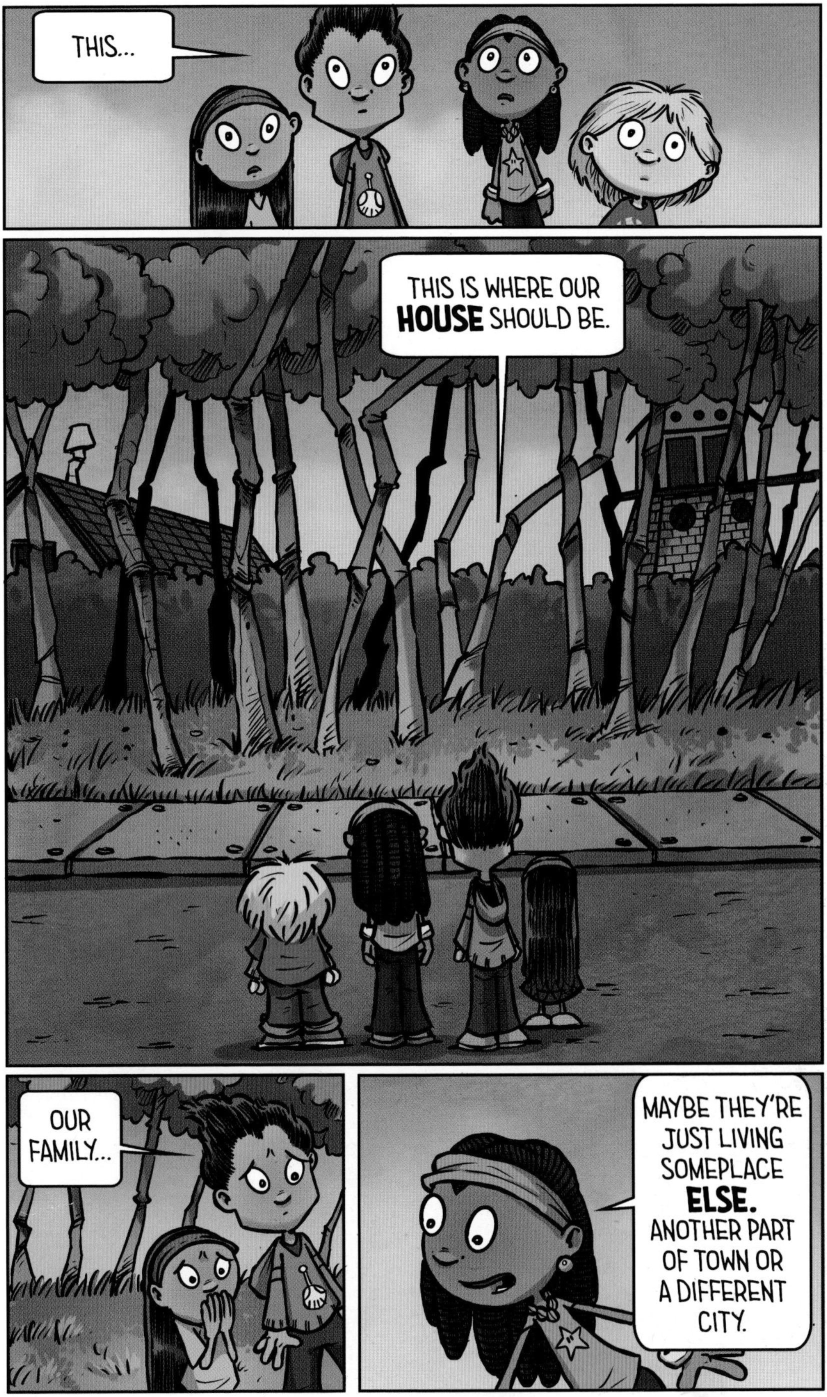
THIS...
THIS IS WHERE OUR HOUSE SHOULD BE.
OUR FAMILY...
MAYBE THEY'RE JUST LIVING SOMEPLACE ELSE. ANOTHER PART OF TOWN OR A DIFFERENT CITY.

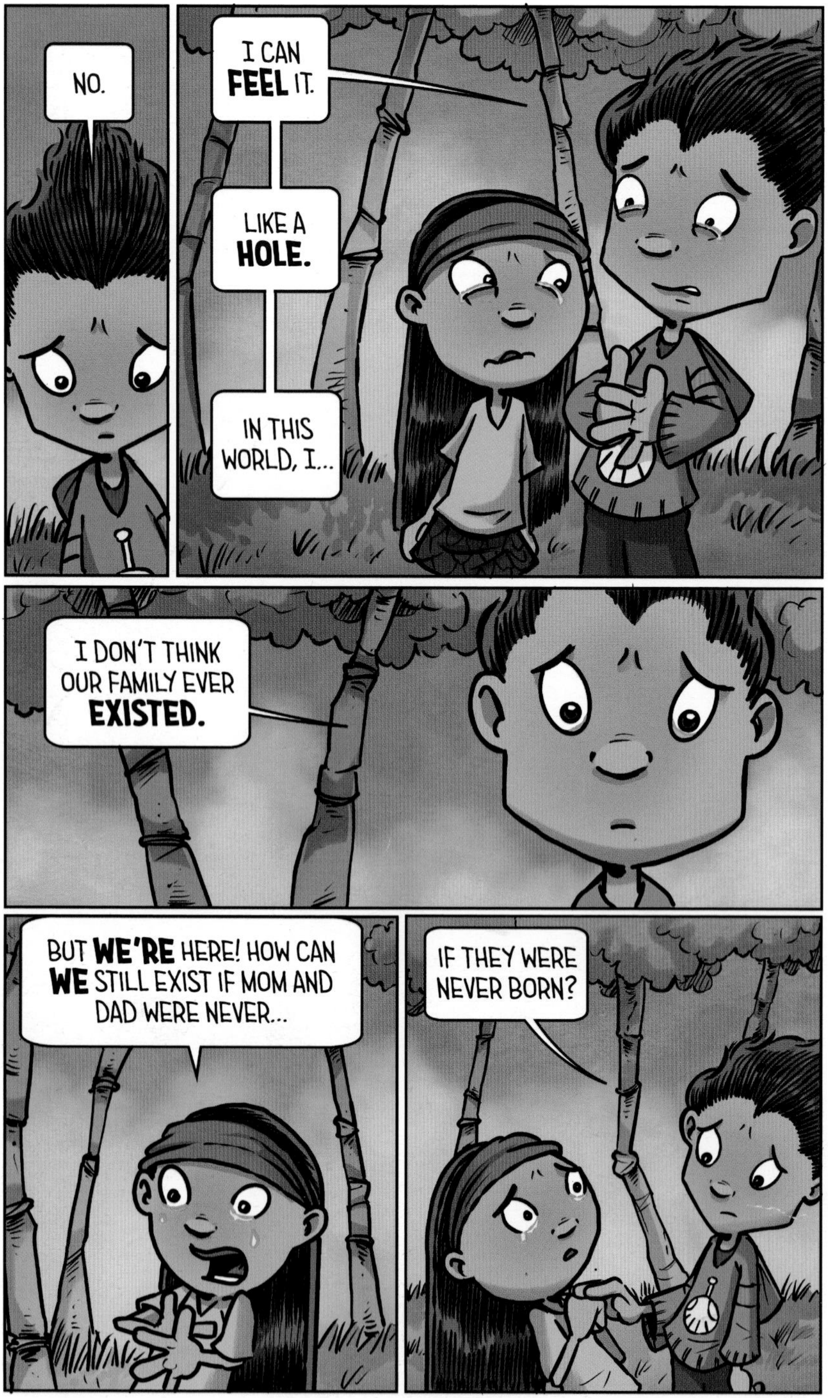
NO.
I CAN **FEEL** IT.
LIKE A **HOLE.**
IN THIS WORLD, I...
I DON'T THINK OUR FAMILY EVER **EXISTED.**
BUT **WE'RE** HERE! HOW CAN **WE** STILL EXIST IF MOM AND DAD WERE NEVER...
IF THEY WERE NEVER BORN?

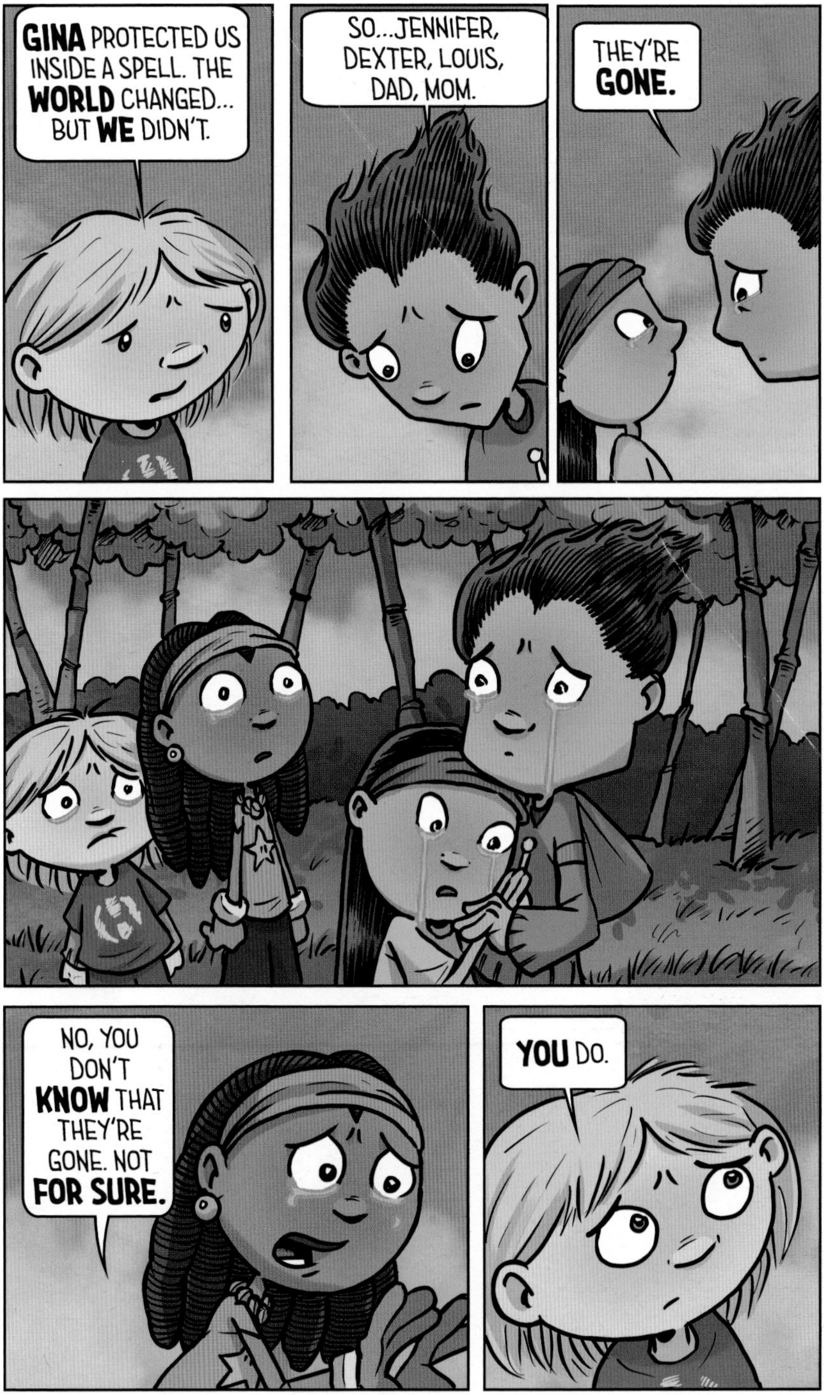
GINA PROTECTED US INSIDE A SPELL. THE WORLD CHANGED... BUT WE DIDN'T.
SO...JENNIFER, DEXTER, LOUIS, DAD, MOM.
THEY'RE GONE.
NO, YOU DON'T KNOW THAT THEY'RE GONE. NOT FOR SURE.
YOU DO.

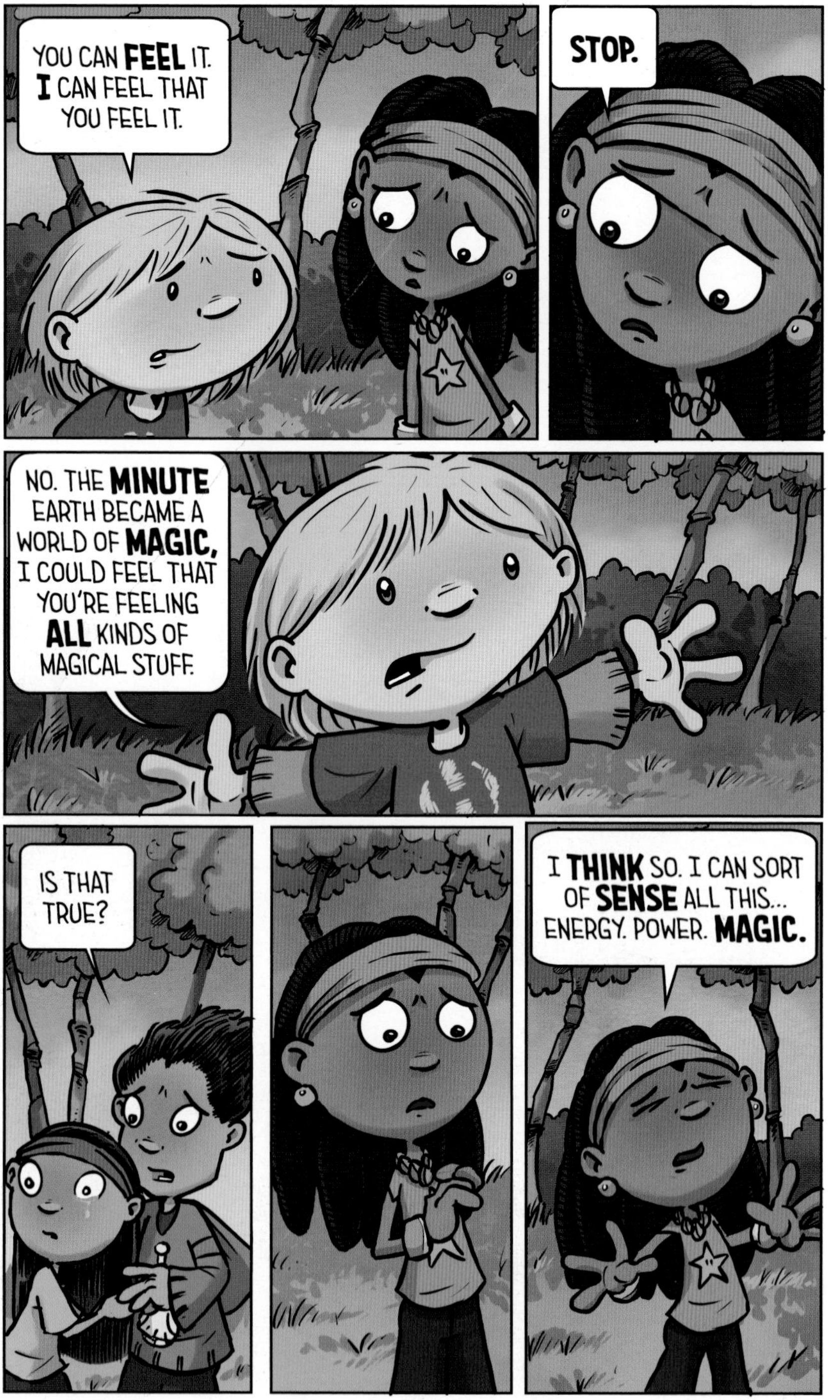
YOU CAN **FEEL** IT. **I** CAN FEEL THAT YOU FEEL IT.
STOP.
NO. THE **MINUTE** EARTH BECAME A WORLD OF **MAGIC,** I COULD FEEL THAT YOU'RE FEELING **ALL** KINDS OF MAGICAL STUFF.
IS THAT TRUE?
I **THINK** SO. I CAN SORT OF **SENSE** ALL THIS... ENERGY. POWER. **MAGIC.**

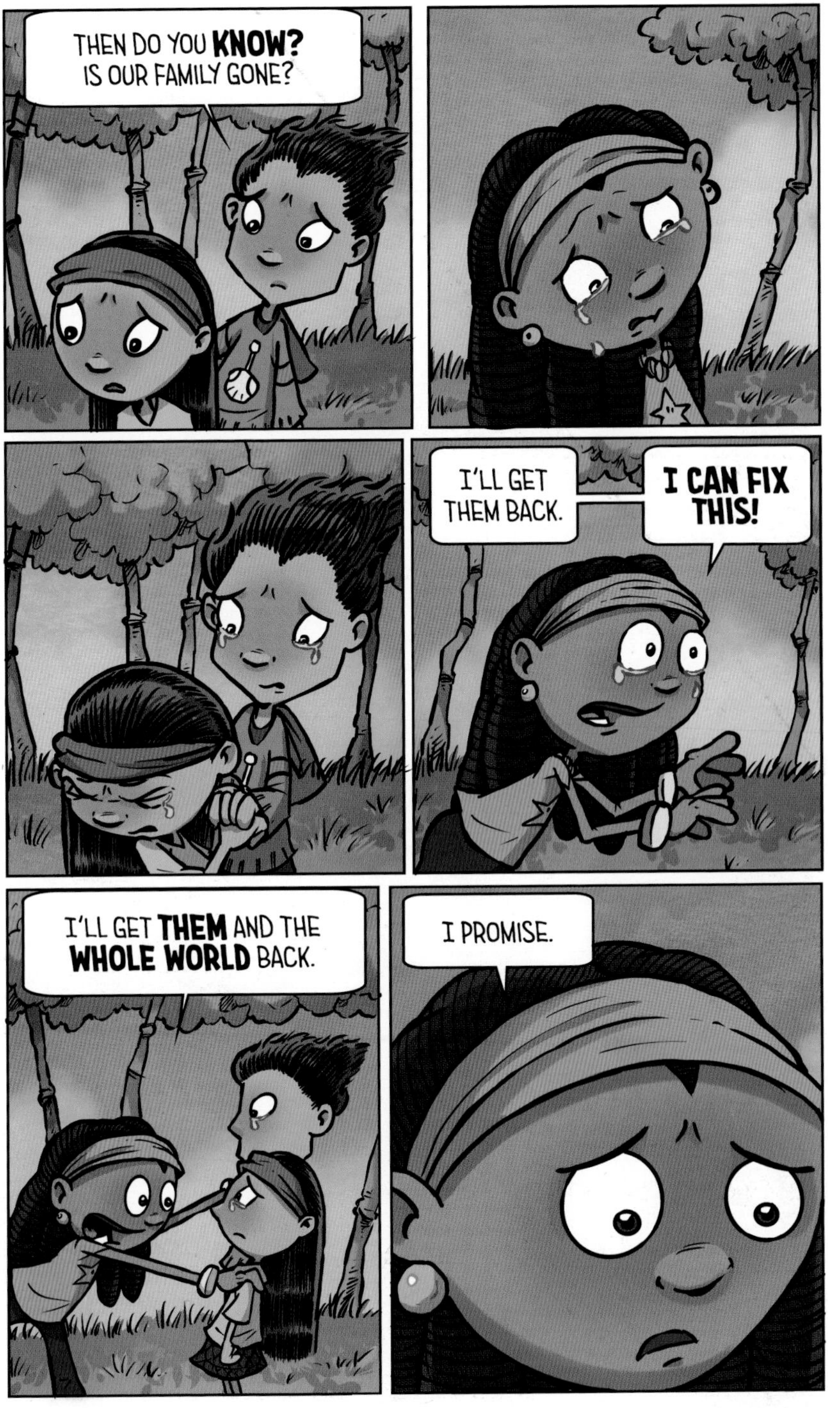
THEN DO YOU **KNOW?** IS OUR FAMILY GONE?
I'LL GET THEM BACK.
I CAN FIX THIS!
I'LL GET **THEM** AND THE **WHOLE WORLD** BACK.
I PROMISE.

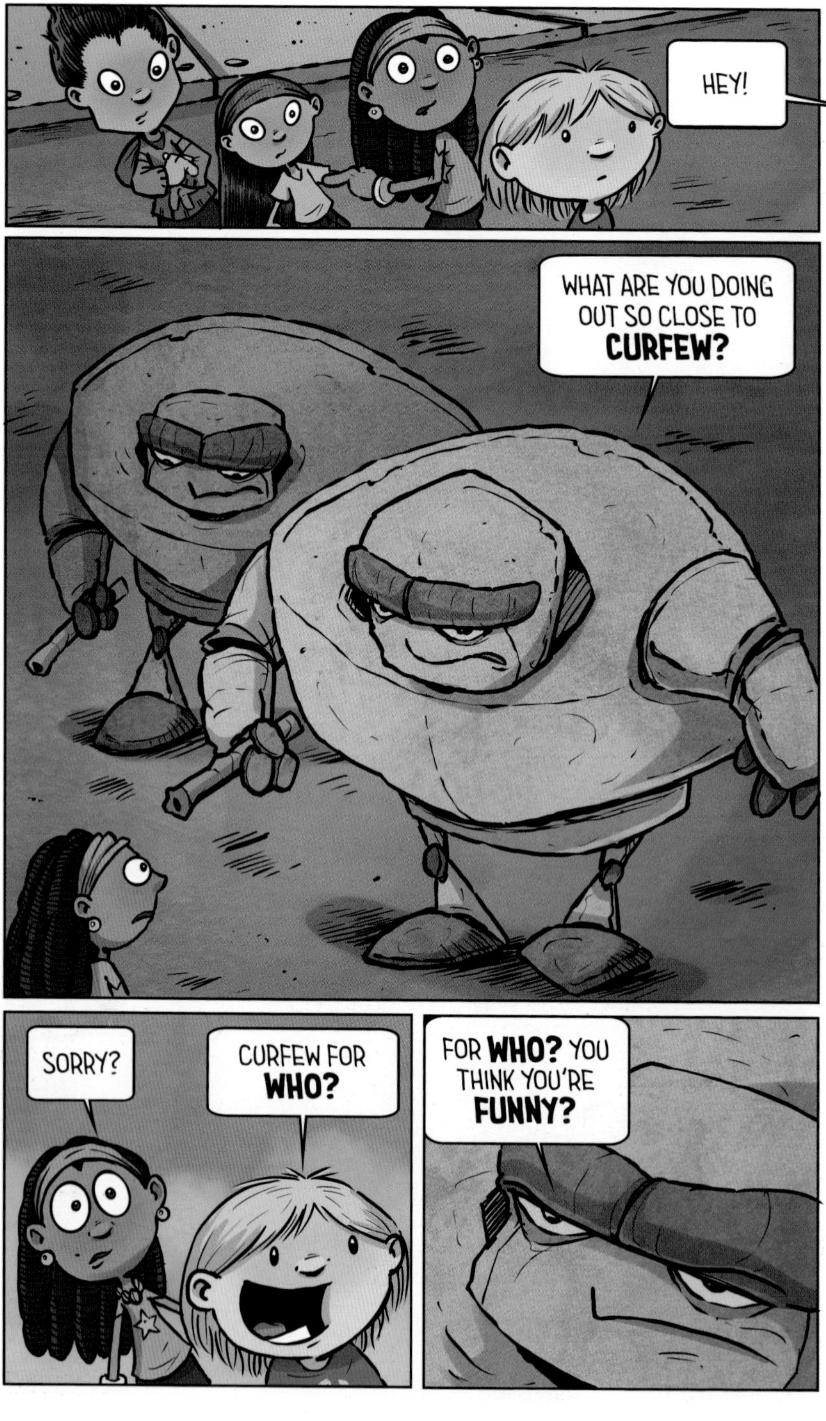
HEY!
WHAT ARE YOU DOING OUT SO CLOSE TO **CURFEW?**
SORRY?
CURFEW FOR **WHO?**
FOR **WHO?** YOU THINK YOU'RE **FUNNY?**

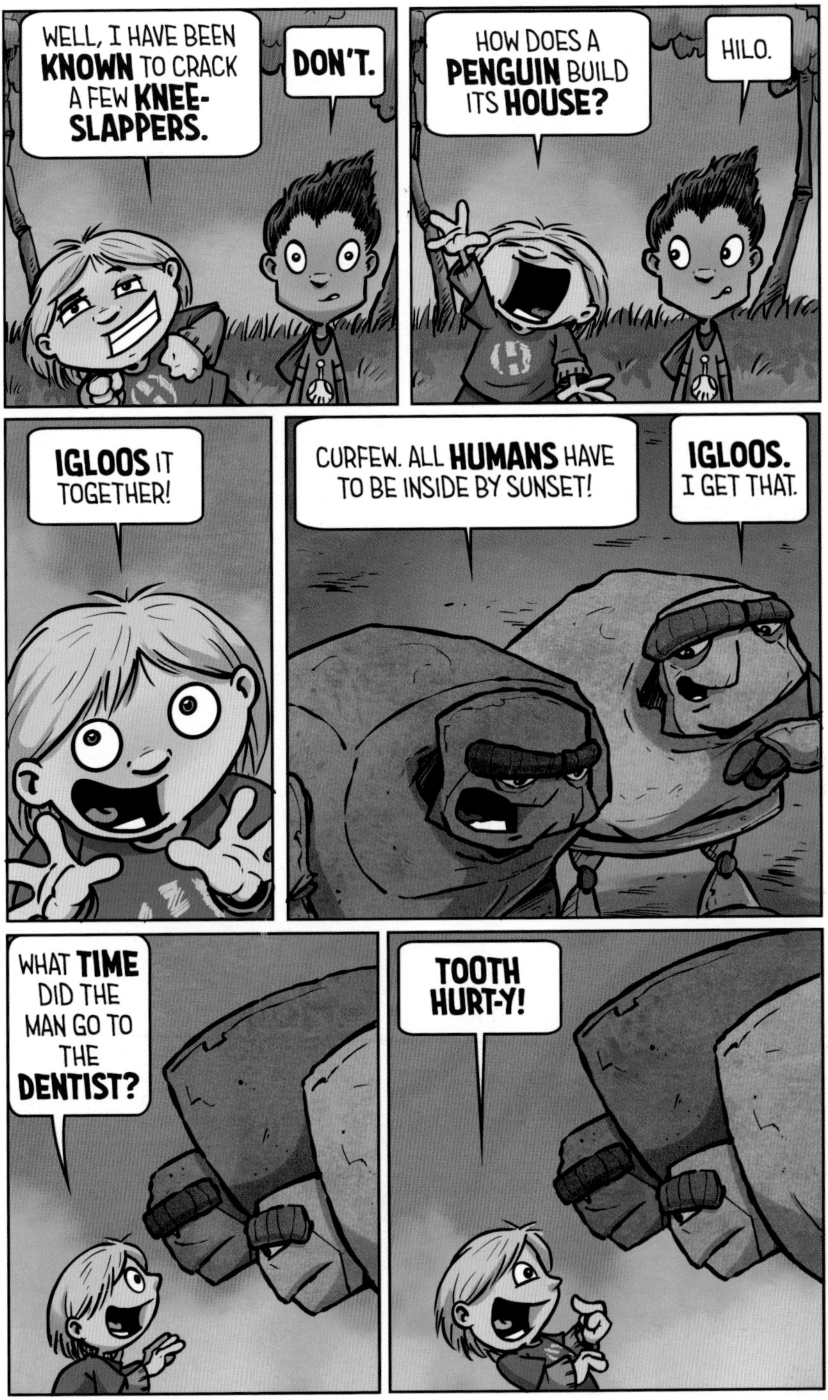

WELL, I HAVE BEEN KNOWN TO CRACK A FEW KNEE-SLAPPERS.
DON'T.
HOW DOES A PENGUIN BUILD ITS HOUSE?
HILO.
IGLOOS IT TOGETHER!
CURFEW. ALL HUMANS HAVE TO BE INSIDE BY SUNSET!
IGLOOS. I GET THAT.
WHAT TIME DID THE MAN GO TO THE DENTIST?
TOOTH HURT-Y!

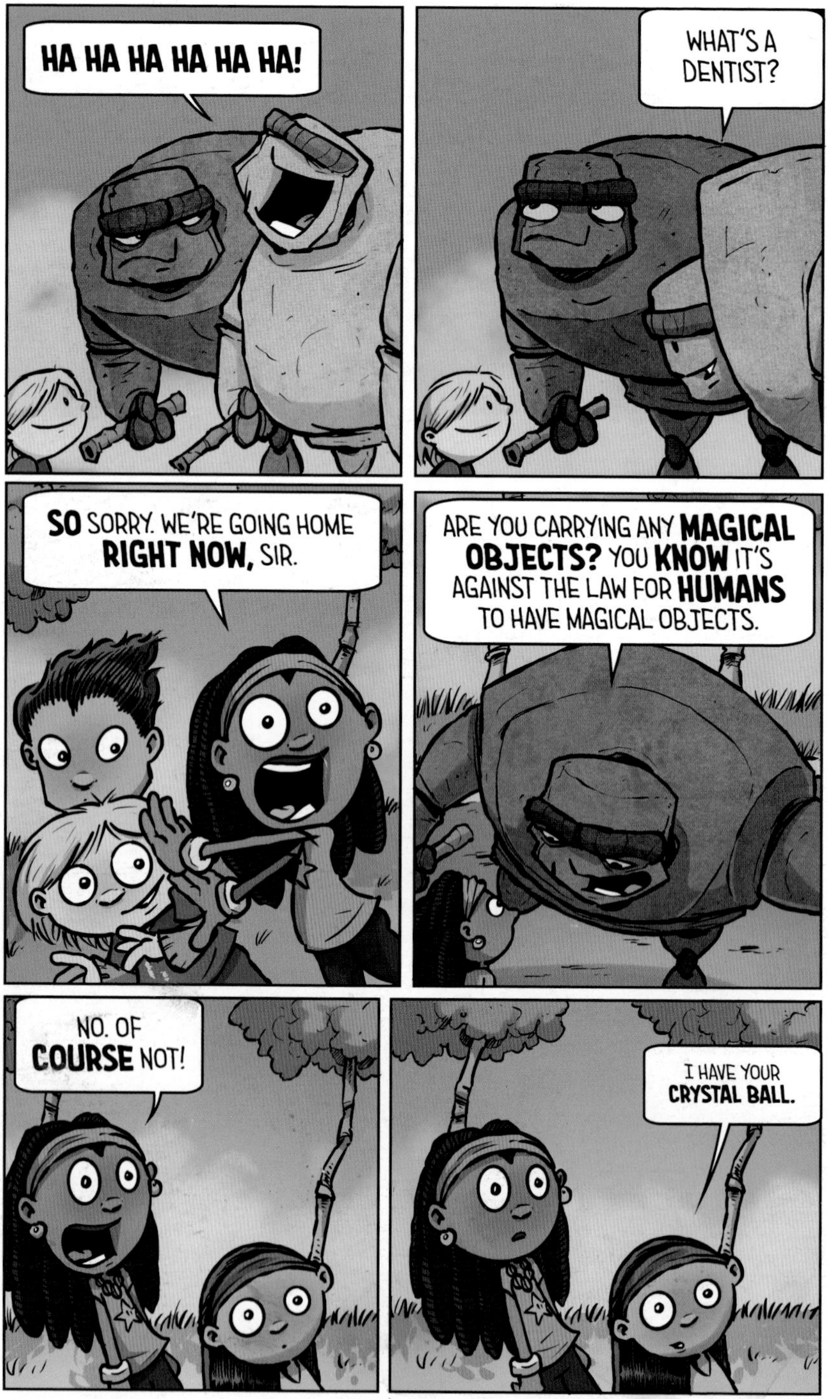
HA HA HA HA HA HA!
WHAT'S A DENTIST?
SO SORRY. WE'RE GOING HOME RIGHT NOW, SIR.
ARE YOU CARRYING ANY MAGICAL OBJECTS? YOU KNOW IT'S AGAINST THE LAW FOR HUMANS TO HAVE MAGICAL OBJECTS.
NO. OF COURSE NOT!
I HAVE YOUR CRYSTAL BALL.

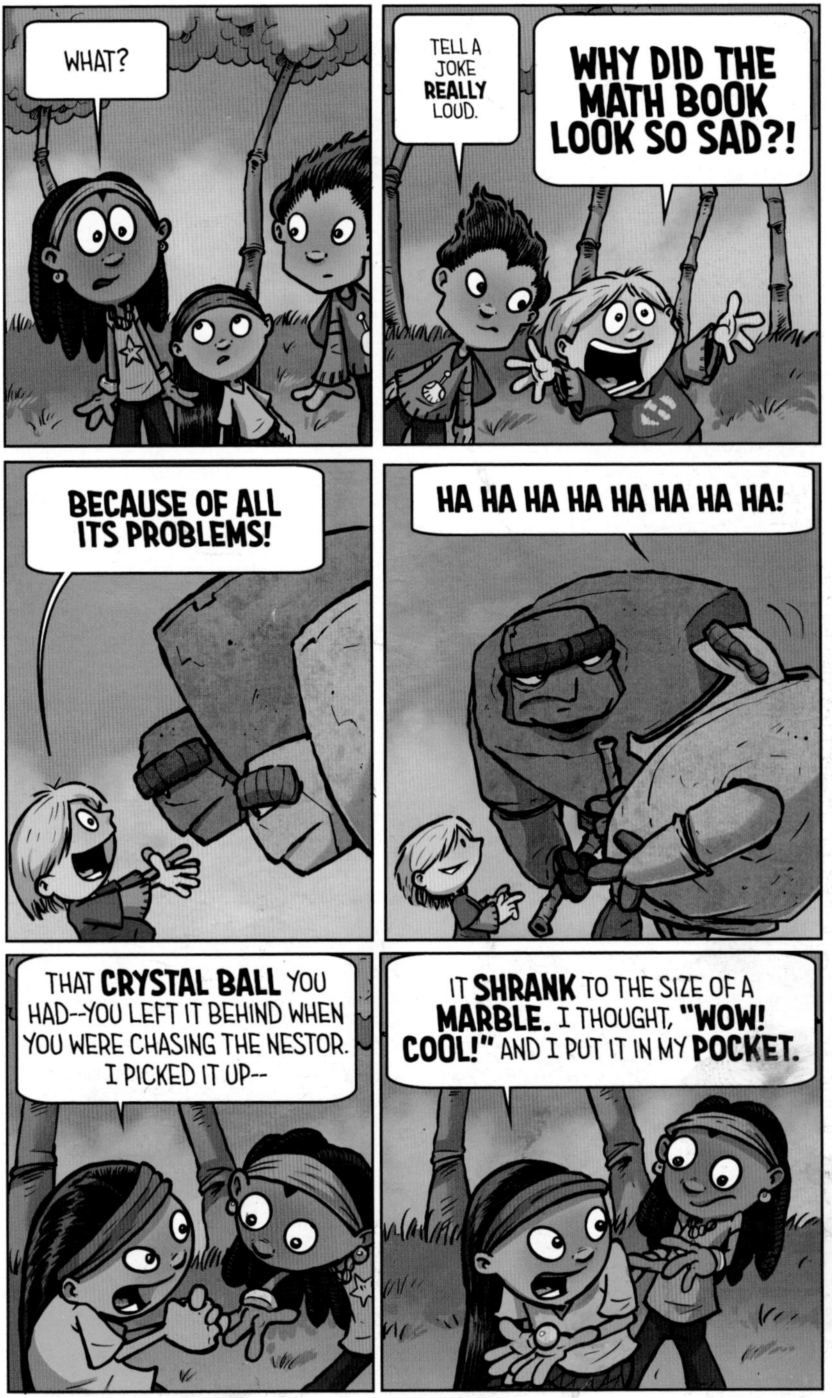
WHAT?
TELL A JOKE REALLY LOUD.
WHY DID THE MATH BOOK LOOK SO SAD?!
BECAUSE OF ALL ITS PROBLEMS!
HA HA HA HA HA HA HA HA!
THAT CRYSTAL BALL YOU HAD--YOU LEFT IT BEHIND WHEN YOU WERE CHASING THE NESTOR. I PICKED IT UP--
IT SHRANK TO THE SIZE OF A MARBLE. I THOUGHT, "WOW! COOL!" AND I PUT IT IN MY POCKET.

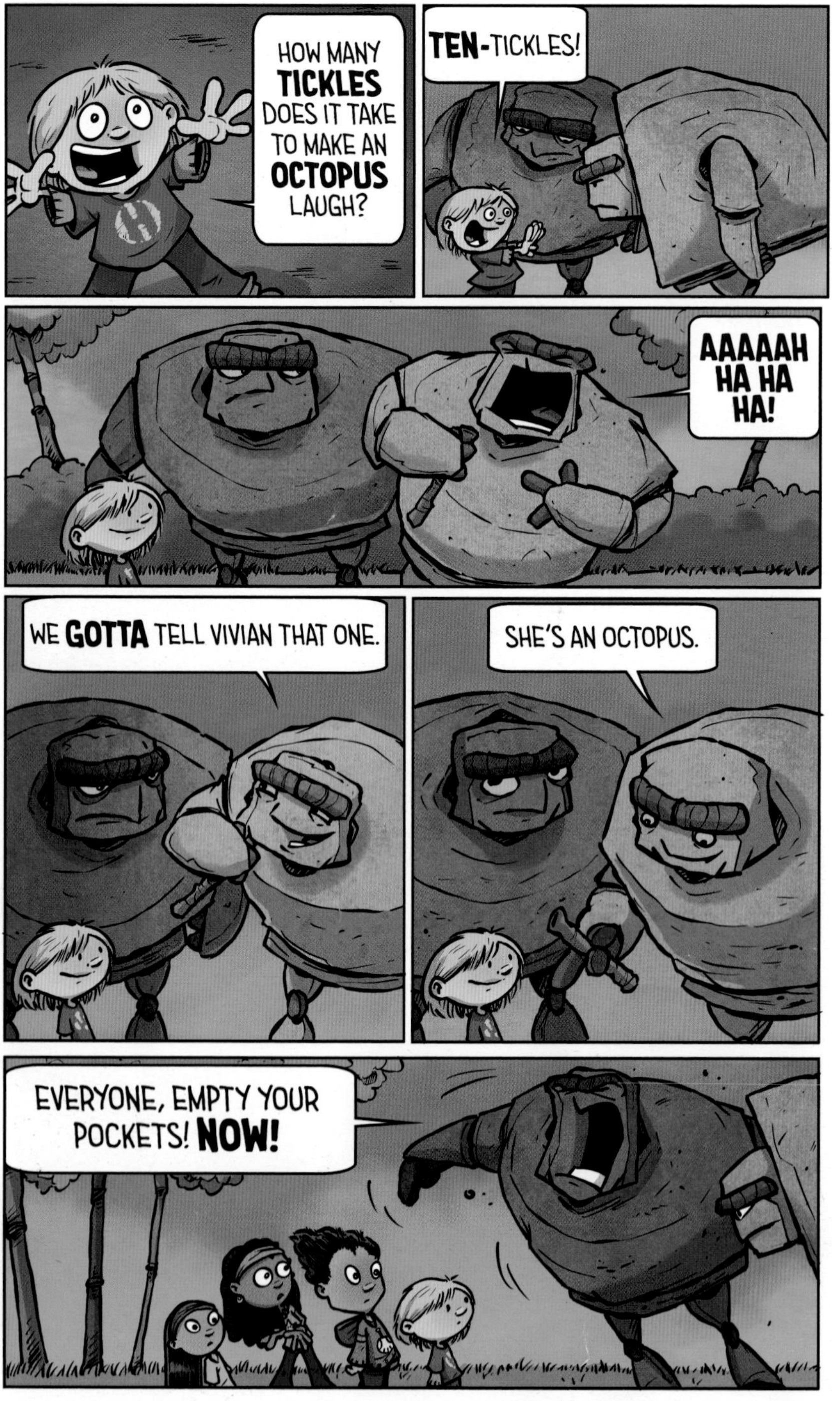
HOW MANY **TICKLES** DOES IT TAKE TO MAKE AN **OCTOPUS** LAUGH?
TEN-TICKLES!
AAAAAH HA HA HA!
WE **GOTTA** TELL VIVIAN THAT ONE.
SHE'S AN OCTOPUS.
EVERYONE, EMPTY YOUR POCKETS! **NOW!**

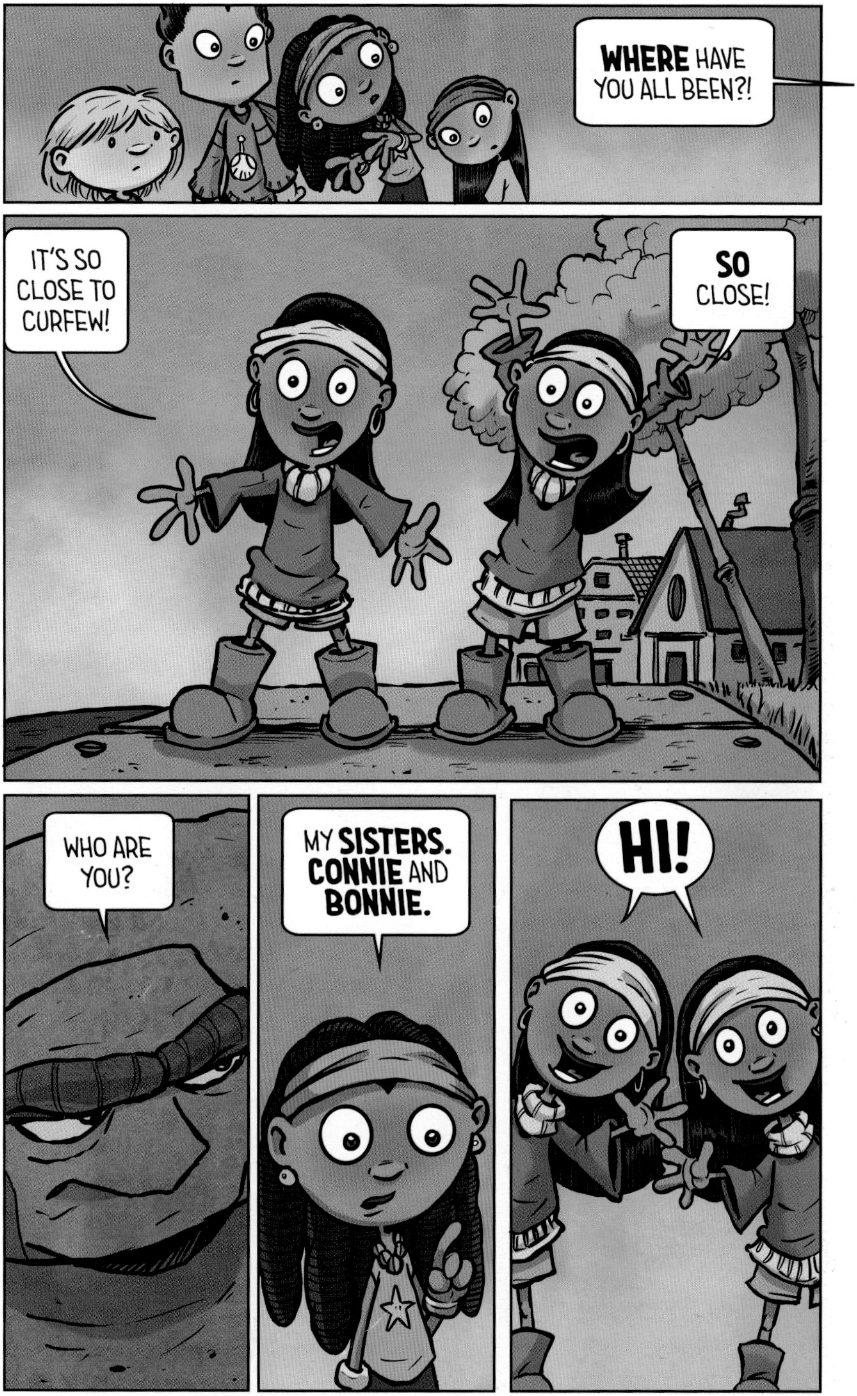

WHERE HAVE YOU ALL BEEN?!
IT'S SO CLOSE TO CURFEW!
SO CLOSE!
WHO ARE YOU?
MY SISTERS. CONNIE AND BONNIE.
HI!

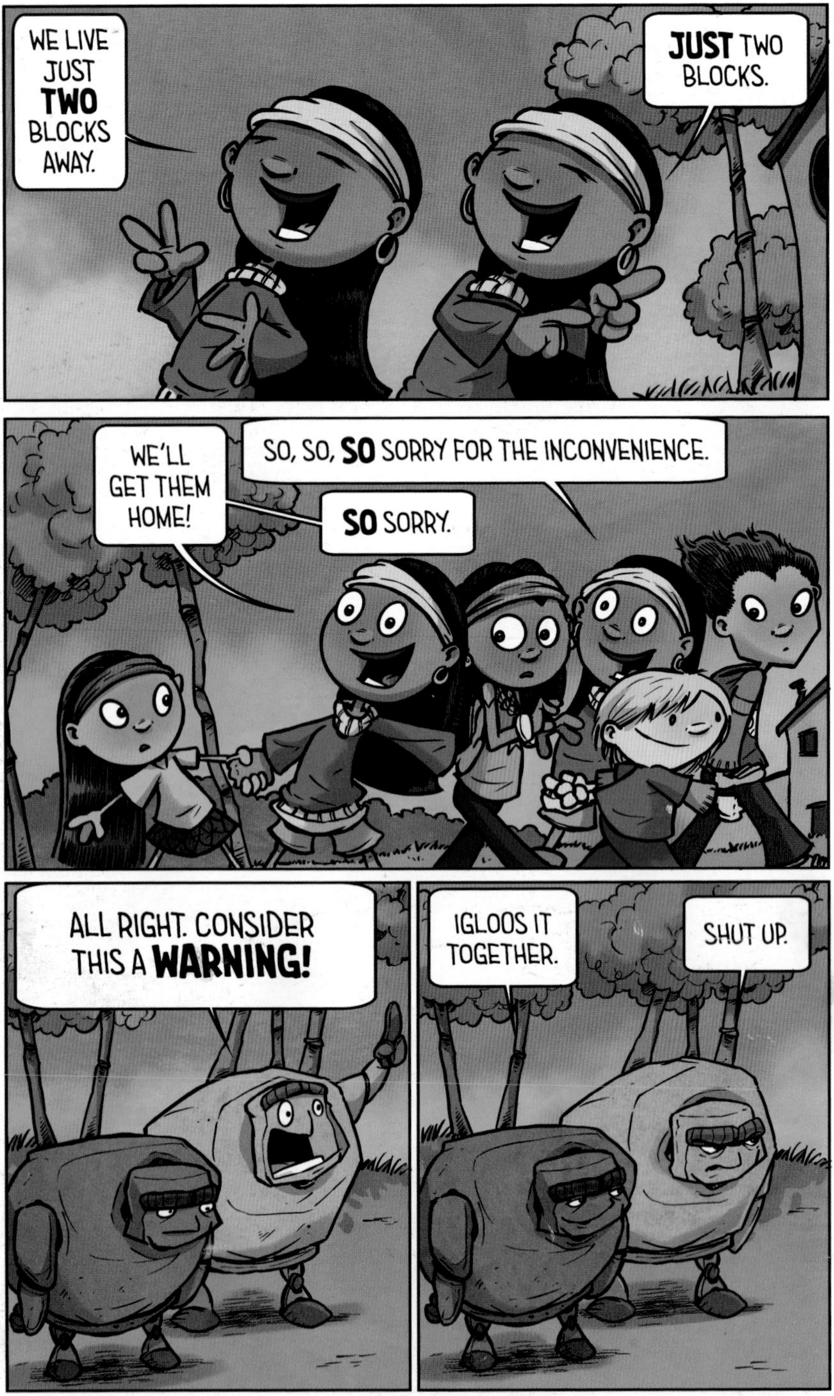
WE LIVE JUST TWO BLOCKS AWAY.
JUST TWO BLOCKS.
WE'LL GET THEM HOME!
SO, SO, SO SORRY FOR THE INCONVENIENCE.
SO SORRY.
ALL RIGHT. CONSIDER THIS A WARNING!
IGLOOS IT TOGETHER.
SHUT UP.

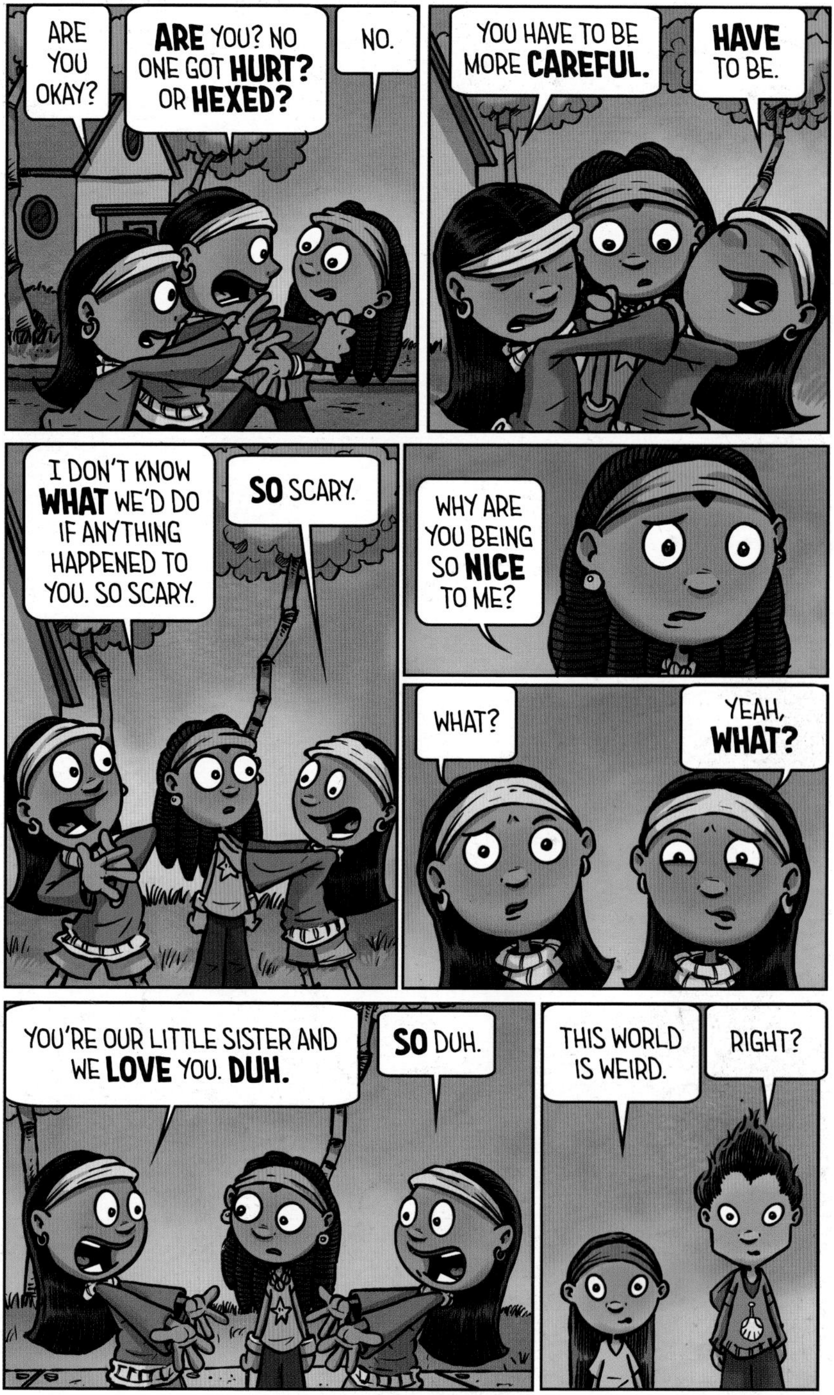
ARE YOU OKAY?
ARE YOU? NO ONE GOT HURT? OR HEXED?
NO.
YOU HAVE TO BE MORE CAREFUL.
HAVE TO BE.
I DON'T KNOW WHAT WE'D DO IF ANYTHING HAPPENED TO YOU. SO SCARY.
SO SCARY.
WHY ARE YOU BEING SO NICE TO ME?
WHAT?
YEAH, WHAT?
YOU'RE OUR LITTLE SISTER AND WE LOVE YOU. DUH.
SO DUH.
THIS WORLD IS WEIRD.
RIGHT?

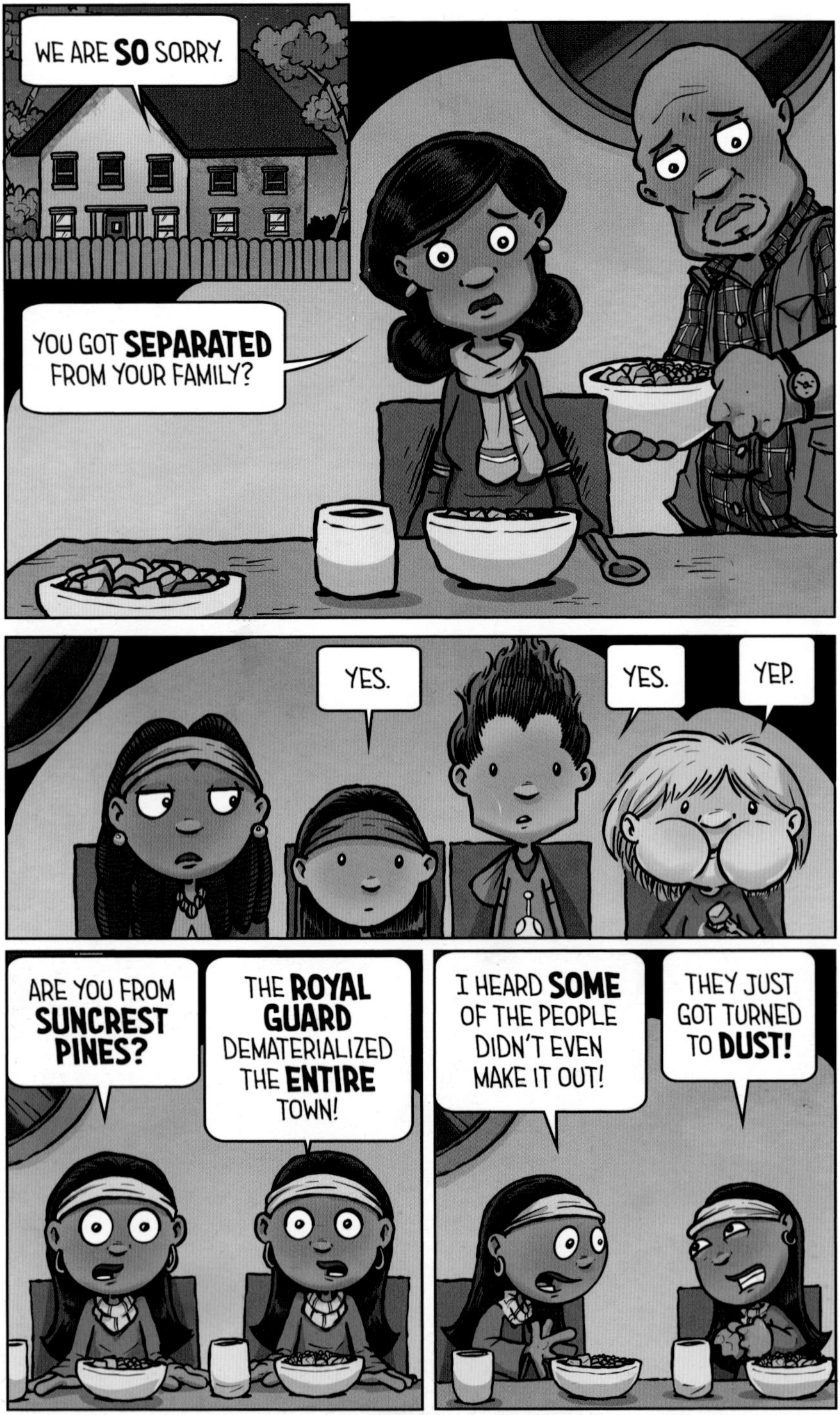
WE ARE **SO** SORRY.
YOU GOT **SEPARATED** FROM YOUR FAMILY?
YES.
YES.
YEP.
ARE YOU FROM **SUNCREST PINES?**
THE **ROYAL GUARD** DEMATERIALIZED THE **ENTIRE** TOWN!
I HEARD **SOME** OF THE PEOPLE DIDN'T EVEN MAKE IT OUT!
THEY JUST GOT TURNED TO **DUST!**

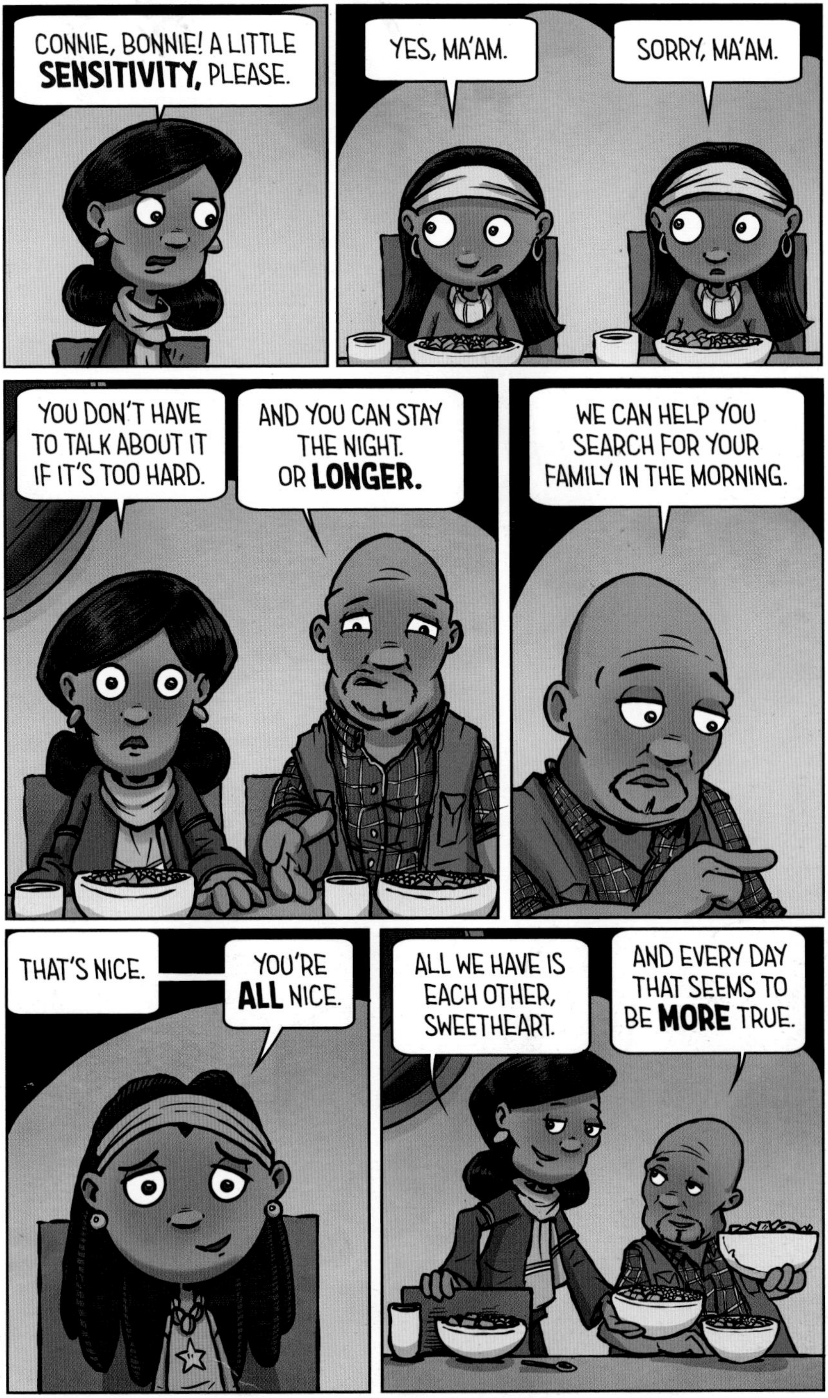
CONNIE, BONNIE! A LITTLE **SENSITIVITY,** PLEASE.
YES, MA'AM.
SORRY, MA'AM.
YOU DON'T HAVE TO TALK ABOUT IT IF IT'S TOO HARD.
AND YOU CAN STAY THE NIGHT. OR **LONGER.**
WE CAN HELP YOU SEARCH FOR YOUR FAMILY IN THE MORNING.
THAT'S NICE.
YOU'RE **ALL** NICE.
ALL WE HAVE IS EACH OTHER, SWEETHEART.
AND EVERY DAY THAT SEEMS TO BE **MORE** TRUE.

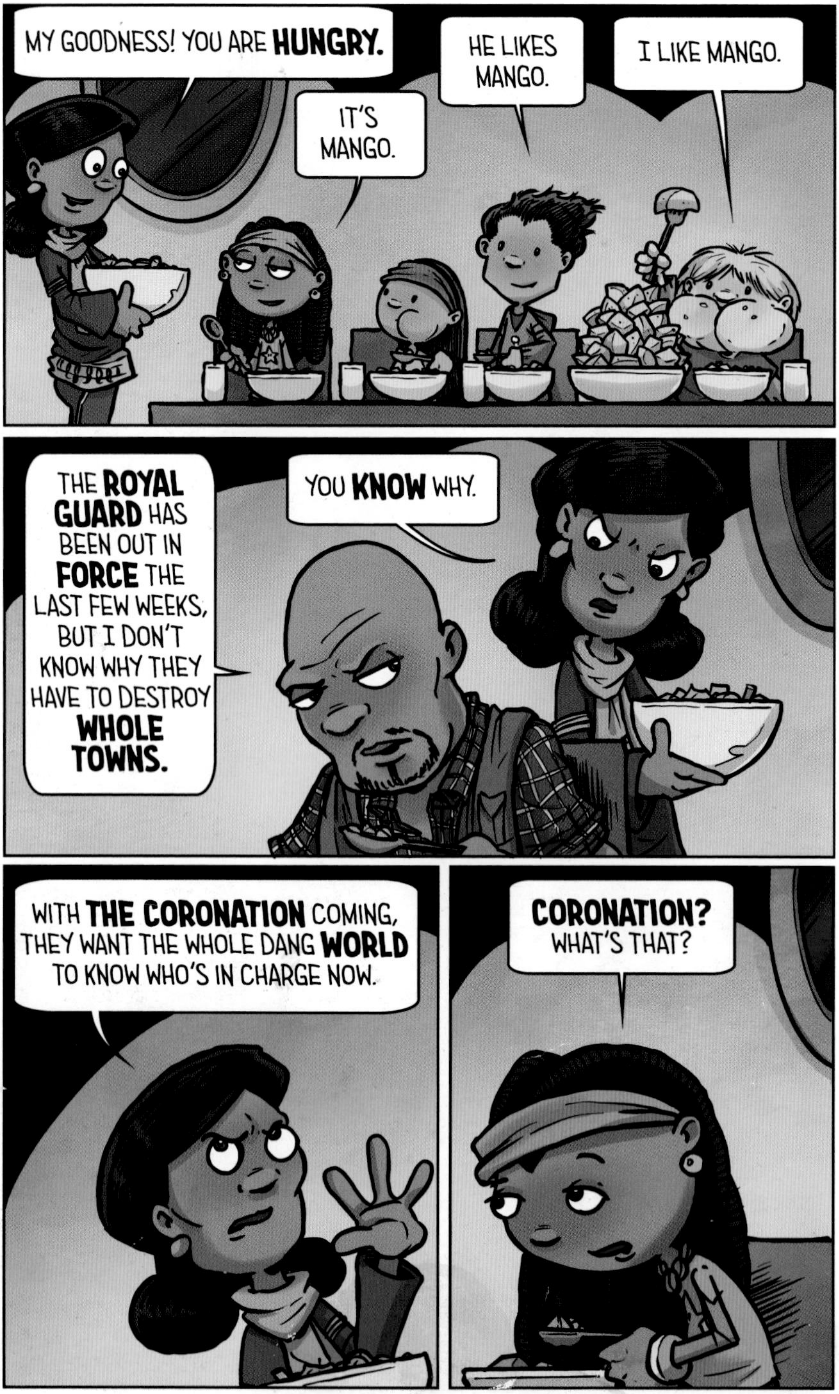
MY GOODNESS! YOU ARE **HUNGRY.**
IT'S MANGO.
HE LIKES MANGO.
I LIKE MANGO.
THE **ROYAL GUARD** HAS BEEN OUT IN **FORCE** THE LAST FEW WEEKS, BUT I DON'T KNOW WHY THEY HAVE TO DESTROY **WHOLE TOWNS.**
YOU **KNOW** WHY.
WITH **THE CORONATION** COMING, THEY WANT THE WHOLE DANG **WORLD** TO KNOW WHO'S IN CHARGE NOW.
CORONATION? WHAT'S THAT?

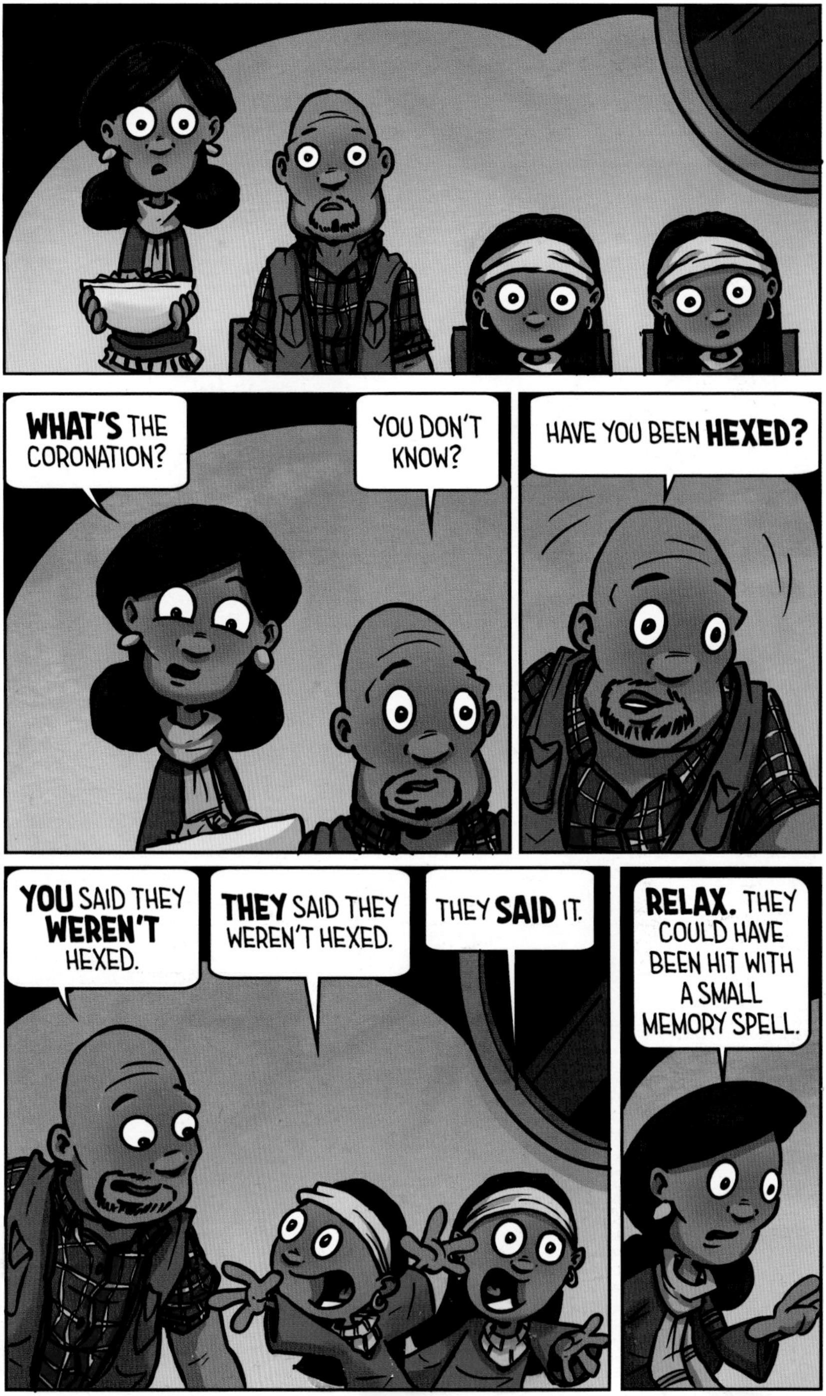
WHAT'S THE CORONATION?
YOU DON'T KNOW?
HAVE YOU BEEN HEXED?
YOU SAID THEY WEREN'T HEXED.
THEY SAID THEY WEREN'T HEXED.
THEY SAID IT.
RELAX. THEY COULD HAVE BEEN HIT WITH A SMALL MEMORY SPELL.

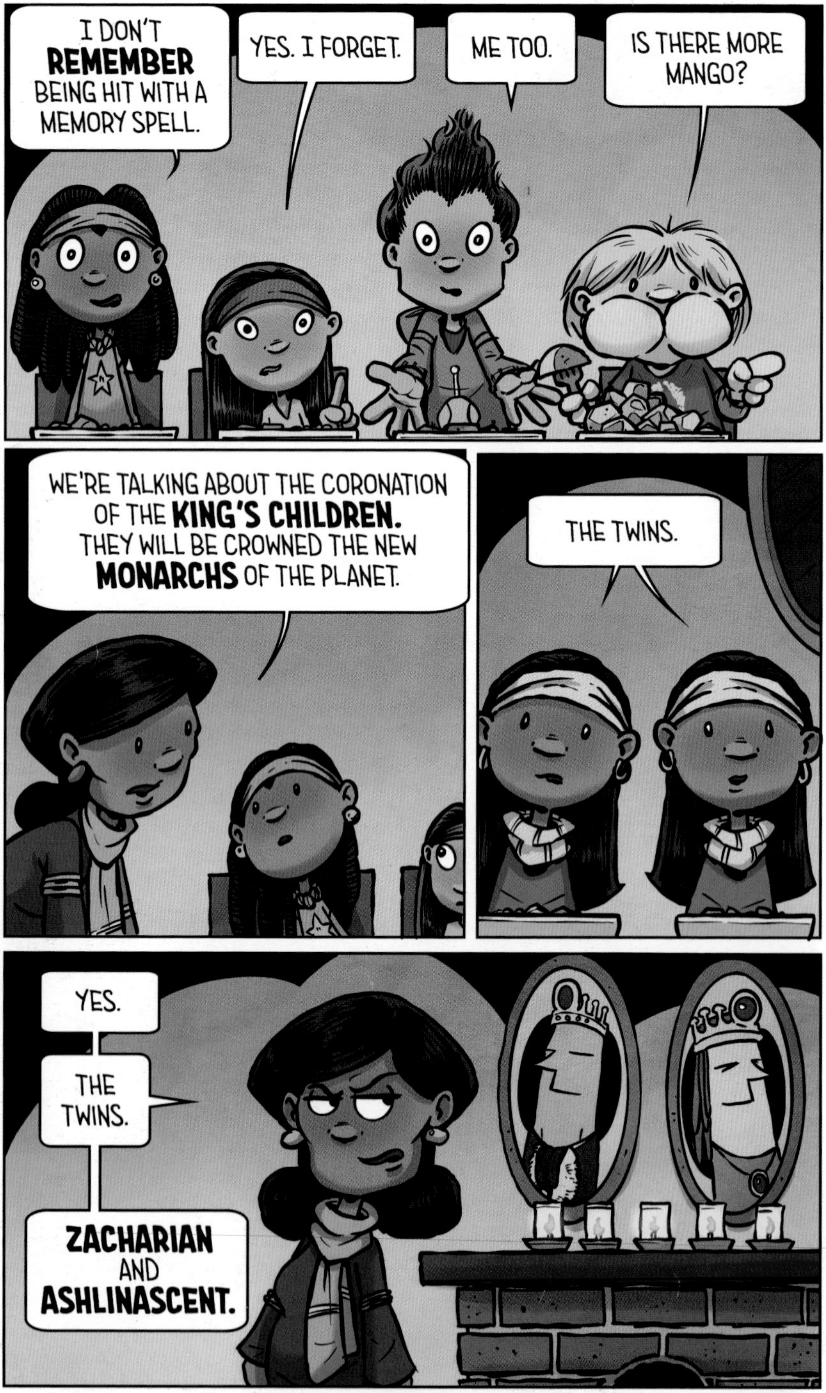

I DON'T REMEMBER BEING HIT WITH A MEMORY SPELL.
YES. I FORGET.
ME TOO.
IS THERE MORE MANGO?
WE'RE TALKING ABOUT THE CORONATION OF THE KING'S CHILDREN. THEY WILL BE CROWNED THE NEW MONARCHS OF THE PLANET.
THE TWINS.
YES.
THE TWINS.
ZACHARIAN AND ASHLINASCENT.

CHAPTER 3

ROYAL PAINS

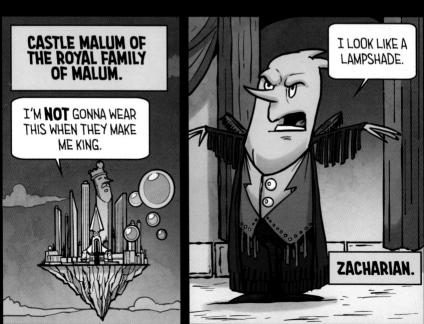

CASTLE MALUM OF THE ROYAL FAMILY OF MALUM.

I'M **NOT** GONNA WEAR THIS WHEN THEY MAKE ME KING.

I LOOK LIKE A LAMPSHADE.

ZACHARIAN.

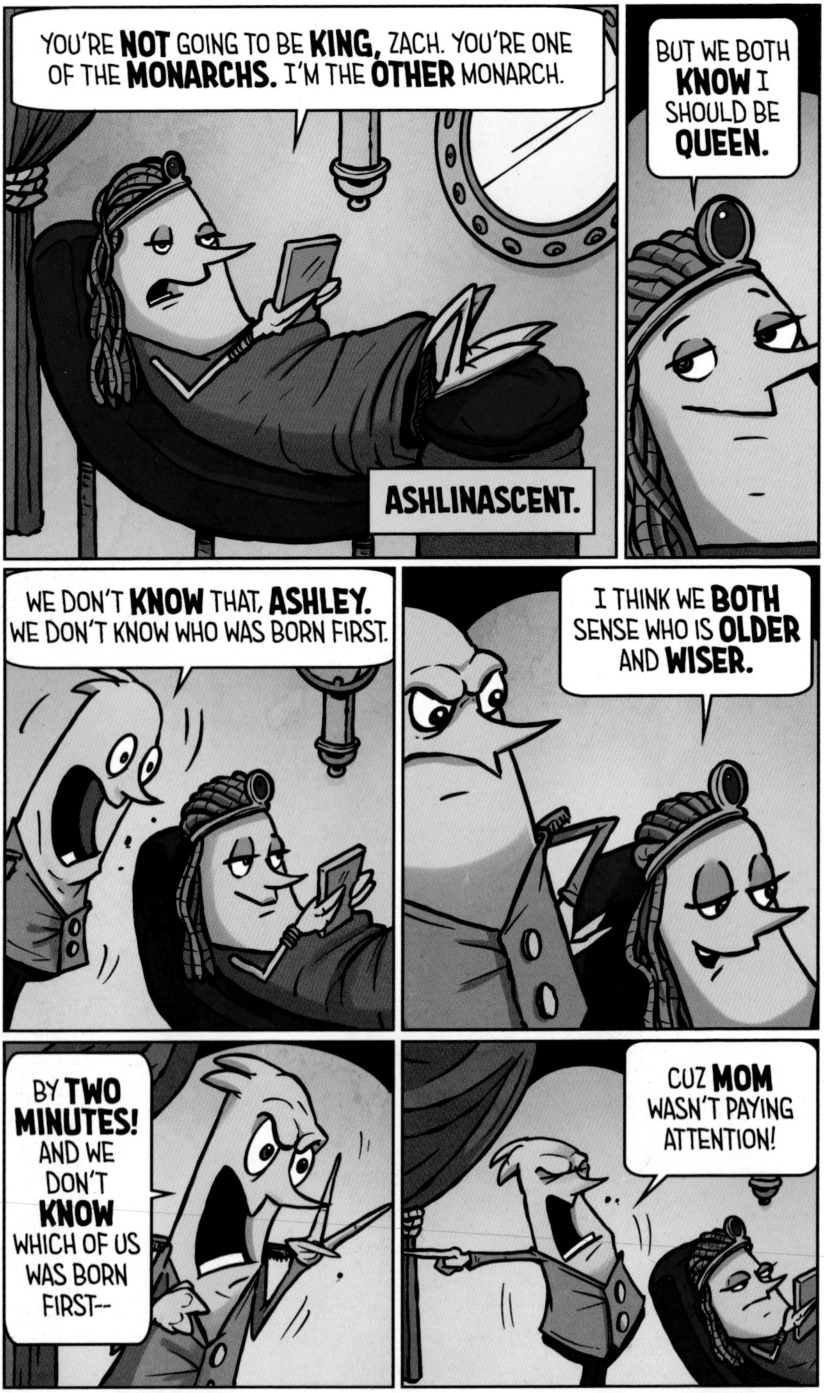
YOU'RE **NOT** GOING TO BE **KING,** ZACH. YOU'RE ONE OF THE **MONARCHS.** I'M THE **OTHER** MONARCH.
ASHLINASCENT.
BUT WE BOTH **KNOW** I SHOULD BE **QUEEN.**
WE DON'T **KNOW** THAT, **ASHLEY.** WE DON'T KNOW WHO WAS BORN FIRST.
I THINK WE **BOTH** SENSE WHO IS **OLDER** AND **WISER.**
BY **TWO MINUTES!** AND WE DON'T **KNOW** WHICH OF US WAS BORN FIRST--
CUZ **MOM** WASN'T PAYING ATTENTION!

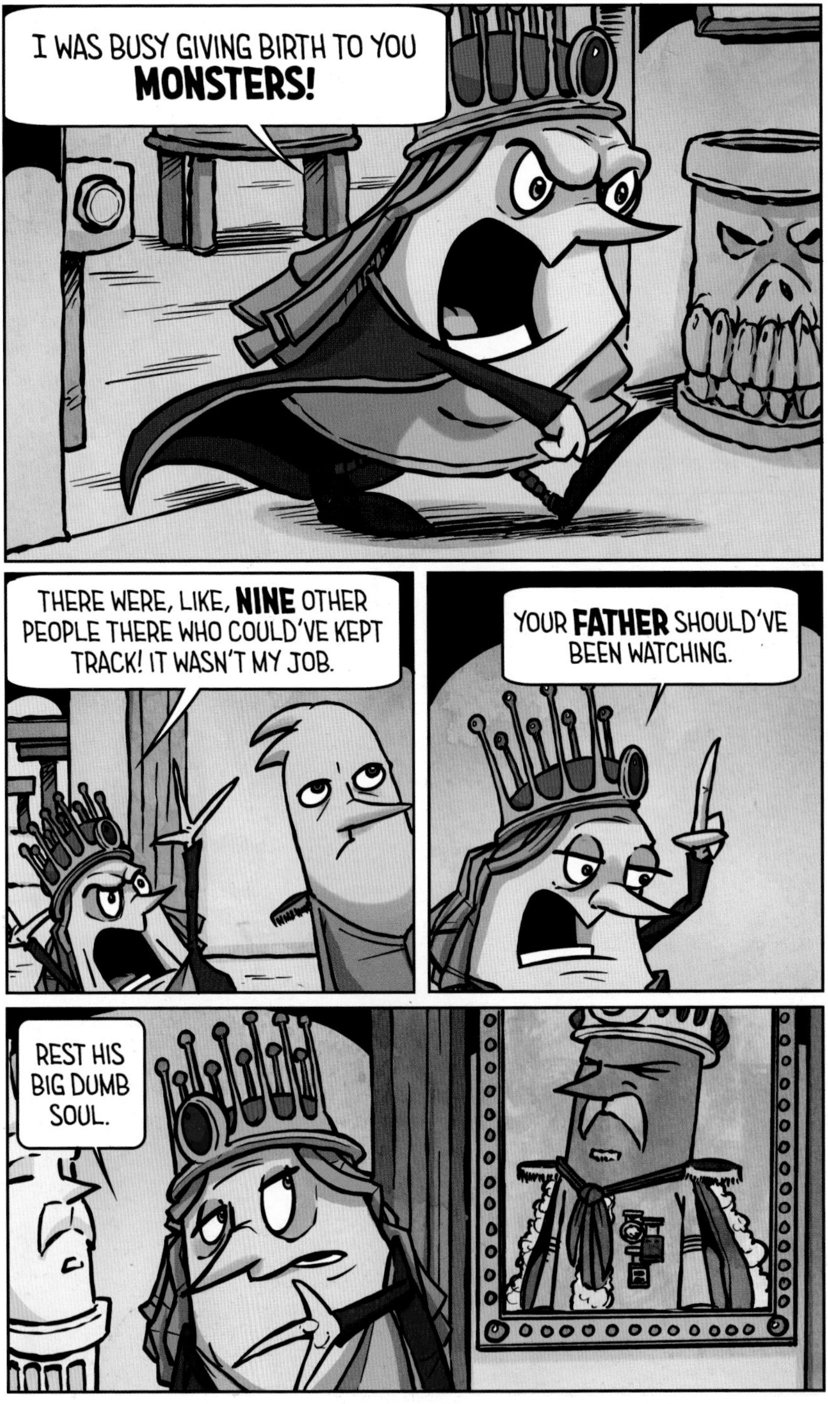
I WAS BUSY GIVING BIRTH TO YOU **MONSTERS!**
THERE WERE, LIKE, **NINE** OTHER PEOPLE THERE WHO COULD'VE KEPT TRACK! IT WASN'T MY JOB.
YOUR **FATHER** SHOULD'VE BEEN WATCHING.
REST HIS BIG DUMB SOUL.

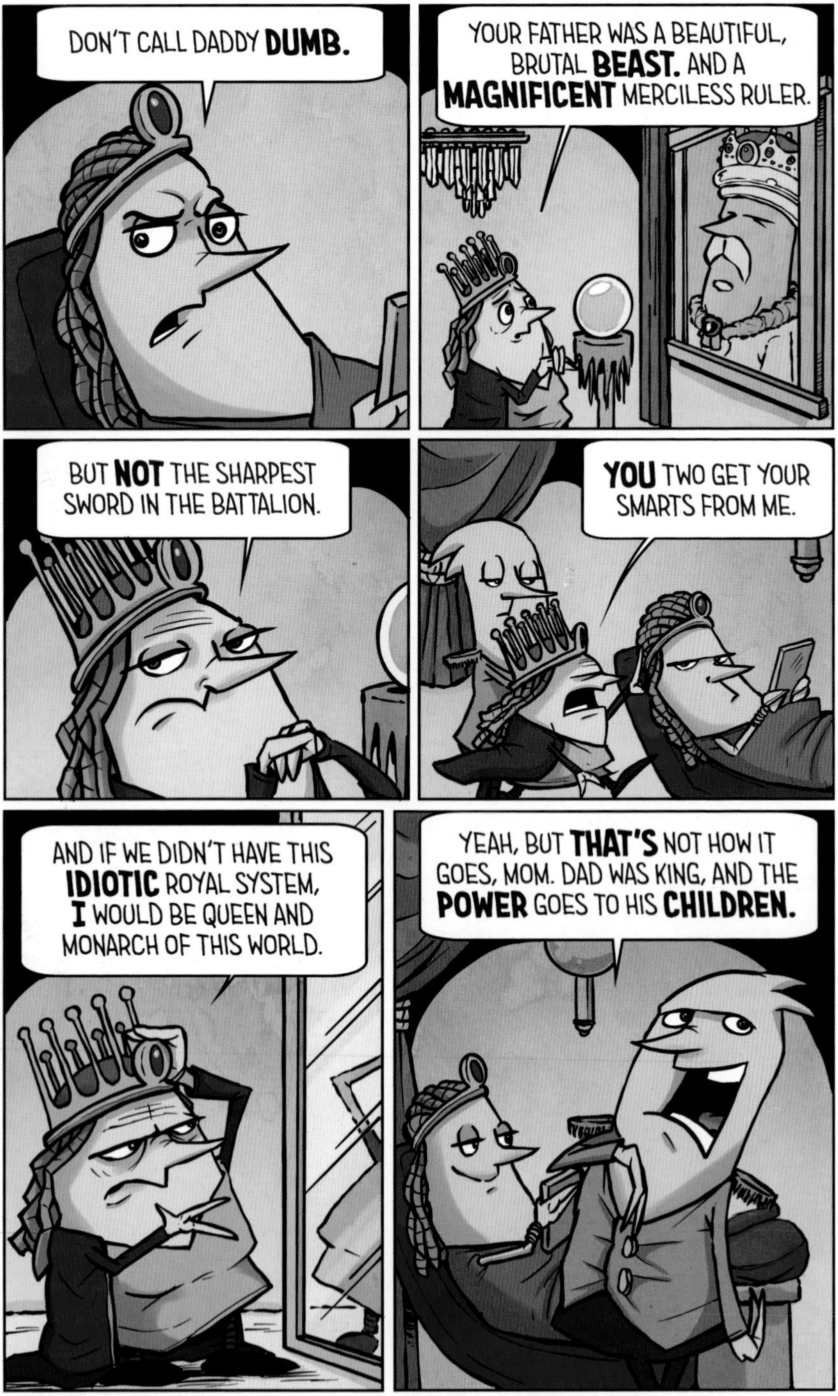
DON'T CALL DADDY **DUMB.**
YOUR FATHER WAS A BEAUTIFUL, BRUTAL **BEAST.** AND A **MAGNIFICENT** MERCILESS RULER.
BUT **NOT** THE SHARPEST SWORD IN THE BATTALION.
YOU TWO GET YOUR SMARTS FROM ME.
AND IF WE DIDN'T HAVE THIS **IDIOTIC** ROYAL SYSTEM, **I** WOULD BE QUEEN AND MONARCH OF THIS WORLD.
YEAH, BUT **THAT'S** NOT HOW IT GOES, MOM. DAD WAS KING, AND THE **POWER** GOES TO HIS **CHILDREN.**

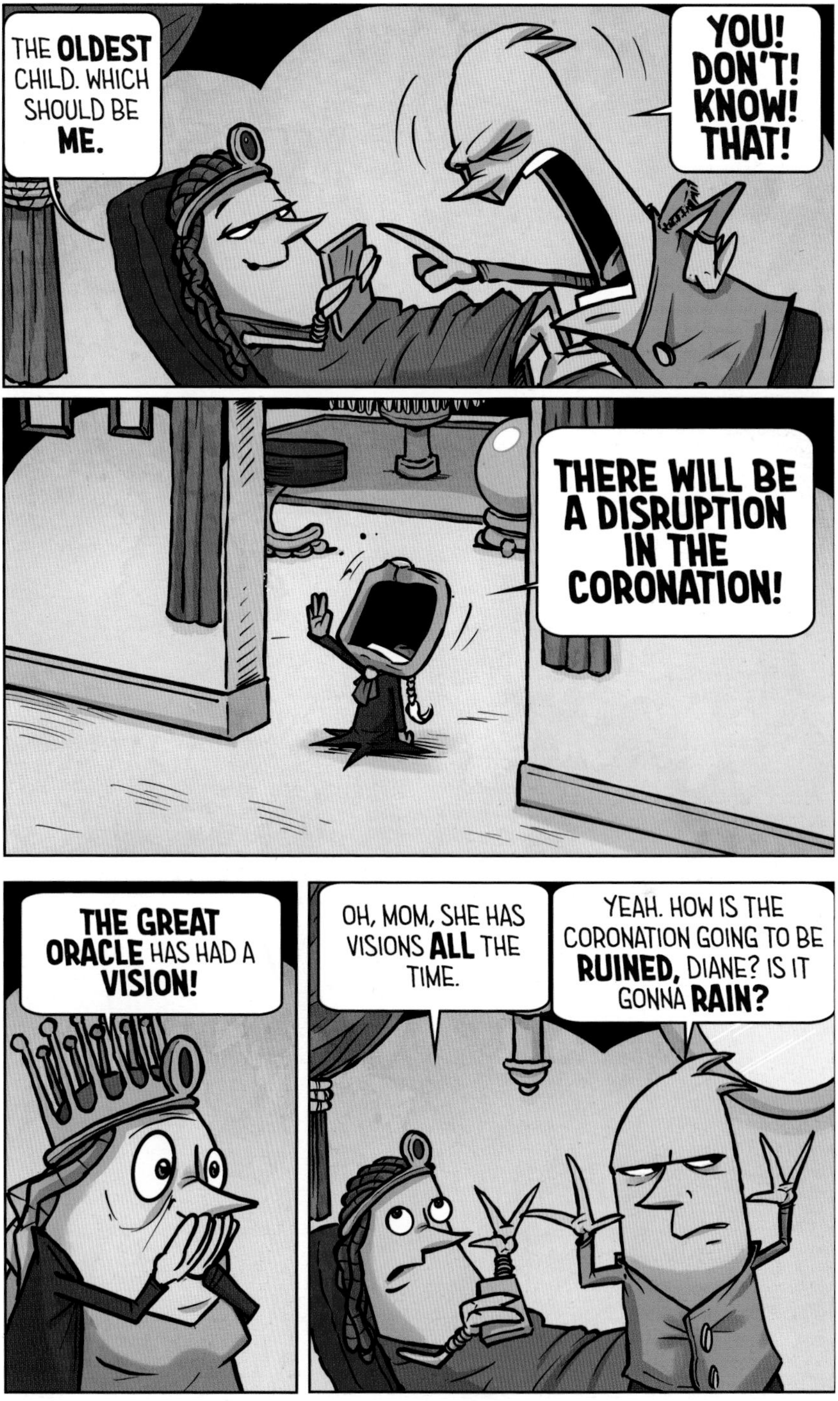
THE **OLDEST** CHILD. WHICH SHOULD BE **ME.**
YOU! DON'T! KNOW! THAT!
THERE WILL BE A DISRUPTION IN THE CORONATION!
THE GREAT ORACLE HAS HAD A **VISION!**
OH, MOM, SHE HAS VISIONS **ALL** THE TIME.
YEAH. HOW IS THE CORONATION GOING TO BE **RUINED,** DIANE? IS IT GONNA **RAIN?**

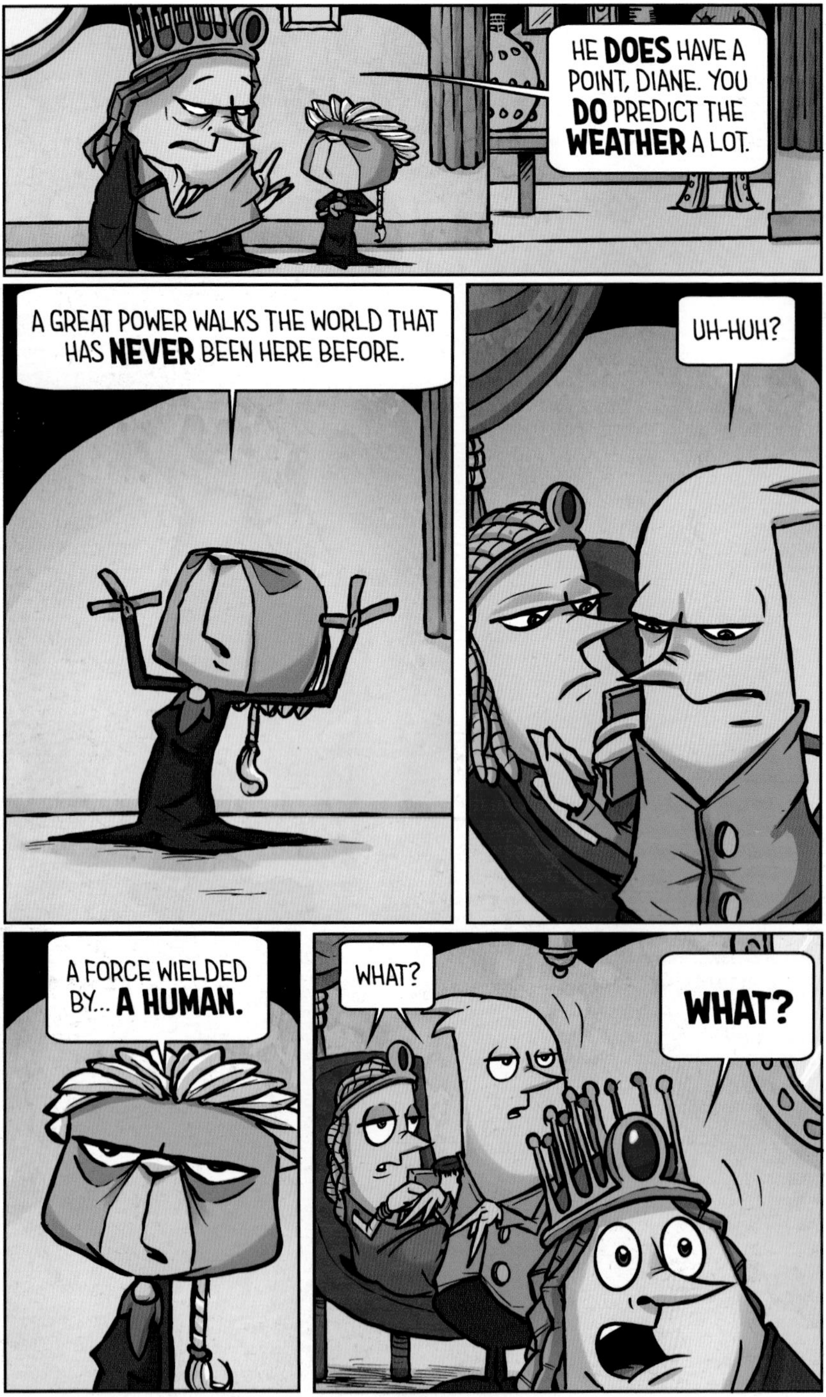
HE **DOES** HAVE A POINT, DIANE. YOU **DO** PREDICT THE **WEATHER** A LOT.
A GREAT POWER WALKS THE WORLD THAT HAS **NEVER** BEEN HERE BEFORE.
UH-HUH?
A FORCE WIELDED BY... **A HUMAN.**
WHAT?
WHAT?

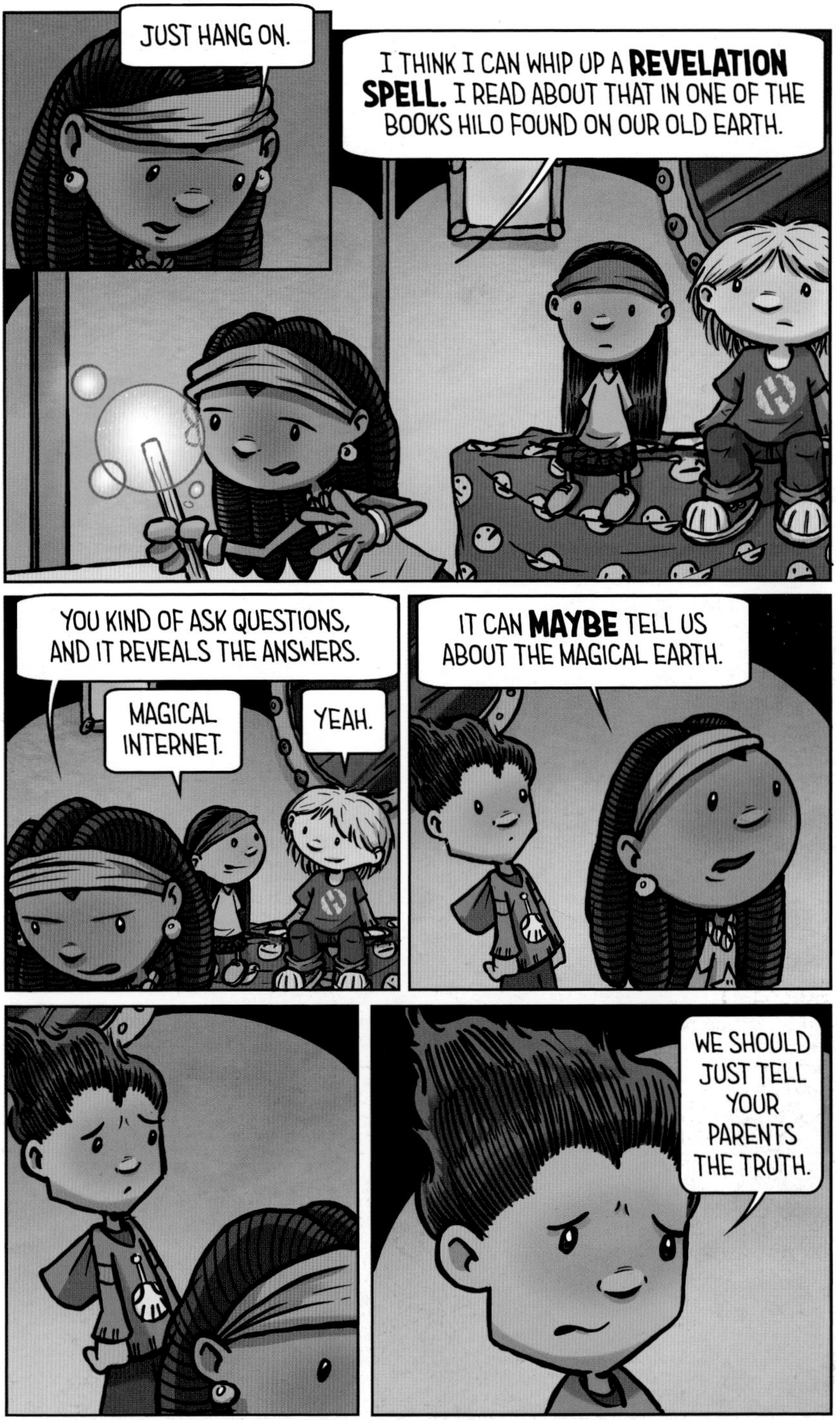
JUST HANG ON.
I THINK I CAN WHIP UP A **REVELATION SPELL.** I READ ABOUT THAT IN ONE OF THE BOOKS HILO FOUND ON OUR OLD EARTH.
YOU KIND OF ASK QUESTIONS, AND IT REVEALS THE ANSWERS.
MAGICAL INTERNET.
YEAH.
IT CAN **MAYBE** TELL US ABOUT THE MAGICAL EARTH.
WE SHOULD JUST TELL YOUR PARENTS THE TRUTH.

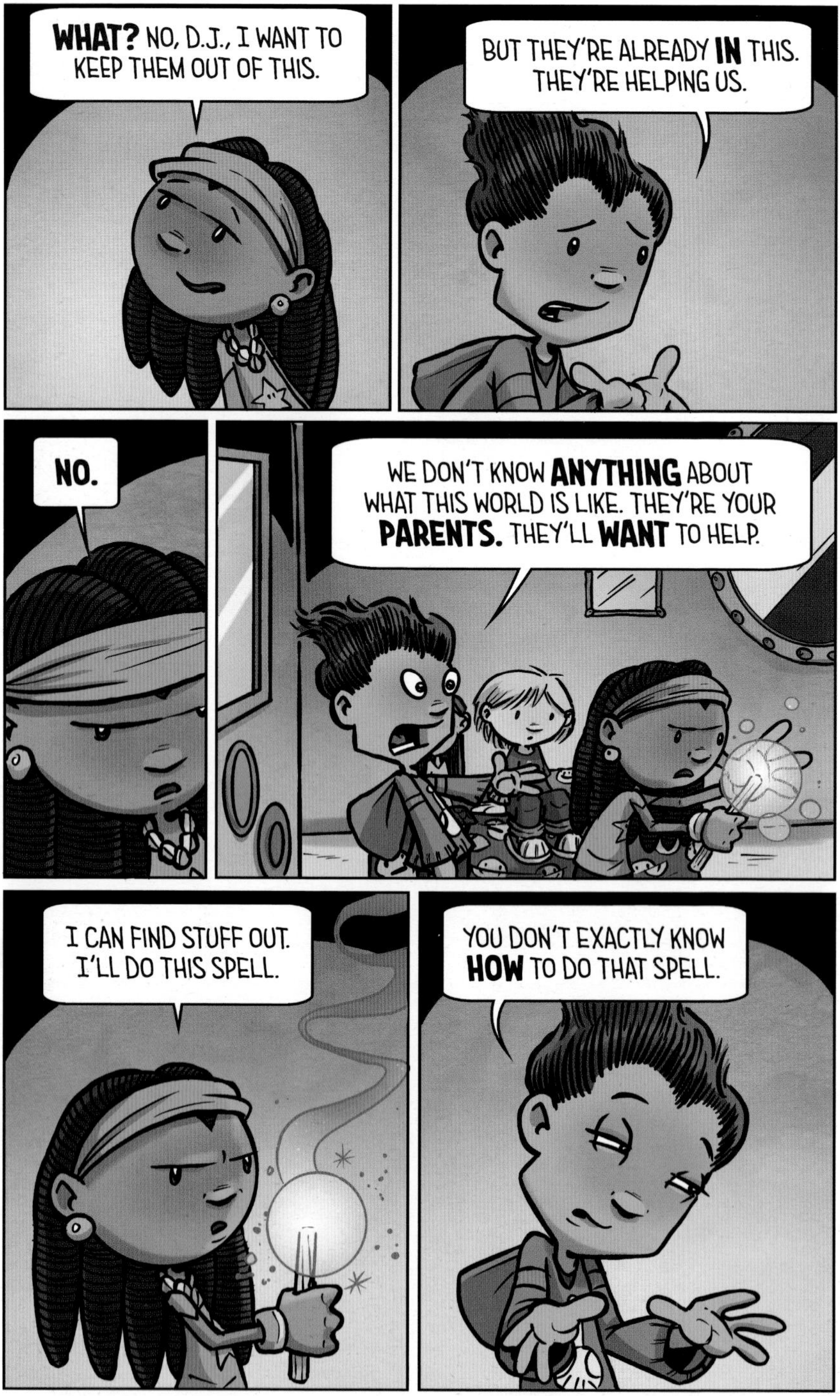
WHAT? NO, D.J., I WANT TO KEEP THEM OUT OF THIS.
BUT THEY'RE ALREADY IN THIS. THEY'RE HELPING US.
NO.
WE DON'T KNOW ANYTHING ABOUT WHAT THIS WORLD IS LIKE. THEY'RE YOUR PARENTS. THEY'LL WANT TO HELP.
I CAN FIND STUFF OUT. I'LL DO THIS SPELL.
YOU DON'T EXACTLY KNOW HOW TO DO THAT SPELL.

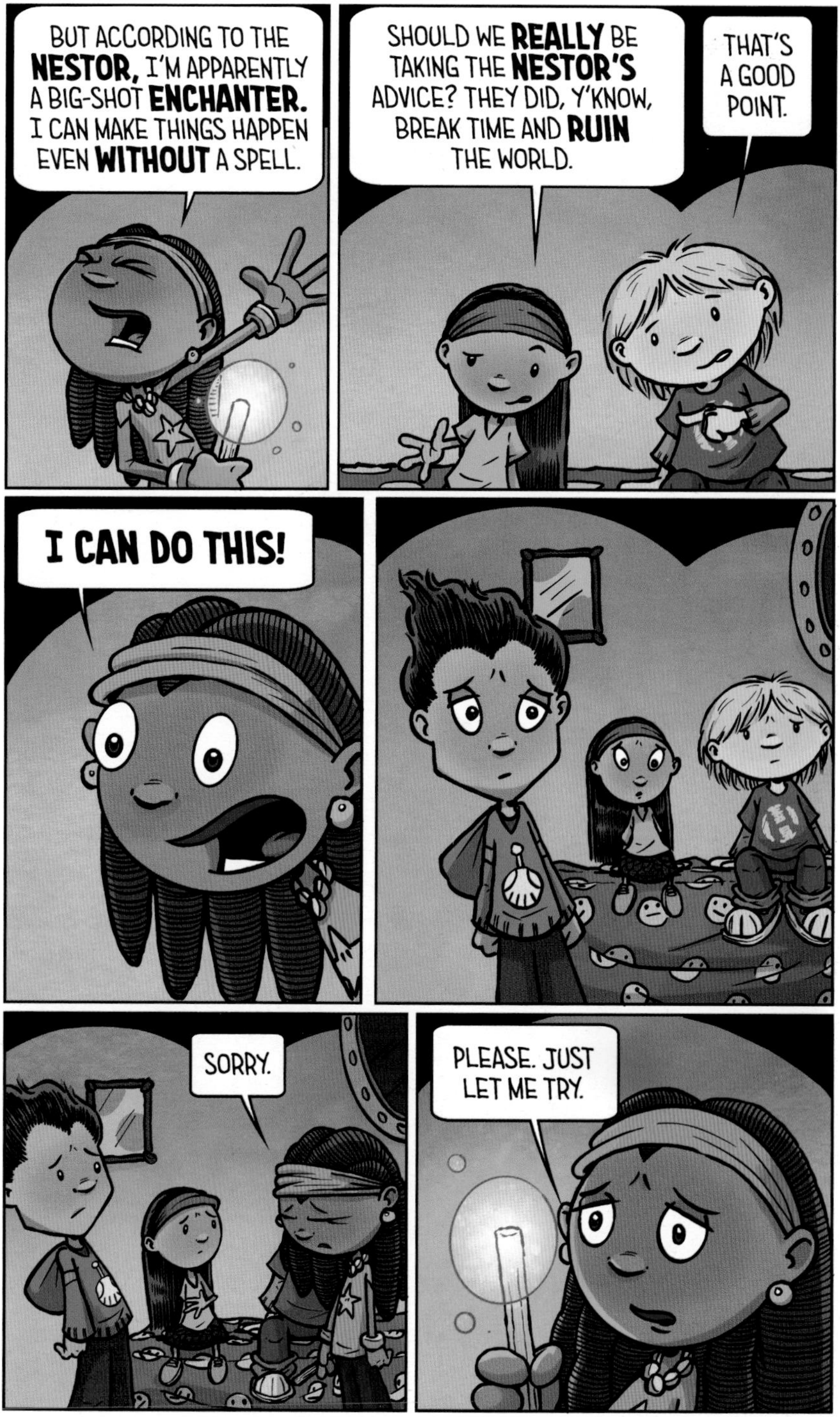
BUT ACCORDING TO THE NESTOR, I'M APPARENTLY A BIG-SHOT ENCHANTER. I CAN MAKE THINGS HAPPEN EVEN WITHOUT A SPELL.
SHOULD WE REALLY BE TAKING THE NESTOR'S ADVICE? THEY DID, Y'KNOW, BREAK TIME AND RUIN THE WORLD.
THAT'S A GOOD POINT.
I CAN DO THIS!
SORRY.
PLEASE. JUST LET ME TRY.

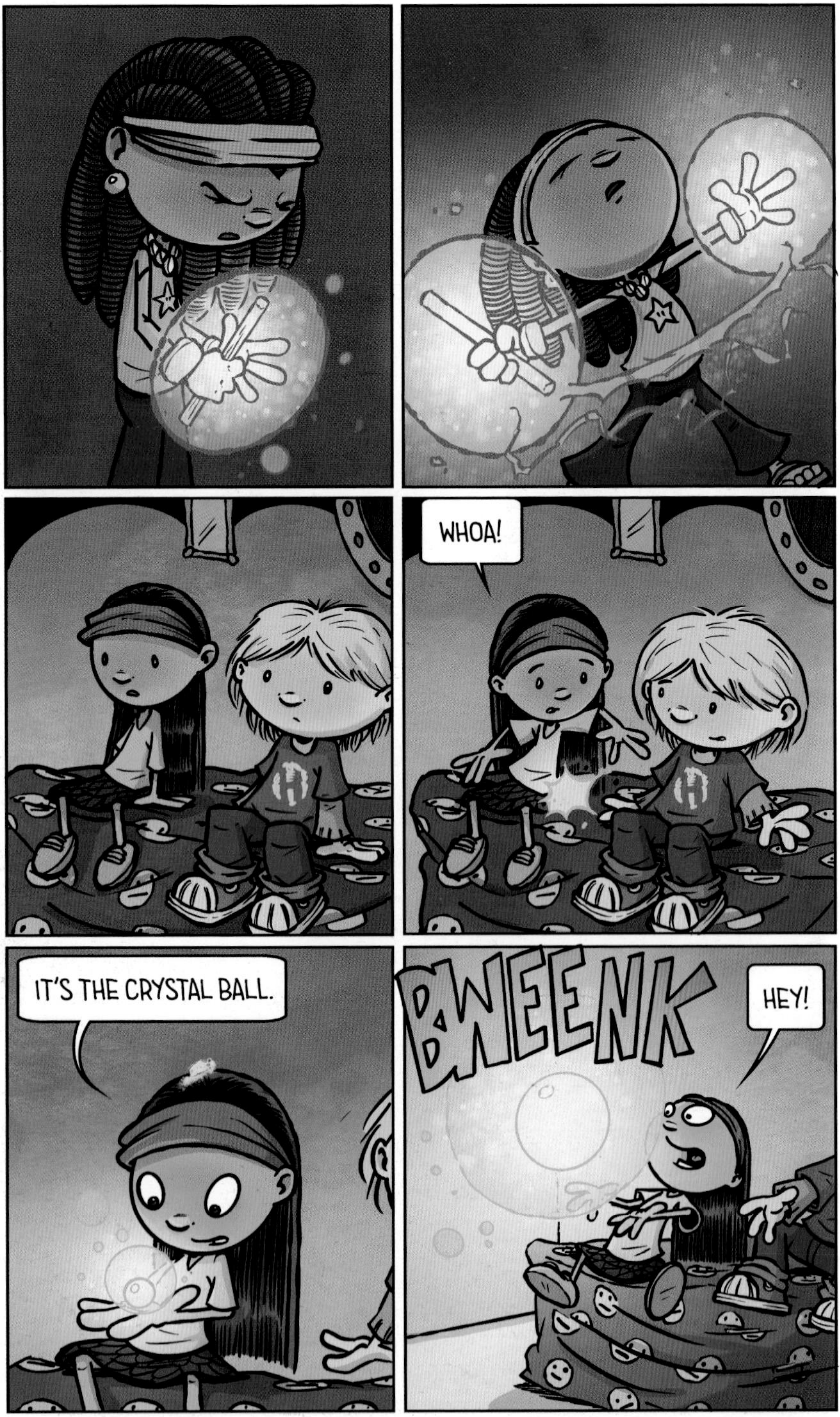
WHOA!
IT'S THE CRYSTAL BALL.
BWEENK
HEY!

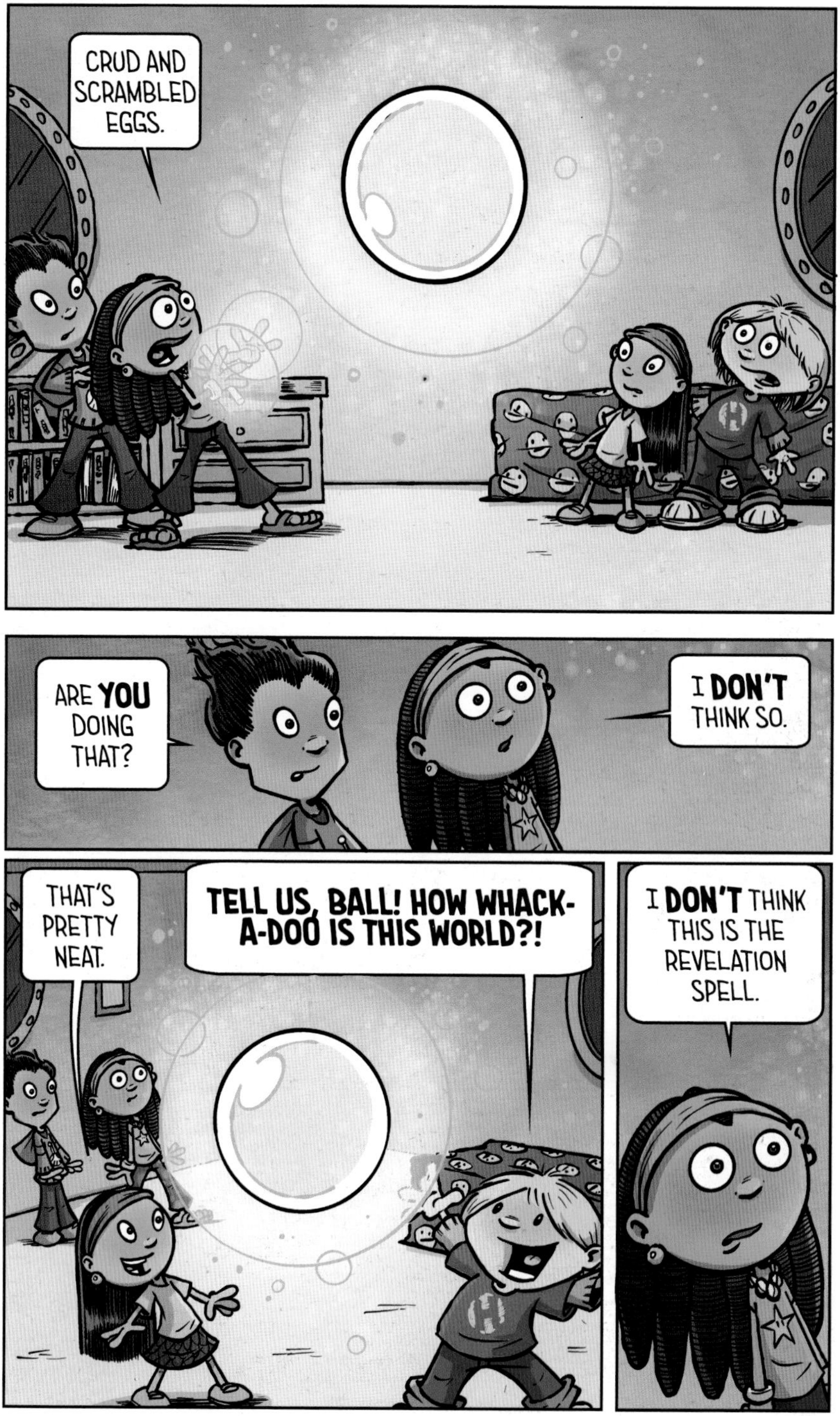
CRUD AND SCRAMBLED EGGS.
ARE **YOU** DOING THAT?
I **DON'T** THINK SO.
THAT'S PRETTY NEAT.
TELL US, BALL! HOW WHACK-A-DOO IS THIS WORLD?!
I **DON'T** THINK THIS IS THE REVELATION SPELL.

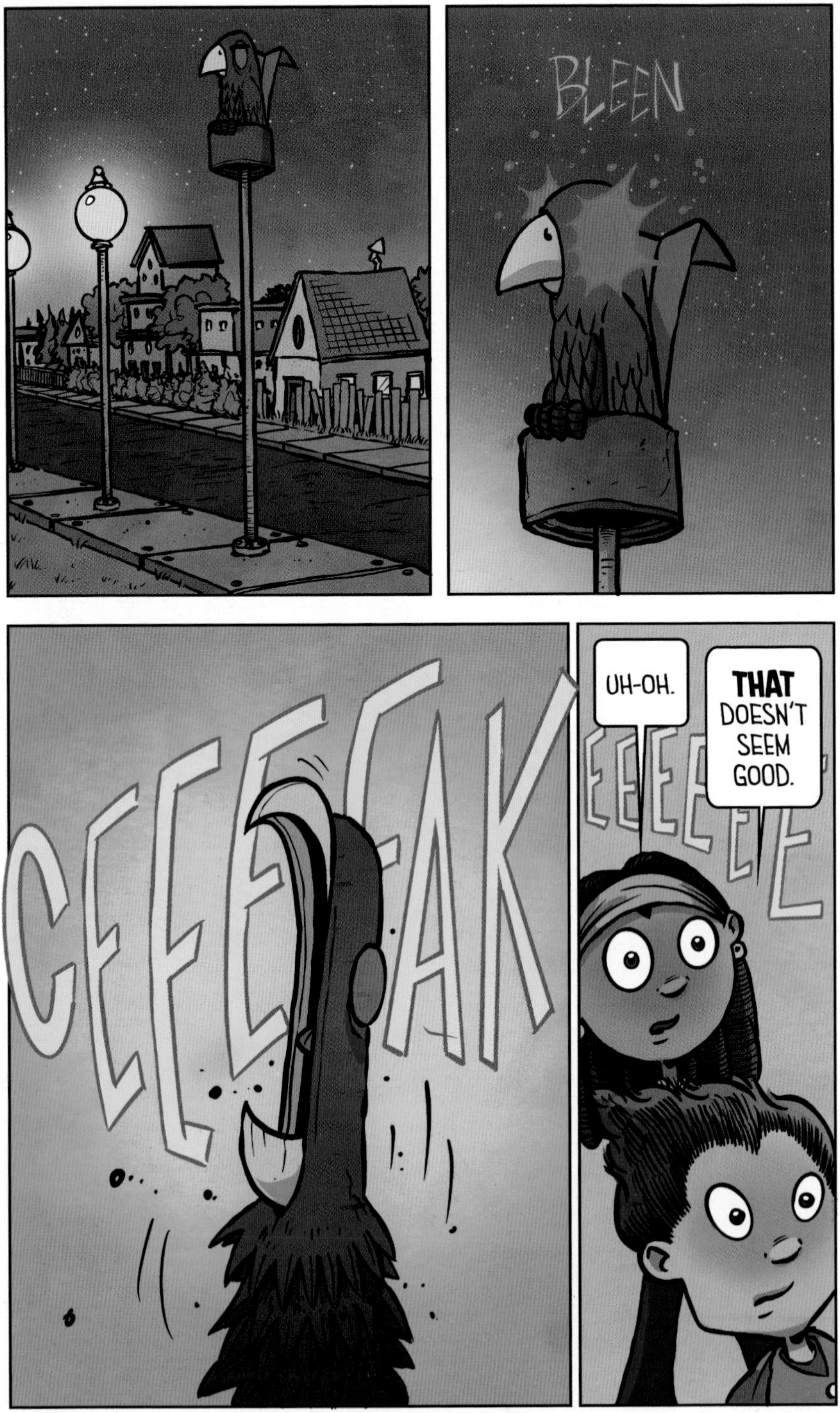
BLEEN
CEEEEAK
EEEEEEE
UH-OH.
THAT DOESN'T SEEM GOOD.

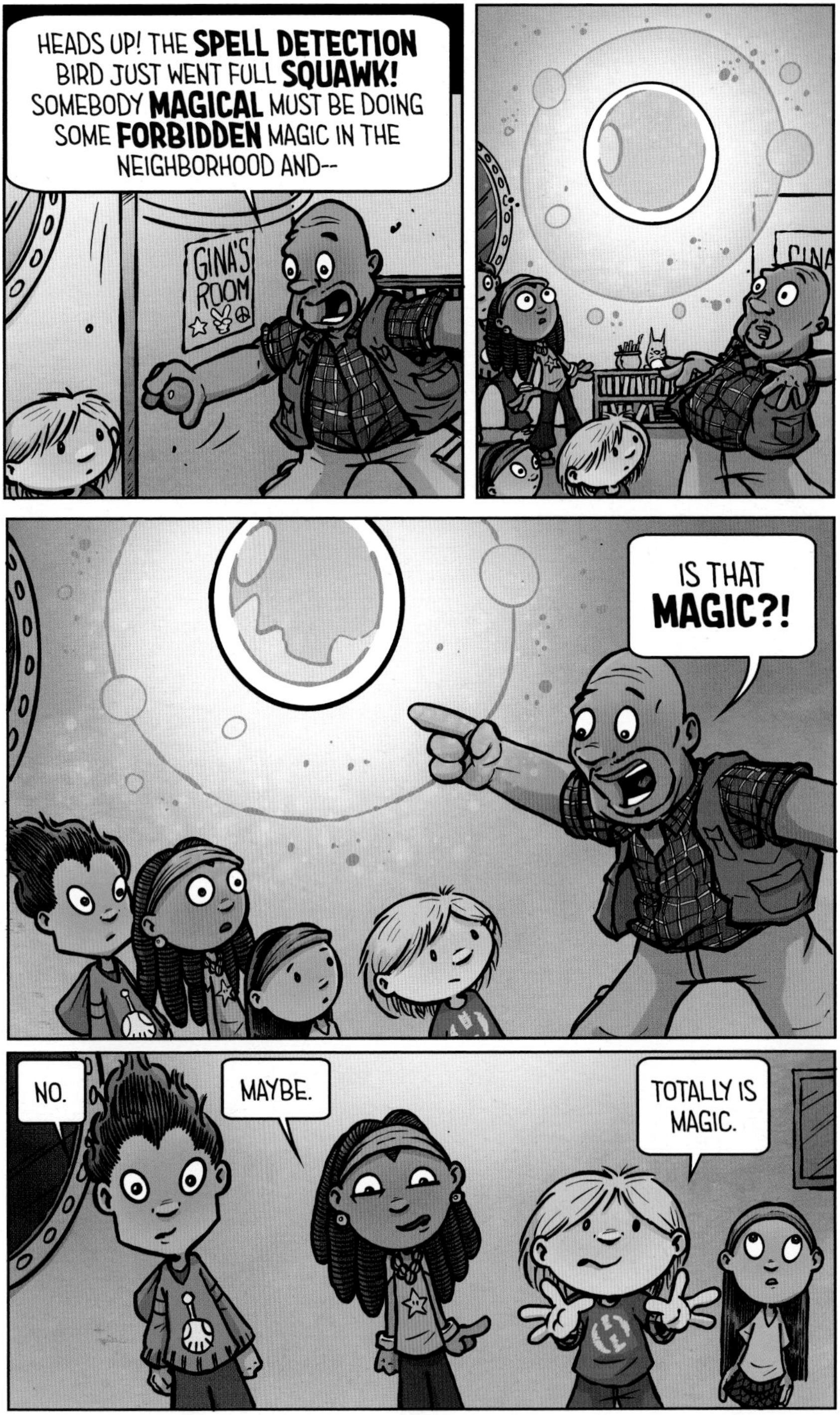
HEADS UP! THE **SPELL DETECTION** BIRD JUST WENT FULL **SQUAWK!** SOMEBODY **MAGICAL** MUST BE DOING SOME **FORBIDDEN** MAGIC IN THE NEIGHBORHOOD AND--
GINA'S ROOM
IS THAT **MAGIC?!**
NO.
MAYBE.
TOTALLY IS MAGIC.

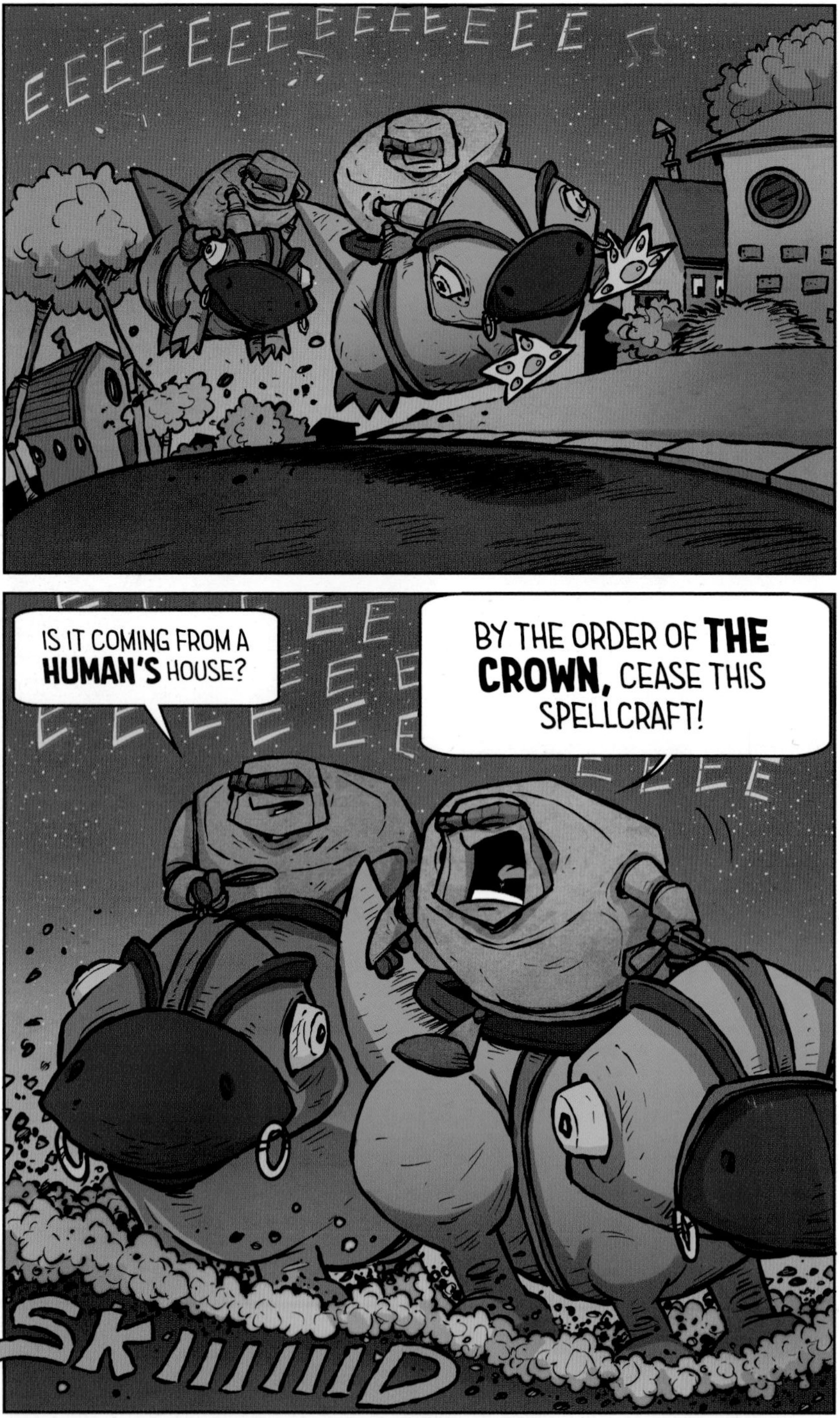
IS IT COMING FROM A HUMAN'S HOUSE?
BY THE ORDER OF THE CROWN, CEASE THIS SPELLCRAFT!
SKIIIIIIID

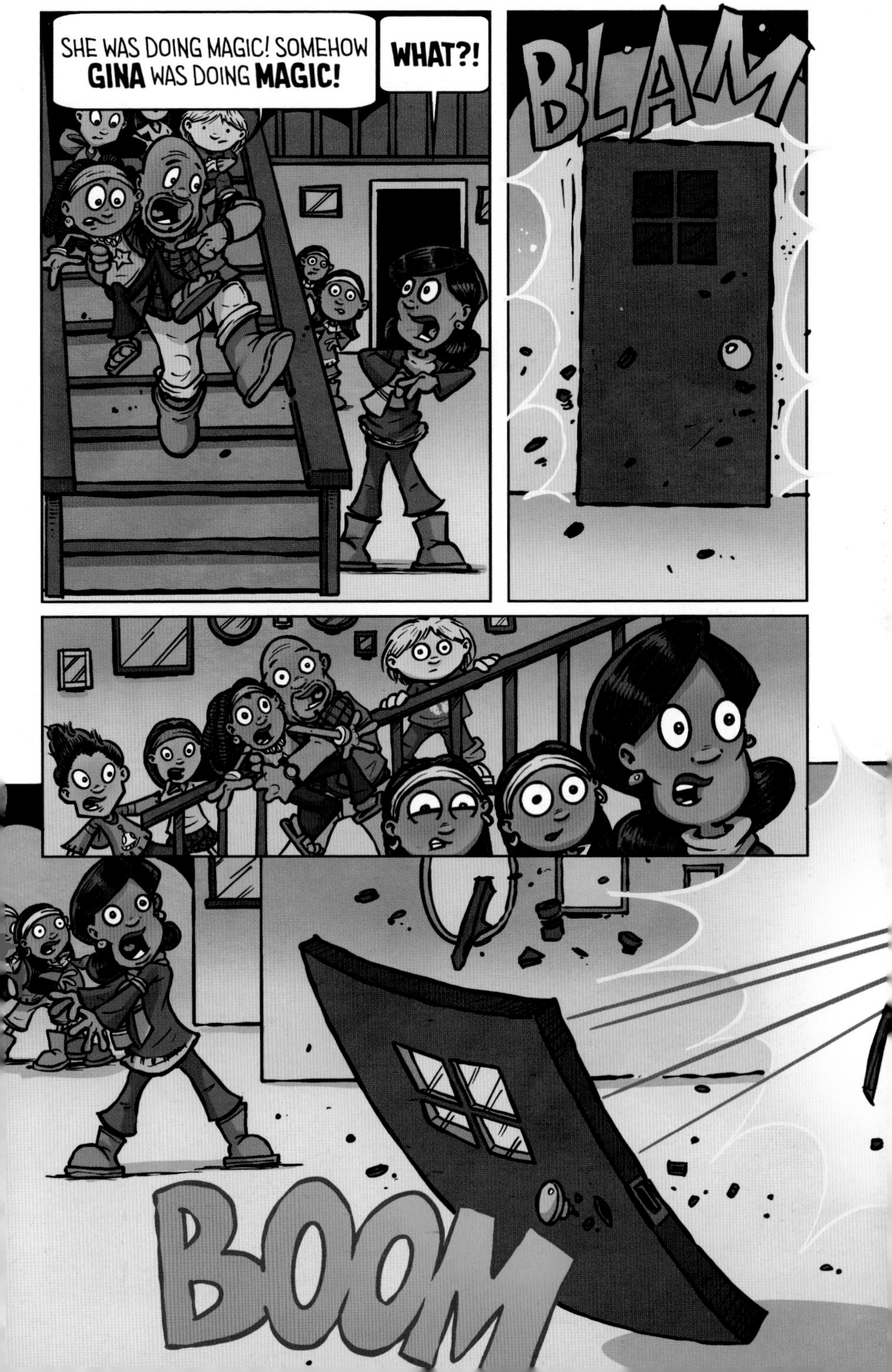
SHE WAS DOING MAGIC! SOMEHOW GINA WAS DOING MAGIC!
WHAT?!
BLAM
BOOM

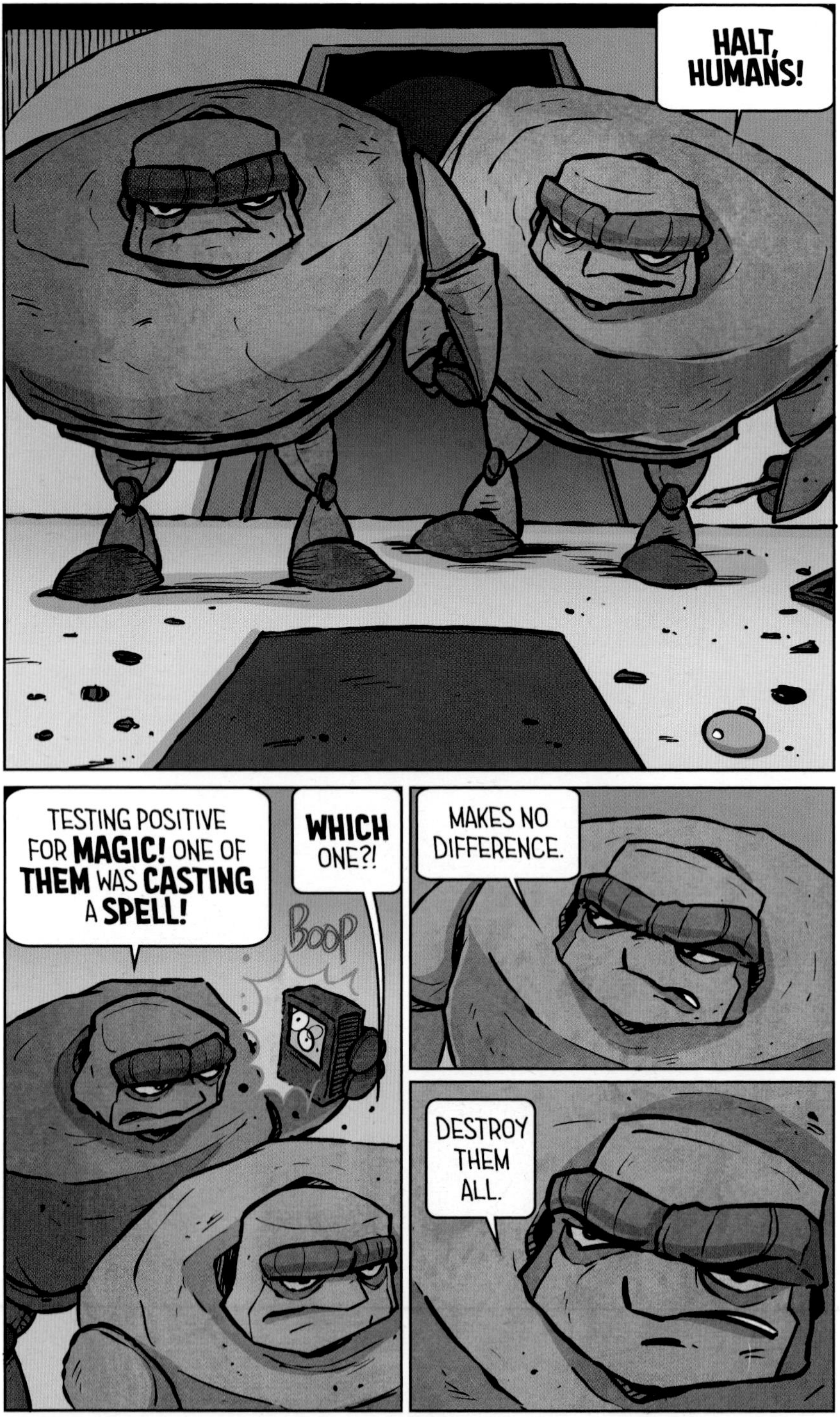
HALT, HUMANS!
TESTING POSITIVE FOR **MAGIC!** ONE OF **THEM** WAS **CASTING** A **SPELL!**
WHICH ONE?!
BOOP
MAKES NO DIFFERENCE.
DESTROY THEM ALL.

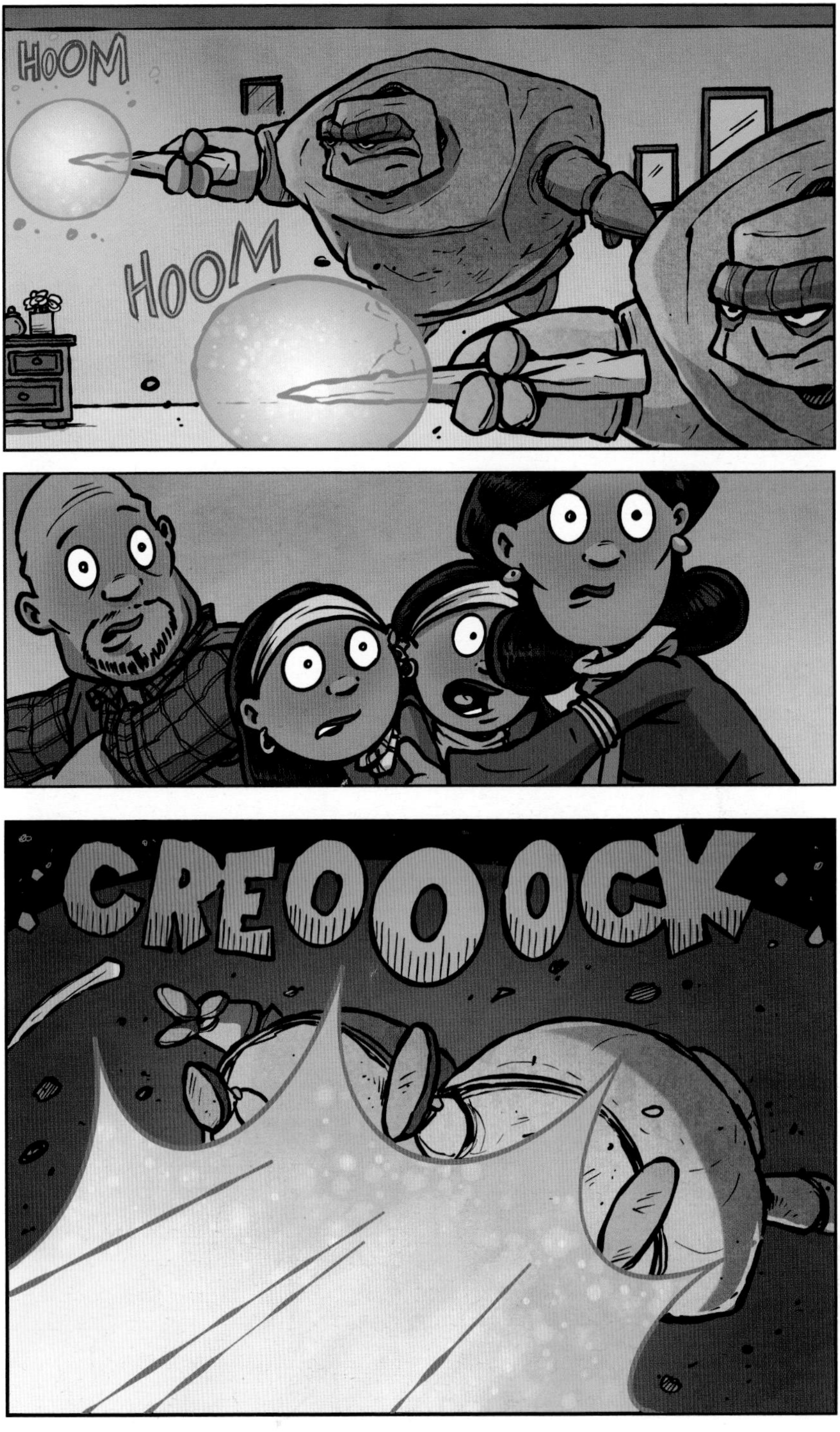
HOOM
HOOM
CREOOOCK

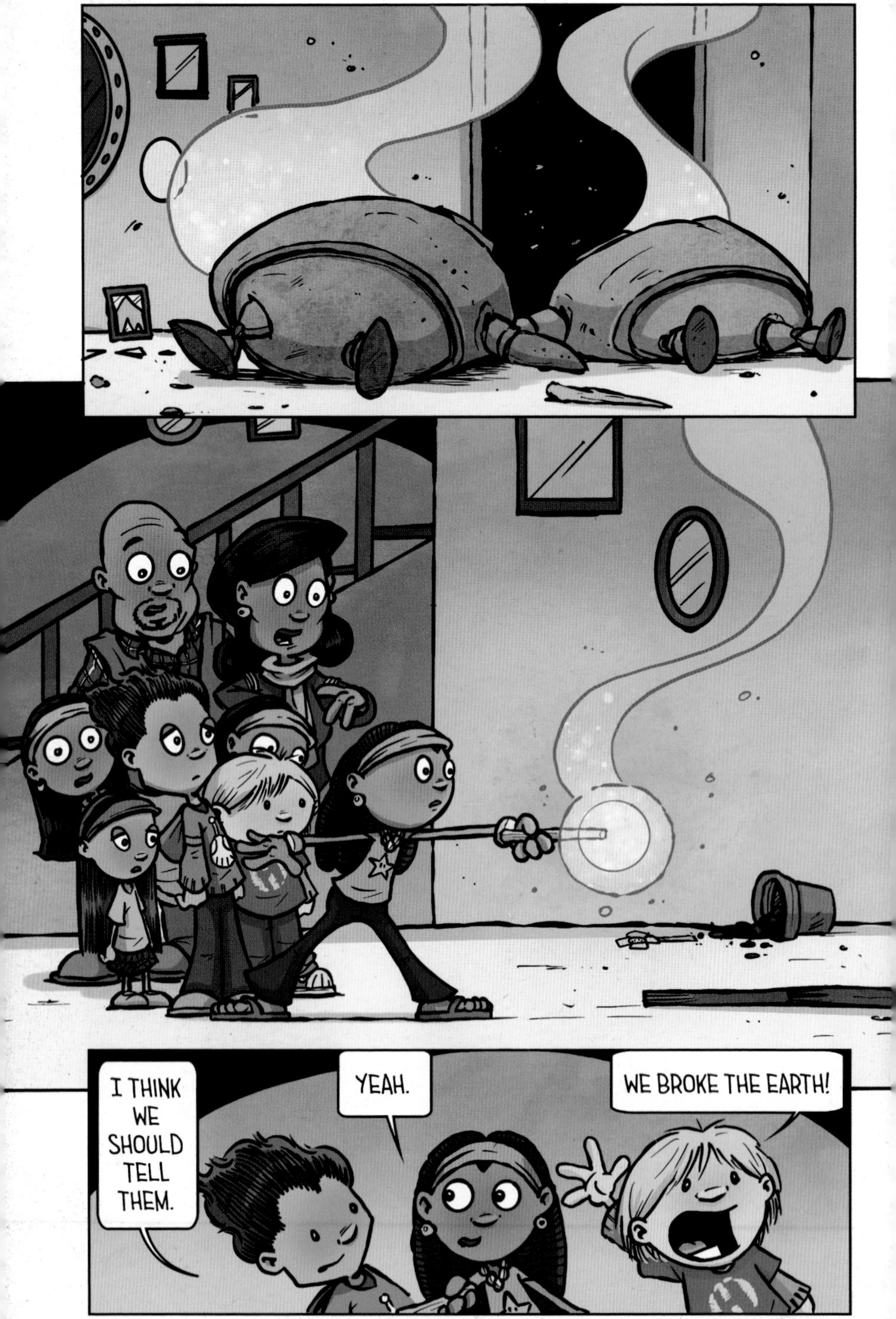
I THINK WE SHOULD TELL THEM.
YEAH.
WE BROKE THE EARTH!

CHAPTER 4

GO

THERE'S AN EARTH **WITHOUT** MAGIC?
YES. THAT'S HOW IT WAS **SUPPOSED** TO BE.
AND IT WAS BETTER?

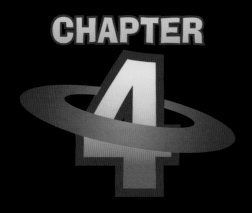

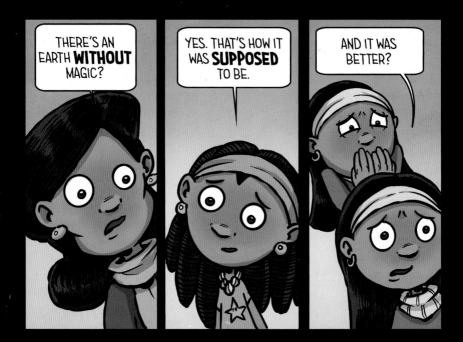

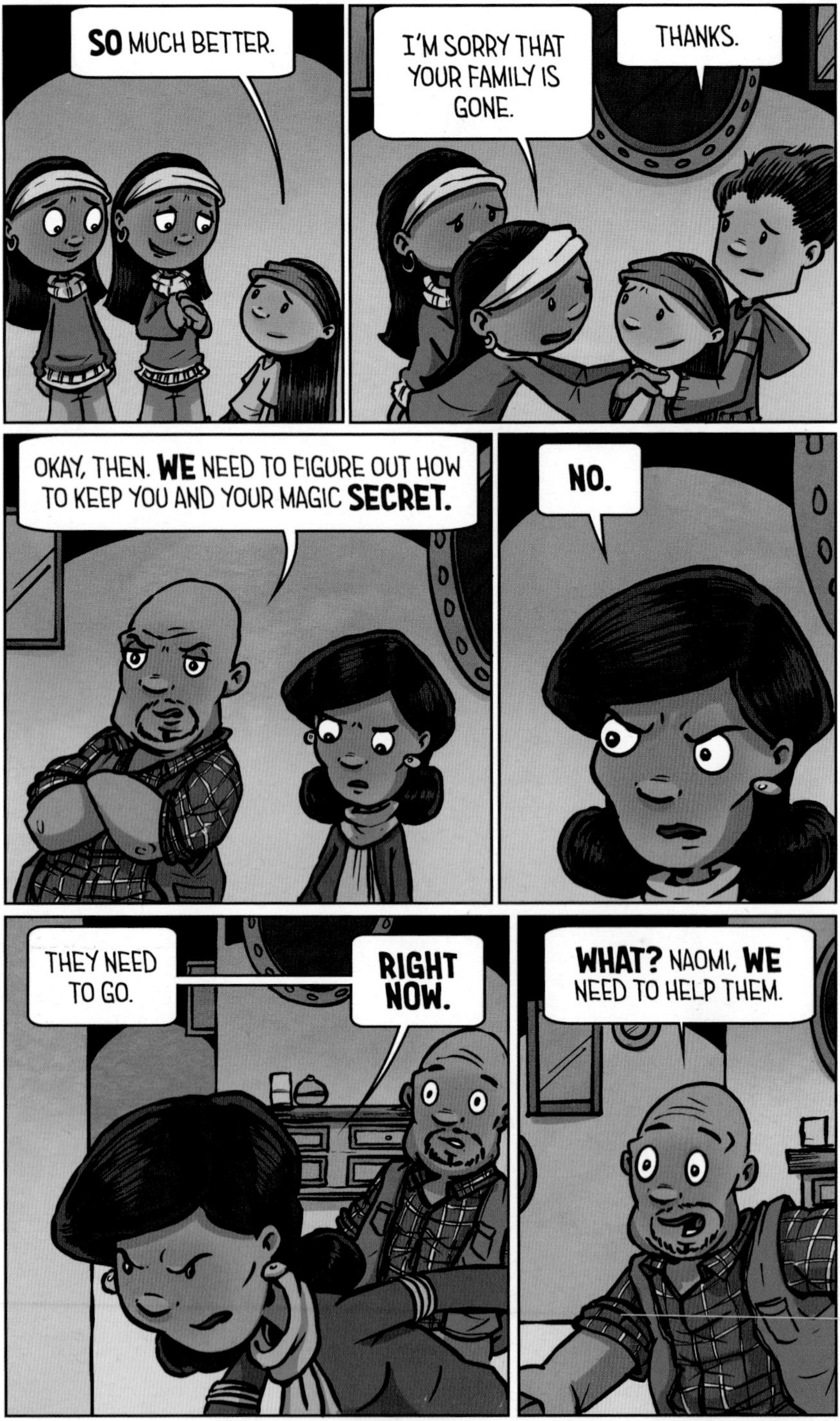
SO MUCH BETTER.
I'M SORRY THAT YOUR FAMILY IS GONE.
THANKS.
OKAY, THEN. WE NEED TO FIGURE OUT HOW TO KEEP YOU AND YOUR MAGIC SECRET.
NO.
THEY NEED TO GO.
RIGHT NOW.
WHAT? NAOMI, WE NEED TO HELP THEM.

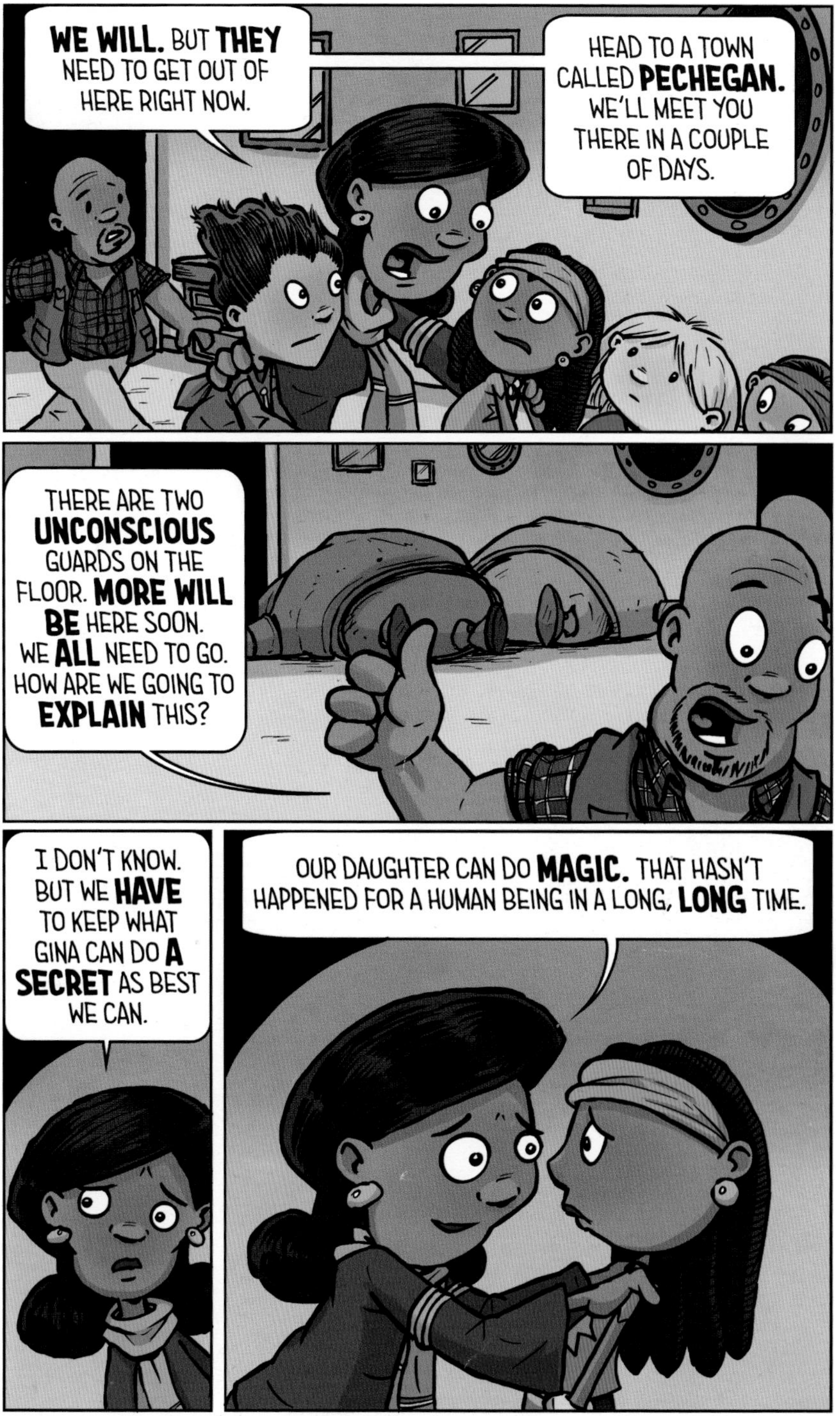
WE WILL. BUT THEY NEED TO GET OUT OF HERE RIGHT NOW.
HEAD TO A TOWN CALLED PECHEGAN. WE'LL MEET YOU THERE IN A COUPLE OF DAYS.
THERE ARE TWO UNCONSCIOUS GUARDS ON THE FLOOR. MORE WILL BE HERE SOON. WE ALL NEED TO GO. HOW ARE WE GOING TO EXPLAIN THIS?
I DON'T KNOW. BUT WE HAVE TO KEEP WHAT GINA CAN DO A SECRET AS BEST WE CAN.
OUR DAUGHTER CAN DO MAGIC. THAT HASN'T HAPPENED FOR A HUMAN BEING IN A LONG, LONG TIME.

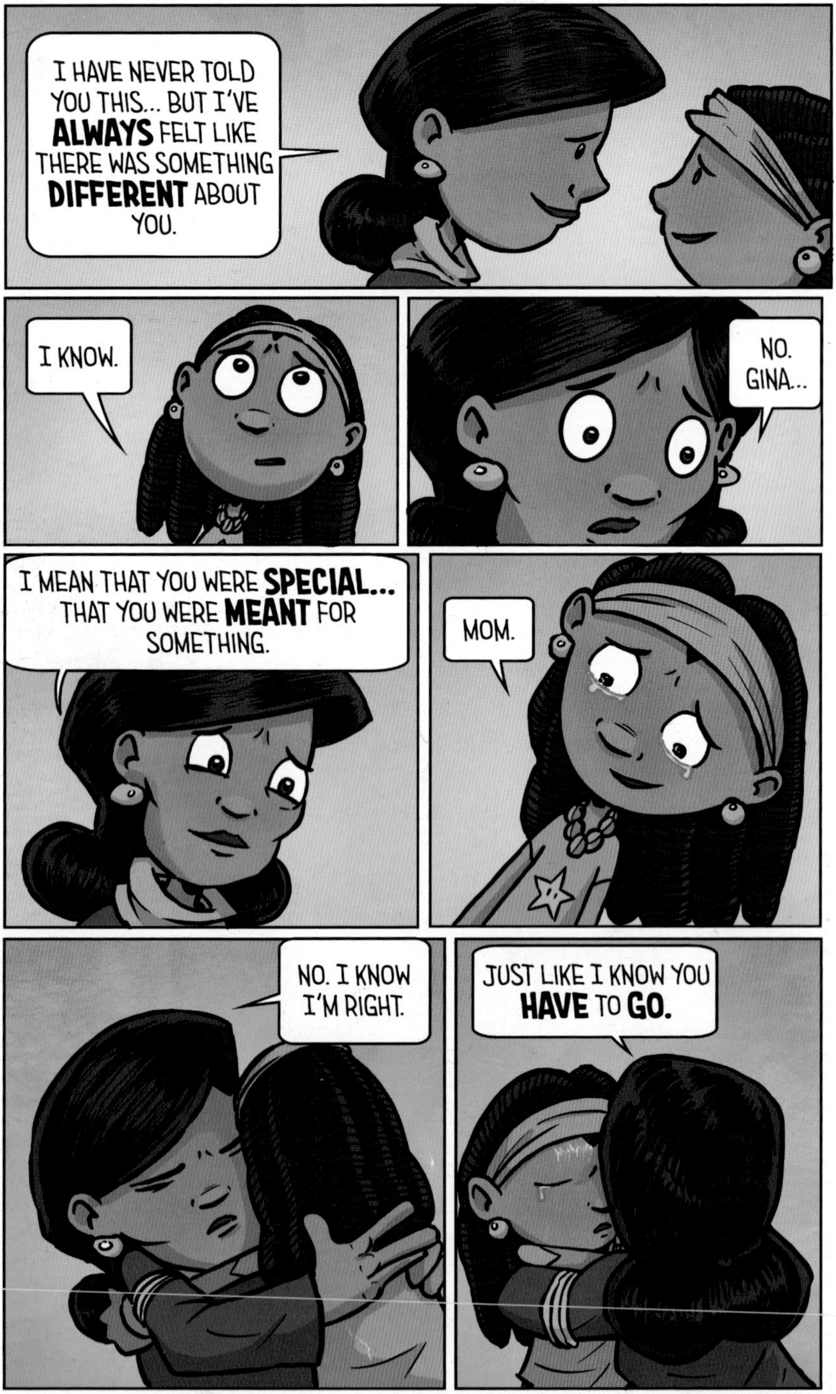

I HAVE NEVER TOLD YOU THIS... BUT I'VE **ALWAYS** FELT LIKE THERE WAS SOMETHING **DIFFERENT** ABOUT YOU.
I KNOW.
NO. GINA...
I MEAN THAT YOU WERE **SPECIAL...** THAT YOU WERE **MEANT** FOR SOMETHING.
MOM.
NO. I KNOW I'M RIGHT.
JUST LIKE I KNOW YOU **HAVE** TO **GO.**

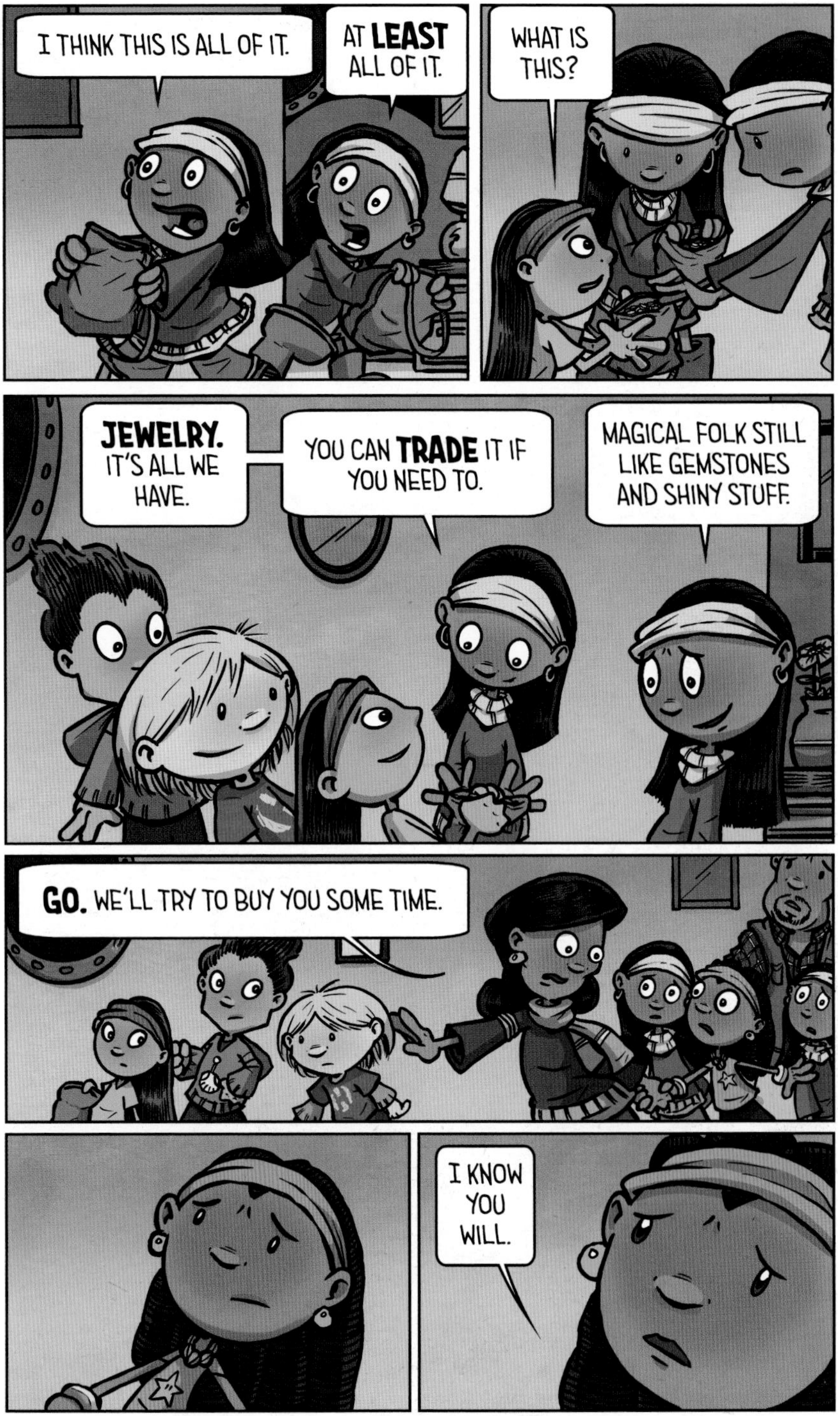
I THINK THIS IS ALL OF IT.
AT LEAST ALL OF IT.
WHAT IS THIS?
JEWELRY. IT'S ALL WE HAVE.
YOU CAN TRADE IT IF YOU NEED TO.
MAGICAL FOLK STILL LIKE GEMSTONES AND SHINY STUFF.
GO. WE'LL TRY TO BUY YOU SOME TIME.
I KNOW YOU WILL.

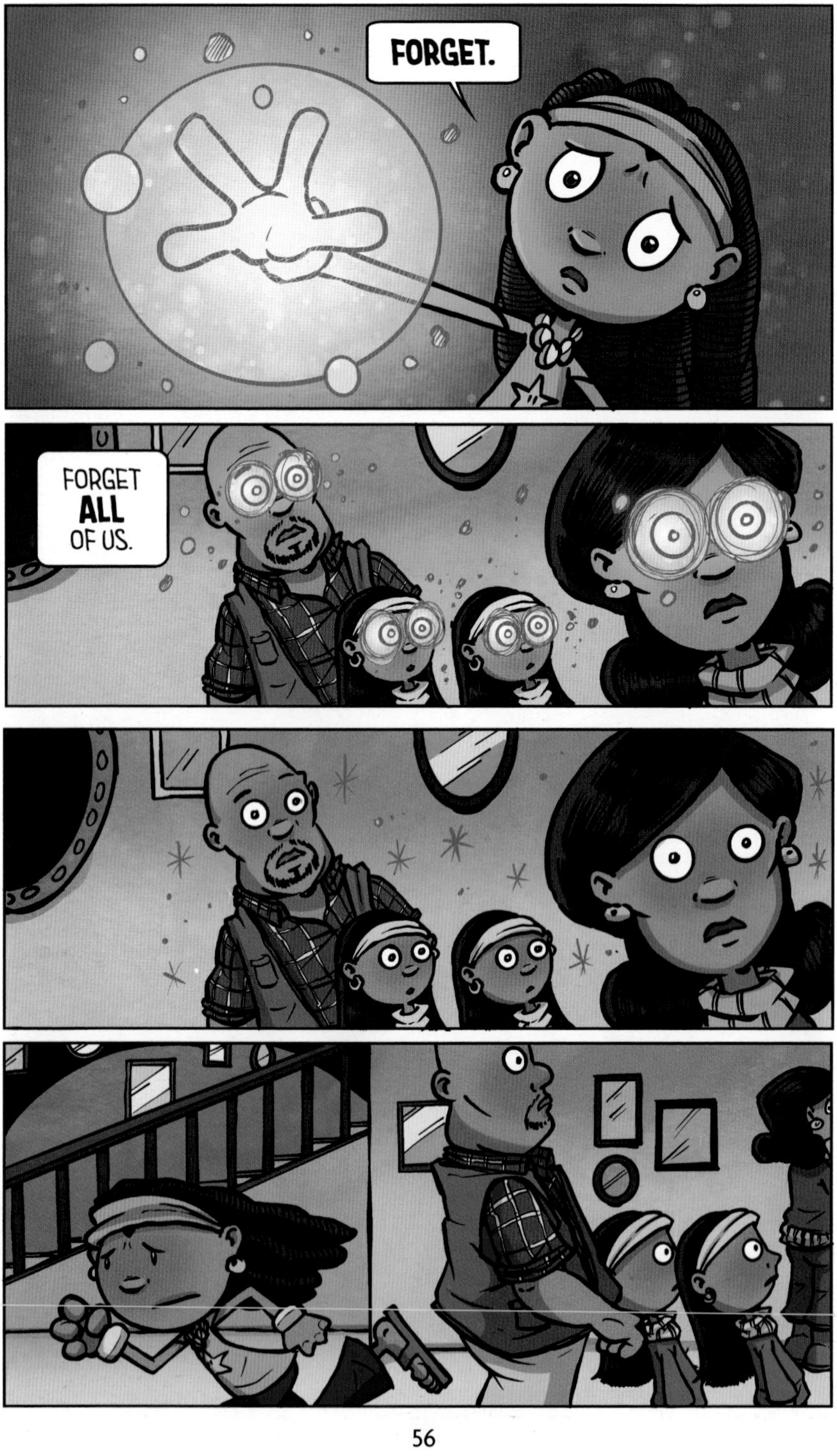
FORGET.
FORGET ALL OF US.

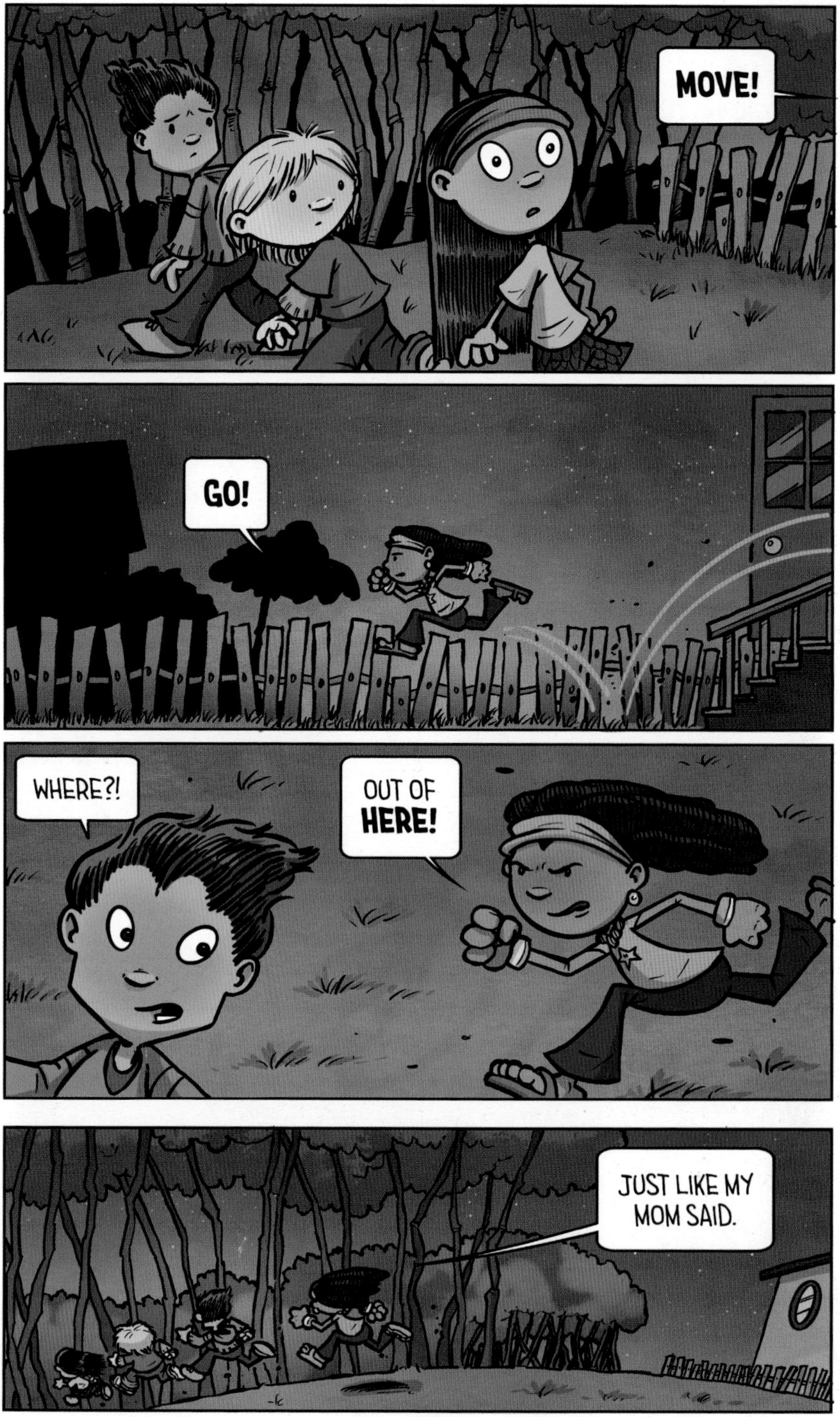
MOVE!
GO!
WHERE?!
OUT OF HERE!
JUST LIKE MY MOM SAID.

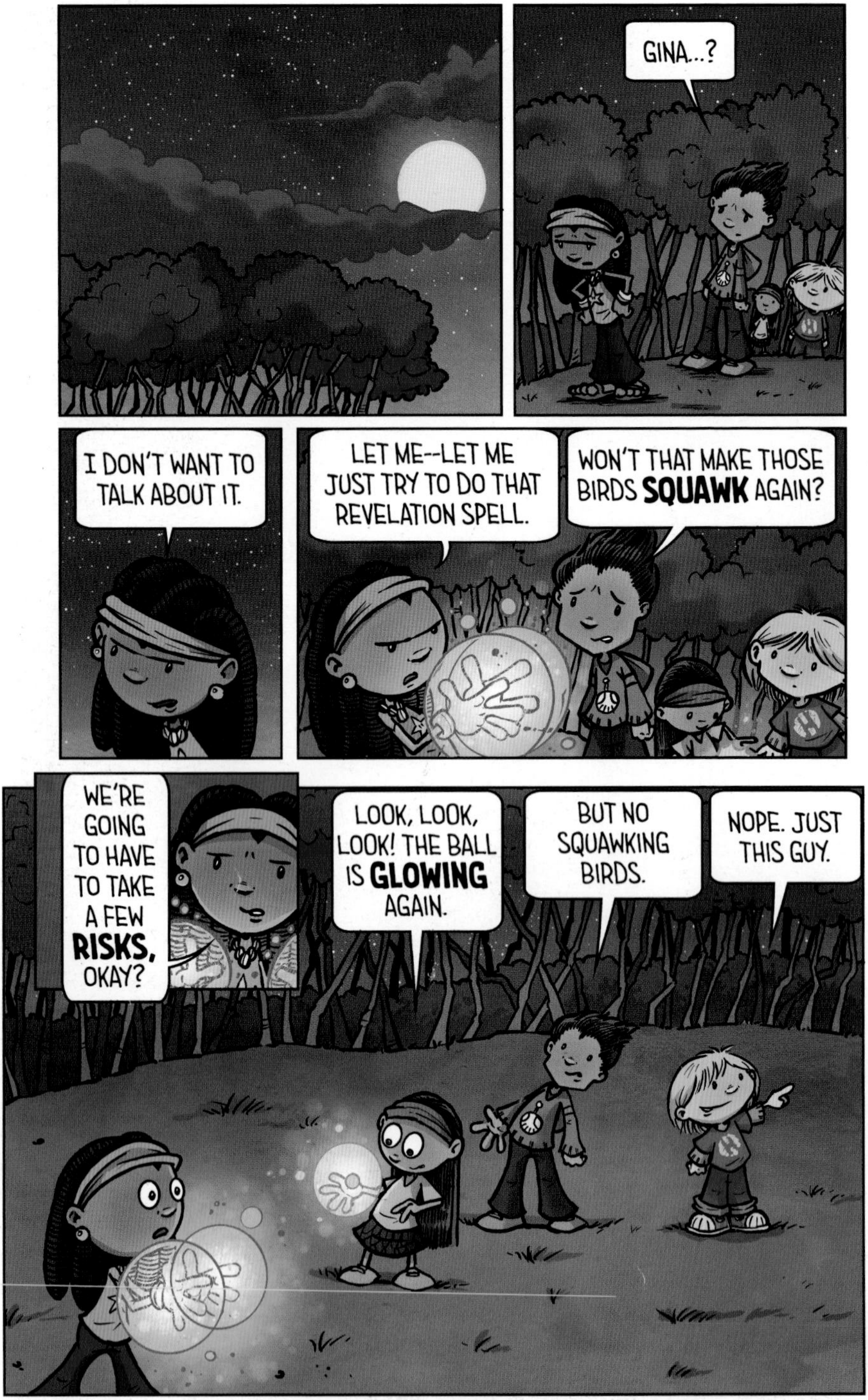
GINA...?
I DON'T WANT TO TALK ABOUT IT.
LET ME--LET ME JUST TRY TO DO THAT REVELATION SPELL.
WON'T THAT MAKE THOSE BIRDS **SQUAWK** AGAIN?
WE'RE GOING TO HAVE TO TAKE A FEW **RISKS,** OKAY?
LOOK, LOOK, LOOK! THE BALL IS **GLOWING** AGAIN.
BUT NO SQUAWKING BIRDS.
NOPE. JUST THIS GUY.

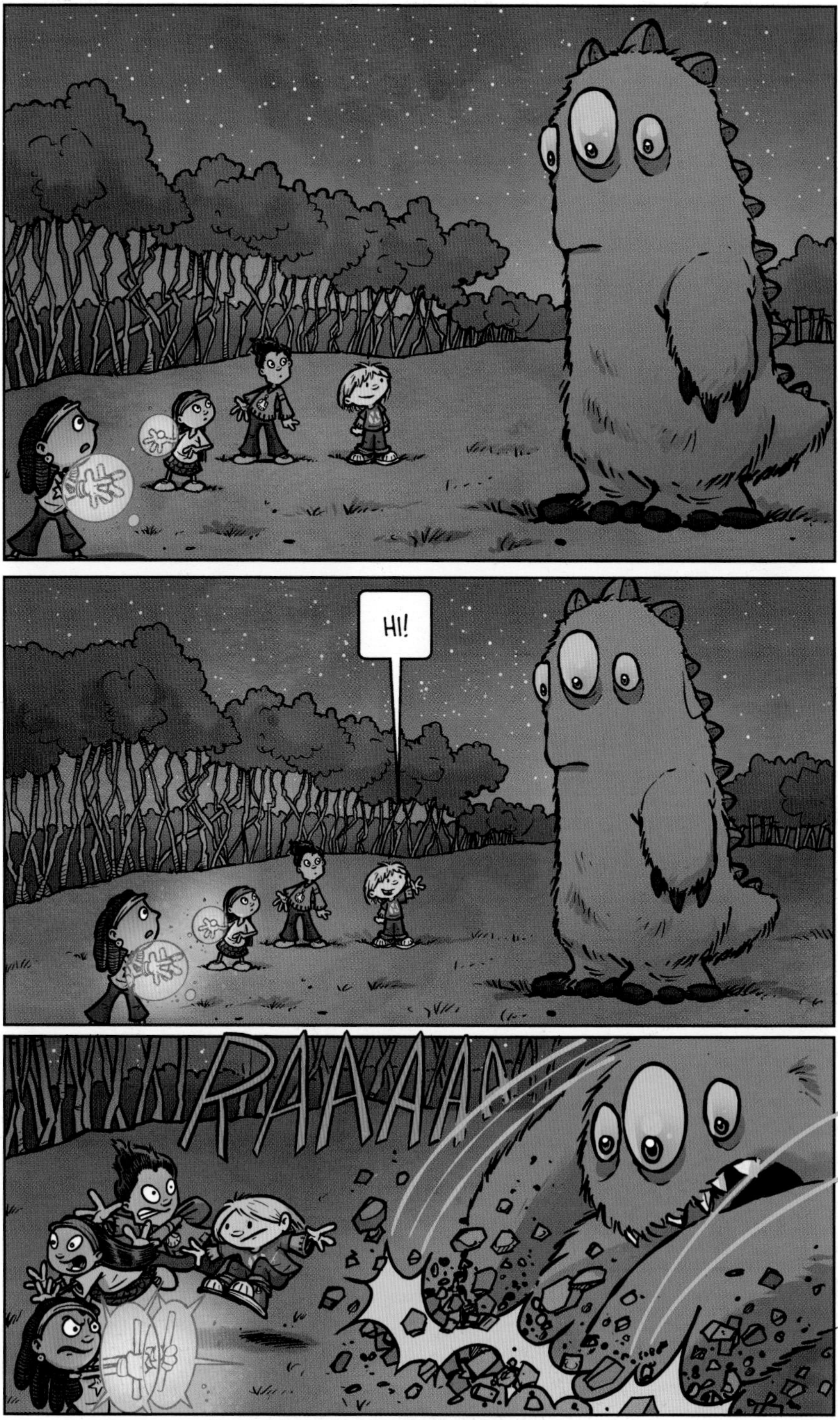
HI!
RAAAAA

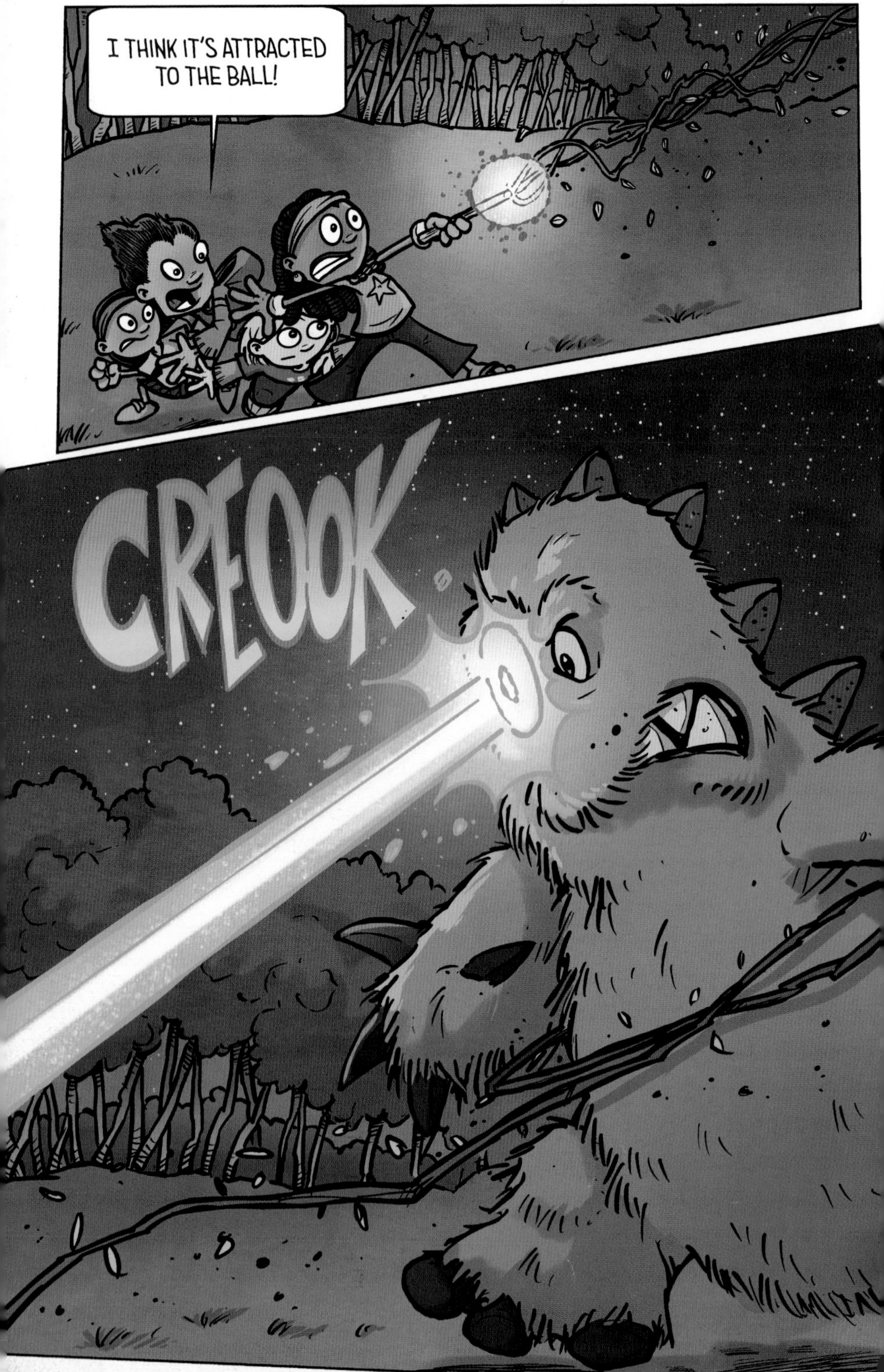
I THINK IT'S ATTRACTED TO THE BALL!
CREOOK

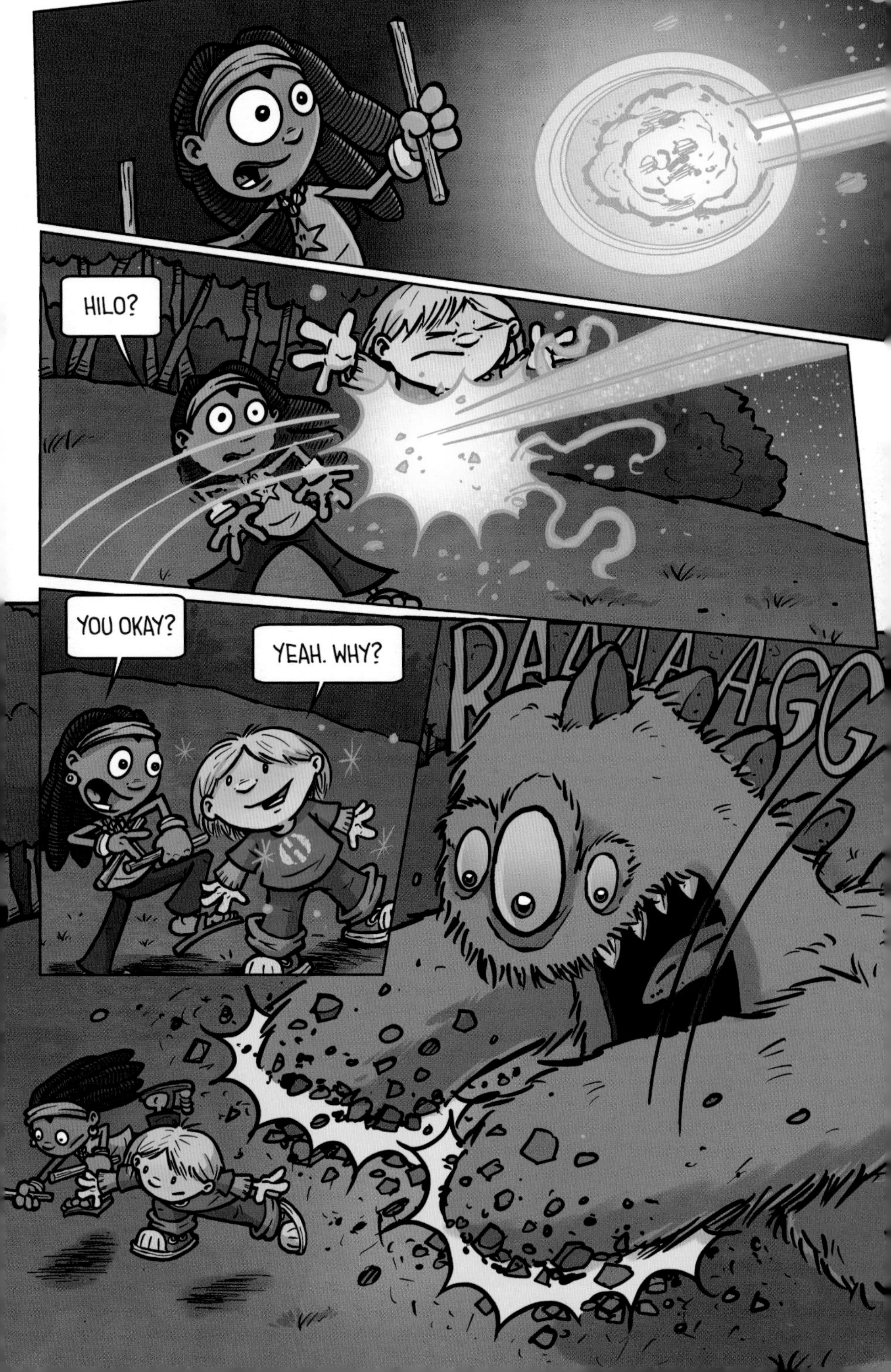
HILO?
YOU OKAY?
YEAH. WHY?
RAAAAAGG

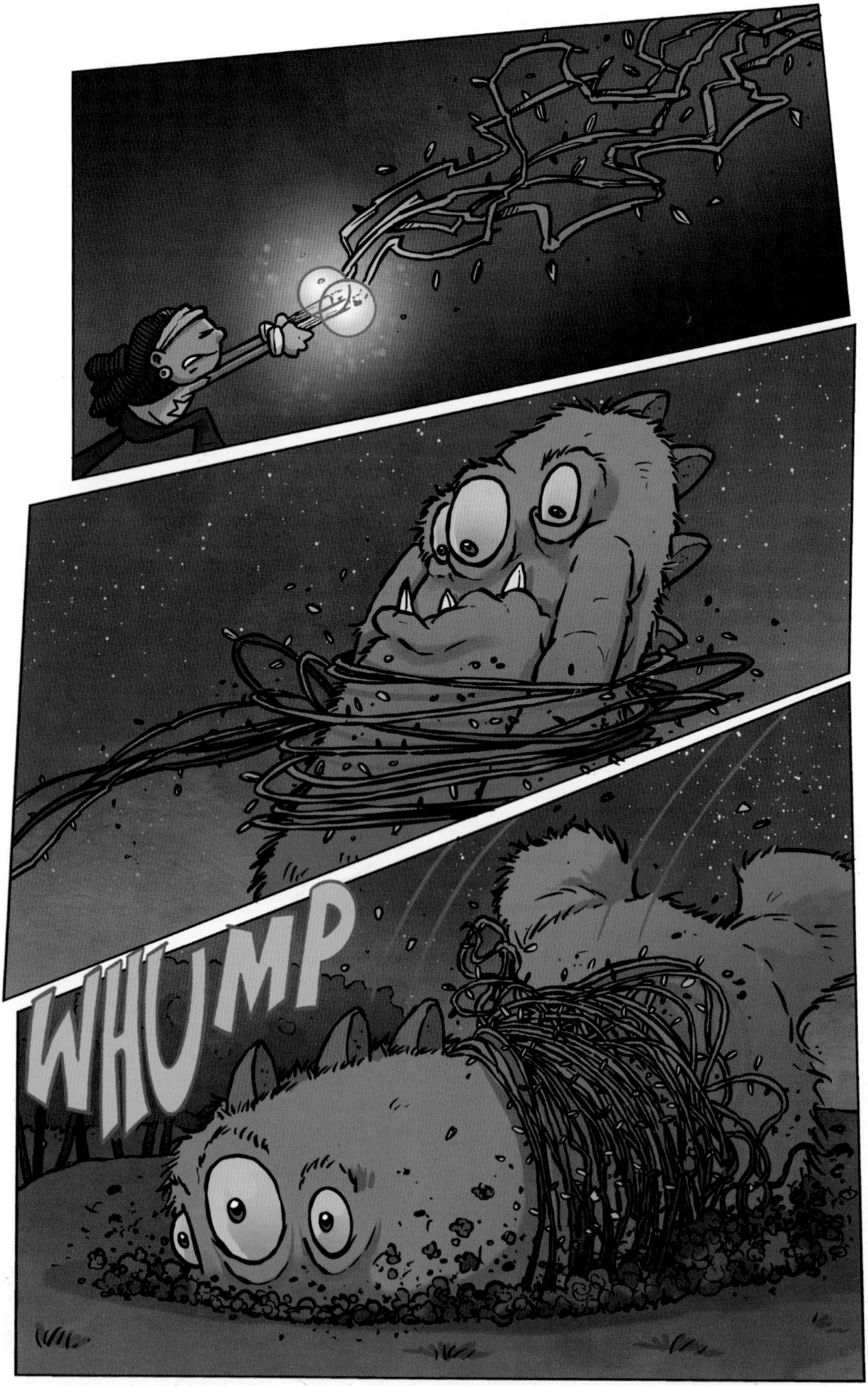
WHUMP

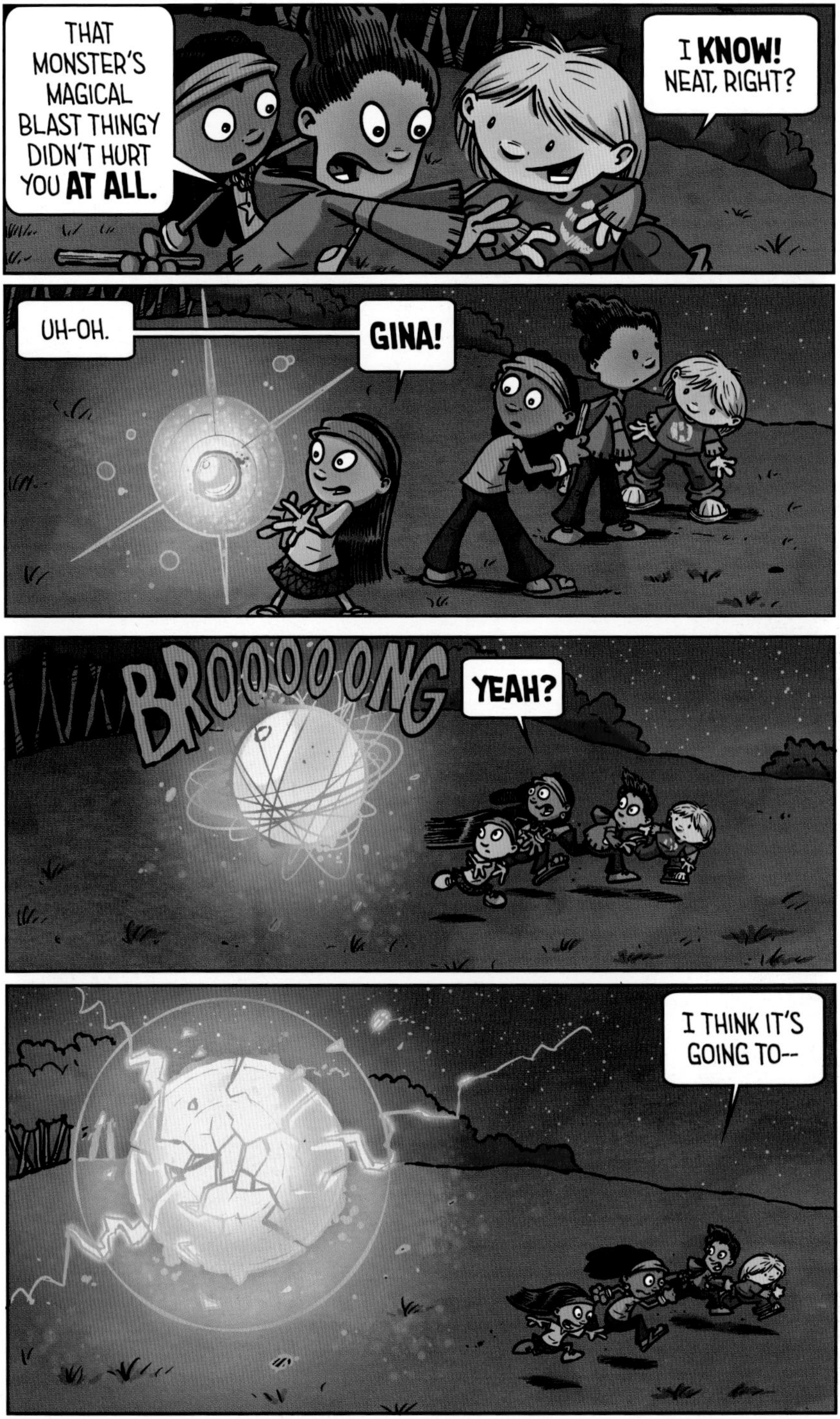
THAT MONSTER'S MAGICAL BLAST THINGY DIDN'T HURT YOU **AT ALL.**
I **KNOW!** NEAT, RIGHT?
UH-OH.
GINA!
BROOOOONG
YEAH?
I THINK IT'S GOING TO--

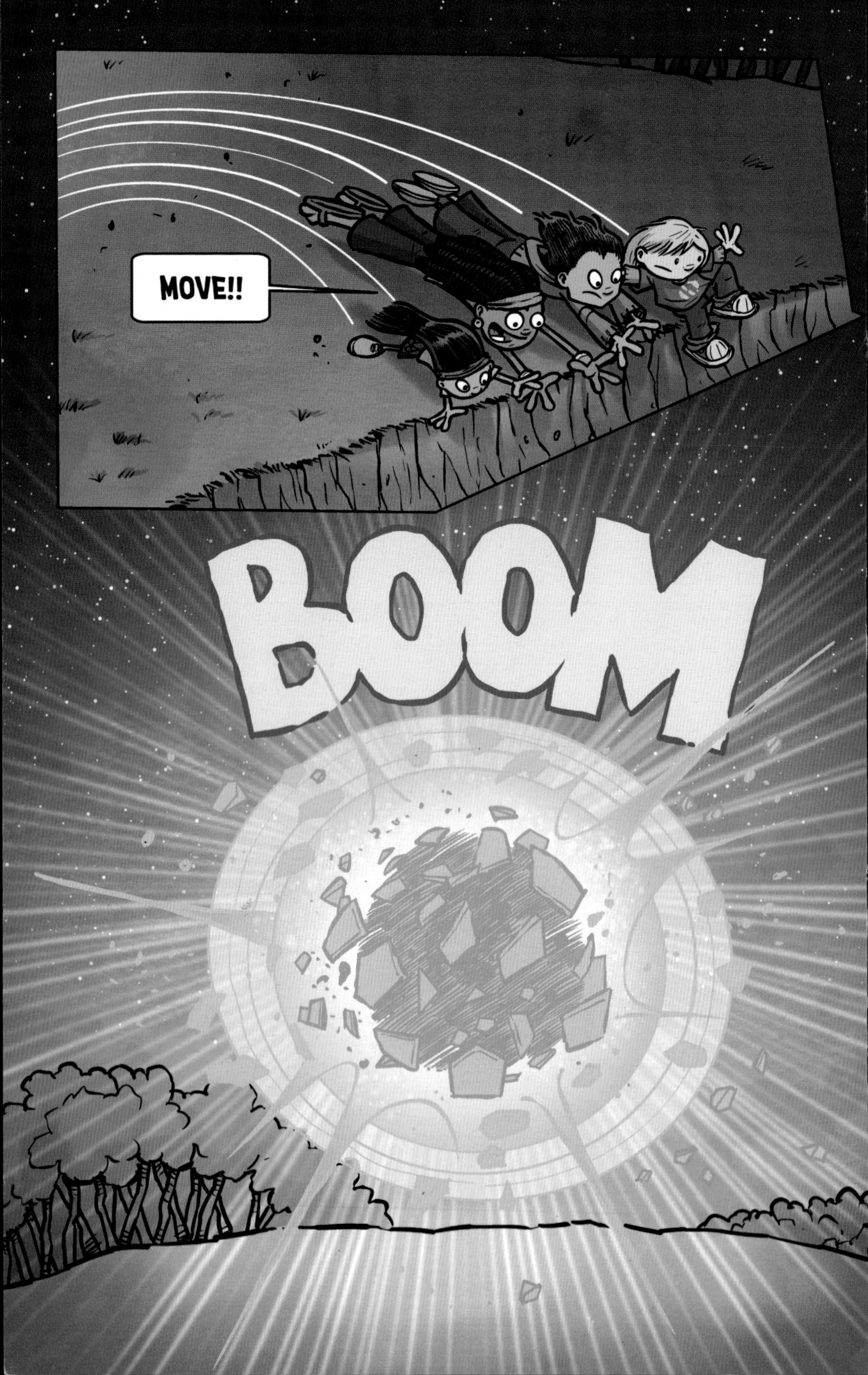
MOVE!!
BOOM

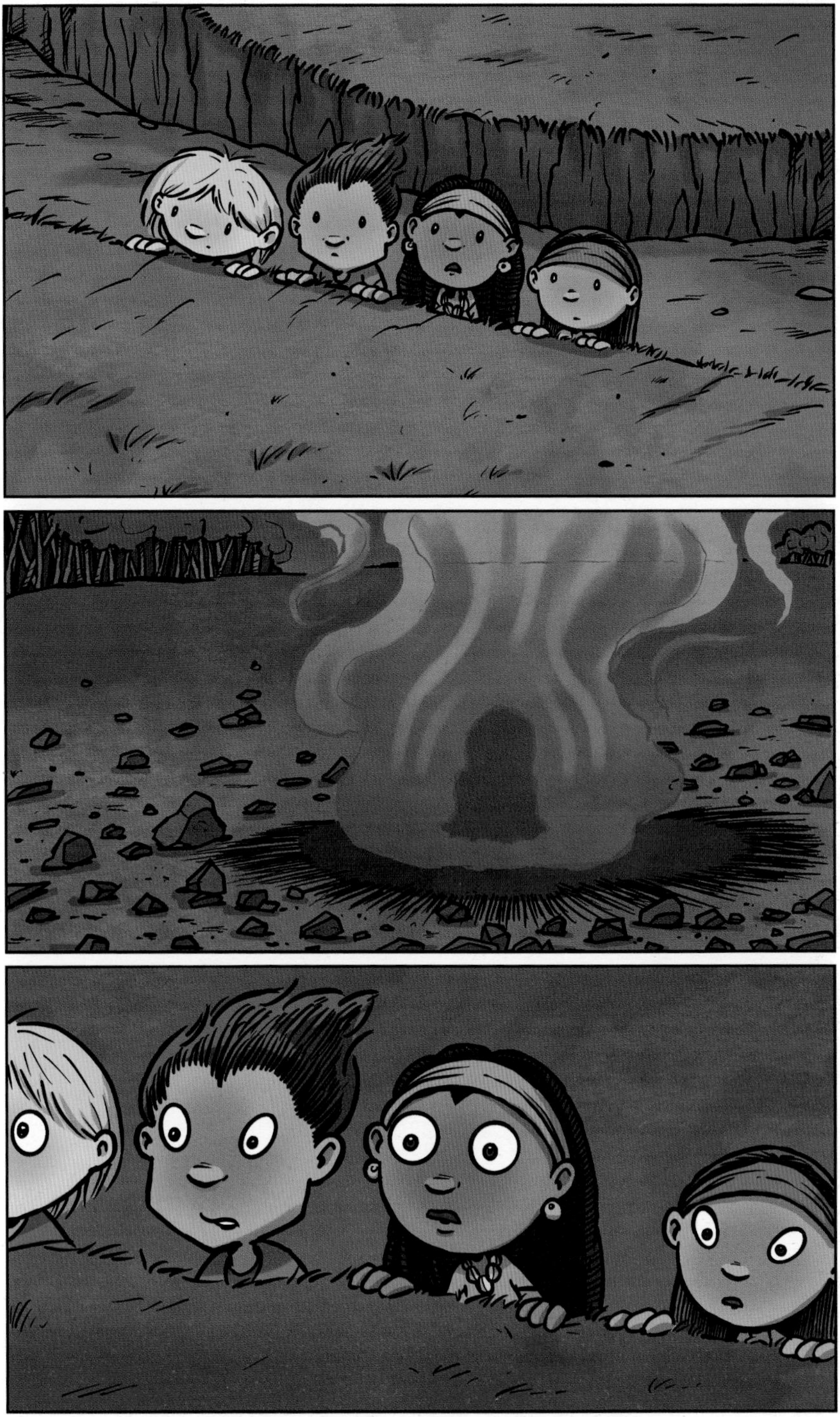

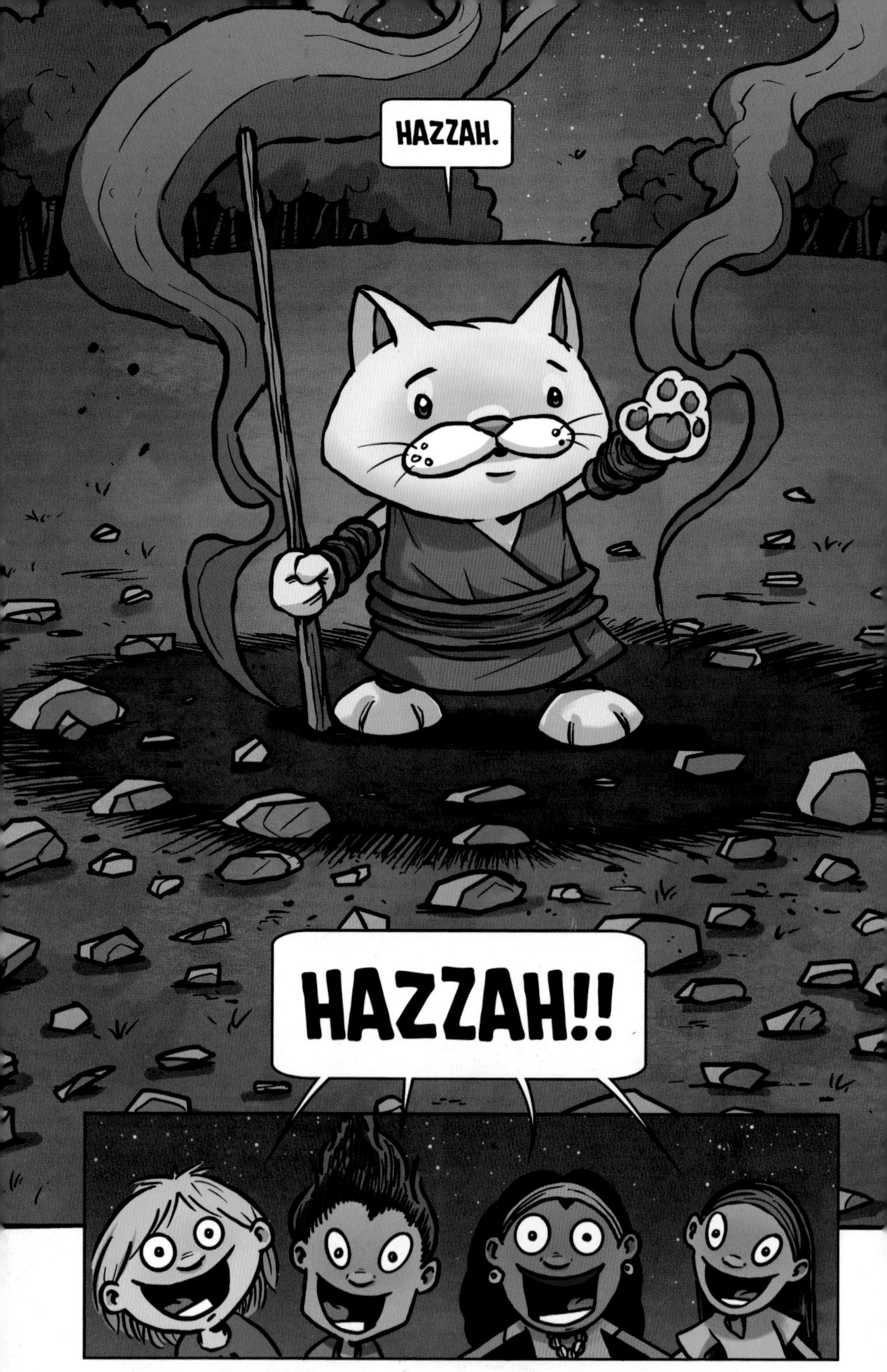
HAZZAH.
HAZZAH!!

CHAPTER 5

PHILLIP IGNATIUS SEBASTIAN KORIMAKO

THE BAND IS BACK TOGETHER!
POLLY! WHAT ARE YOU DOING HERE?!

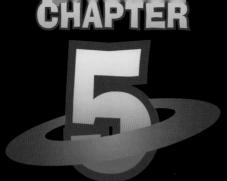

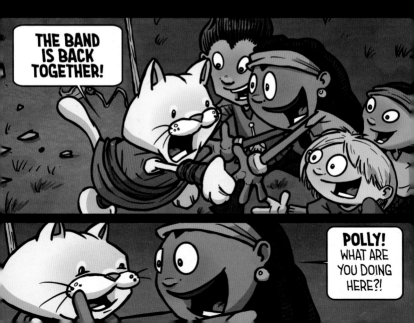

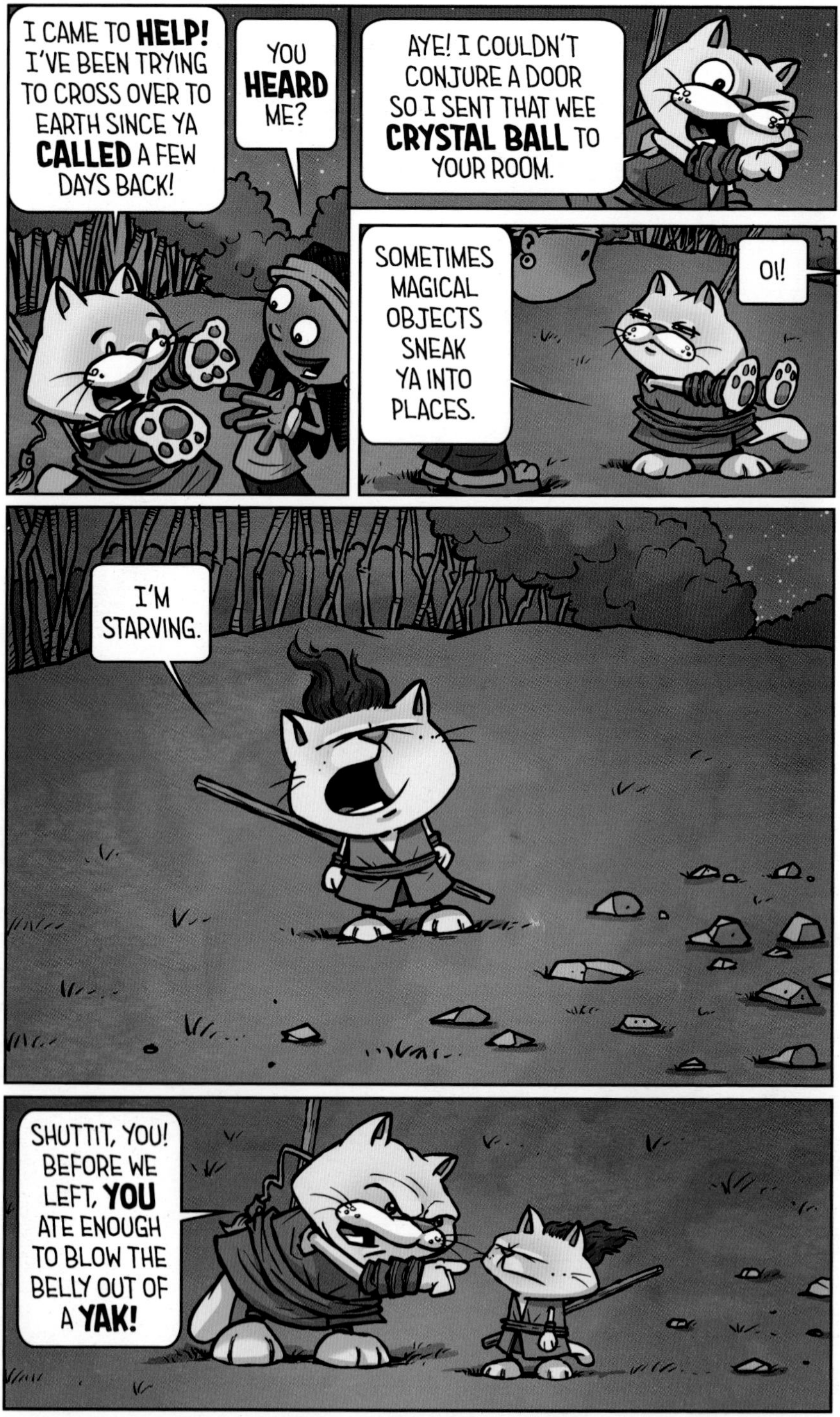
I CAME TO HELP! I'VE BEEN TRYING TO CROSS OVER TO EARTH SINCE YA CALLED A FEW DAYS BACK!
YOU HEARD ME?
AYE! I COULDN'T CONJURE A DOOR SO I SENT THAT WEE CRYSTAL BALL TO YOUR ROOM.
SOMETIMES MAGICAL OBJECTS SNEAK YA INTO PLACES.
OI!
I'M STARVING.
SHUTTIT, YOU! BEFORE WE LEFT, YOU ATE ENOUGH TO BLOW THE BELLY OUT OF A YAK!

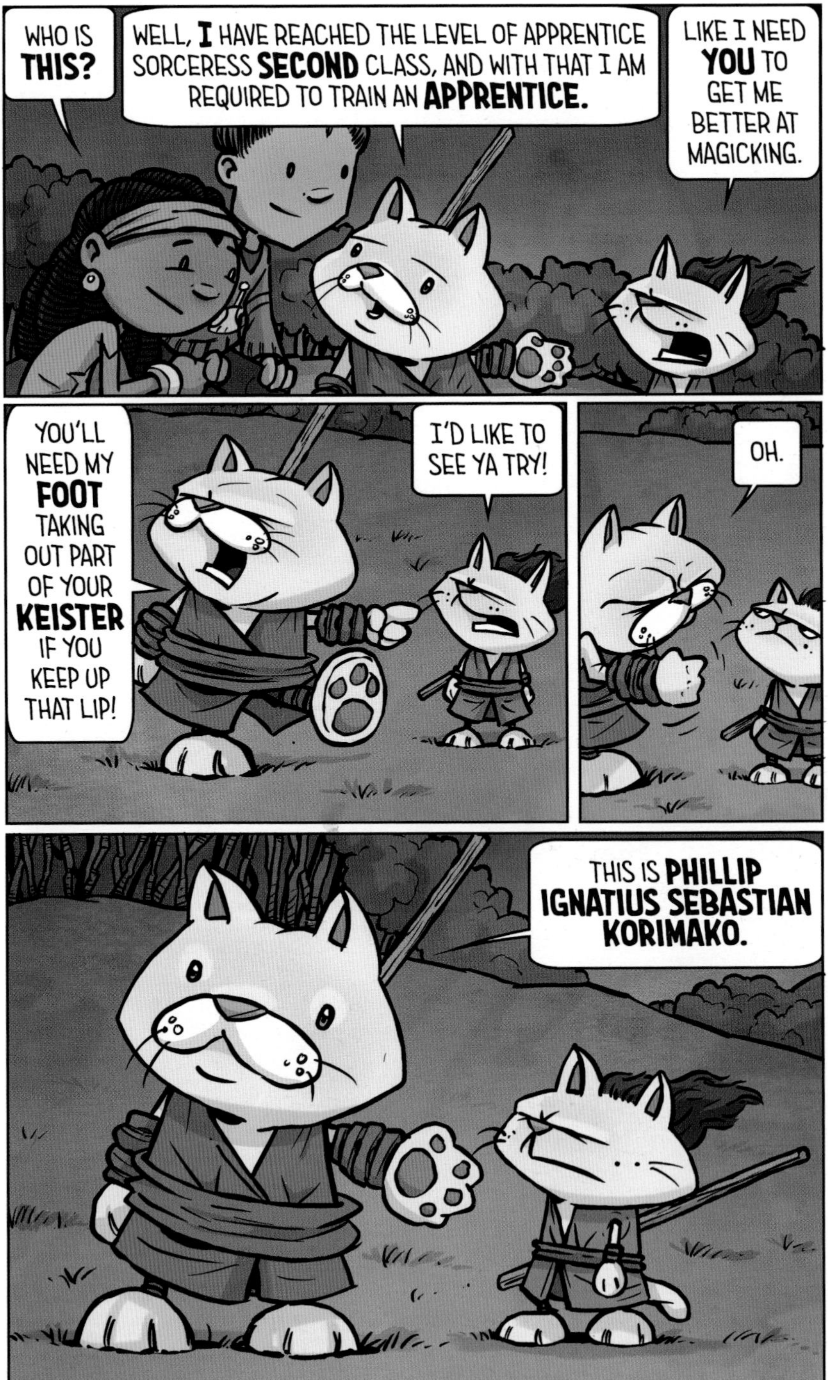
WHO IS THIS?
WELL, I HAVE REACHED THE LEVEL OF APPRENTICE SORCERESS SECOND CLASS, AND WITH THAT I AM REQUIRED TO TRAIN AN APPRENTICE.
LIKE I NEED YOU TO GET ME BETTER AT MAGICKING.
YOU'LL NEED MY FOOT TAKING OUT PART OF YOUR KEISTER IF YOU KEEP UP THAT LIP!
I'D LIKE TO SEE YA TRY!
OH.
THIS IS PHILLIP IGNATIUS SEBASTIAN KORIMAKO.

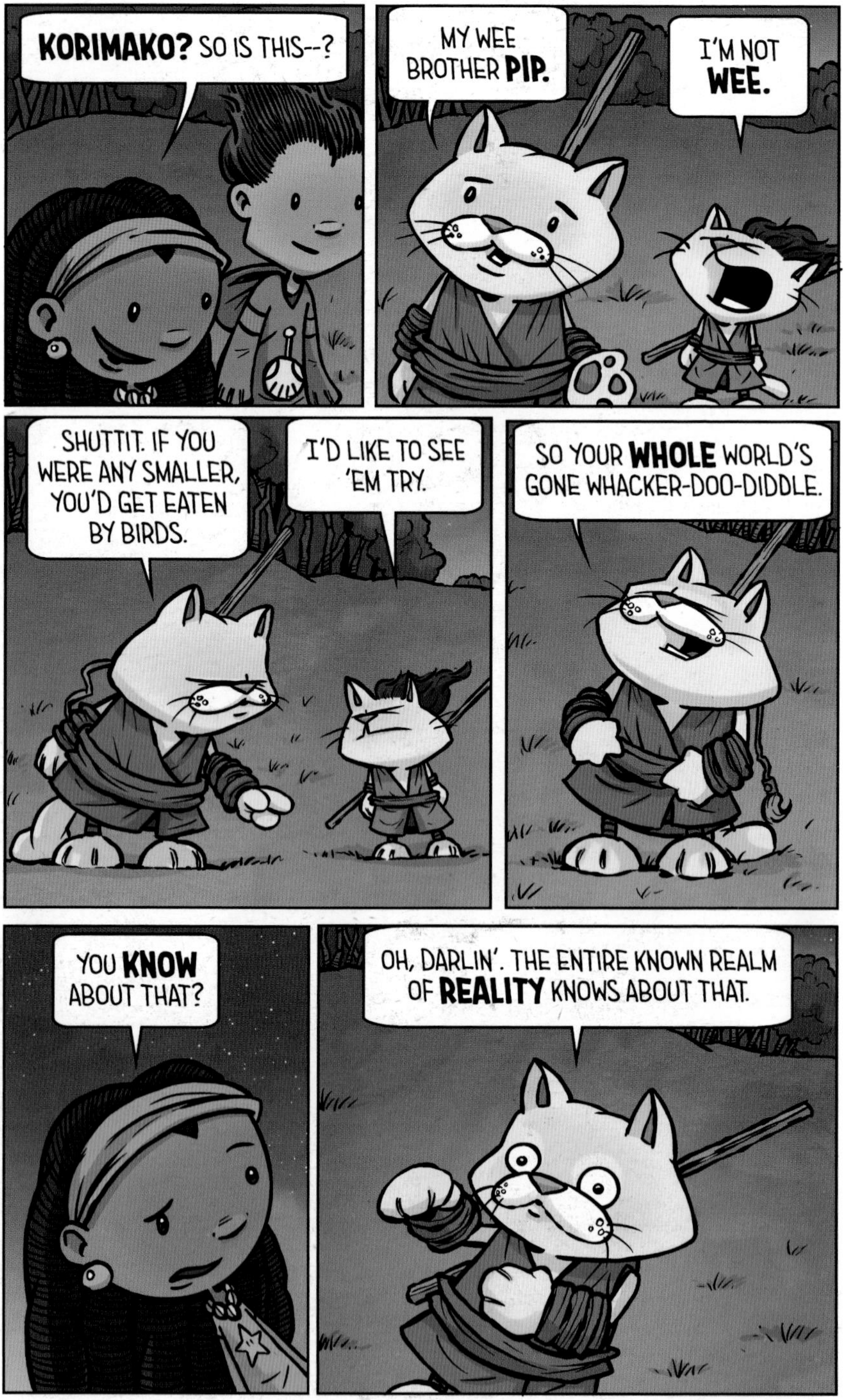
KORIMAKO? SO IS THIS--?
MY WEE BROTHER PIP.
I'M NOT WEE.
SHUTTIT. IF YOU WERE ANY SMALLER, YOU'D GET EATEN BY BIRDS.
I'D LIKE TO SEE 'EM TRY.
SO YOUR WHOLE WORLD'S GONE WHACKER-DOO-DIDDLE.
YOU KNOW ABOUT THAT?
OH, DARLIN'. THE ENTIRE KNOWN REALM OF REALITY KNOWS ABOUT THAT.

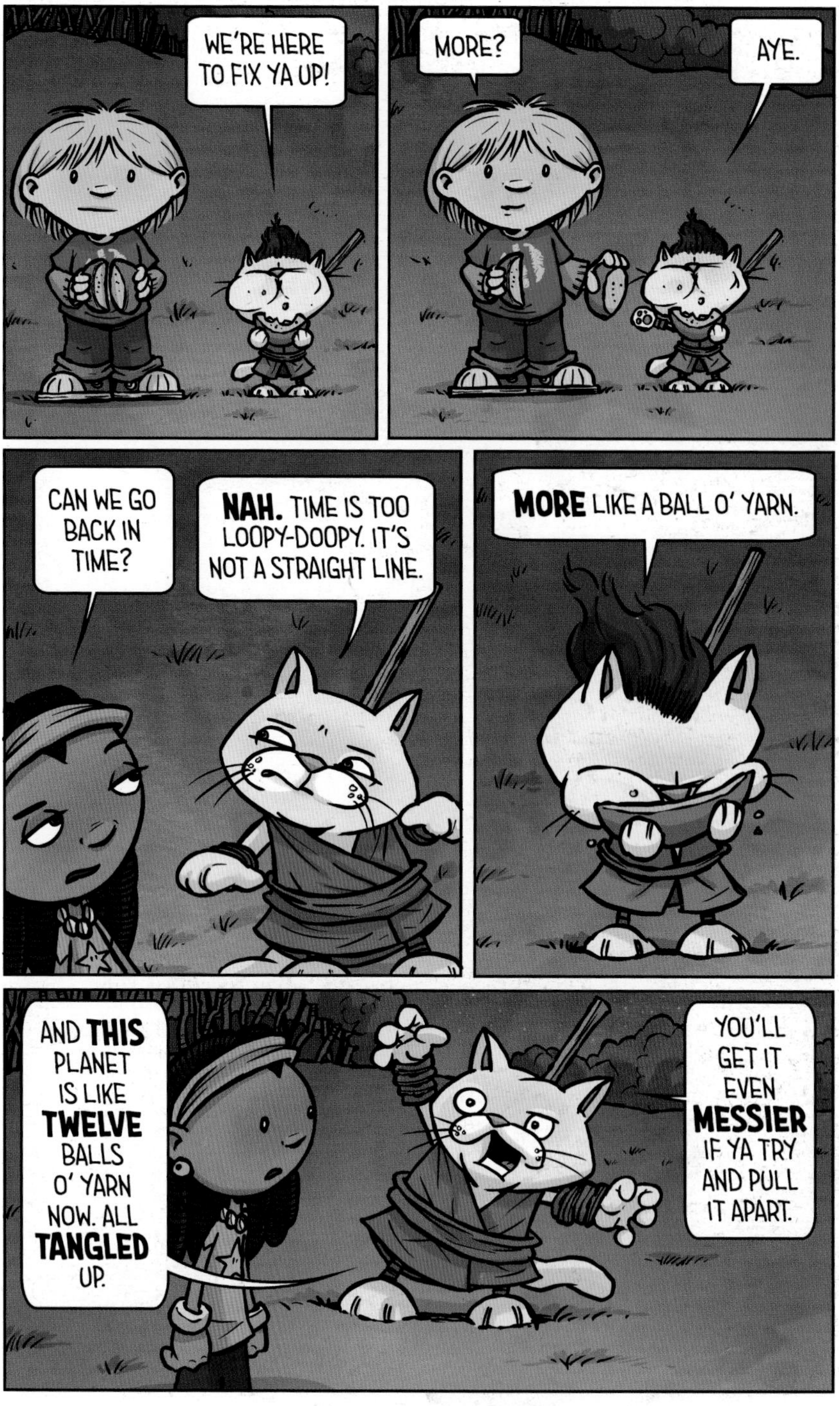
WE'RE HERE TO FIX YA UP!
MORE?
AYE.
CAN WE GO BACK IN TIME?
NAH. TIME IS TOO LOOPY-DOOPY. IT'S NOT A STRAIGHT LINE.
MORE LIKE A BALL O' YARN.
AND THIS PLANET IS LIKE TWELVE BALLS O' YARN NOW. ALL TANGLED UP.
YOU'LL GET IT EVEN MESSIER IF YA TRY AND PULL IT APART.

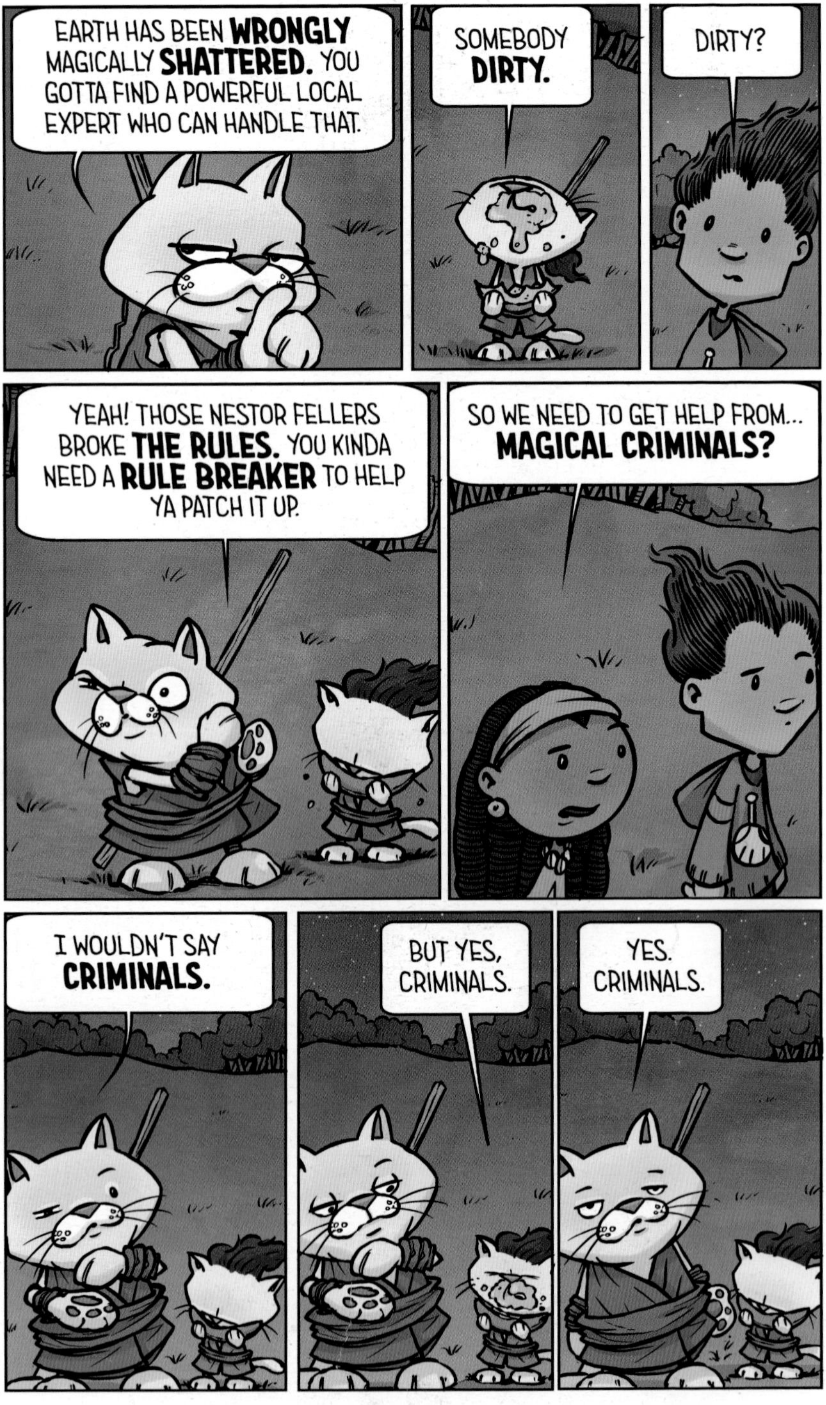
EARTH HAS BEEN WRONGLY MAGICALLY SHATTERED. YOU GOTTA FIND A POWERFUL LOCAL EXPERT WHO CAN HANDLE THAT.
SOMEBODY DIRTY.
DIRTY?
YEAH! THOSE NESTOR FELLERS BROKE THE RULES. YOU KINDA NEED A RULE BREAKER TO HELP YA PATCH IT UP.
SO WE NEED TO GET HELP FROM... MAGICAL CRIMINALS?
I WOULDN'T SAY CRIMINALS.
BUT YES, CRIMINALS.
YES. CRIMINALS.

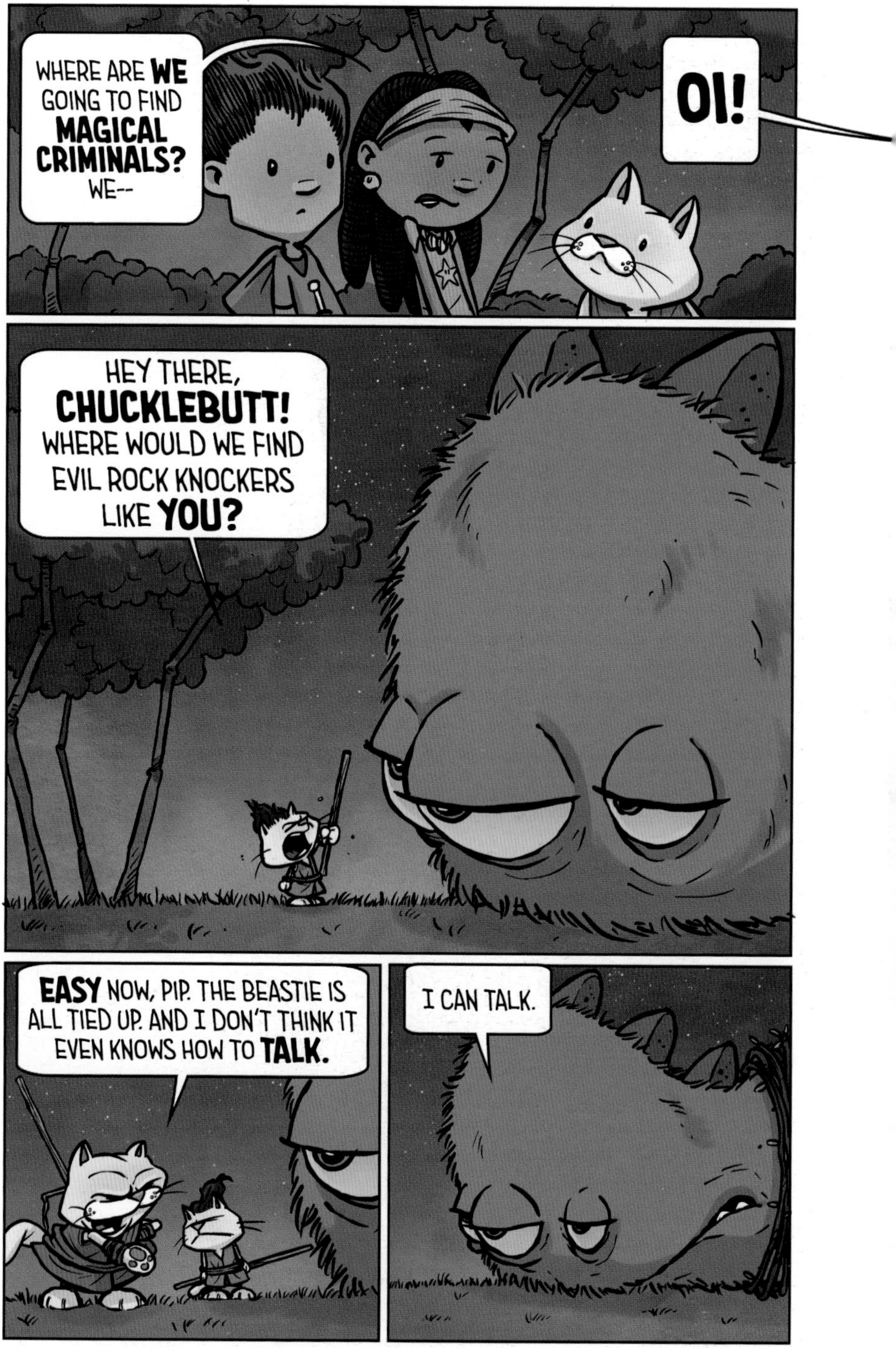
WHERE ARE **WE** GOING TO FIND **MAGICAL CRIMINALS?** WE--
OI!
HEY THERE, **CHUCKLEBUTT!** WHERE WOULD WE FIND EVIL ROCK KNOCKERS LIKE **YOU?**
EASY NOW, PIP. THE BEASTIE IS ALL TIED UP. AND I DON'T THINK IT EVEN KNOWS HOW TO **TALK.**
I CAN TALK.

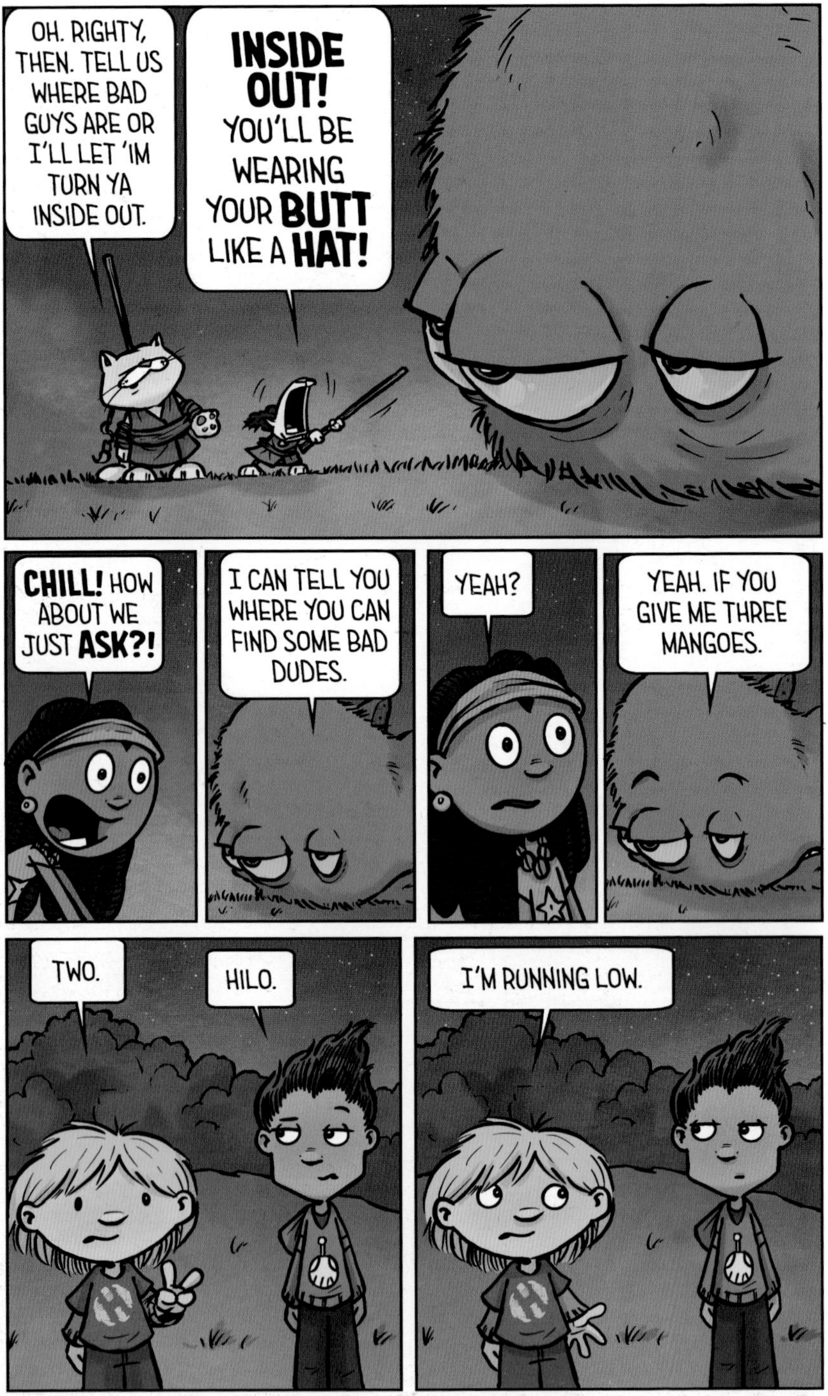
OH. RIGHTY, THEN. TELL US WHERE BAD GUYS ARE OR I'LL LET 'IM TURN YA INSIDE OUT.
INSIDE OUT! YOU'LL BE WEARING YOUR BUTT LIKE A HAT!
CHILL! HOW ABOUT WE JUST ASK?!
I CAN TELL YOU WHERE YOU CAN FIND SOME BAD DUDES.
YEAH?
YEAH. IF YOU GIVE ME THREE MANGOES.
TWO.
HILO.
I'M RUNNING LOW.

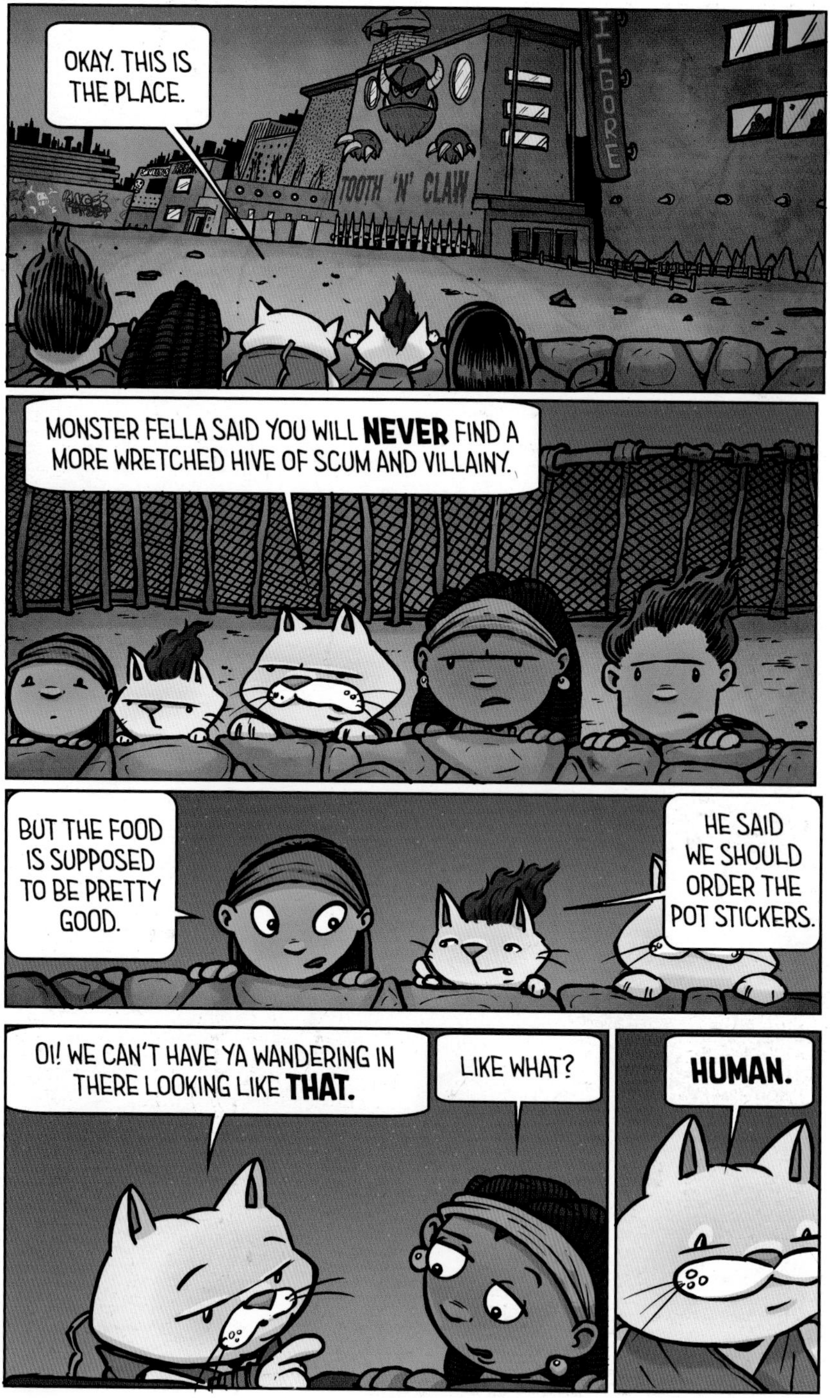
OKAY. THIS IS THE PLACE.
TOOTH 'N' CLAW
MONSTER FELLA SAID YOU WILL **NEVER** FIND A MORE WRETCHED HIVE OF SCUM AND VILLAINY.
BUT THE FOOD IS SUPPOSED TO BE PRETTY GOOD.
HE SAID WE SHOULD ORDER THE POT STICKERS.
OI! WE CAN'T HAVE YA WANDERING IN THERE LOOKING LIKE **THAT.**
LIKE WHAT?
HUMAN.

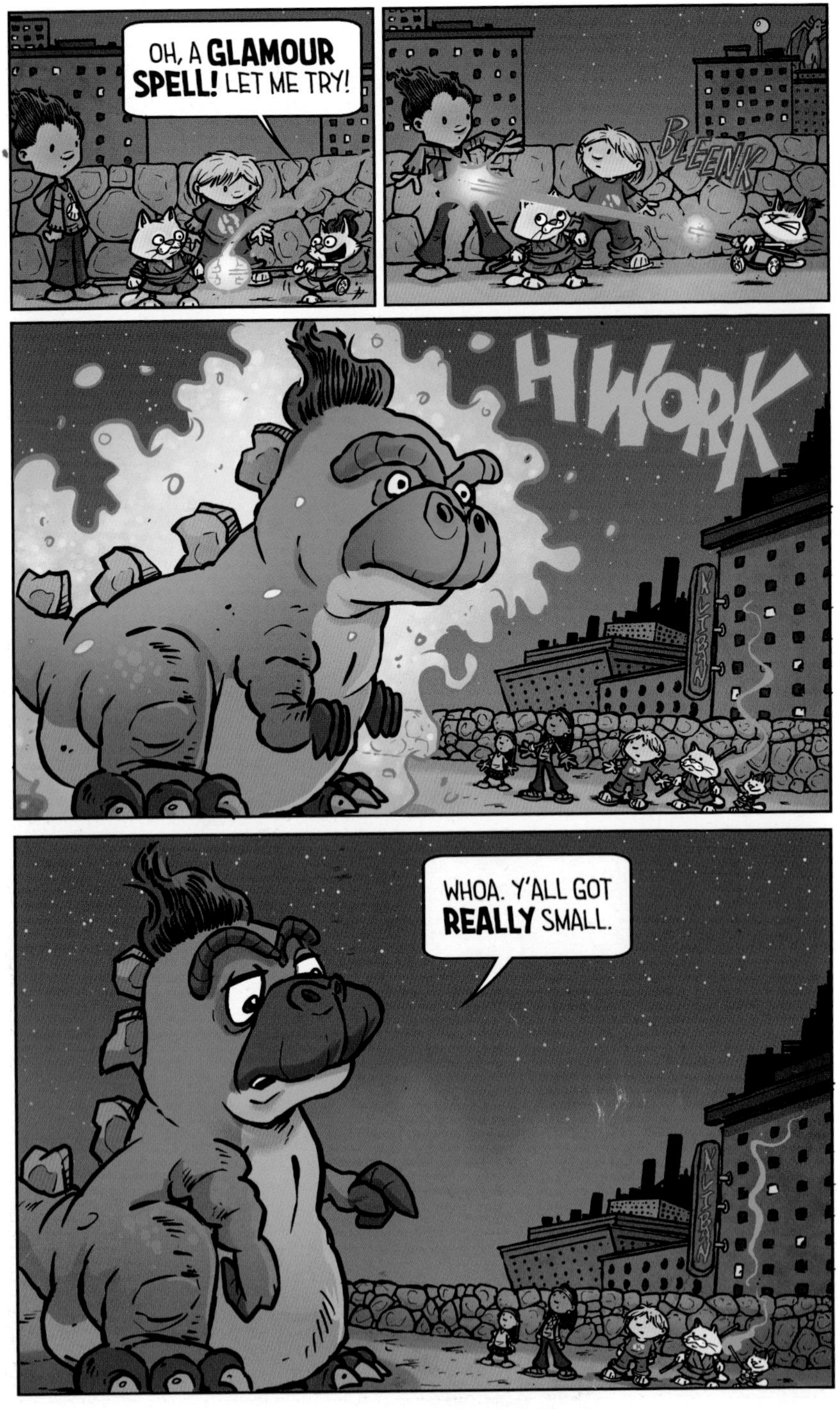
OH, A **GLAMOUR SPELL!** LET ME TRY!
BLEENK
HWORK
WHOA. Y'ALL GOT **REALLY** SMALL.

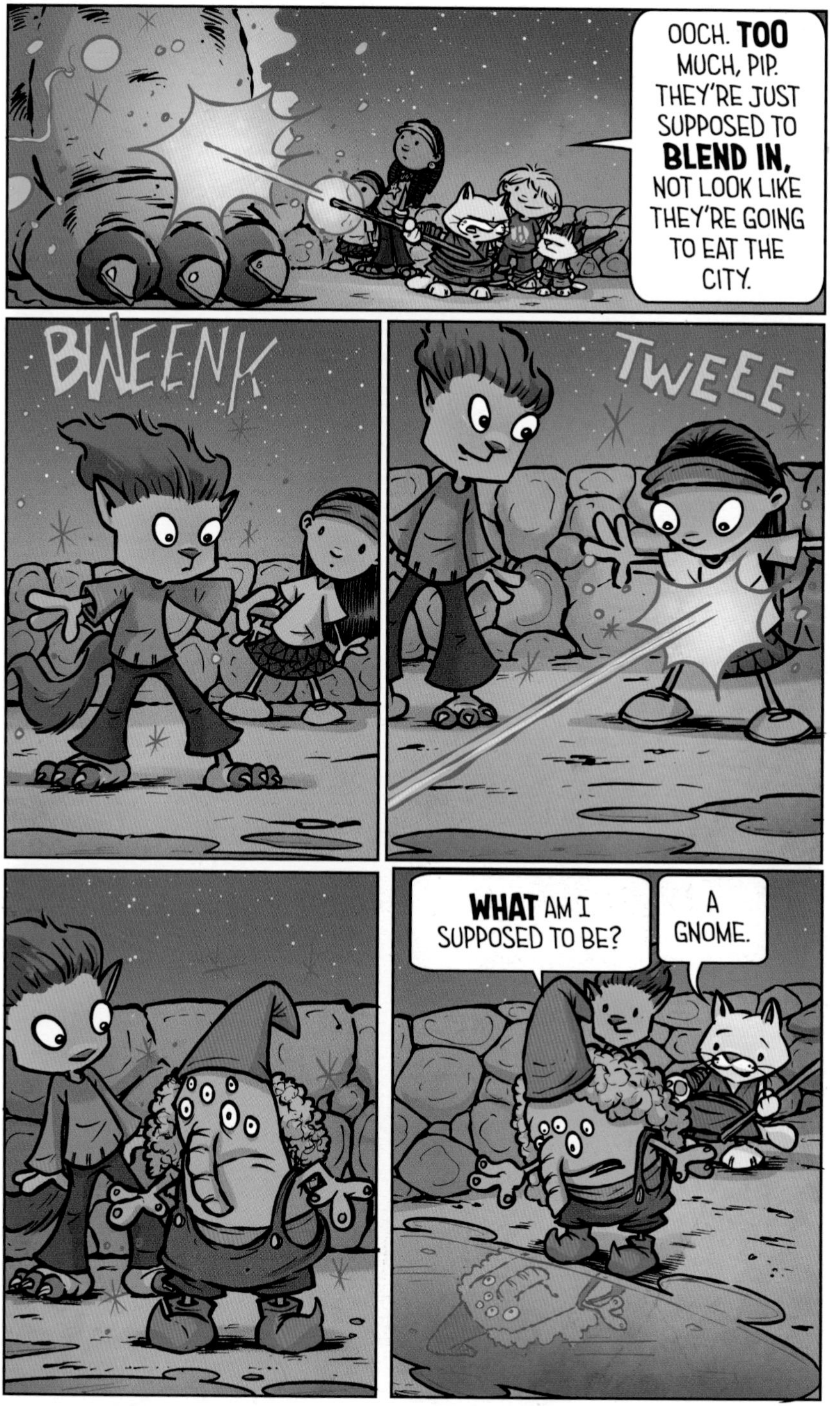
OOCH. TOO MUCH, PIP. THEY'RE JUST SUPPOSED TO BLEND IN, NOT LOOK LIKE THEY'RE GOING TO EAT THE CITY.
BWEENK
TWEEE
WHAT AM I SUPPOSED TO BE?
A GNOME.

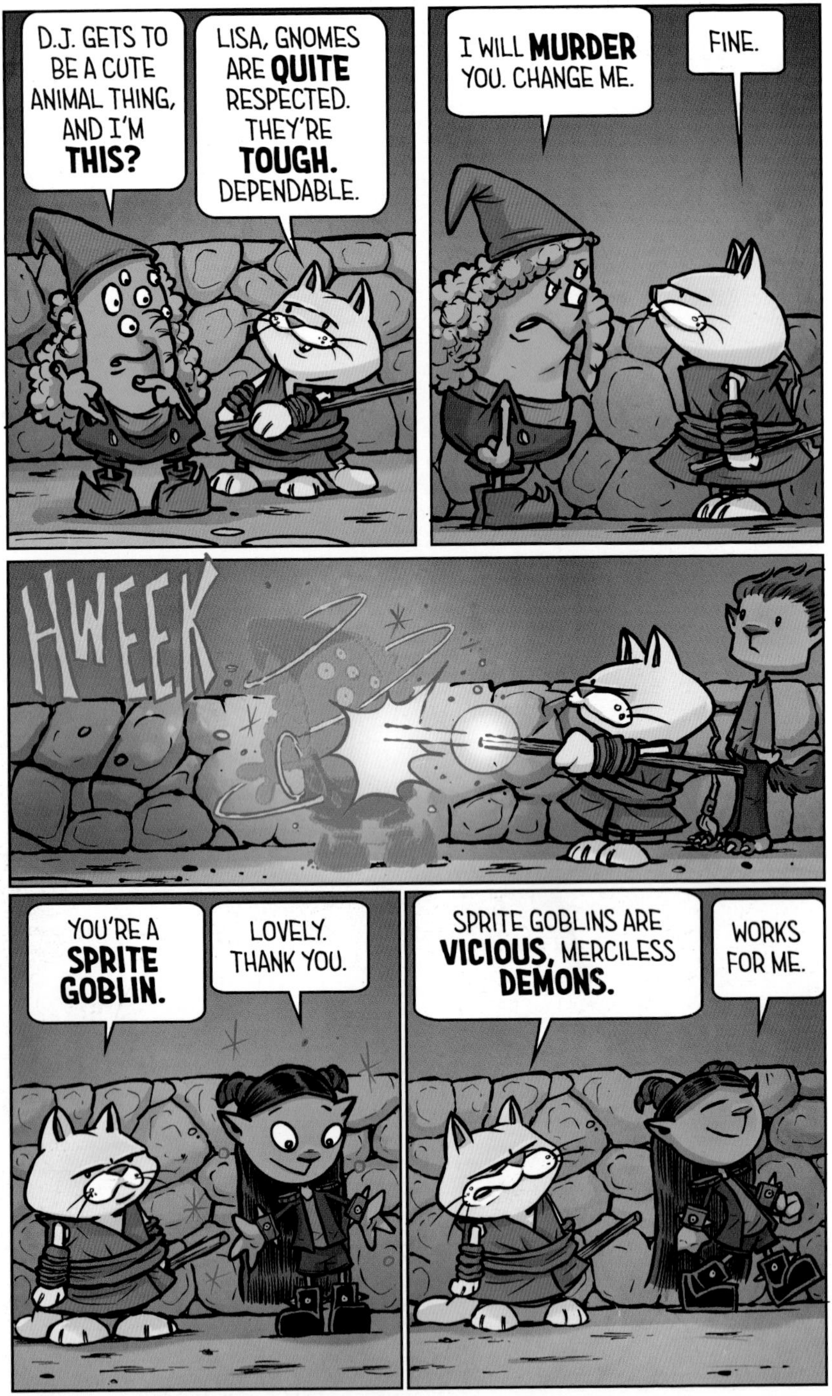
D.J. GETS TO BE A CUTE ANIMAL THING, AND I'M **THIS?**
LISA, GNOMES ARE **QUITE** RESPECTED. THEY'RE **TOUGH.** DEPENDABLE.
I WILL **MURDER** YOU. CHANGE ME.
FINE.
HWEEK
YOU'RE A **SPRITE GOBLIN.**
LOVELY. THANK YOU.
SPRITE GOBLINS ARE **VICIOUS,** MERCILESS **DEMONS.**
WORKS FOR ME.

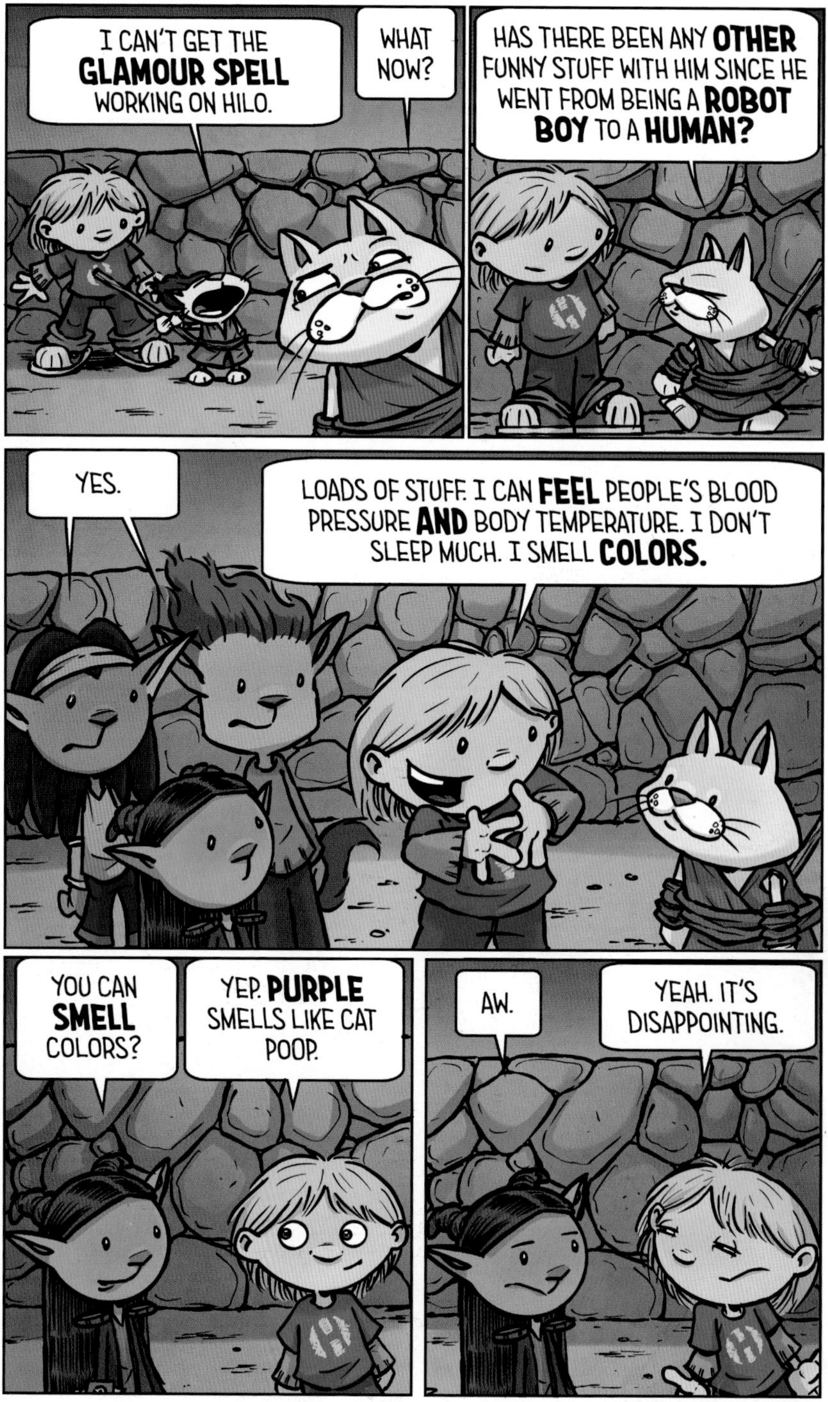
I CAN'T GET THE GLAMOUR SPELL WORKING ON HILO.
WHAT NOW?
HAS THERE BEEN ANY OTHER FUNNY STUFF WITH HIM SINCE HE WENT FROM BEING A ROBOT BOY TO A HUMAN?
YES.
LOADS OF STUFF. I CAN FEEL PEOPLE'S BLOOD PRESSURE AND BODY TEMPERATURE. I DON'T SLEEP MUCH. I SMELL COLORS.
YOU CAN SMELL COLORS?
YEP. PURPLE SMELLS LIKE CAT POOP.
AW.
YEAH. IT'S DISAPPOINTING.

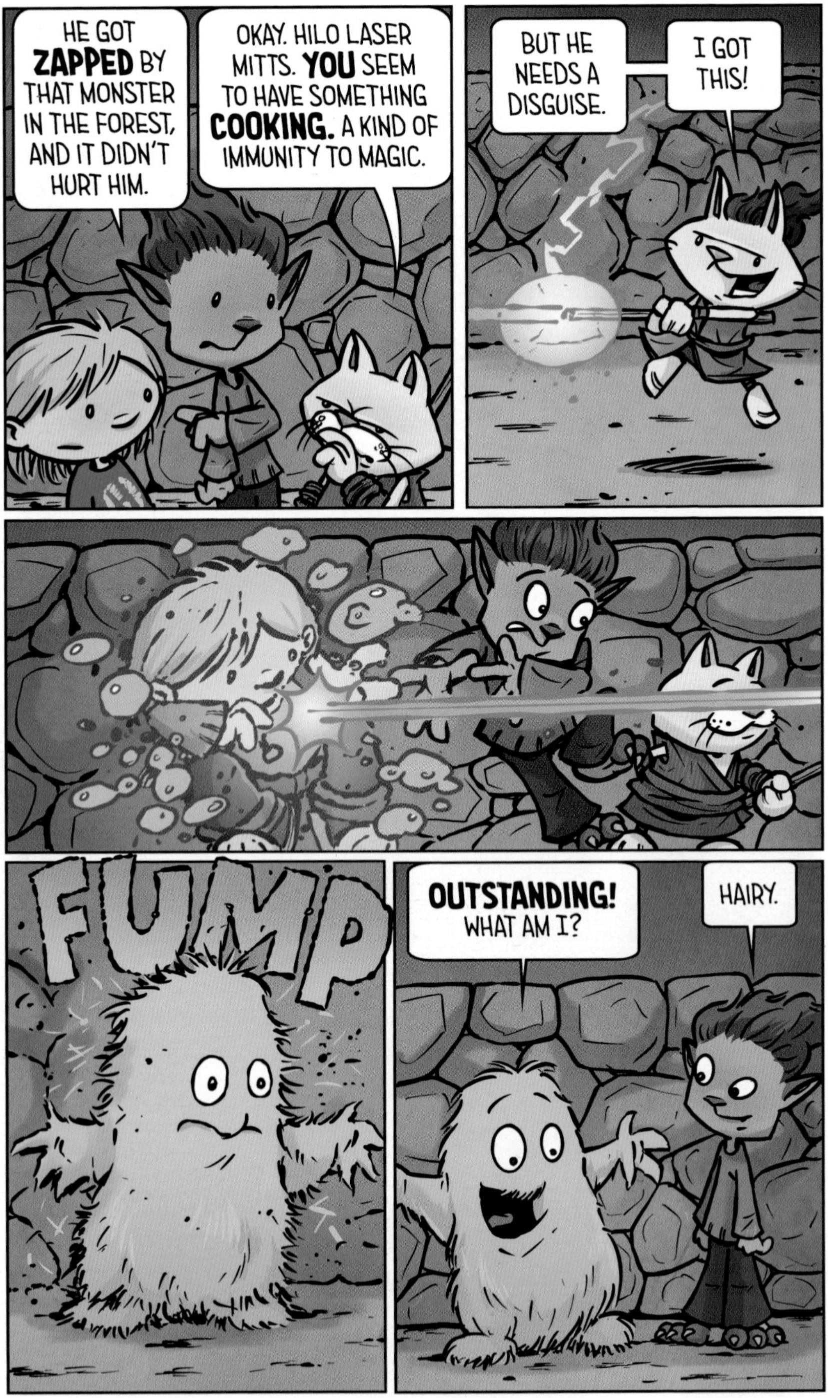
HE GOT ZAPPED BY THAT MONSTER IN THE FOREST, AND IT DIDN'T HURT HIM.
OKAY. HILO LASER MITTS. YOU SEEM TO HAVE SOMETHING COOKING. A KIND OF IMMUNITY TO MAGIC.
BUT HE NEEDS A DISGUISE.
I GOT THIS!
FUMP
OUTSTANDING! WHAT AM I?
HAIRY.

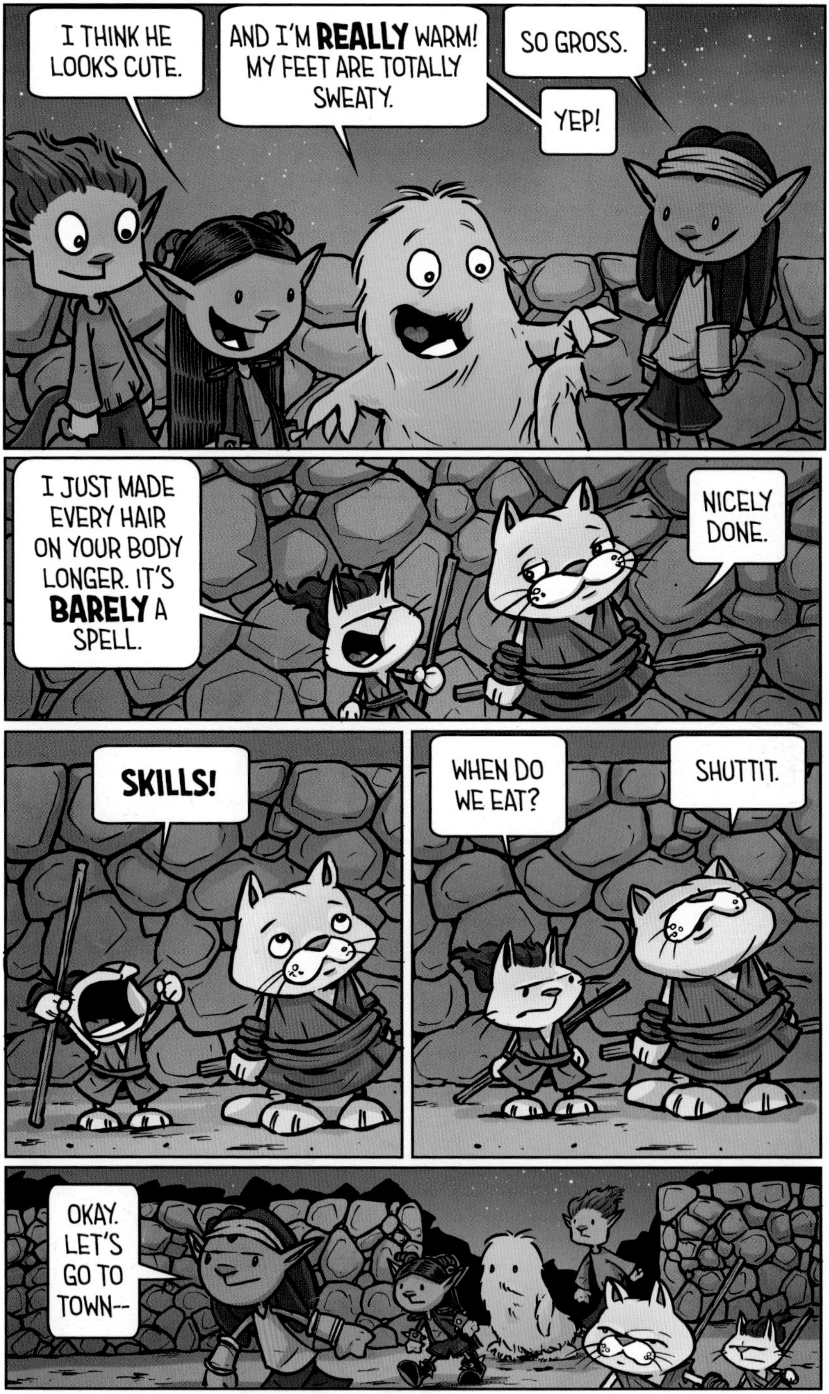
I THINK HE LOOKS CUTE.
AND I'M **REALLY** WARM! MY FEET ARE TOTALLY SWEATY.
SO GROSS.
YEP!
I JUST MADE EVERY HAIR ON YOUR BODY LONGER. IT'S **BARELY** A SPELL.
NICELY DONE.
SKILLS!
WHEN DO WE EAT?
SHUTTIT.
OKAY. LET'S GO TO TOWN--

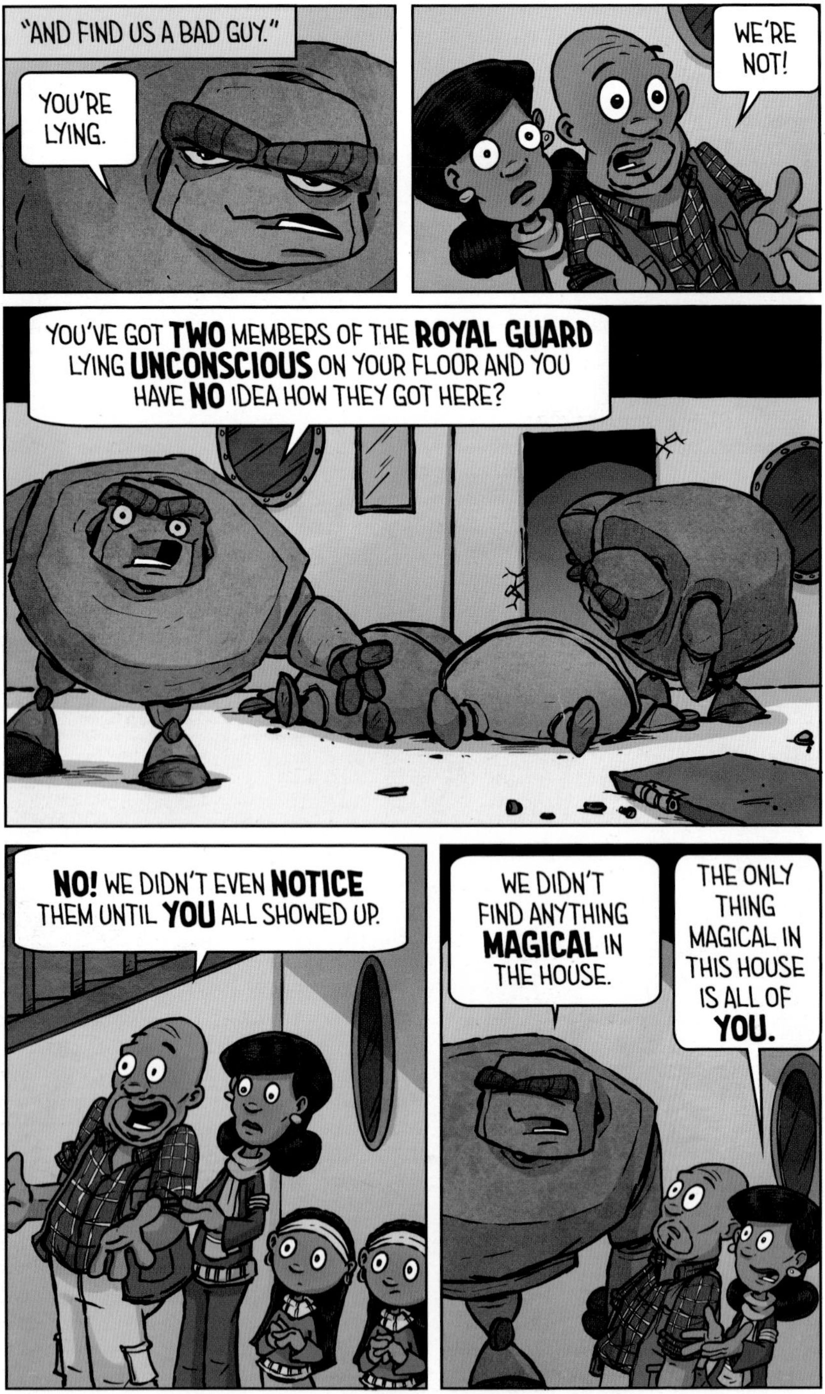
"AND FIND US A BAD GUY."
YOU'RE LYING.
WE'RE NOT!
YOU'VE GOT **TWO** MEMBERS OF THE **ROYAL GUARD** LYING **UNCONSCIOUS** ON YOUR FLOOR AND YOU HAVE **NO** IDEA HOW THEY GOT HERE?
NO! WE DIDN'T EVEN **NOTICE** THEM UNTIL **YOU** ALL SHOWED UP.
WE DIDN'T FIND ANYTHING **MAGICAL** IN THE HOUSE.
THE ONLY THING MAGICAL IN THIS HOUSE IS ALL OF **YOU.**

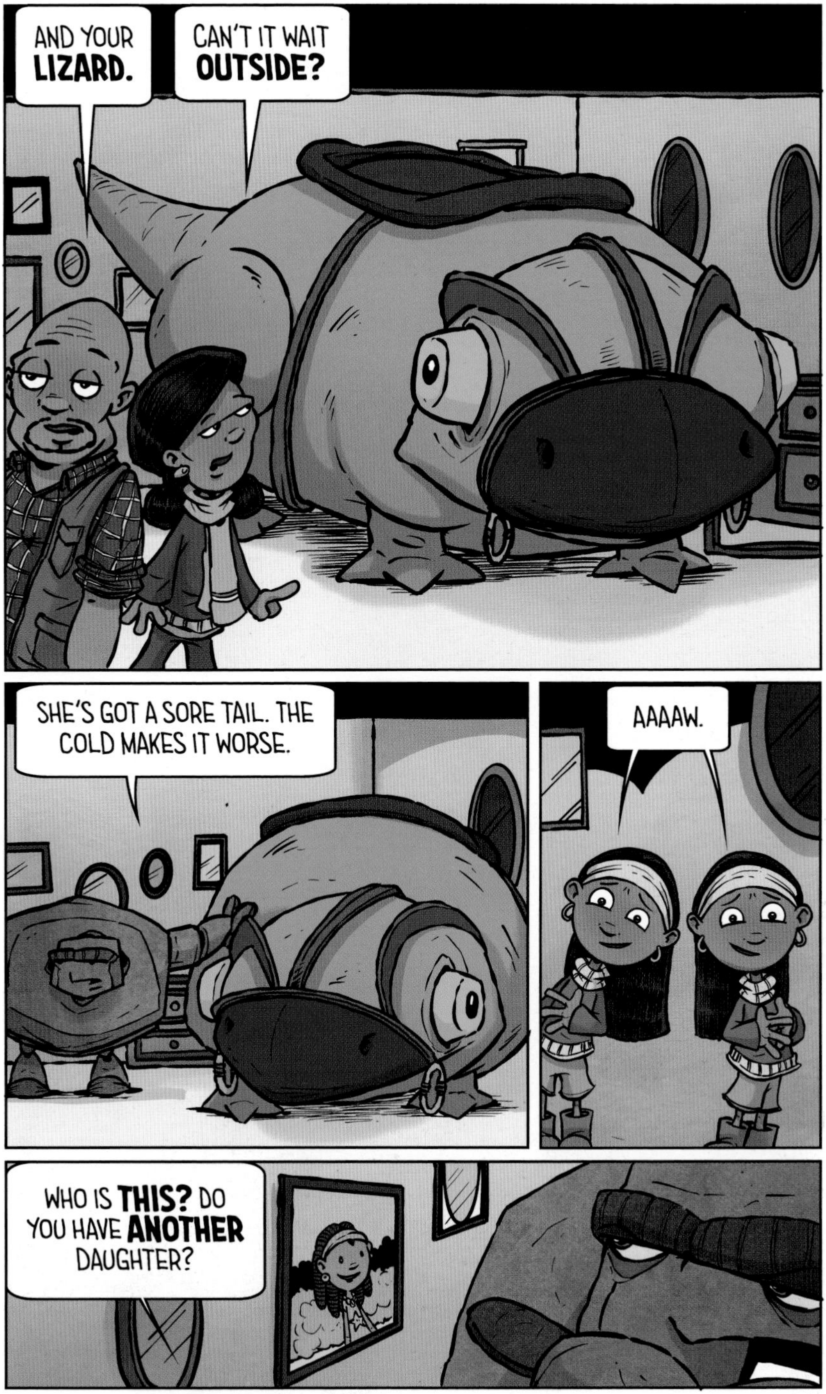
AND YOUR **LIZARD.**
CAN'T IT WAIT **OUTSIDE?**
SHE'S GOT A SORE TAIL. THE COLD MAKES IT WORSE.
AAAAW.
WHO IS **THIS?** DO YOU HAVE **ANOTHER** DAUGHTER?

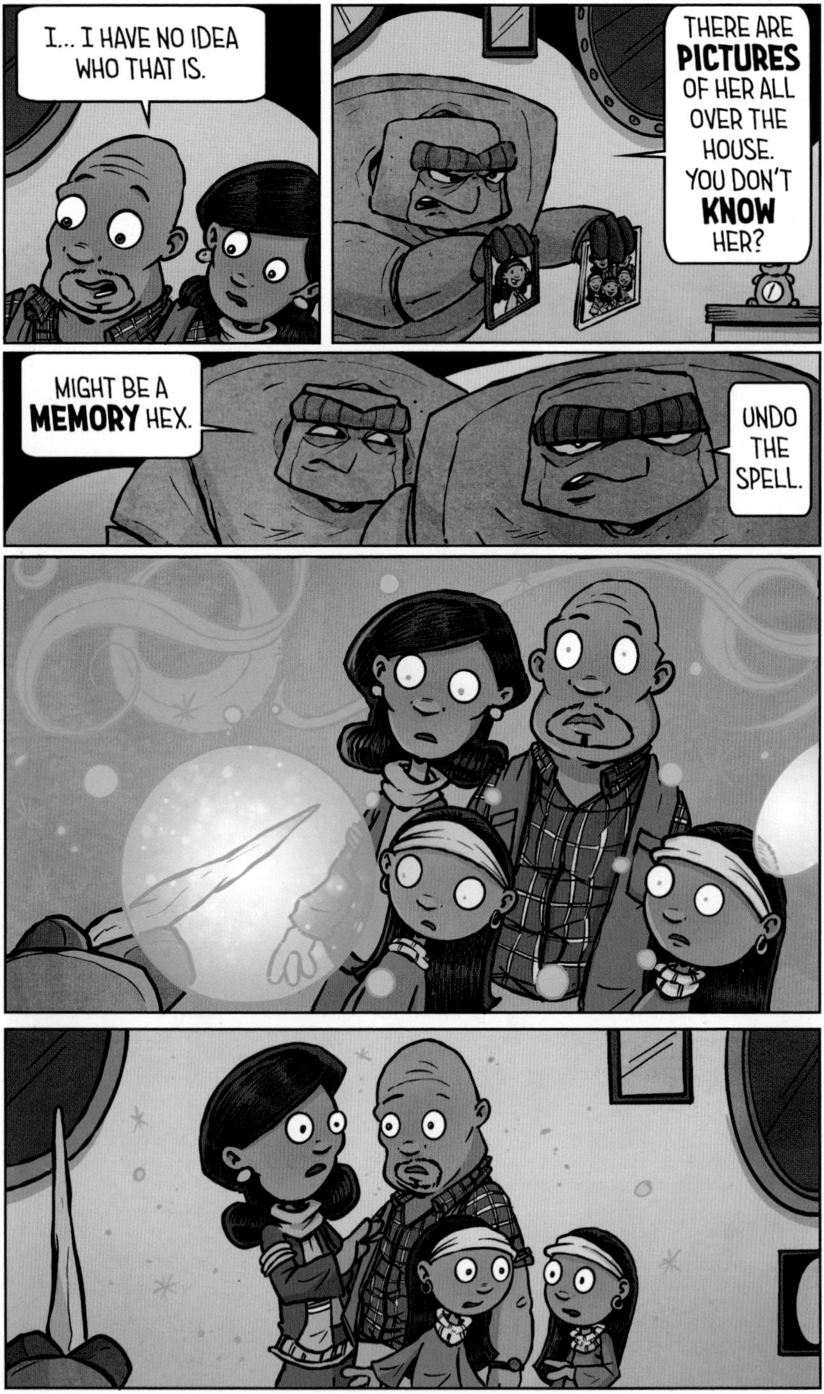
I... I HAVE NO IDEA WHO THAT IS.
THERE ARE **PICTURES** OF HER ALL OVER THE HOUSE. YOU DON'T **KNOW** HER?
MIGHT BE A **MEMORY** HEX.
UNDO THE SPELL.

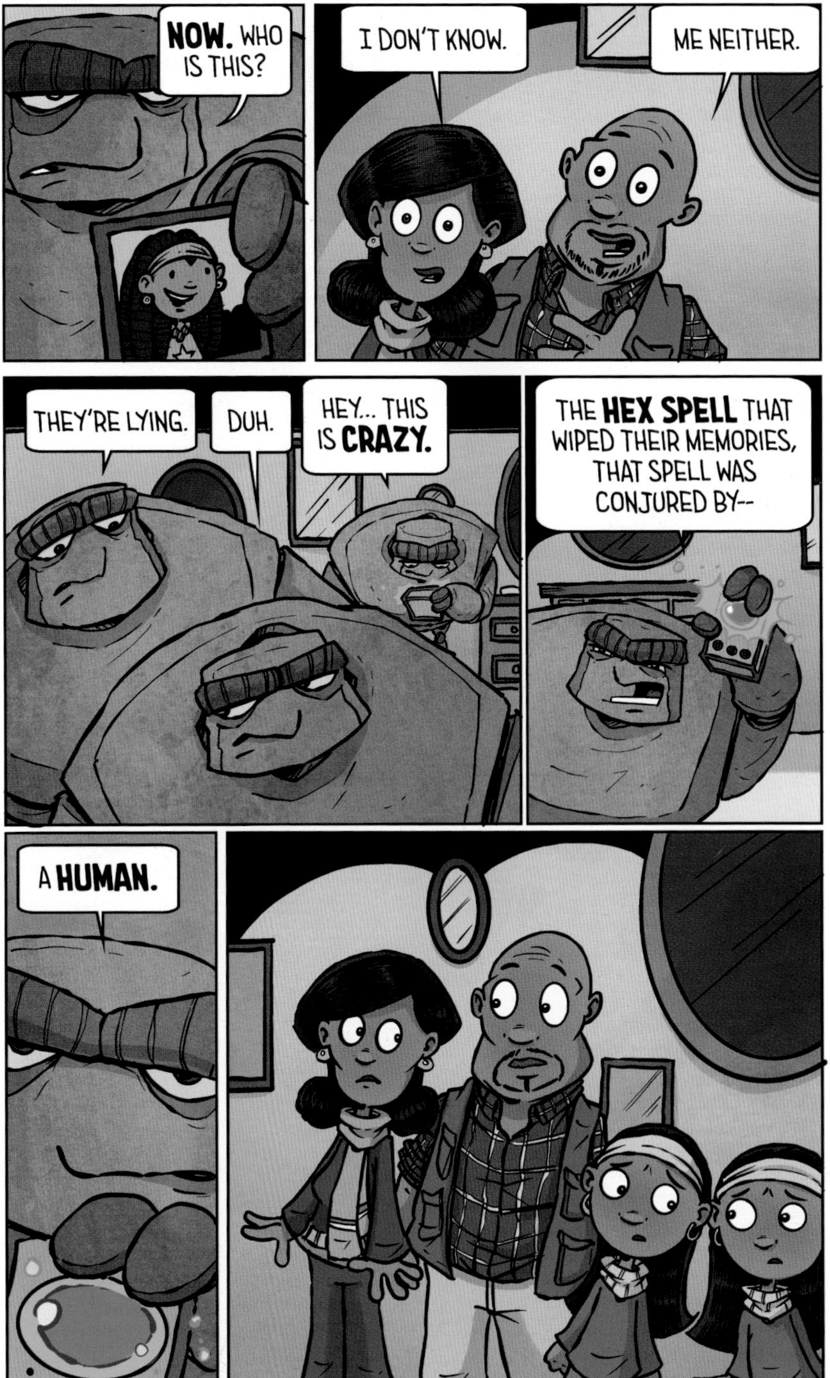
NOW. WHO IS THIS?
I DON'T KNOW.
ME NEITHER.
THEY'RE LYING.
DUH.
HEY... THIS IS CRAZY.
THE HEX SPELL THAT WIPED THEIR MEMORIES, THAT SPELL WAS CONJURED BY--
A HUMAN.

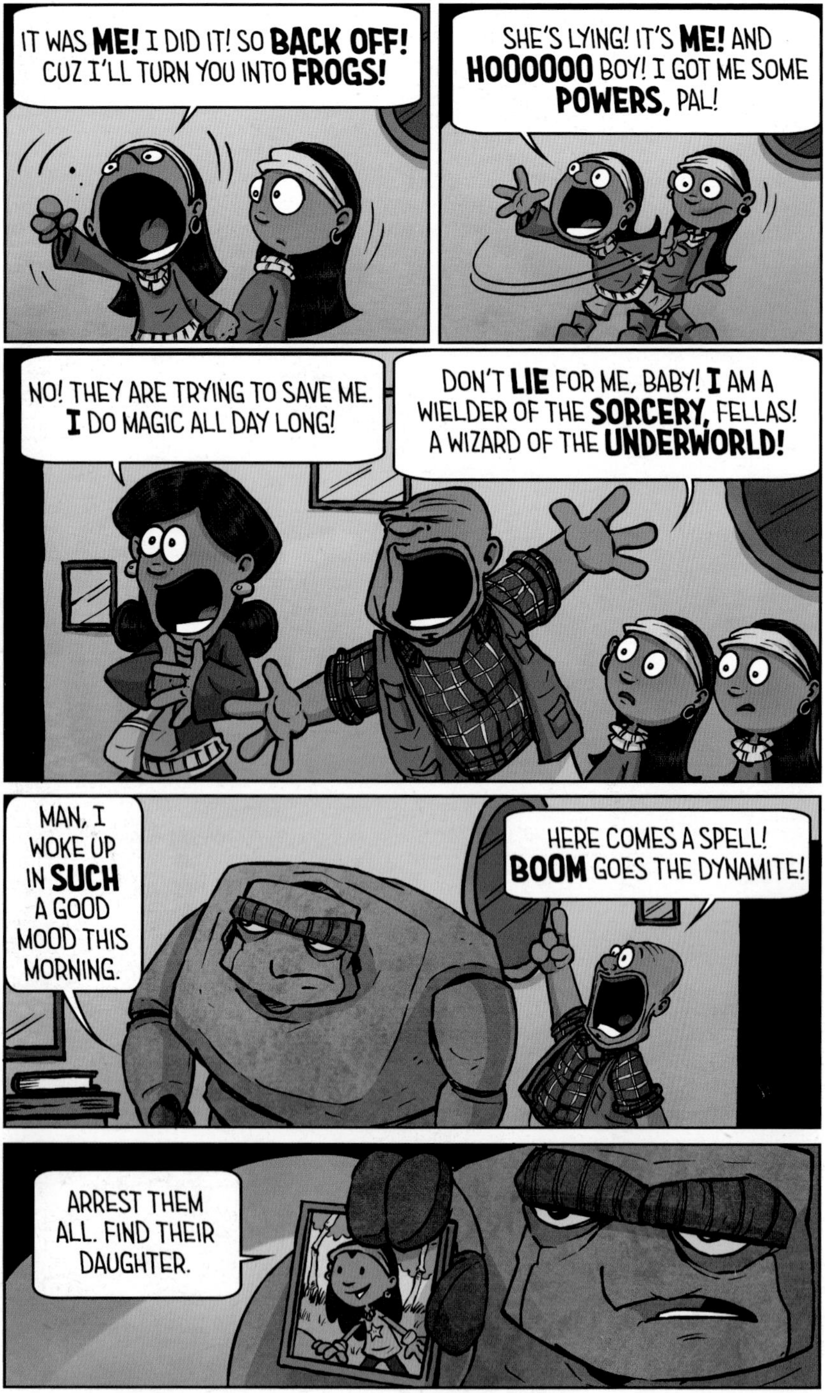
IT WAS ME! I DID IT! SO BACK OFF! CUZ I'LL TURN YOU INTO FROGS!
SHE'S LYING! IT'S ME! AND HOOOOOO BOY! I GOT ME SOME POWERS, PAL!
NO! THEY ARE TRYING TO SAVE ME. I DO MAGIC ALL DAY LONG!
DON'T LIE FOR ME, BABY! I AM A WIELDER OF THE SORCERY, FELLAS! A WIZARD OF THE UNDERWORLD!
MAN, I WOKE UP IN SUCH A GOOD MOOD THIS MORNING.
HERE COMES A SPELL! BOOM GOES THE DYNAMITE!
ARREST THEM ALL. FIND THEIR DAUGHTER.

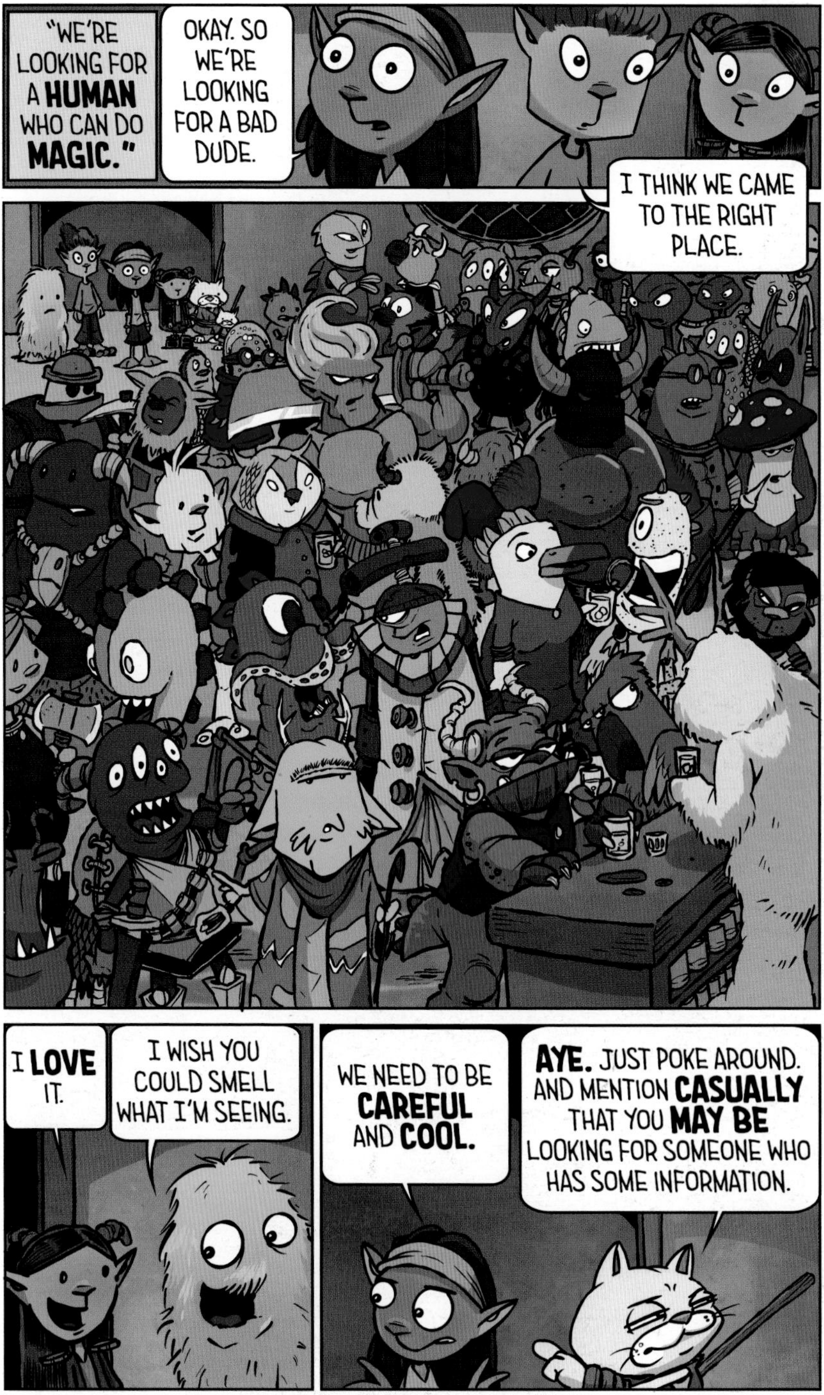
"WE'RE LOOKING FOR A **HUMAN** WHO CAN DO **MAGIC.**"
OKAY. SO WE'RE LOOKING FOR A BAD DUDE.
I THINK WE CAME TO THE RIGHT PLACE.
I **LOVE** IT.
I WISH YOU COULD SMELL WHAT I'M SEEING.
WE NEED TO BE **CAREFUL** AND **COOL.**
AYE. JUST POKE AROUND. AND MENTION **CASUALLY** THAT YOU **MAY BE** LOOKING FOR SOMEONE WHO HAS SOME INFORMATION.

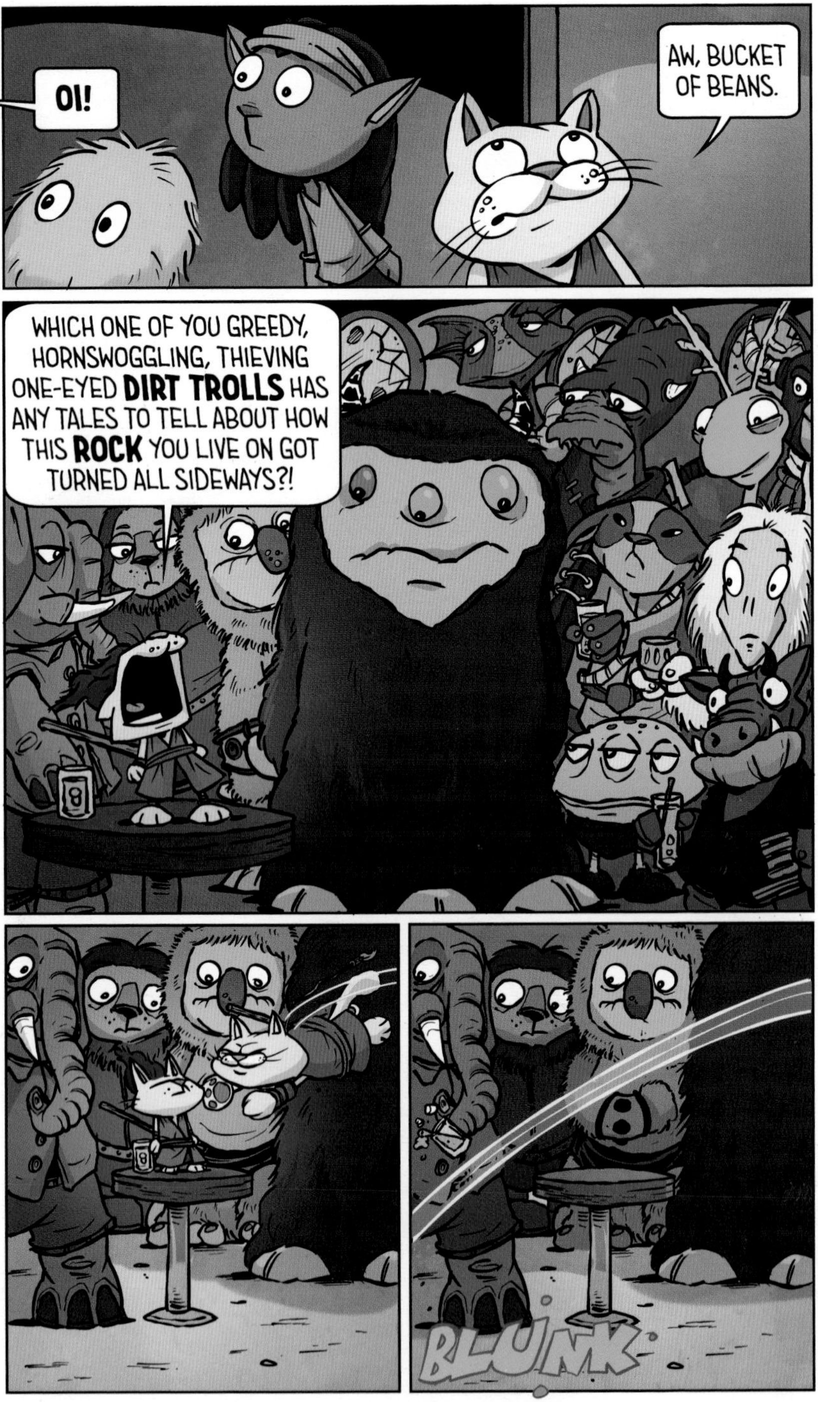
OI!
AW, BUCKET OF BEANS.
WHICH ONE OF YOU GREEDY, HORNSWOGGLING, THIEVING ONE-EYED DIRT TROLLS HAS ANY TALES TO TELL ABOUT HOW THIS ROCK YOU LIVE ON GOT TURNED ALL SIDEWAYS?!
BLUNK

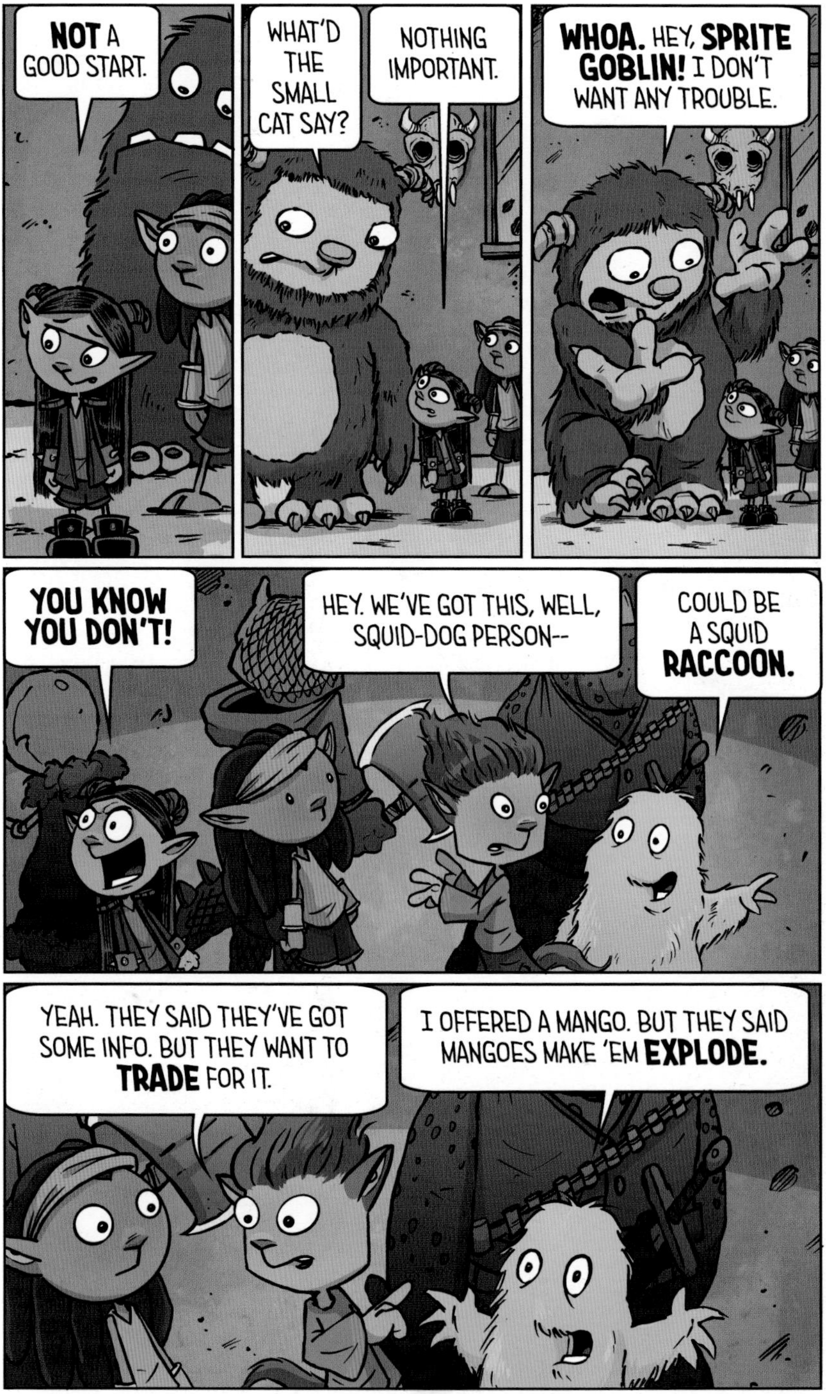
NOT A GOOD START.
WHAT'D THE SMALL CAT SAY?
NOTHING IMPORTANT.
WHOA. HEY, SPRITE GOBLIN! I DON'T WANT ANY TROUBLE.
YOU KNOW YOU DON'T!
HEY. WE'VE GOT THIS, WELL, SQUID-DOG PERSON--
COULD BE A SQUID RACCOON.
YEAH. THEY SAID THEY'VE GOT SOME INFO. BUT THEY WANT TO TRADE FOR IT.
I OFFERED A MANGO. BUT THEY SAID MANGOES MAKE 'EM EXPLODE.

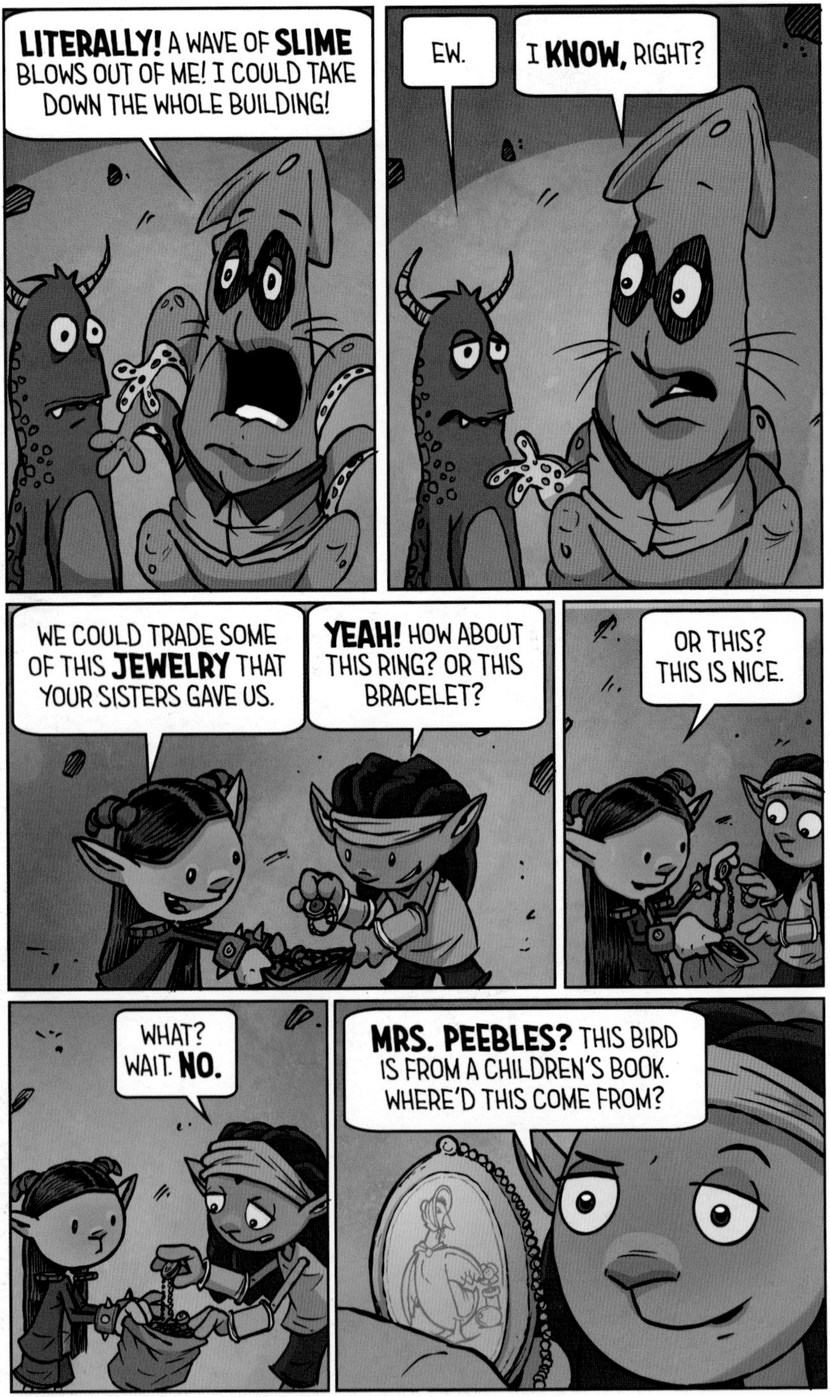
LITERALLY! A WAVE OF SLIME BLOWS OUT OF ME! I COULD TAKE DOWN THE WHOLE BUILDING!
EW.
I KNOW, RIGHT?
WE COULD TRADE SOME OF THIS JEWELRY THAT YOUR SISTERS GAVE US.
YEAH! HOW ABOUT THIS RING? OR THIS BRACELET?
OR THIS? THIS IS NICE.
WHAT? WAIT. NO.
MRS. PEEBLES? THIS BIRD IS FROM A CHILDREN'S BOOK. WHERE'D THIS COME FROM?

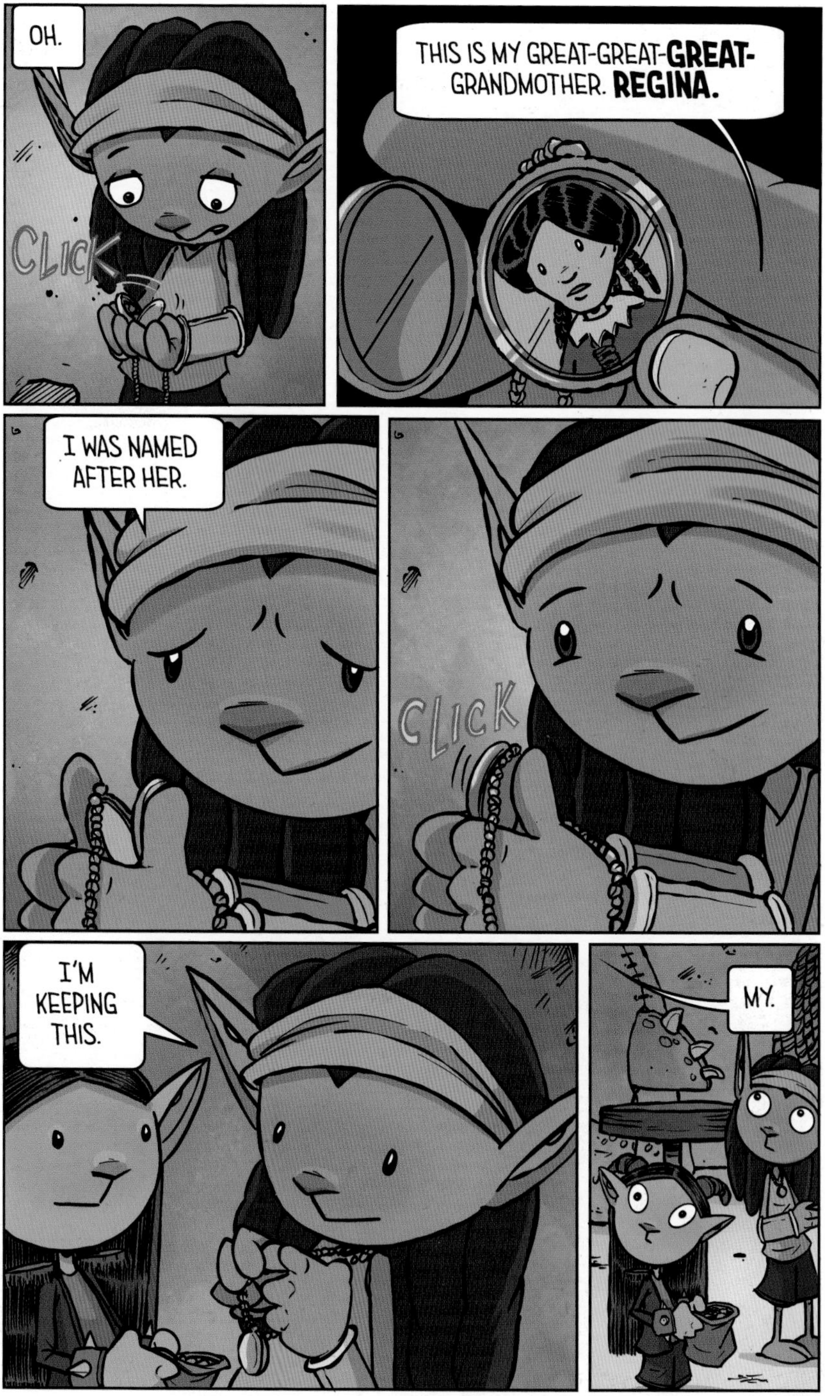
OH.
CLICK
THIS IS MY GREAT-GREAT-GREAT-GRANDMOTHER. REGINA.
I WAS NAMED AFTER HER.
CLICK
I'M KEEPING THIS.
MY.

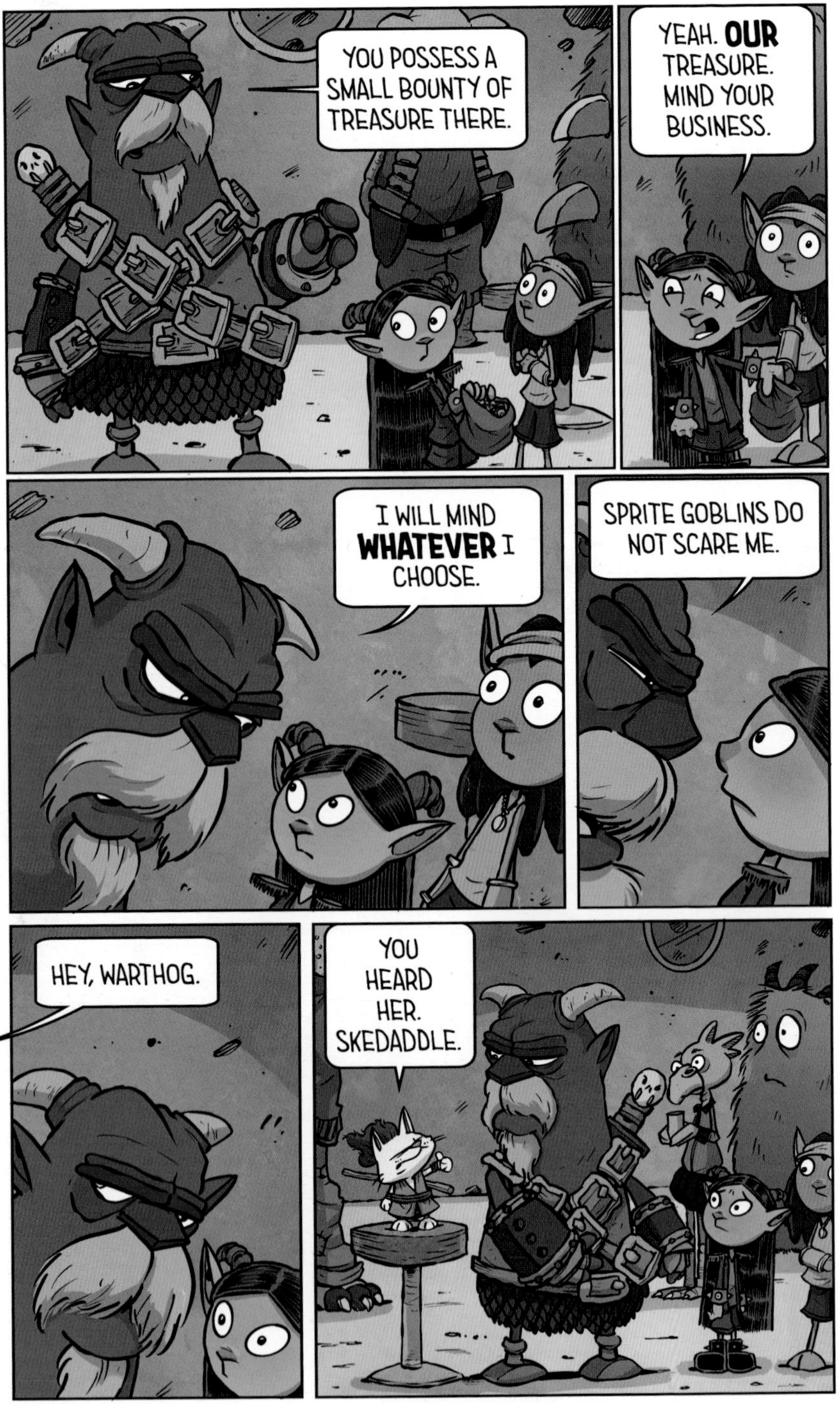
YOU POSSESS A SMALL BOUNTY OF TREASURE THERE.
YEAH. **OUR** TREASURE. MIND YOUR BUSINESS.
I WILL MIND **WHATEVER** I CHOOSE.
SPRITE GOBLINS DO NOT SCARE ME.
HEY, WARTHOG.
YOU HEARD HER. SKEDADDLE.

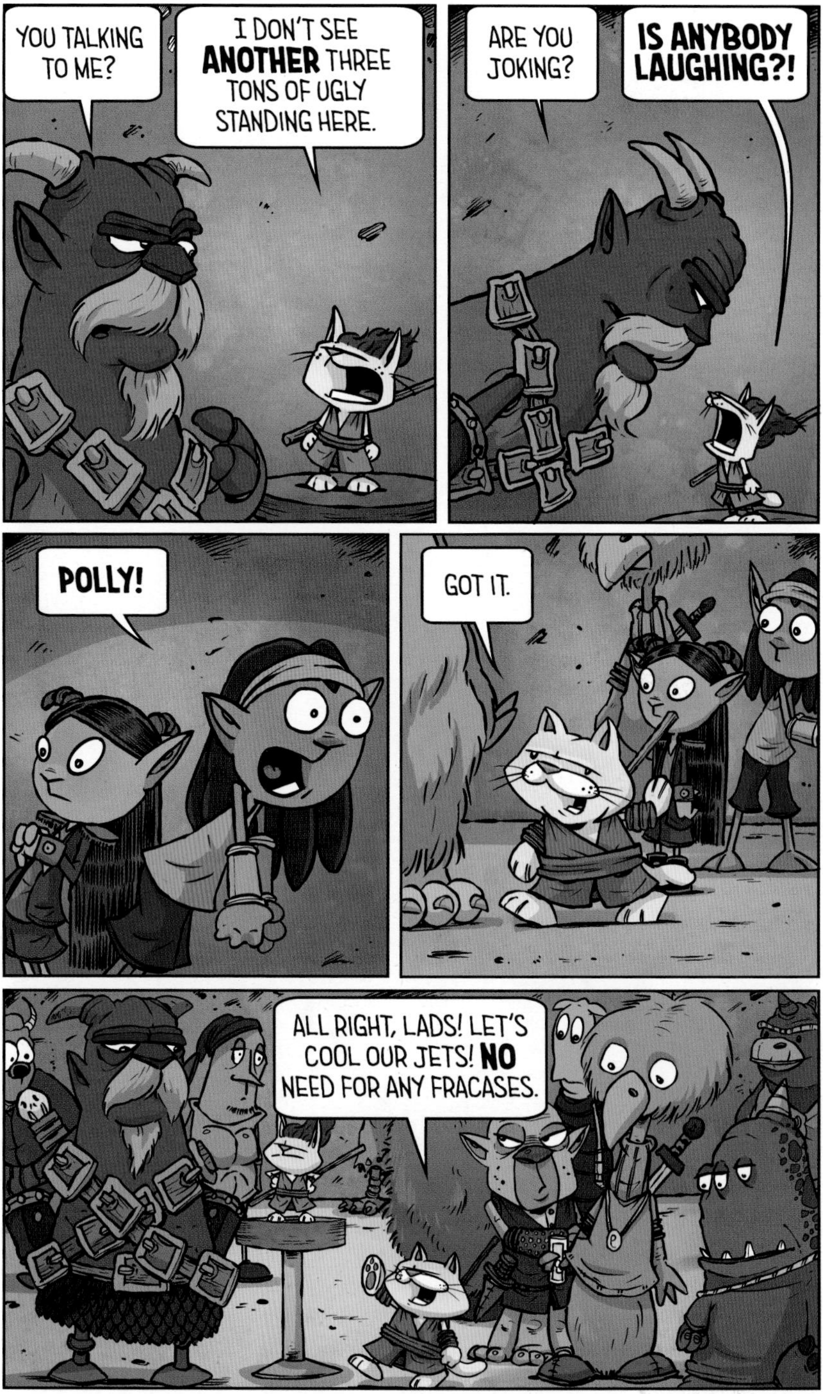
YOU TALKING TO ME?
I DON'T SEE **ANOTHER** THREE TONS OF UGLY STANDING HERE.
ARE YOU JOKING?
IS ANYBODY LAUGHING?!
POLLY!
GOT IT.
ALL RIGHT, LADS! LET'S COOL OUR JETS! **NO** NEED FOR ANY FRACASES.

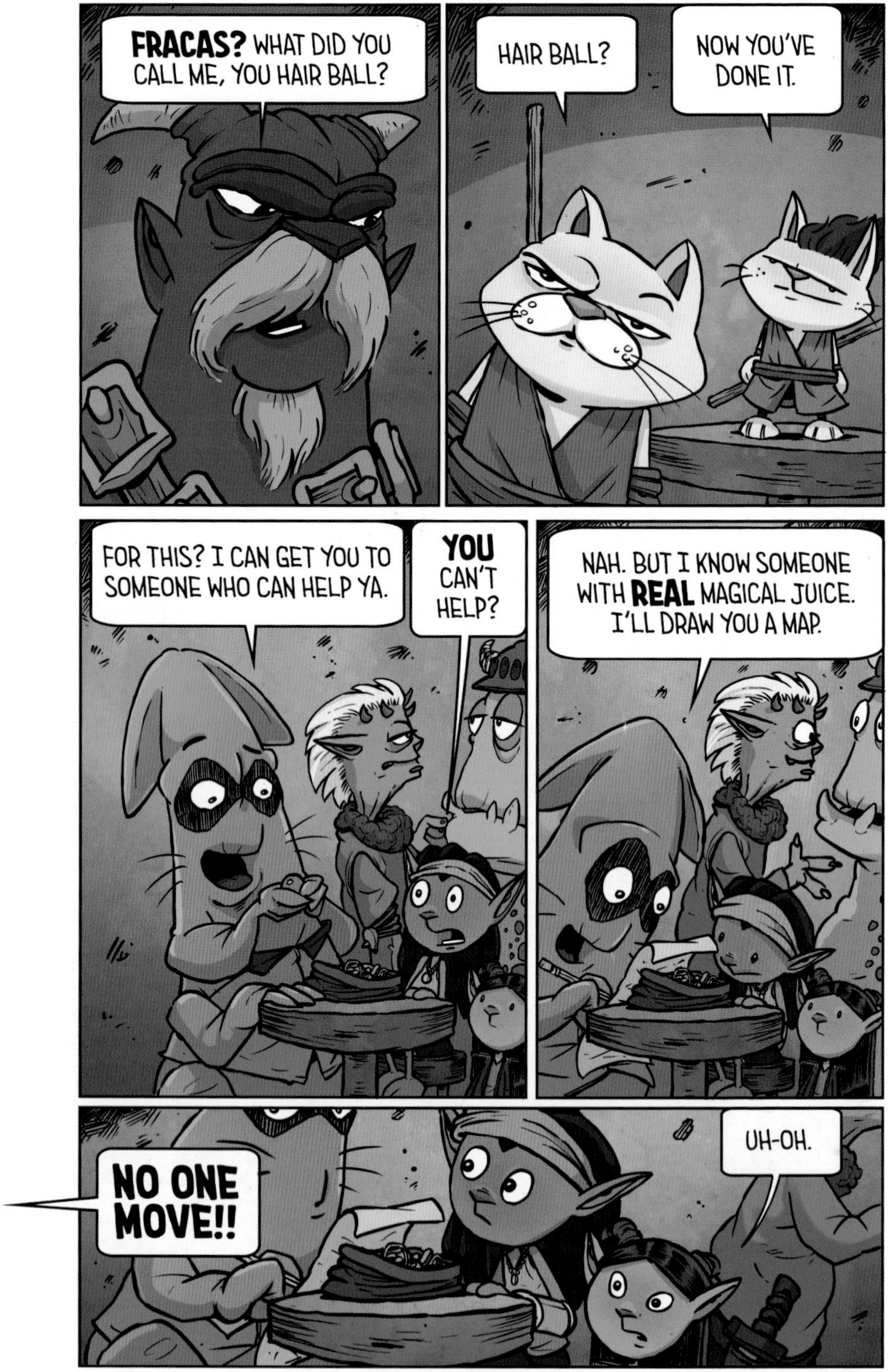
FRACAS? WHAT DID YOU CALL ME, YOU HAIR BALL?
HAIR BALL?
NOW YOU'VE DONE IT.
FOR THIS? I CAN GET YOU TO SOMEONE WHO CAN HELP YA.
YOU CAN'T HELP?
NAH. BUT I KNOW SOMEONE WITH REAL MAGICAL JUICE. I'LL DRAW YOU A MAP.
NO ONE MOVE!!
UH-OH.

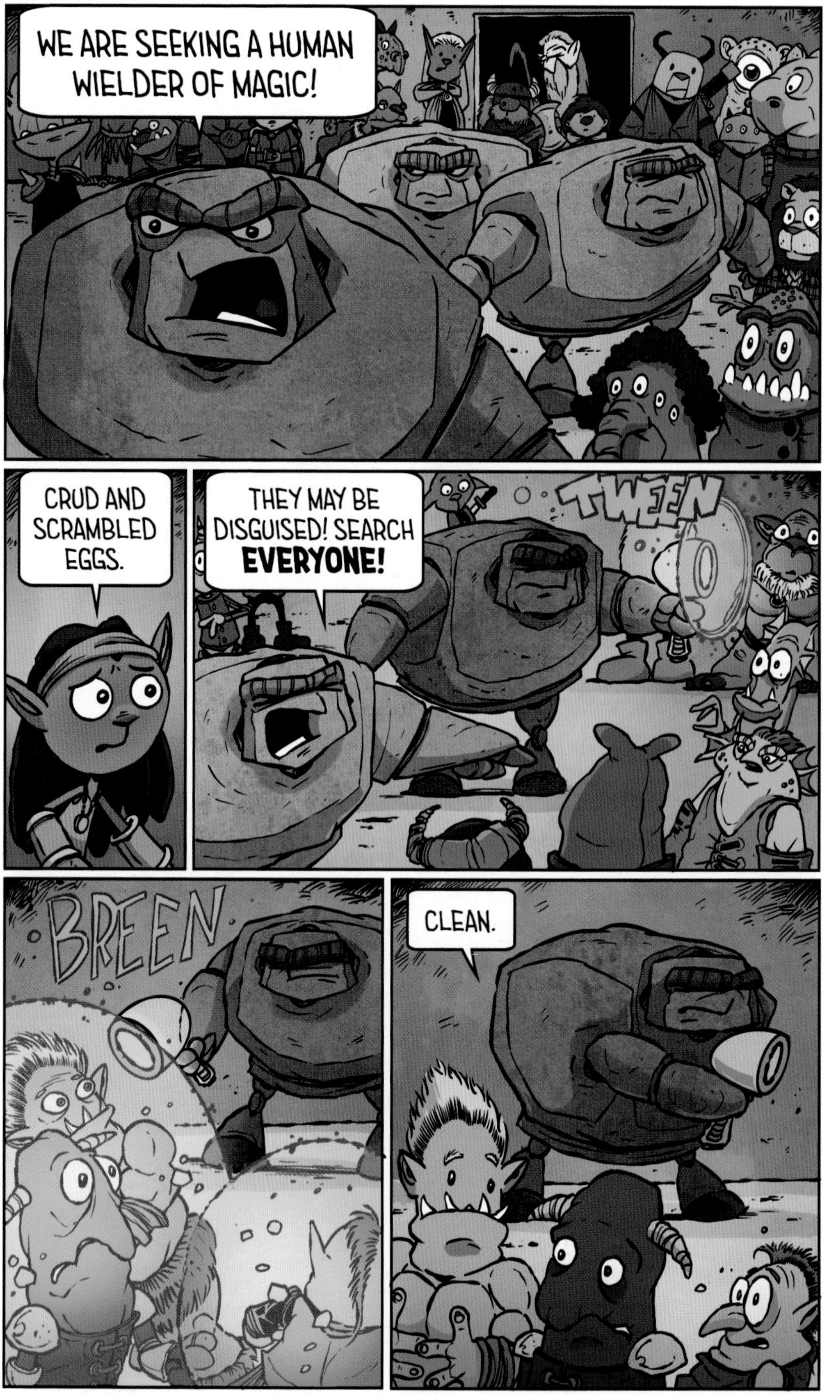
WE ARE SEEKING A HUMAN WIELDER OF MAGIC!
CRUD AND SCRAMBLED EGGS.
THEY MAY BE DISGUISED! SEARCH **EVERYONE!**
TWEEN
BREEN
CLEAN.

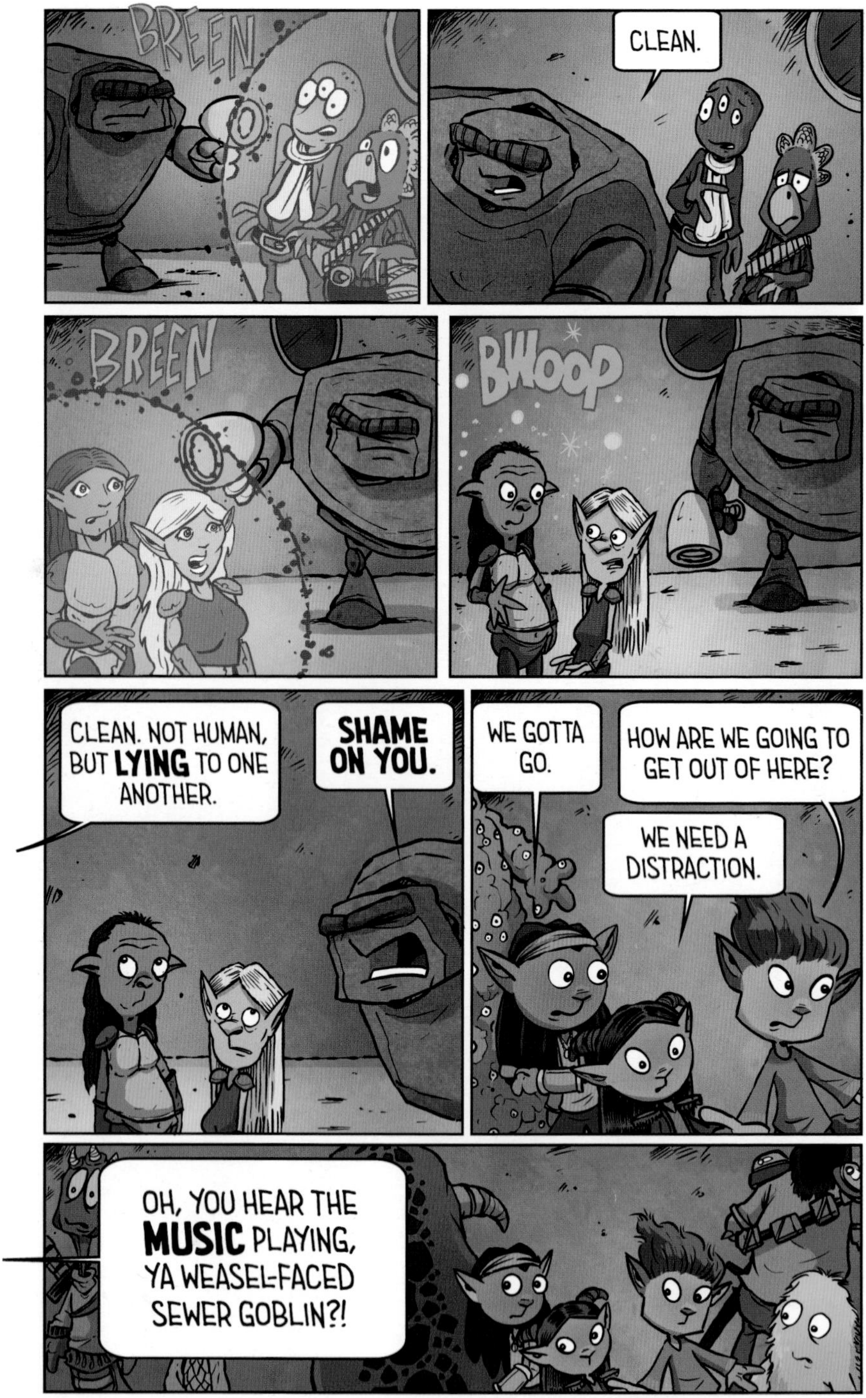
BREEN
CLEAN.
BREEN
BWOOP
CLEAN. NOT HUMAN, BUT LYING TO ONE ANOTHER.
SHAME ON YOU.
WE GOTTA GO.
HOW ARE WE GOING TO GET OUT OF HERE?
WE NEED A DISTRACTION.
OH, YOU HEAR THE MUSIC PLAYING, YA WEASEL-FACED SEWER GOBLIN?!

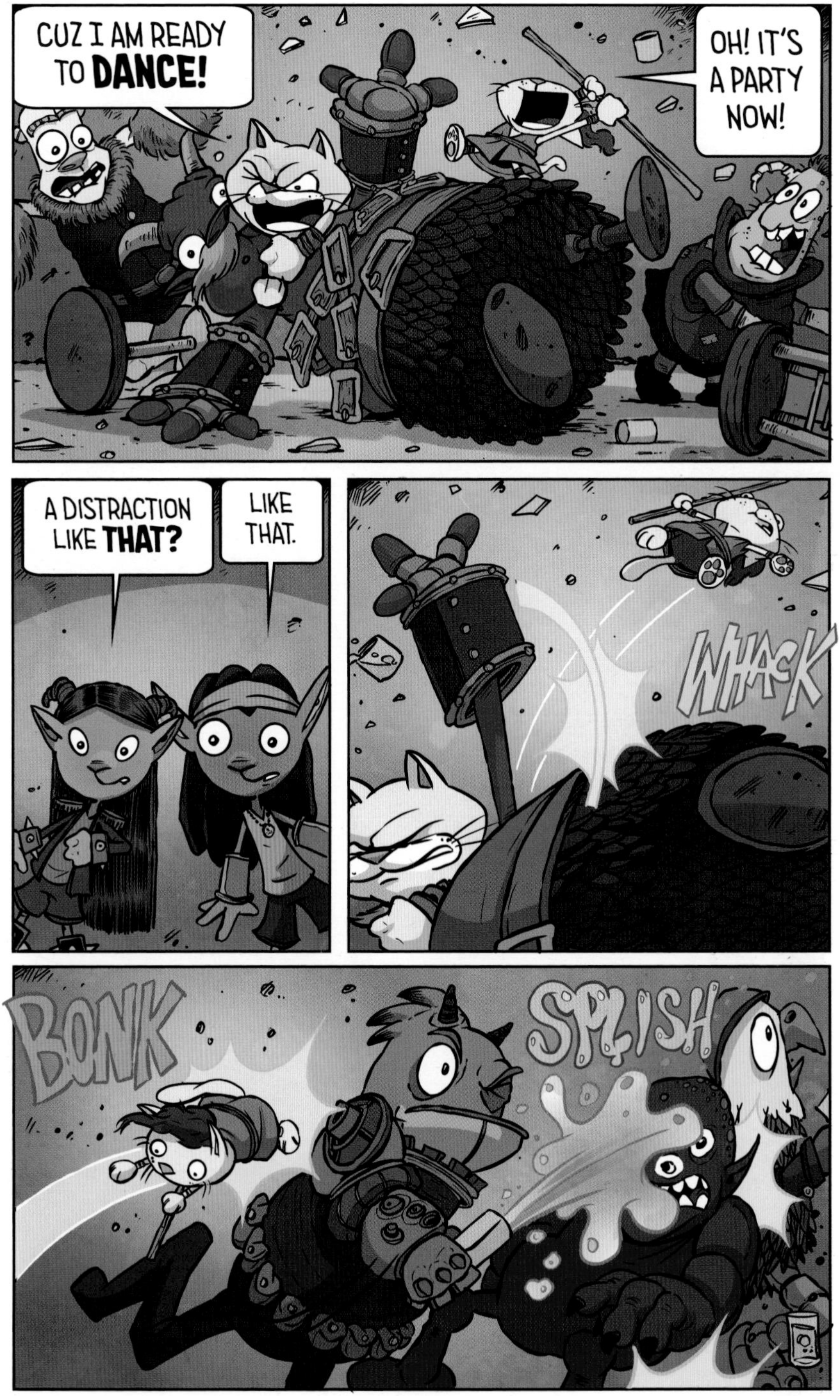
CUZ I AM READY TO DANCE!
OH! IT'S A PARTY NOW!
A DISTRACTION LIKE THAT?
LIKE THAT.
WHACK
BONK
SPLISH

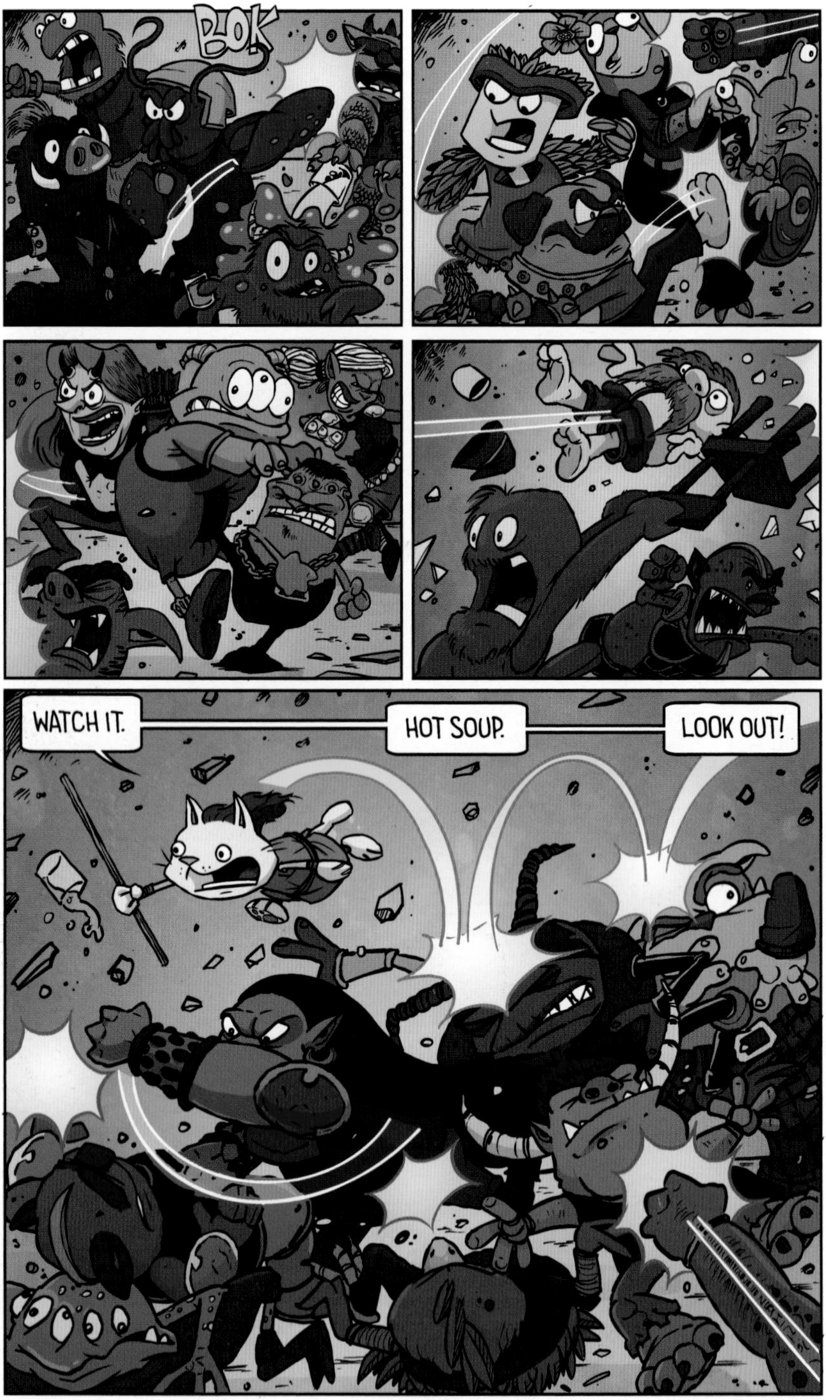
BLOK
WATCH IT.
HOT SOUP.
LOOK OUT!

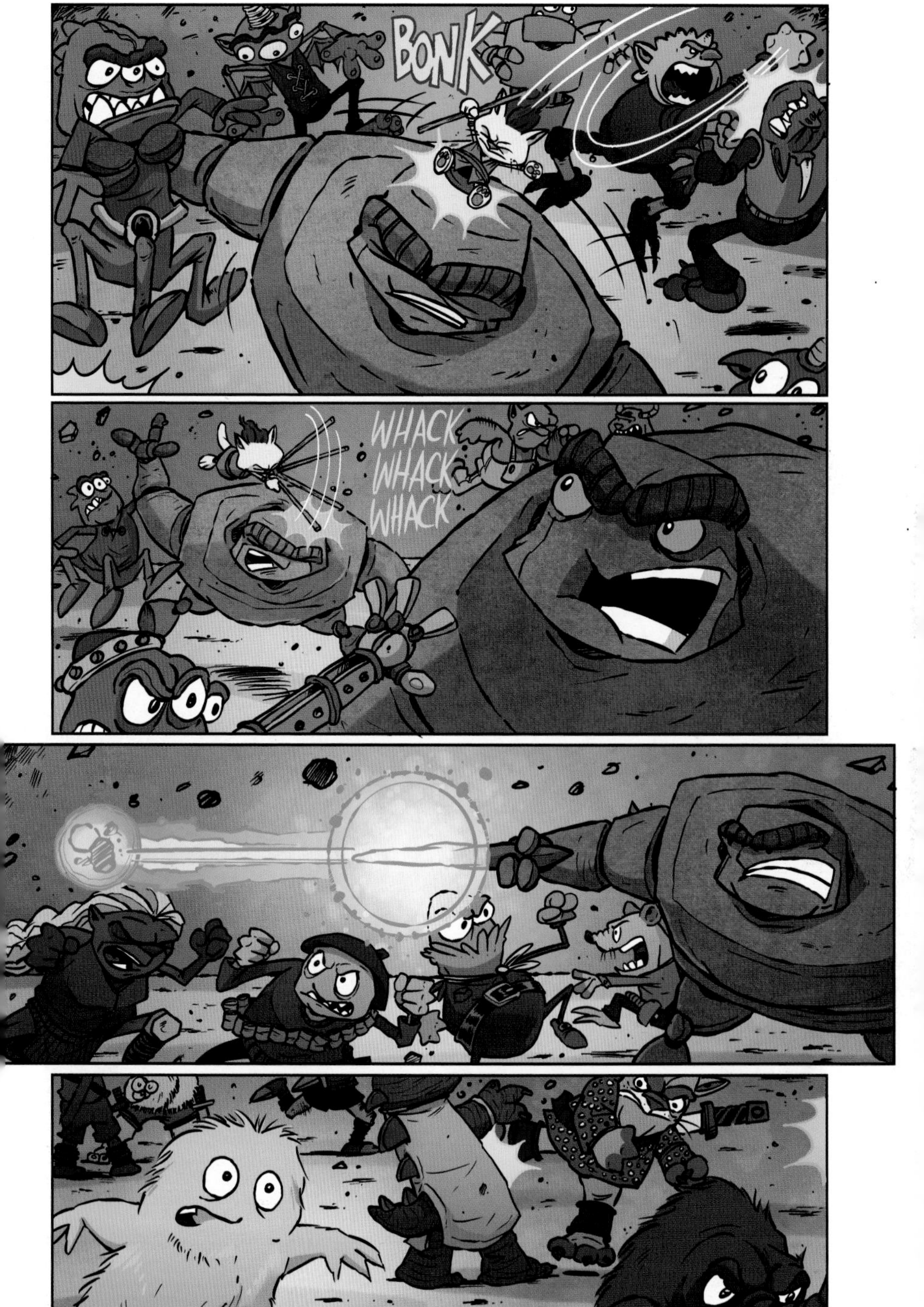
BONK
WHACK
WHACK
WHACK

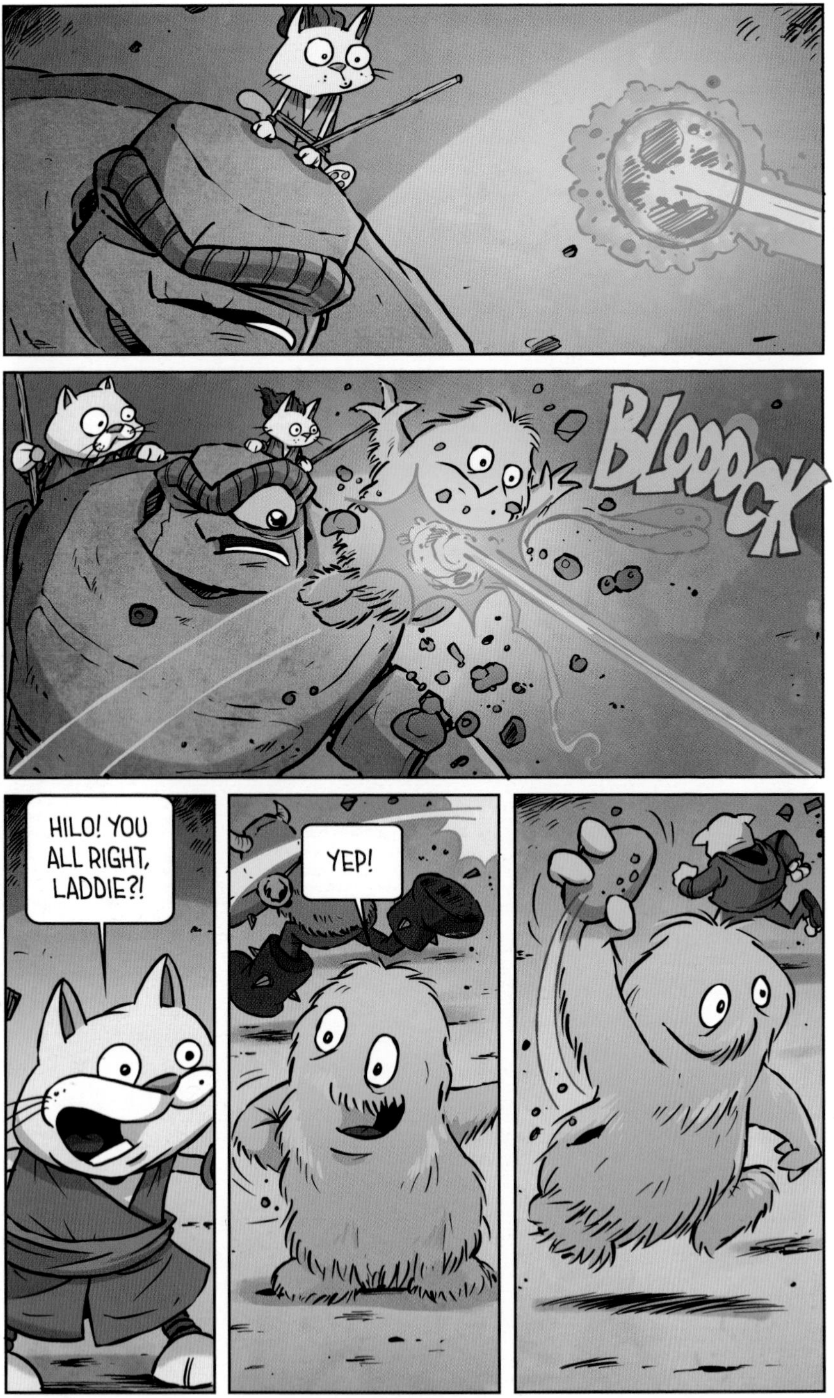
BLOOOCK
HILO! YOU ALL RIGHT, LADDIE?!
YEP!

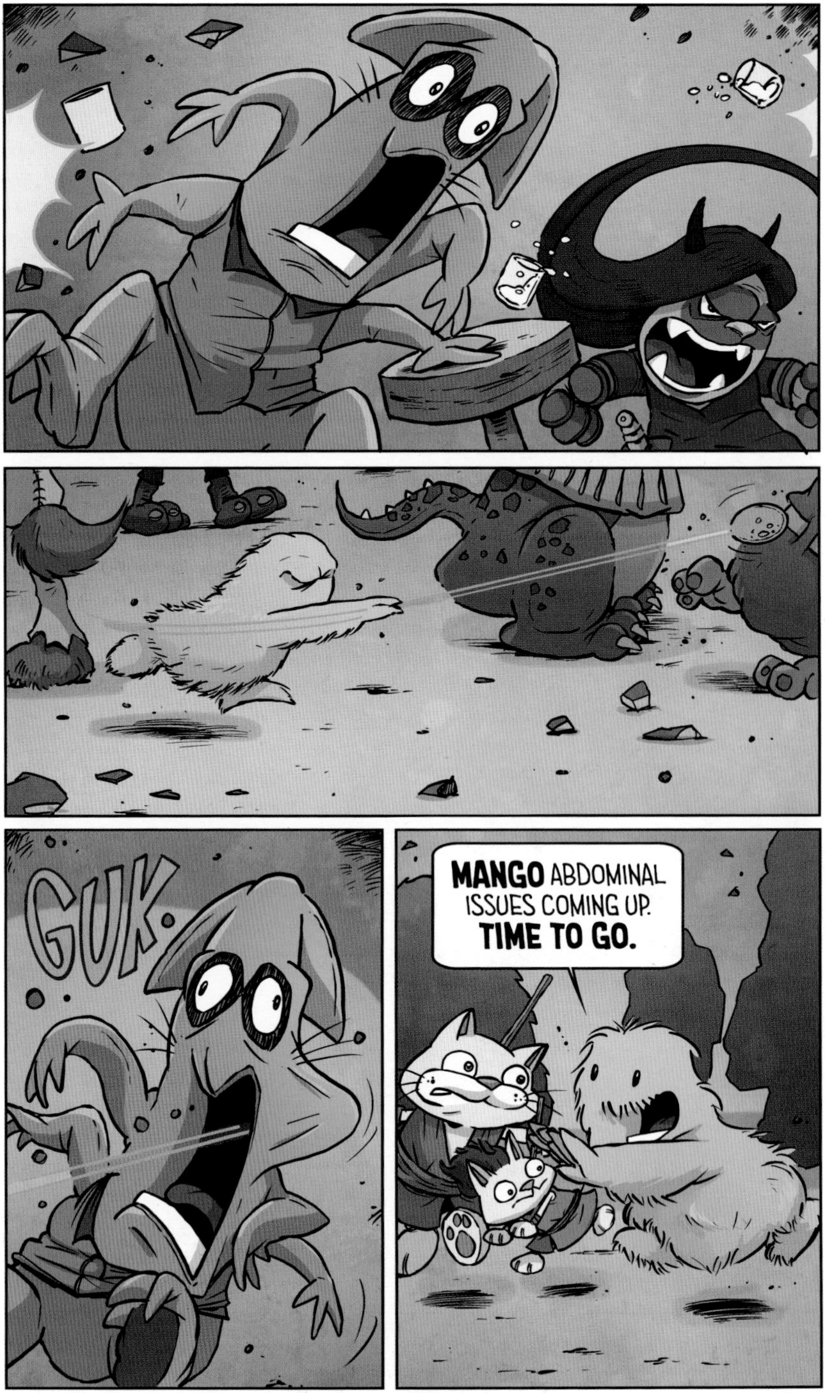
GUK.
MANGO ABDOMINAL ISSUES COMING UP. TIME TO GO.

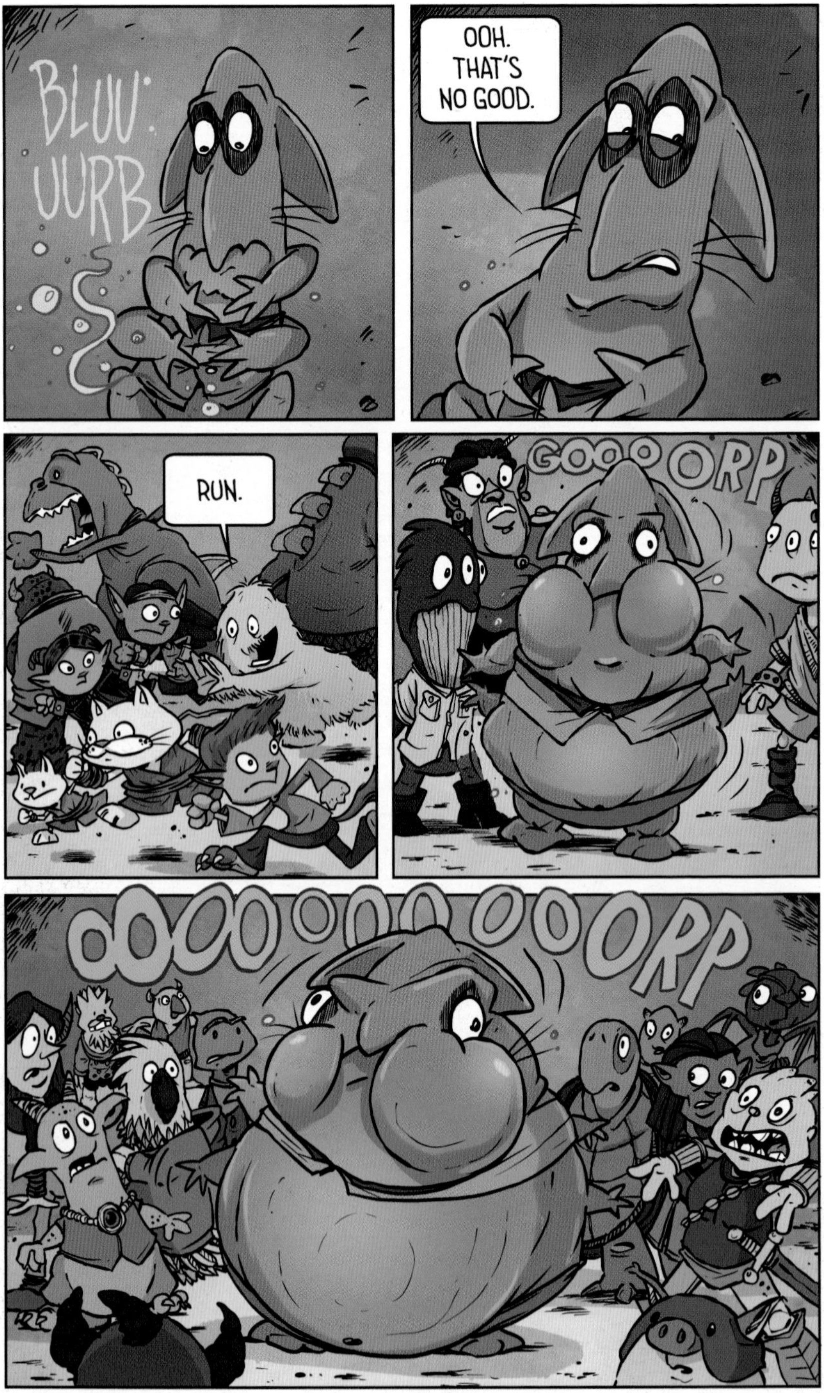
BLUU-UURB
OOH. THAT'S NO GOOD.
RUN.
GOOOORP
OOOOOOOOOORP

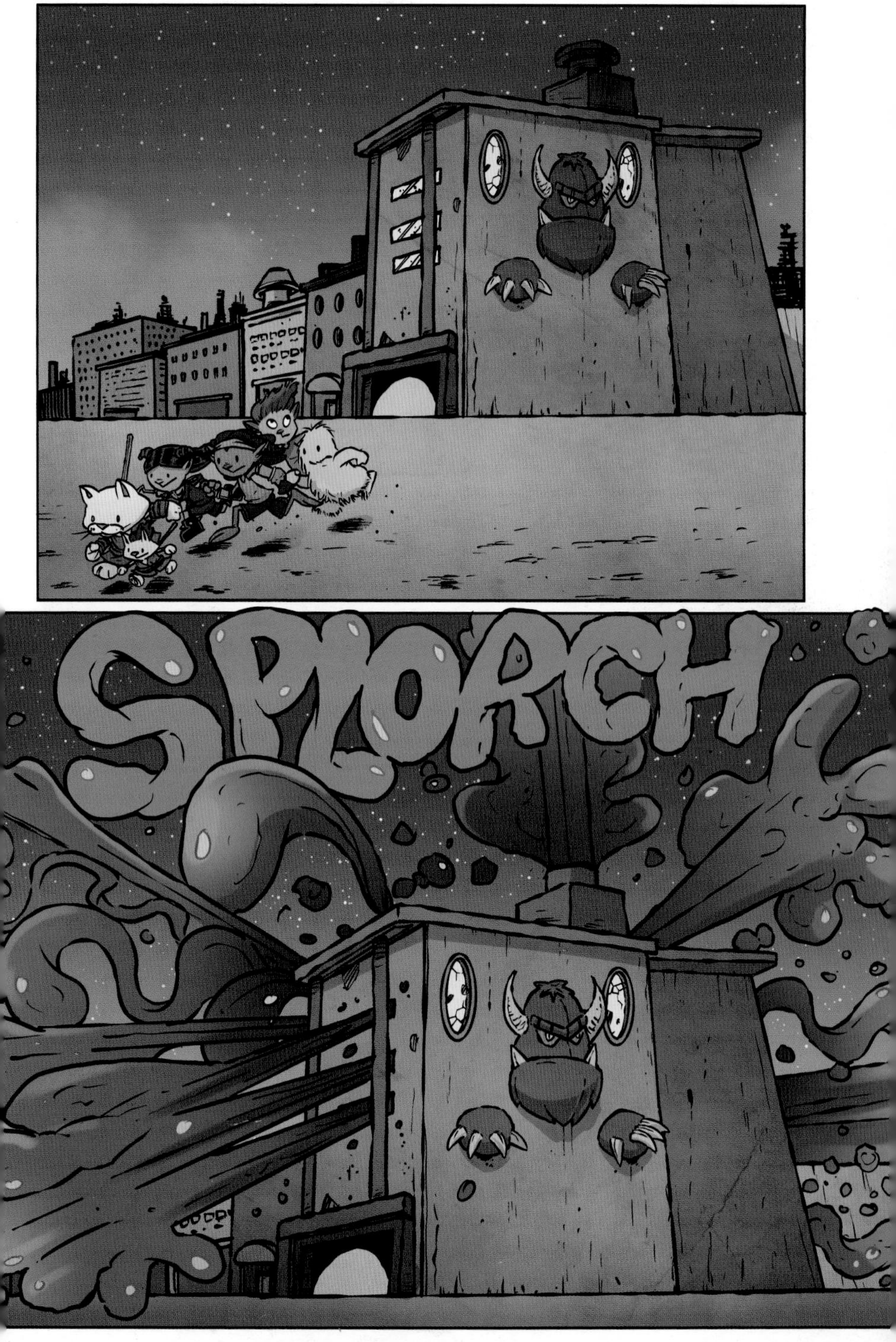
SPLORCH

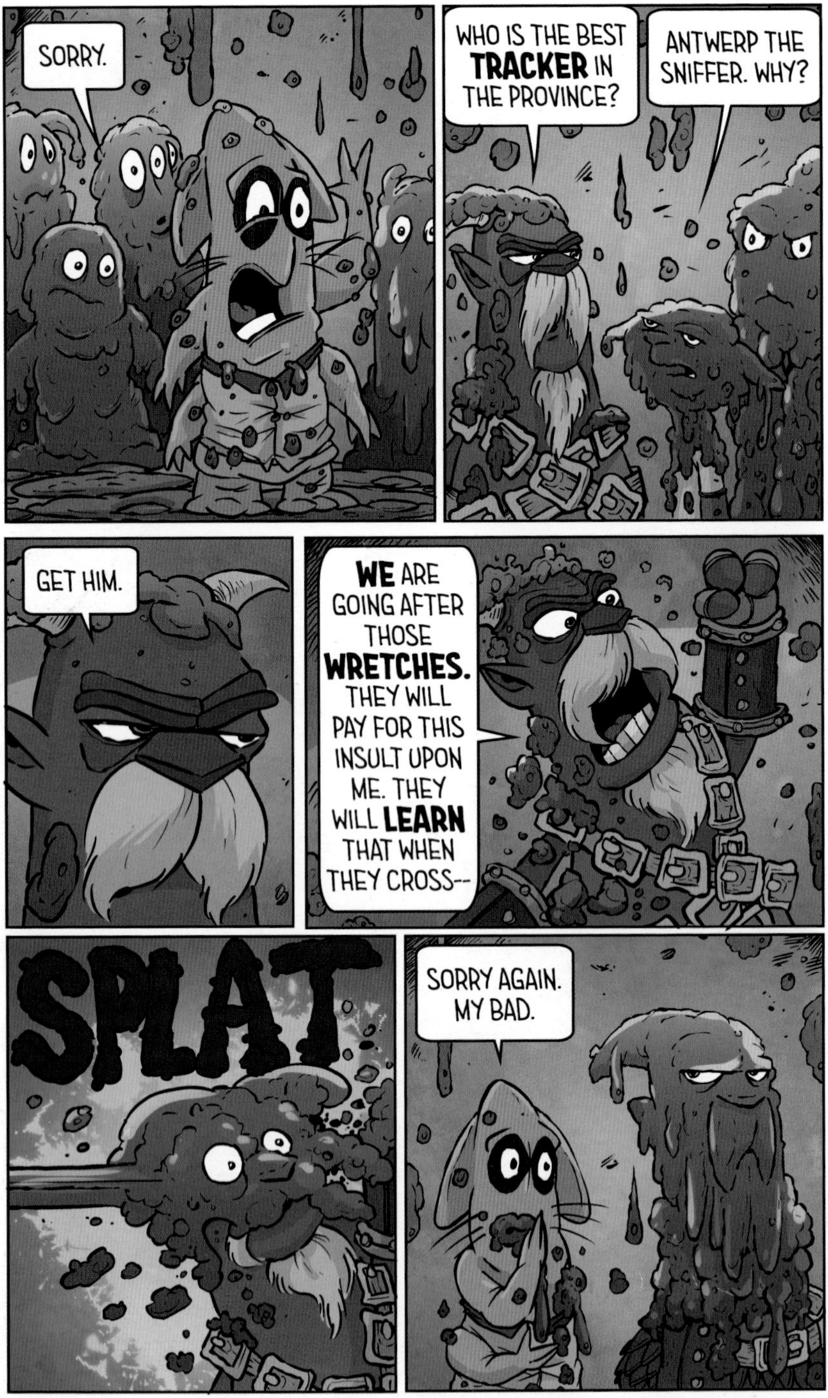
SORRY.
WHO IS THE BEST TRACKER IN THE PROVINCE?
ANTWERP THE SNIFFER. WHY?
GET HIM.
WE ARE GOING AFTER THOSE WRETCHES. THEY WILL PAY FOR THIS INSULT UPON ME. THEY WILL LEARN THAT WHEN THEY CROSS--
SPLAT
SORRY AGAIN. MY BAD.

CHAPTER 6

AN ACTUAL THING

I'M SORRY.
THESE ARE THE FLOWERS FOR OUR CORONATION?
INDEED. THEY ARE LION DAISIES. FRAGRANT AND SO BEAUTIFUL. DO YOU LIKE THEM?

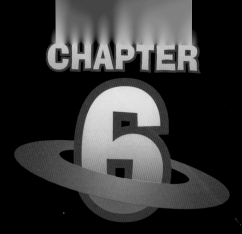

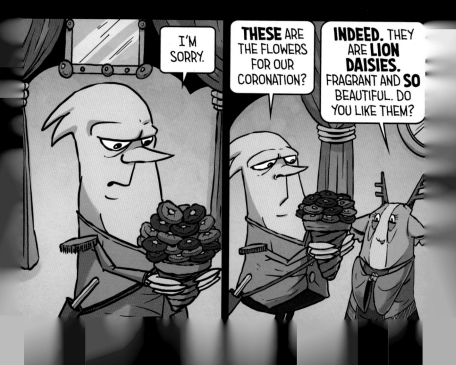

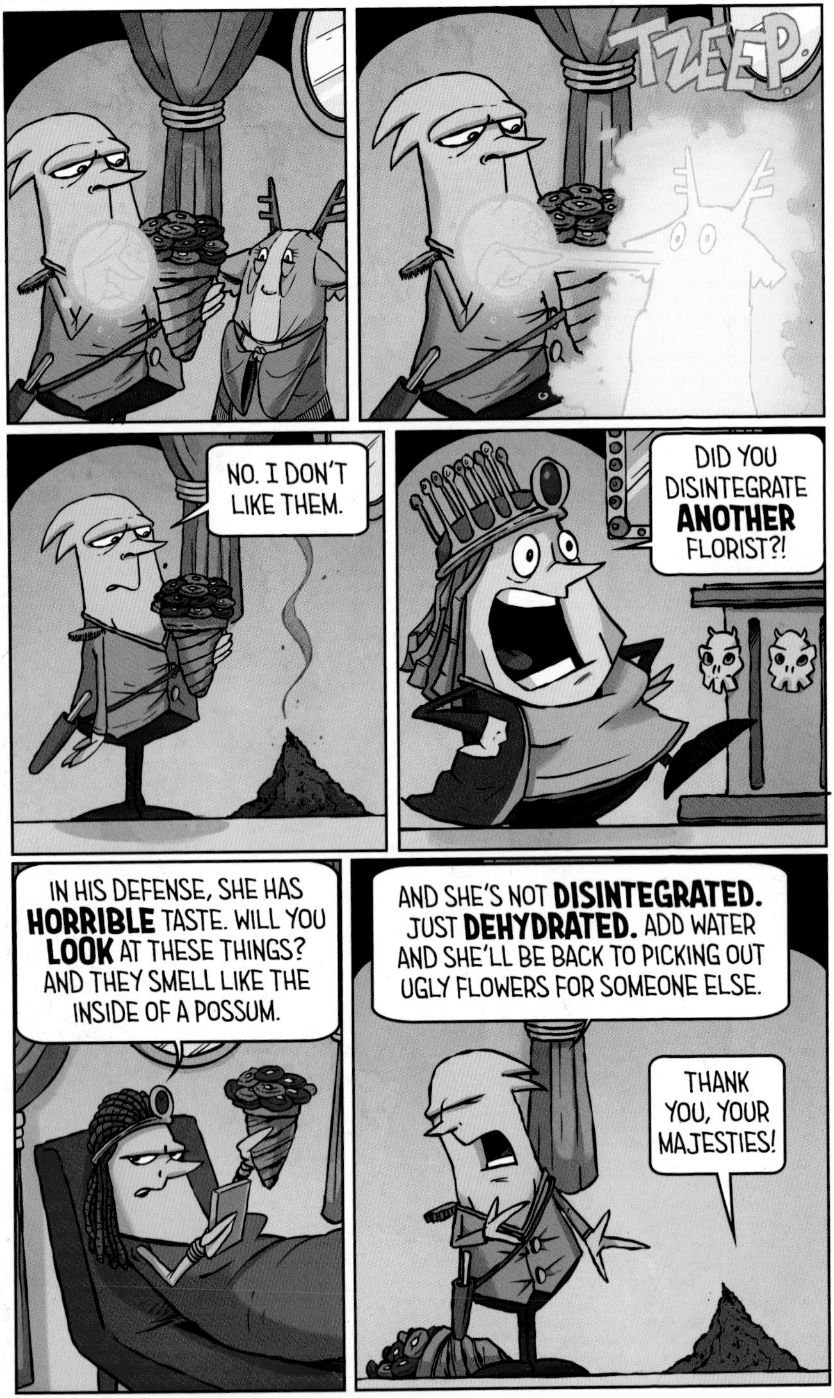
TZEEP.
NO. I DON'T LIKE THEM.
DID YOU DISINTEGRATE ANOTHER FLORIST?!
IN HIS DEFENSE, SHE HAS HORRIBLE TASTE. WILL YOU LOOK AT THESE THINGS? AND THEY SMELL LIKE THE INSIDE OF A POSSUM.
AND SHE'S NOT DISINTEGRATED. JUST DEHYDRATED. ADD WATER AND SHE'LL BE BACK TO PICKING OUT UGLY FLOWERS FOR SOMEONE ELSE.
THANK YOU, YOUR MAJESTIES!

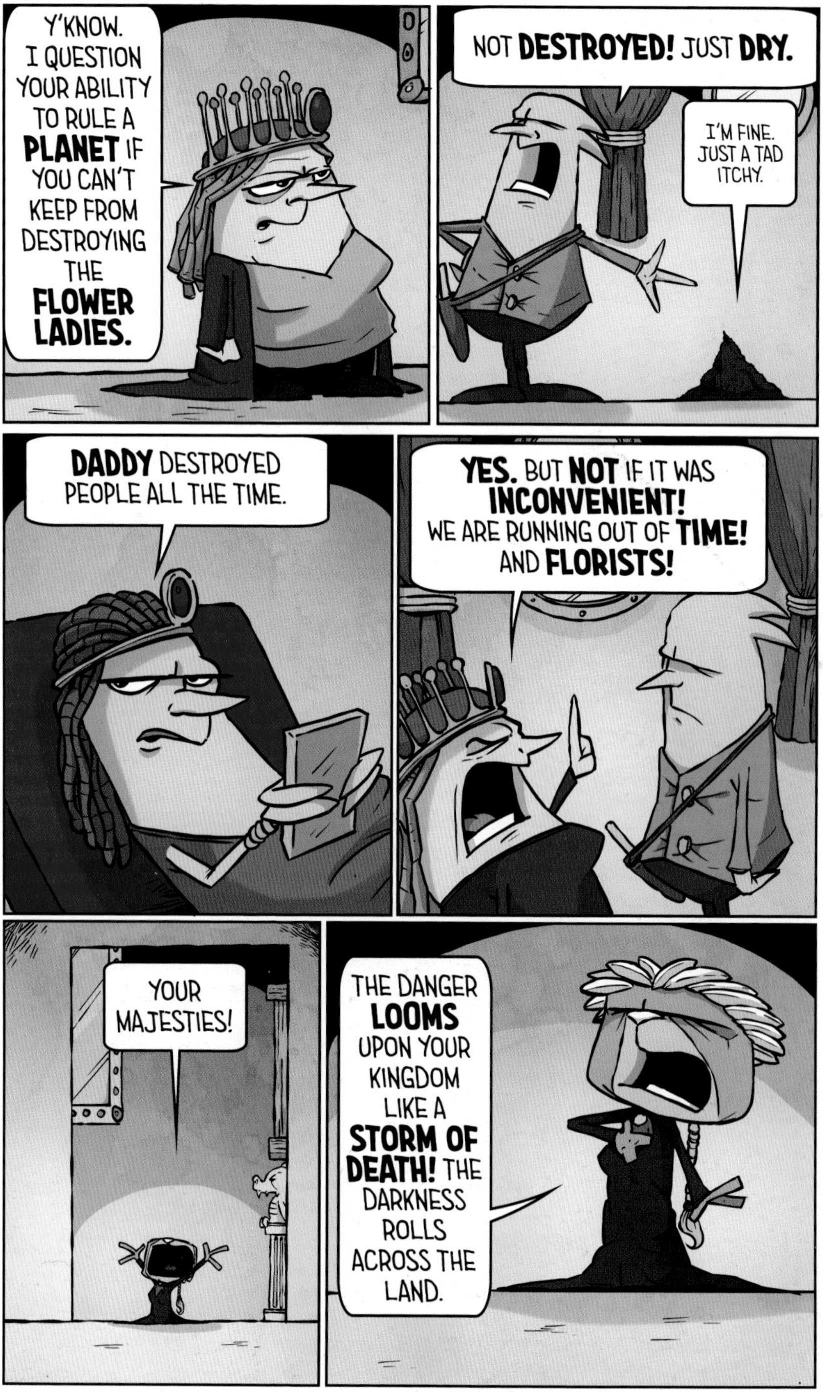
Y'KNOW. I QUESTION YOUR ABILITY TO RULE A PLANET IF YOU CAN'T KEEP FROM DESTROYING THE FLOWER LADIES.
NOT DESTROYED! JUST DRY.
I'M FINE. JUST A TAD ITCHY.
DADDY DESTROYED PEOPLE ALL THE TIME.
YES. BUT NOT IF IT WAS INCONVENIENT! WE ARE RUNNING OUT OF TIME! AND FLORISTS!
YOUR MAJESTIES!
THE DANGER LOOMS UPON YOUR KINGDOM LIKE A STORM OF DEATH! THE DARKNESS ROLLS ACROSS THE LAND.

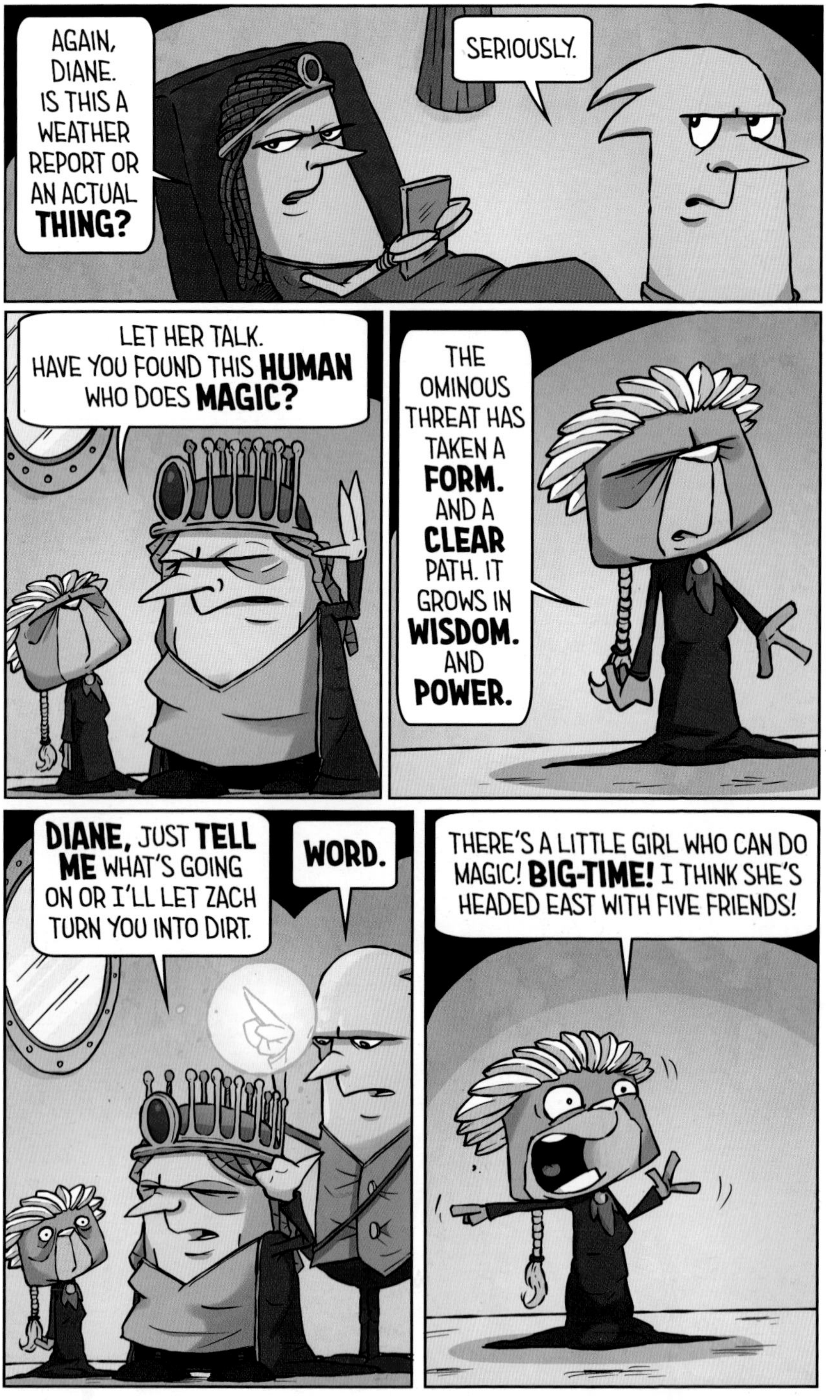
AGAIN, DIANE. IS THIS A WEATHER REPORT OR AN ACTUAL **THING?**
SERIOUSLY.
LET HER TALK. HAVE YOU FOUND THIS **HUMAN** WHO DOES **MAGIC?**
THE OMINOUS THREAT HAS TAKEN A **FORM.** AND A **CLEAR** PATH. IT GROWS IN **WISDOM.** AND **POWER.**
DIANE, JUST **TELL ME** WHAT'S GOING ON OR I'LL LET ZACH TURN YOU INTO DIRT.
WORD.
THERE'S A LITTLE GIRL WHO CAN DO MAGIC! **BIG-TIME!** I THINK SHE'S HEADED EAST WITH FIVE FRIENDS!

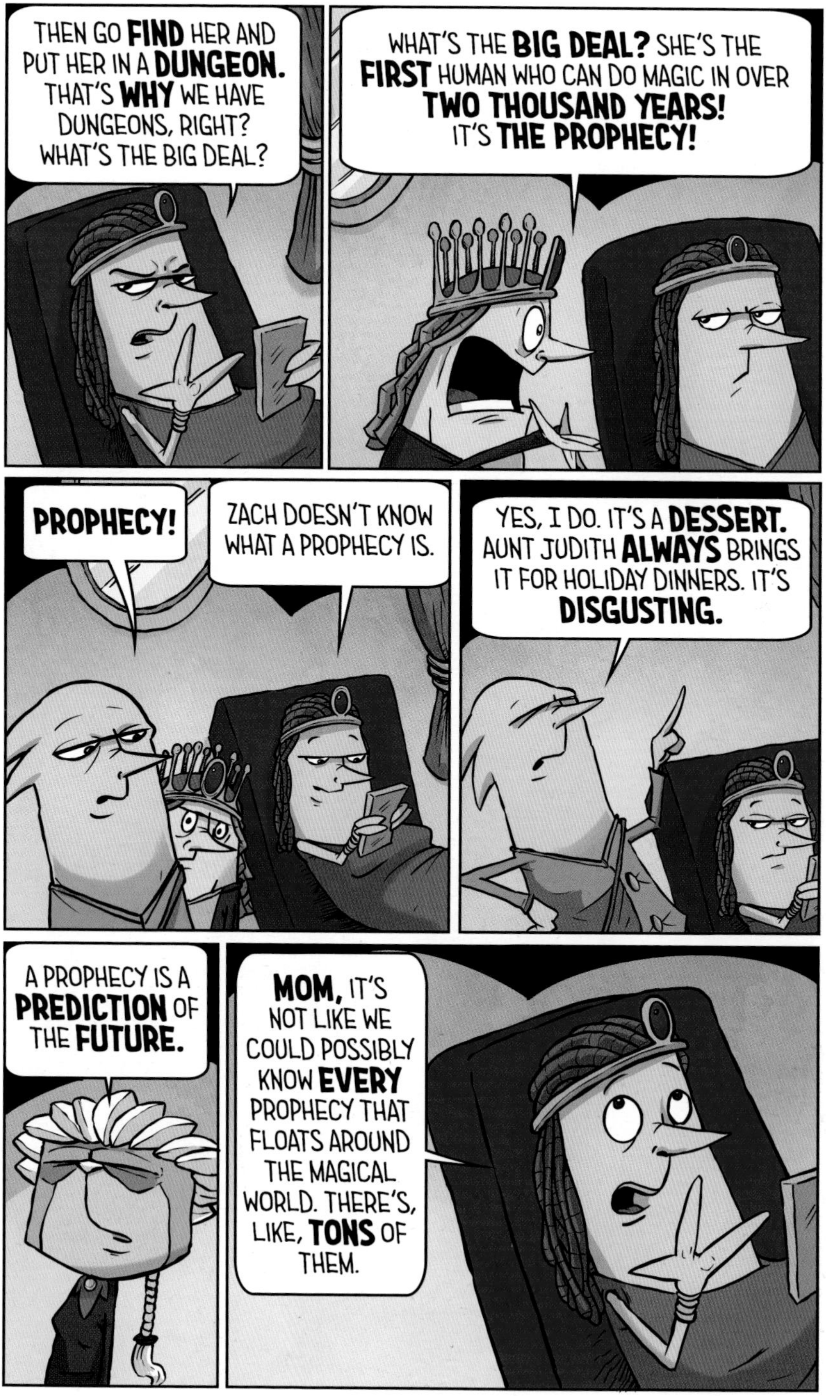
THEN GO FIND HER AND PUT HER IN A DUNGEON. THAT'S WHY WE HAVE DUNGEONS, RIGHT? WHAT'S THE BIG DEAL?
WHAT'S THE BIG DEAL? SHE'S THE FIRST HUMAN WHO CAN DO MAGIC IN OVER TWO THOUSAND YEARS! IT'S THE PROPHECY!
PROPHECY!
ZACH DOESN'T KNOW WHAT A PROPHECY IS.
YES, I DO. IT'S A DESSERT. AUNT JUDITH ALWAYS BRINGS IT FOR HOLIDAY DINNERS. IT'S DISGUSTING.
A PROPHECY IS A PREDICTION OF THE FUTURE.
MOM, IT'S NOT LIKE WE COULD POSSIBLY KNOW EVERY PROPHECY THAT FLOATS AROUND THE MAGICAL WORLD. THERE'S, LIKE, TONS OF THEM.

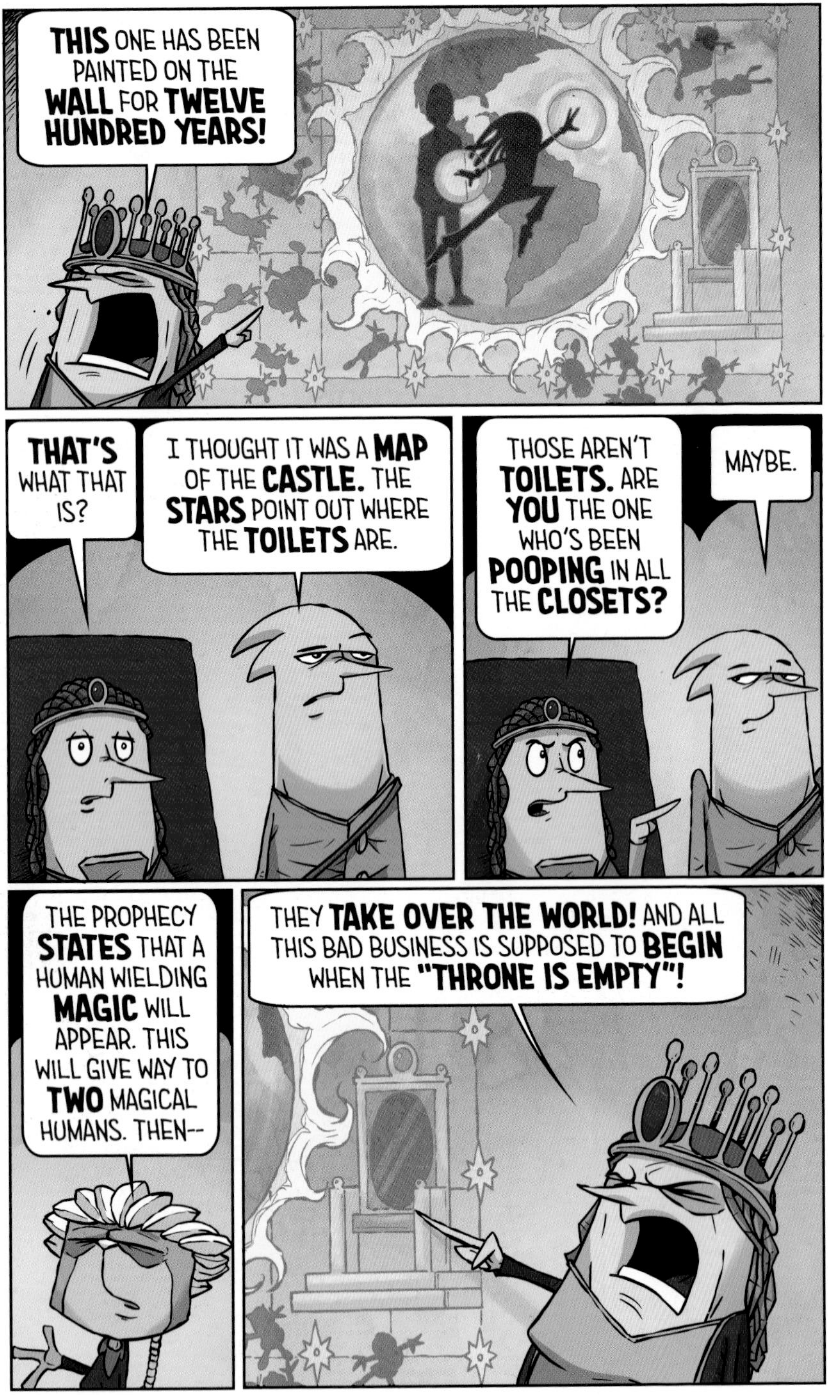
THIS ONE HAS BEEN PAINTED ON THE WALL FOR TWELVE HUNDRED YEARS!
THAT'S WHAT THAT IS?
I THOUGHT IT WAS A MAP OF THE CASTLE. THE STARS POINT OUT WHERE THE TOILETS ARE.
THOSE AREN'T TOILETS. ARE YOU THE ONE WHO'S BEEN POOPING IN ALL THE CLOSETS?
MAYBE.
THE PROPHECY STATES THAT A HUMAN WIELDING MAGIC WILL APPEAR. THIS WILL GIVE WAY TO TWO MAGICAL HUMANS. THEN--
THEY TAKE OVER THE WORLD! AND ALL THIS BAD BUSINESS IS SUPPOSED TO BEGIN WHEN THE "THRONE IS EMPTY"!

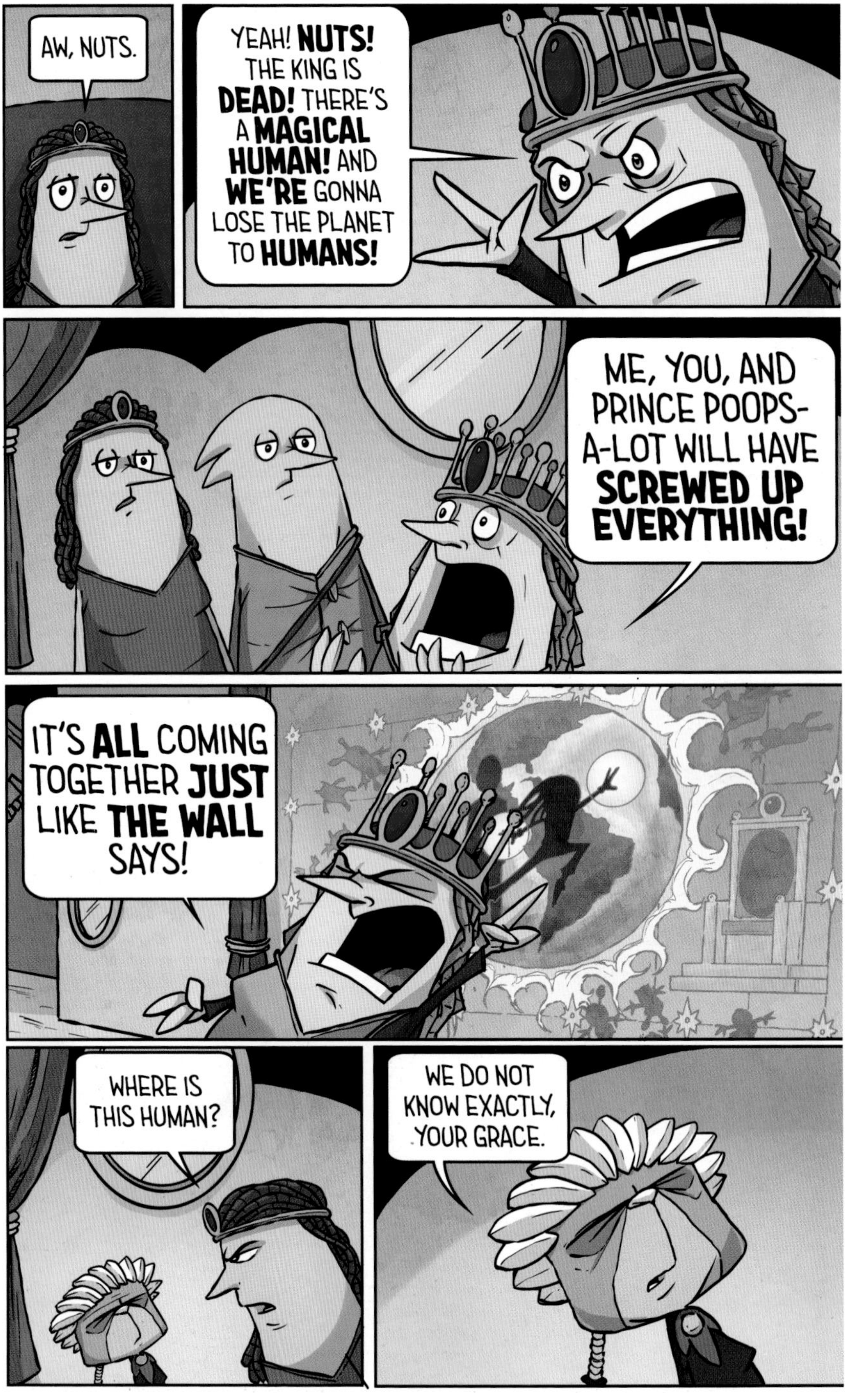
AW, NUTS.
YEAH! NUTS! THE KING IS DEAD! THERE'S A MAGICAL HUMAN! AND WE'RE GONNA LOSE THE PLANET TO HUMANS!
ME, YOU, AND PRINCE POOPS-A-LOT WILL HAVE SCREWED UP EVERYTHING!
IT'S ALL COMING TOGETHER JUST LIKE THE WALL SAYS!
WHERE IS THIS HUMAN?
WE DO NOT KNOW EXACTLY, YOUR GRACE.

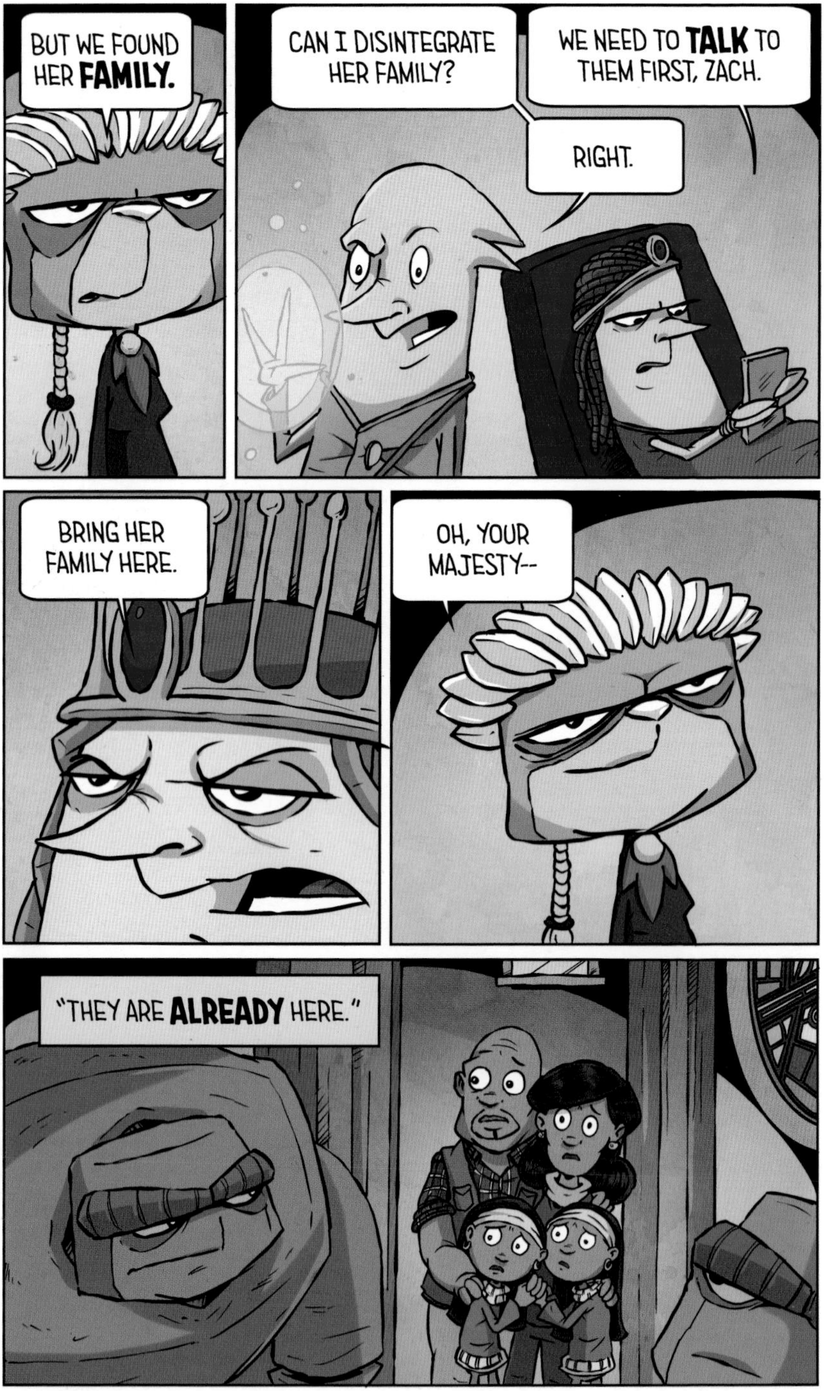
BUT WE FOUND HER **FAMILY.**
CAN I DISINTEGRATE HER FAMILY?
WE NEED TO **TALK** TO THEM FIRST, ZACH.
RIGHT.
BRING HER FAMILY HERE.
OH, YOUR MAJESTY--
"THEY ARE **ALREADY** HERE."

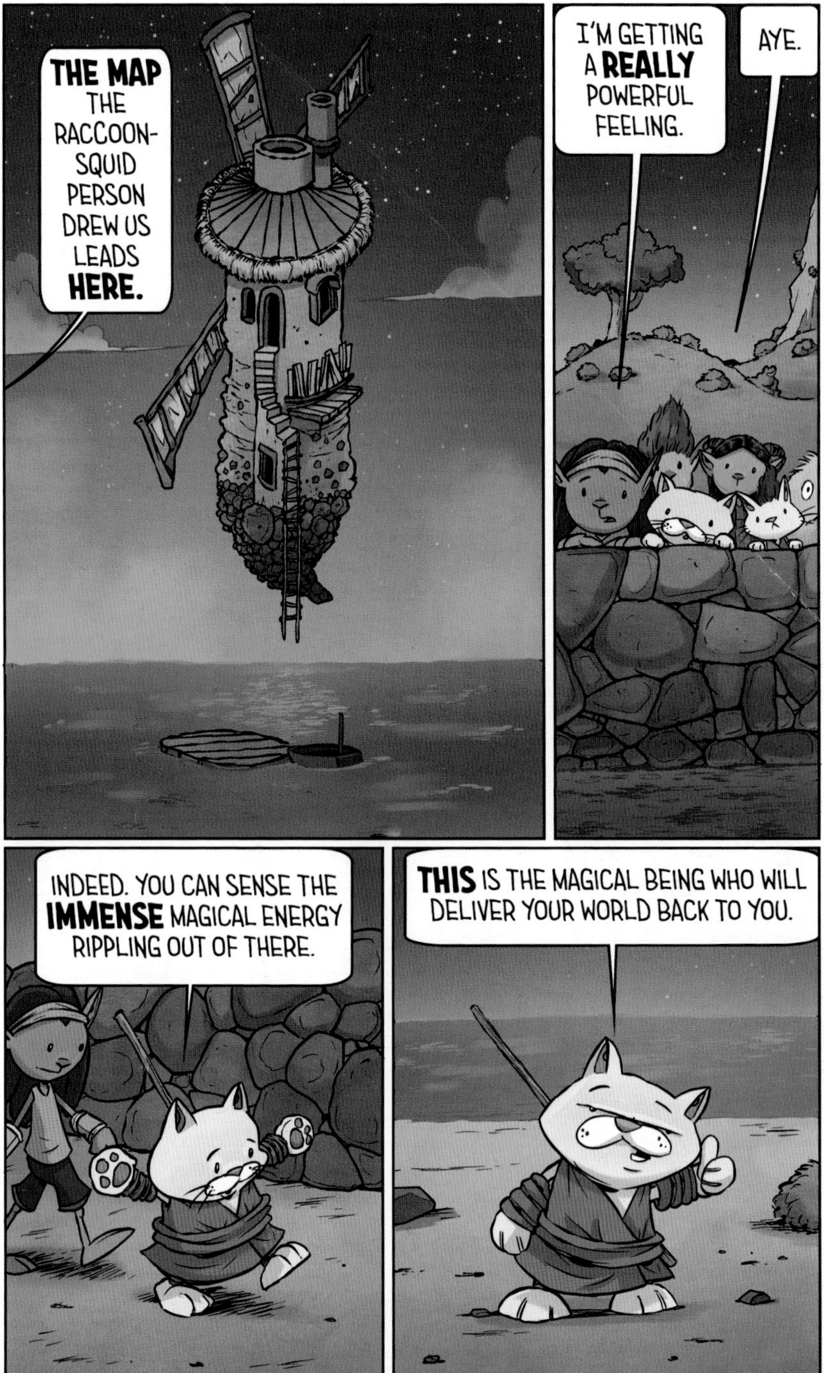
THE MAP THE RACCOON-SQUID PERSON DREW US LEADS HERE.
I'M GETTING A REALLY POWERFUL FEELING.
AYE.
INDEED. YOU CAN SENSE THE IMMENSE MAGICAL ENERGY RIPPLING OUT OF THERE.
THIS IS THE MAGICAL BEING WHO WILL DELIVER YOUR WORLD BACK TO YOU.

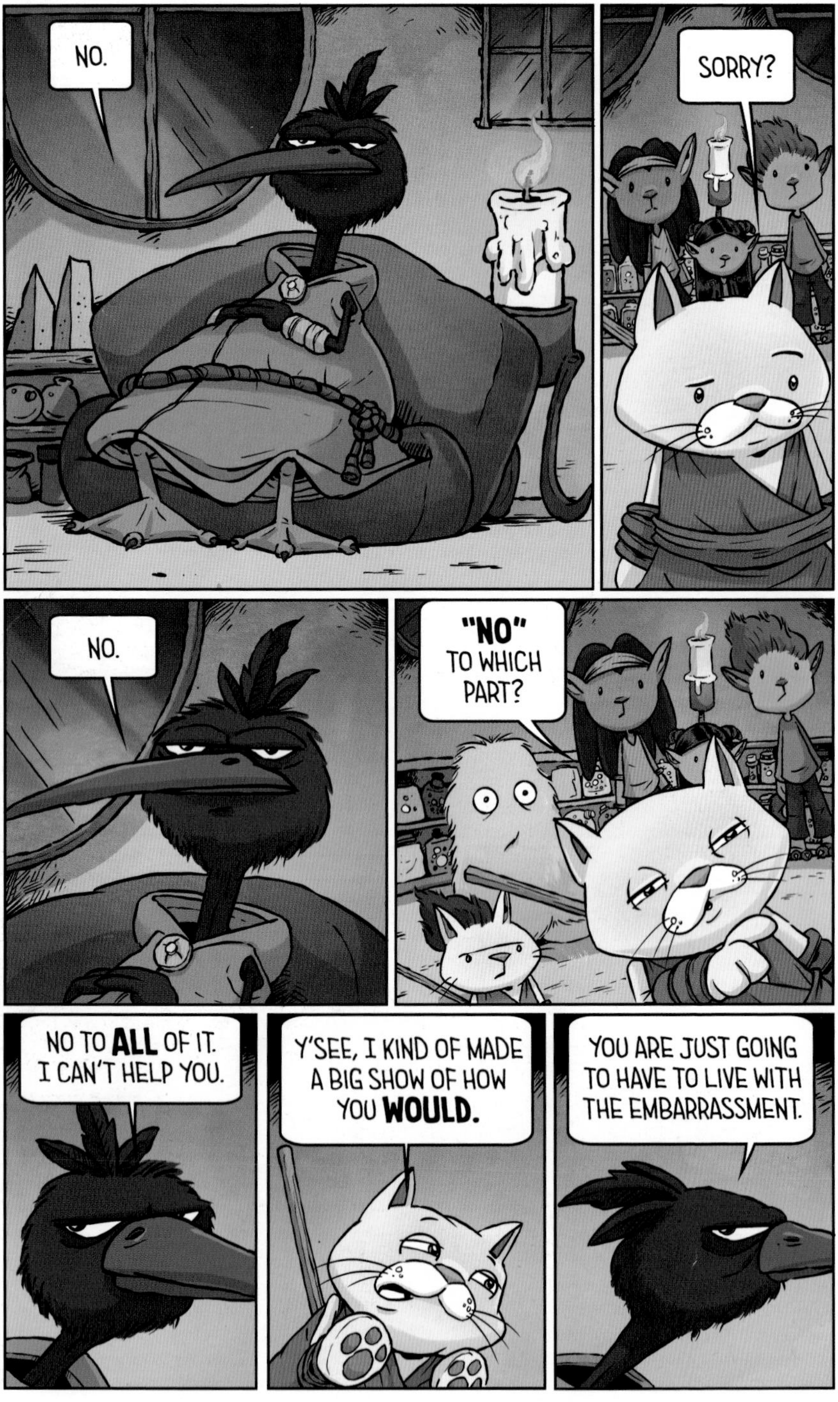
NO.
SORRY?
NO.
"NO" TO WHICH PART?
NO TO **ALL** OF IT. I CAN'T HELP YOU.
Y'SEE, I KIND OF MADE A BIG SHOW OF HOW YOU **WOULD.**
YOU ARE JUST GOING TO HAVE TO LIVE WITH THE EMBARRASSMENT.

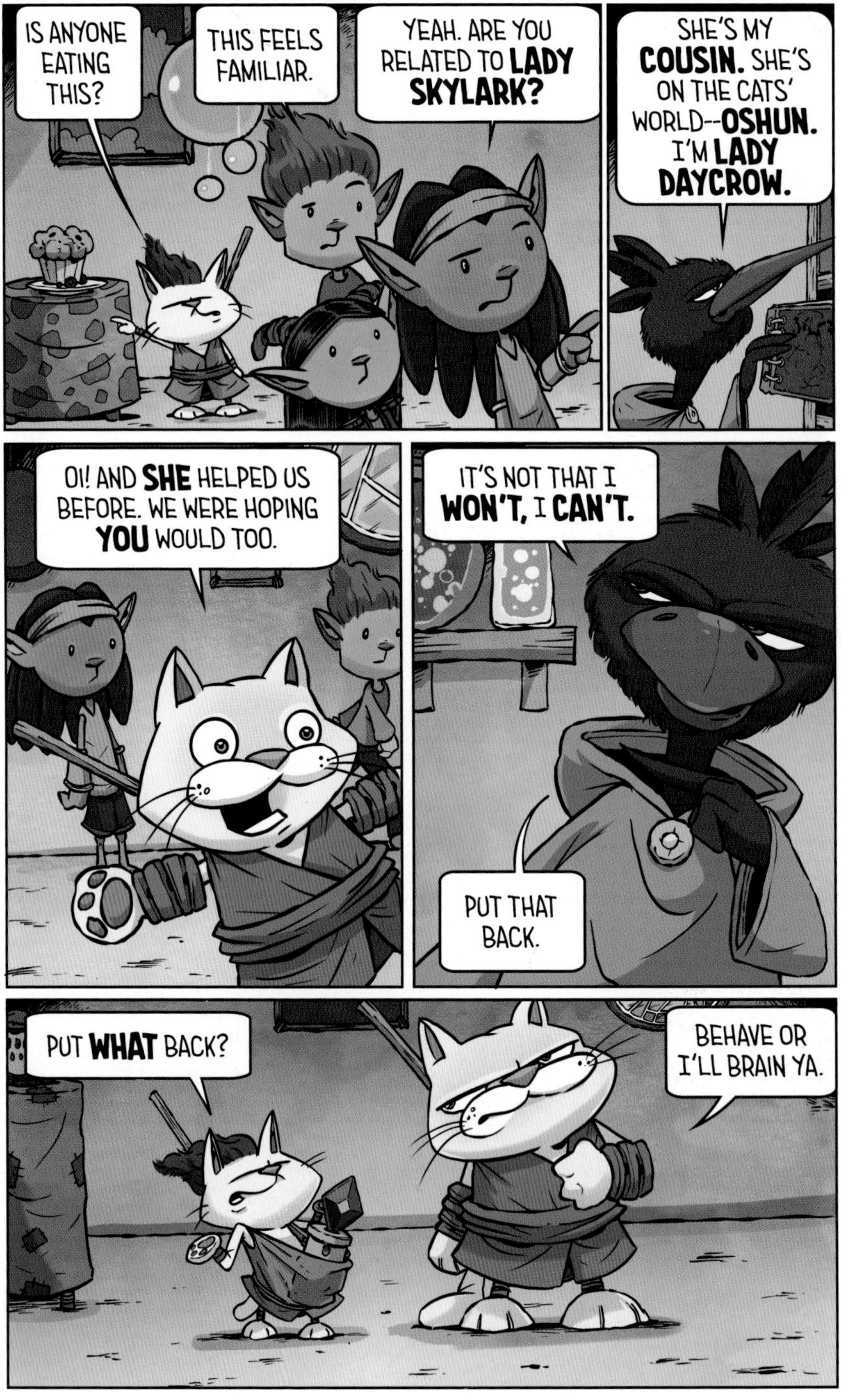
IS ANYONE EATING THIS?
THIS FEELS FAMILIAR.
YEAH. ARE YOU RELATED TO LADY SKYLARK?
SHE'S MY COUSIN. SHE'S ON THE CATS' WORLD--OSHUN. I'M LADY DAYCROW.
OI! AND SHE HELPED US BEFORE. WE WERE HOPING YOU WOULD TOO.
IT'S NOT THAT I WON'T, I CAN'T.
PUT THAT BACK.
PUT WHAT BACK?
BEHAVE OR I'LL BRAIN YA.

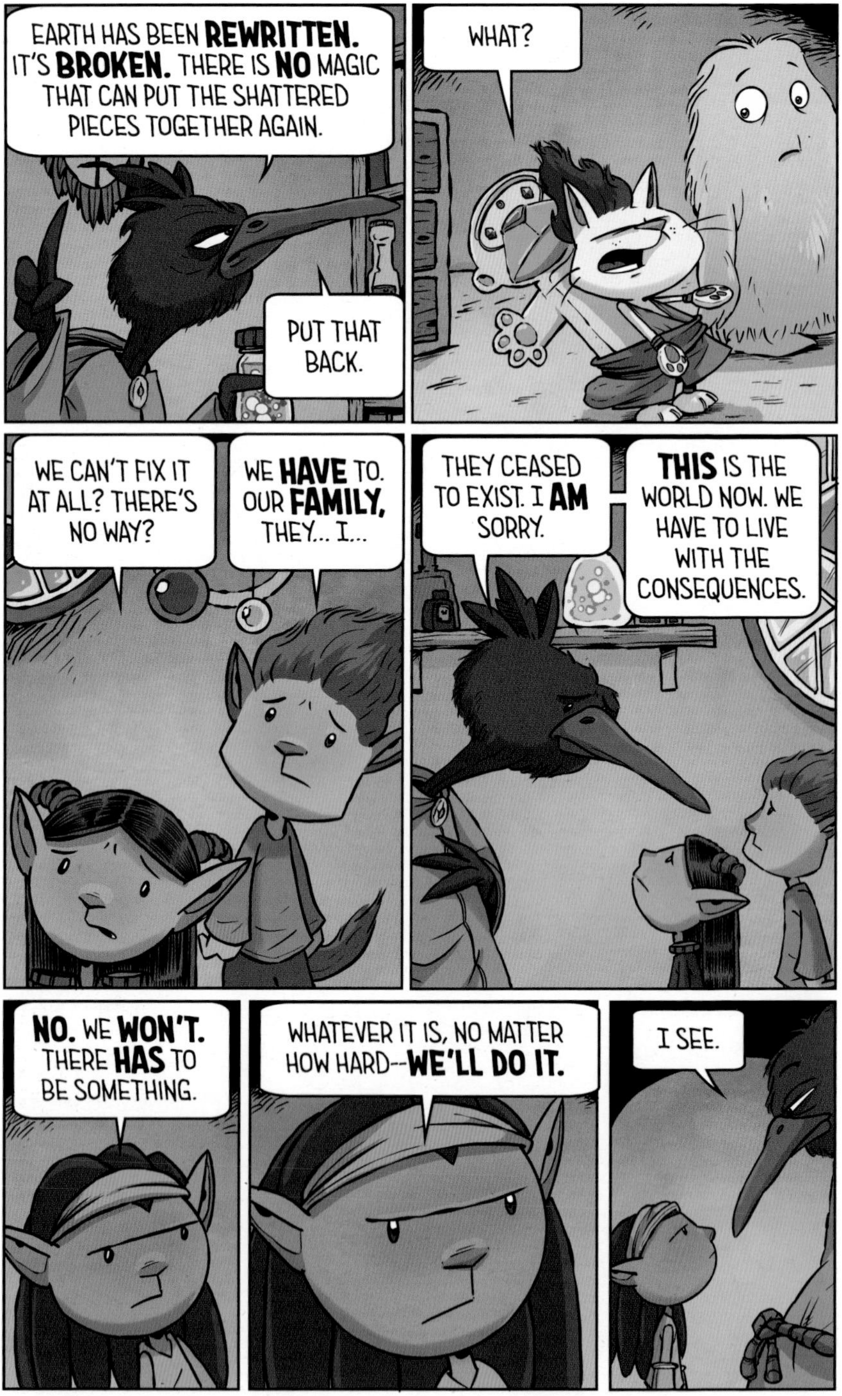
EARTH HAS BEEN **REWRITTEN.** IT'S **BROKEN.** THERE IS **NO** MAGIC THAT CAN PUT THE SHATTERED PIECES TOGETHER AGAIN.
PUT THAT BACK.
WHAT?
WE CAN'T FIX IT AT ALL? THERE'S NO WAY?
WE **HAVE** TO. OUR **FAMILY,** THEY... I...
THEY CEASED TO EXIST. I **AM** SORRY.
THIS IS THE WORLD NOW. WE HAVE TO LIVE WITH THE CONSEQUENCES.
NO. WE **WON'T.** THERE **HAS** TO BE SOMETHING.
WHATEVER IT IS, NO MATTER HOW HARD--**WE'LL DO IT.**
I SEE.

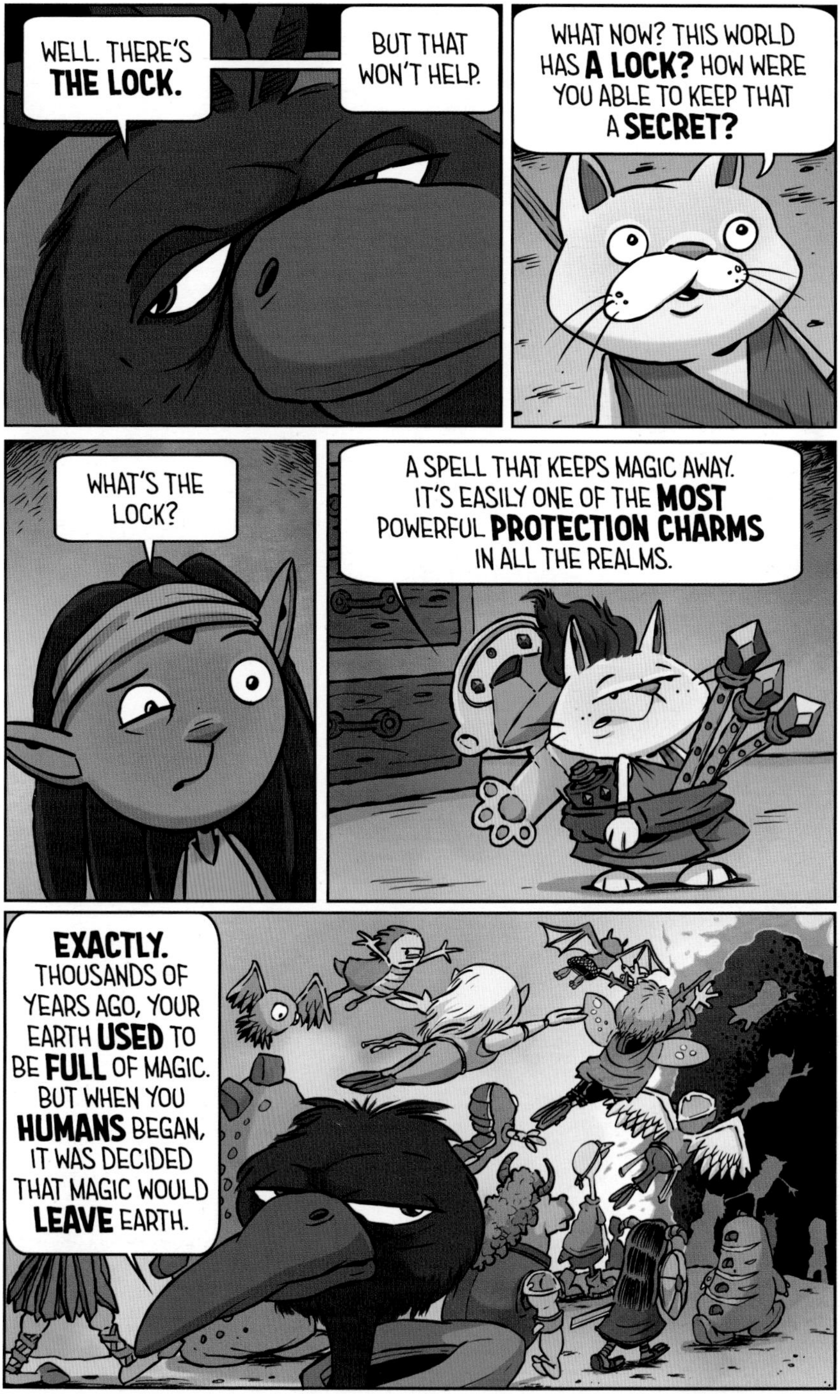
WELL. THERE'S **THE LOCK.**
BUT THAT WON'T HELP.
WHAT NOW? THIS WORLD HAS **A LOCK?** HOW WERE YOU ABLE TO KEEP THAT A **SECRET?**
WHAT'S THE LOCK?
A SPELL THAT KEEPS MAGIC AWAY. IT'S EASILY ONE OF THE **MOST** POWERFUL **PROTECTION CHARMS** IN ALL THE REALMS.
EXACTLY. THOUSANDS OF YEARS AGO, YOUR EARTH **USED** TO BE **FULL** OF MAGIC. BUT WHEN YOU **HUMANS** BEGAN, IT WAS DECIDED THAT MAGIC WOULD **LEAVE** EARTH.

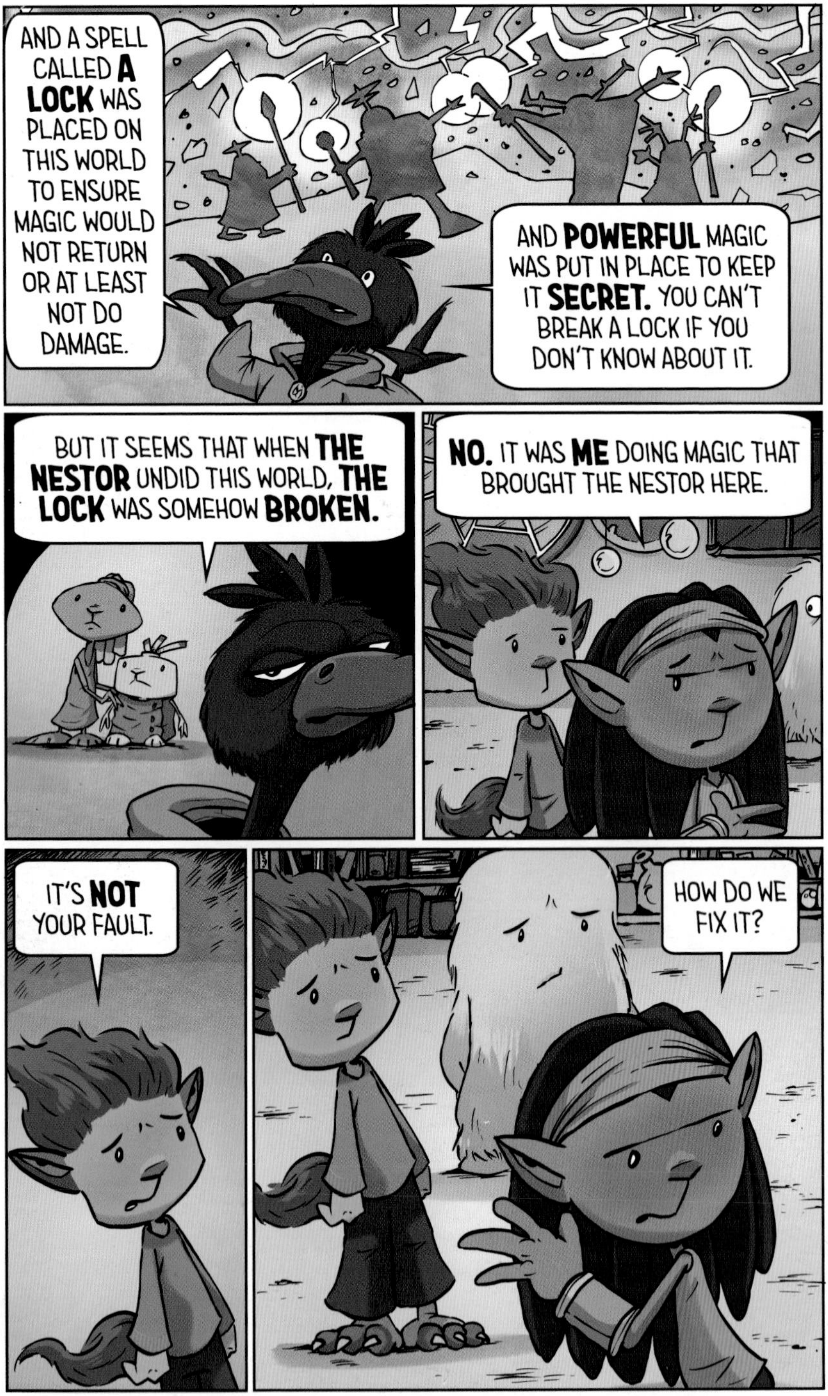
AND A SPELL CALLED **A LOCK** WAS PLACED ON THIS WORLD TO ENSURE MAGIC WOULD NOT RETURN OR AT LEAST NOT DO DAMAGE.
AND **POWERFUL** MAGIC WAS PUT IN PLACE TO KEEP IT **SECRET.** YOU CAN'T BREAK A LOCK IF YOU DON'T KNOW ABOUT IT.
BUT IT SEEMS THAT WHEN **THE NESTOR** UNDID THIS WORLD, **THE LOCK** WAS SOMEHOW **BROKEN.**
NO. IT WAS **ME** DOING MAGIC THAT BROUGHT THE NESTOR HERE.
IT'S **NOT** YOUR FAULT.
HOW DO WE FIX IT?

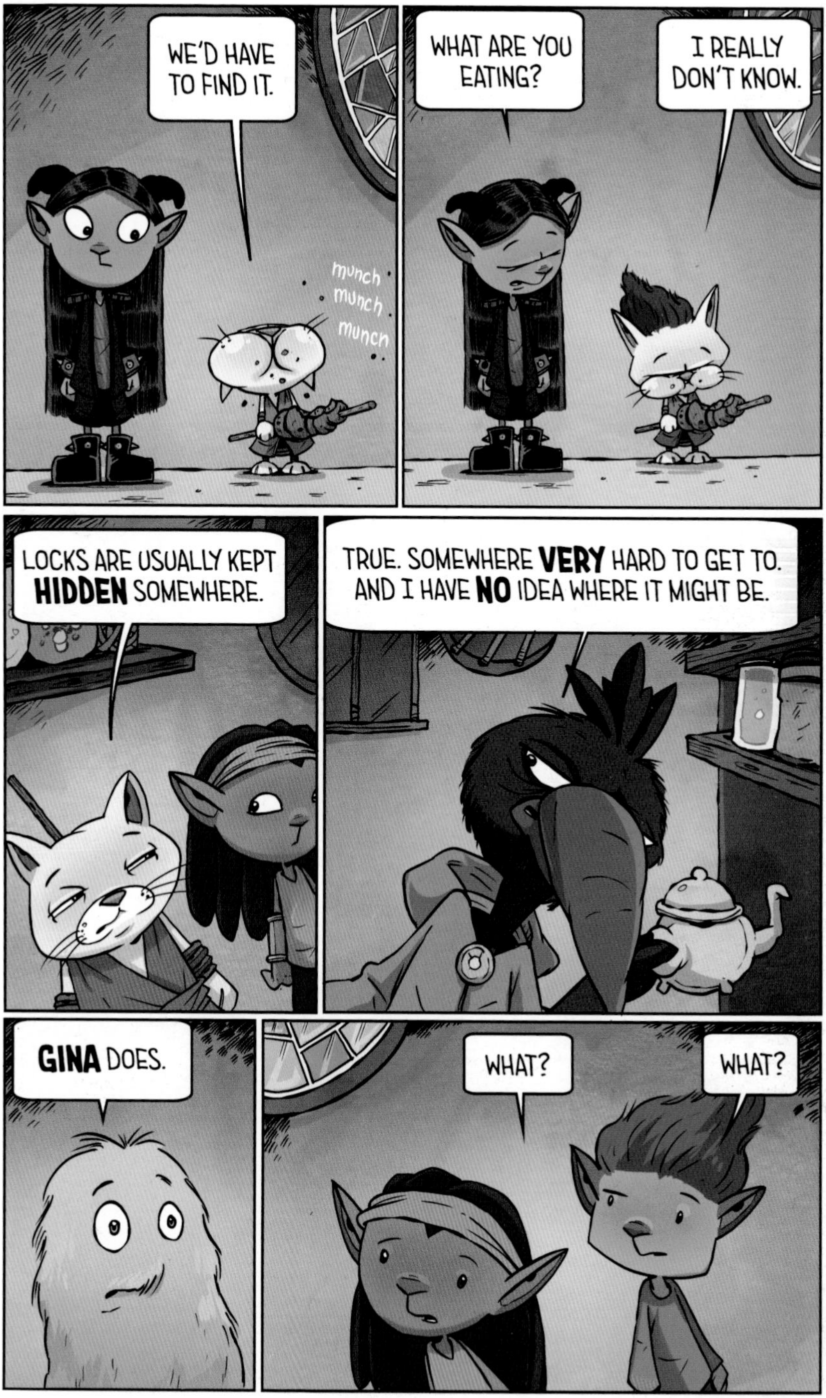
WE'D HAVE TO FIND IT.
munch munch munch
WHAT ARE YOU EATING?
I REALLY DON'T KNOW.
LOCKS ARE USUALLY KEPT **HIDDEN** SOMEWHERE.
TRUE. SOMEWHERE **VERY** HARD TO GET TO. AND I HAVE **NO** IDEA WHERE IT MIGHT BE.
GINA DOES.
WHAT?
WHAT?

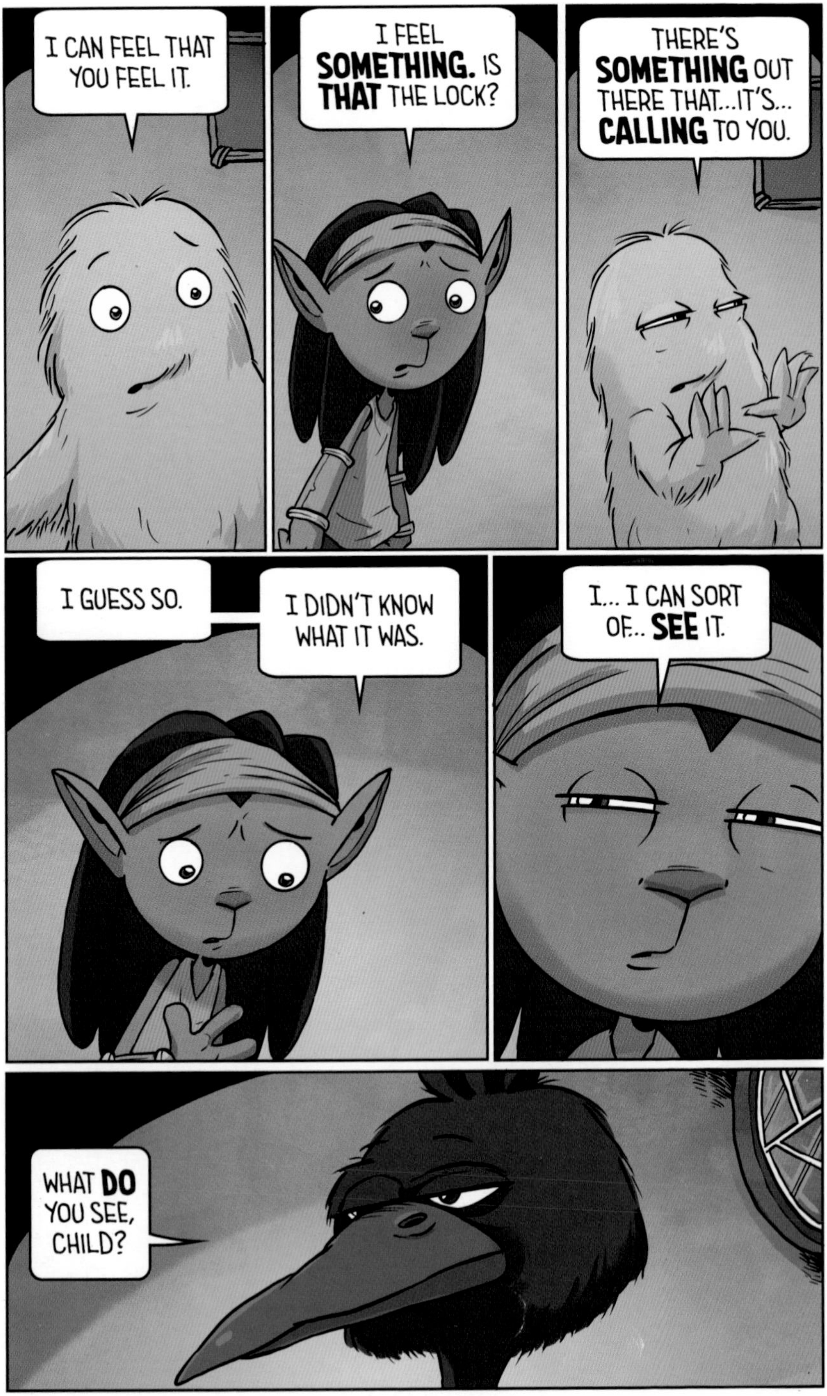
I CAN FEEL THAT YOU FEEL IT.
I FEEL SOMETHING. IS THAT THE LOCK?
THERE'S SOMETHING OUT THERE THAT...IT'S... CALLING TO YOU.
I GUESS SO.
I DIDN'T KNOW WHAT IT WAS.
I... I CAN SORT OF... SEE IT.
WHAT DO YOU SEE, CHILD?

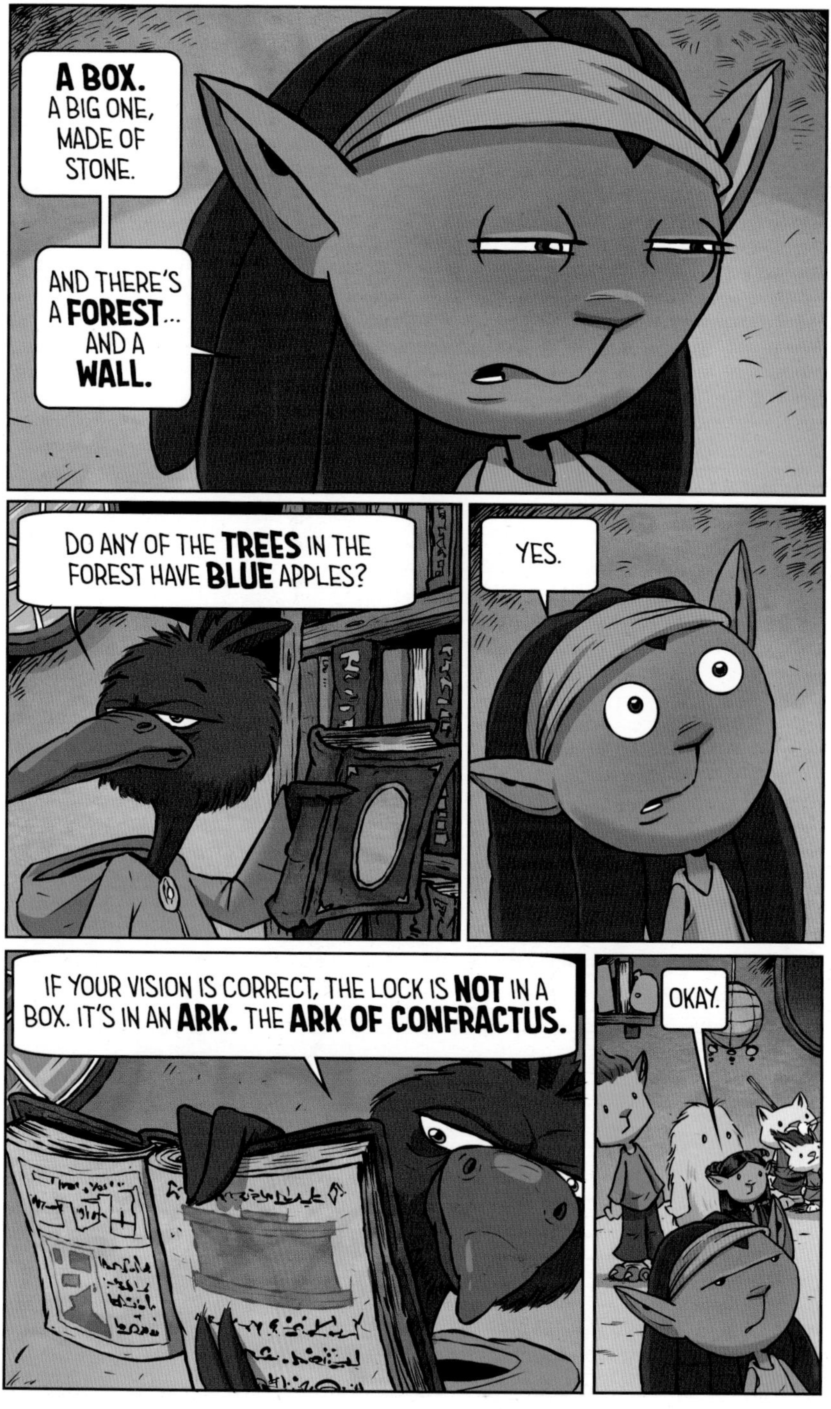
A BOX. A BIG ONE, MADE OF STONE.
AND THERE'S A FOREST... AND A WALL.
DO ANY OF THE TREES IN THE FOREST HAVE BLUE APPLES?
YES.
IF YOUR VISION IS CORRECT, THE LOCK IS NOT IN A BOX. IT'S IN AN ARK. THE ARK OF CONFRACTUS.
OKAY.

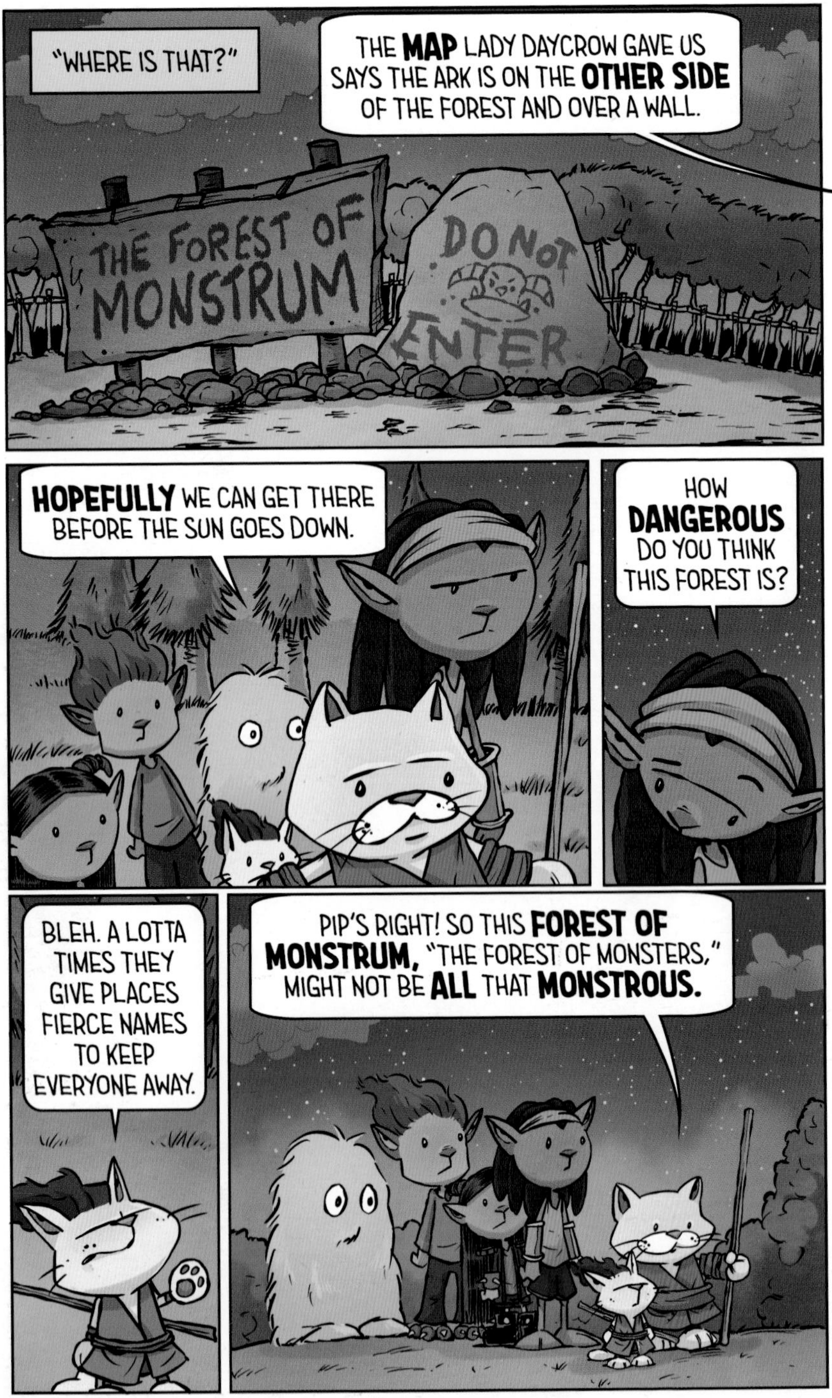
"WHERE IS THAT?"
THE MAP LADY DAYCROW GAVE US SAYS THE ARK IS ON THE OTHER SIDE OF THE FOREST AND OVER A WALL.
THE FOREST OF MONSTRUM
DO NOT ENTER
HOPEFULLY WE CAN GET THERE BEFORE THE SUN GOES DOWN.
HOW DANGEROUS DO YOU THINK THIS FOREST IS?
BLEH. A LOTTA TIMES THEY GIVE PLACES FIERCE NAMES TO KEEP EVERYONE AWAY.
PIP'S RIGHT! SO THIS FOREST OF MONSTRUM, "THE FOREST OF MONSTERS," MIGHT NOT BE ALL THAT MONSTROUS.

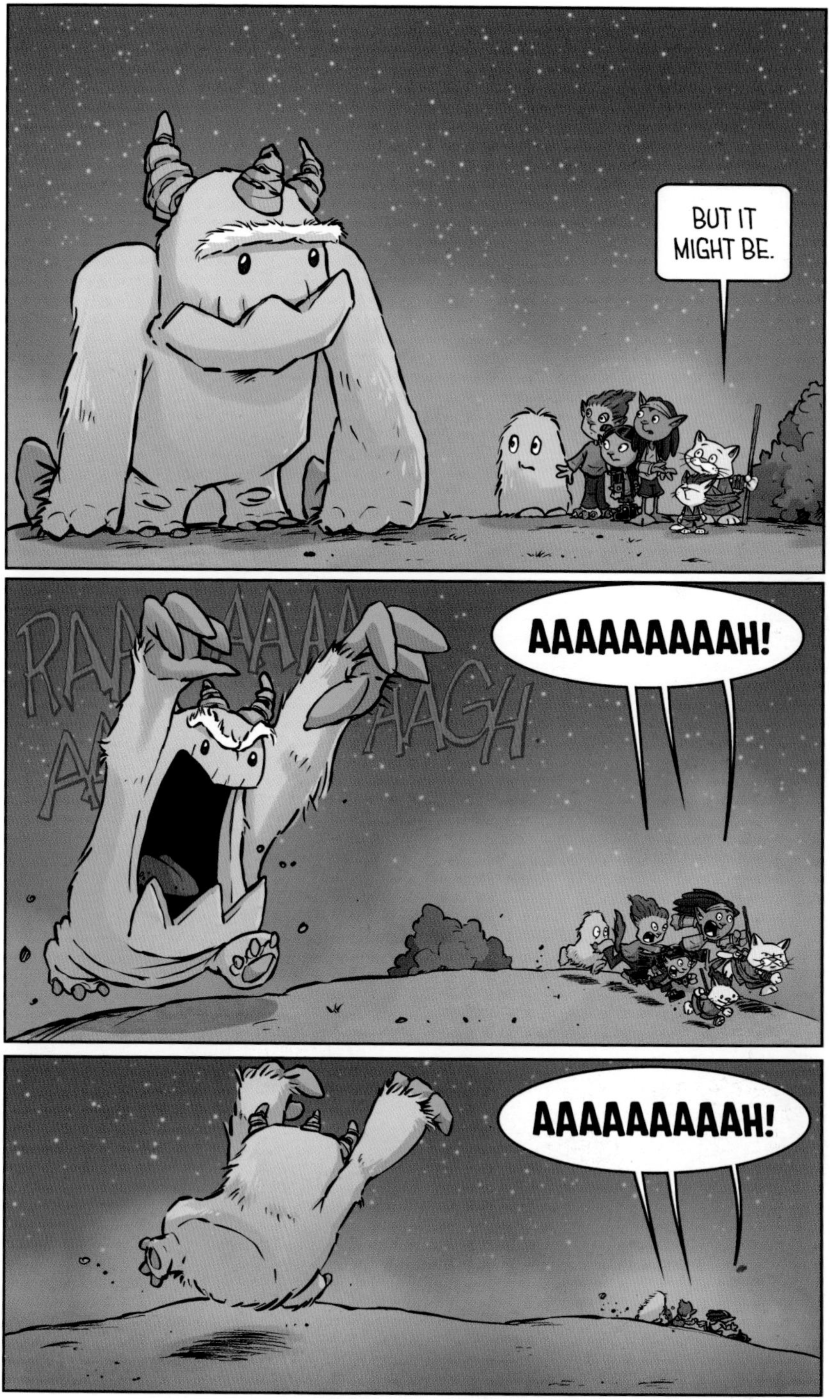
BUT IT MIGHT BE.
RAAAAAAAAAAAAAGH
AAAAAAAAAH!
AAAAAAAAAH!

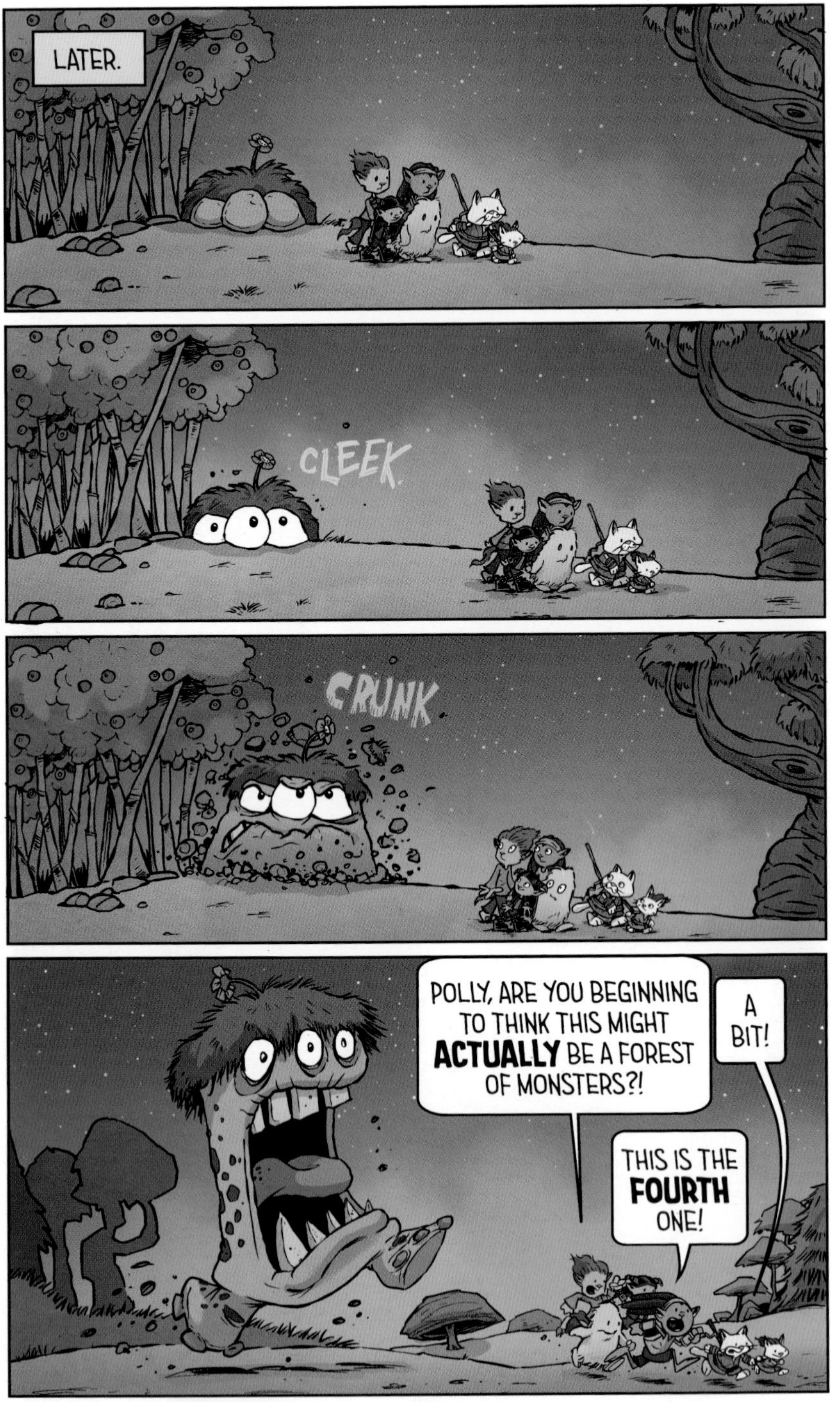
LATER.
CLEEK
CRUNK
POLLY, ARE YOU BEGINNING TO THINK THIS MIGHT **ACTUALLY** BE A FOREST OF MONSTERS?!
A BIT!
THIS IS THE **FOURTH** ONE!

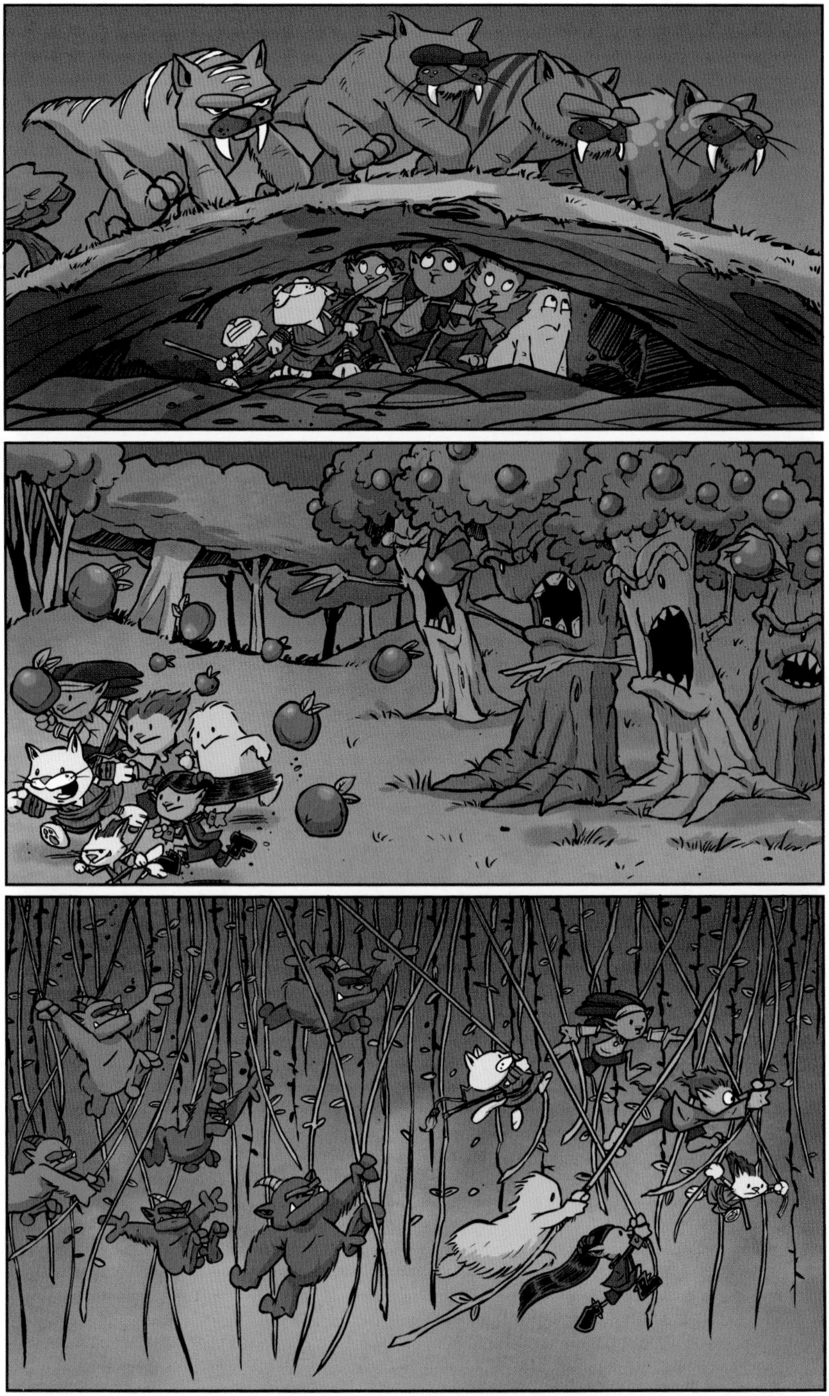

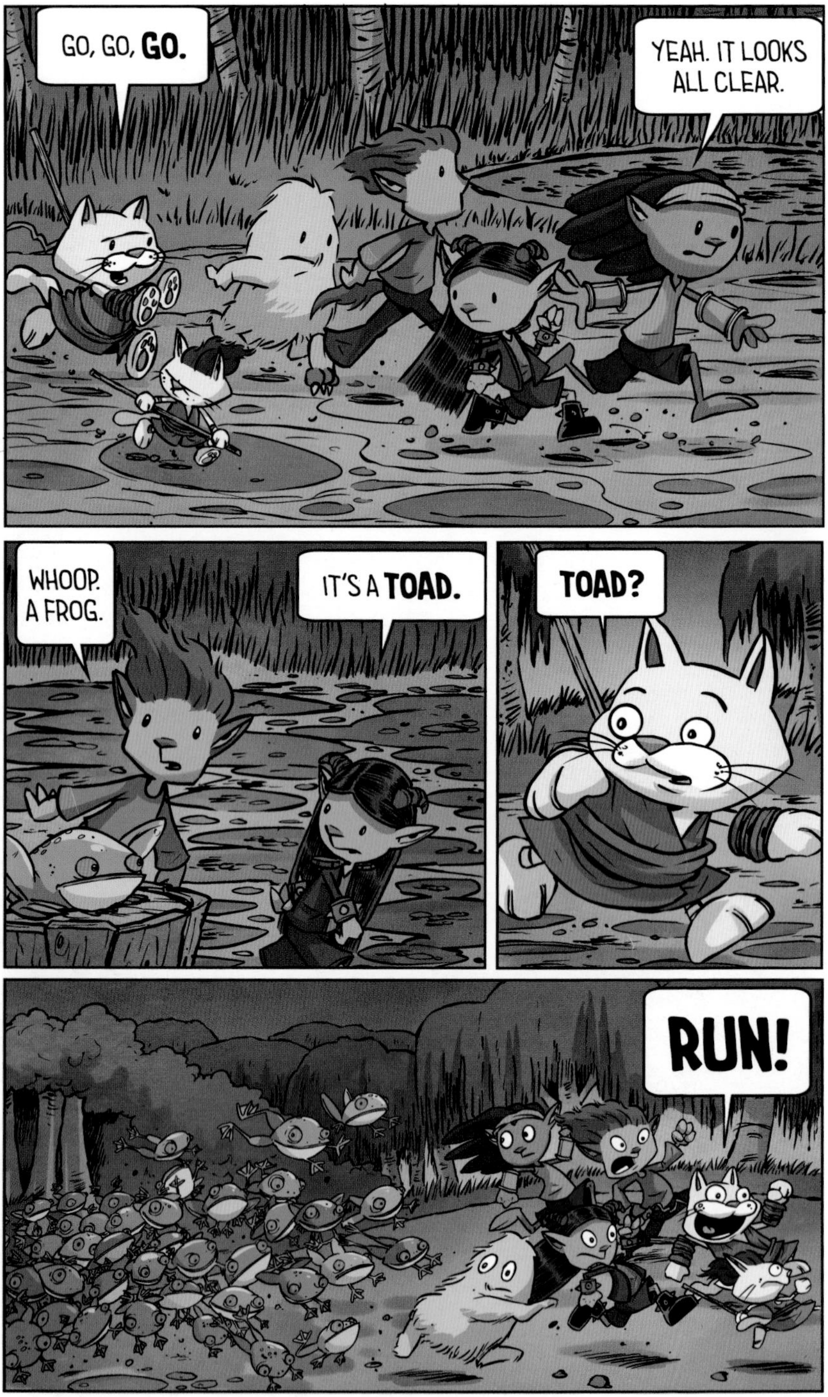
GO, GO, GO.
YEAH. IT LOOKS ALL CLEAR.
WHOOP. A FROG.
IT'S A TOAD.
TOAD?
RUN!

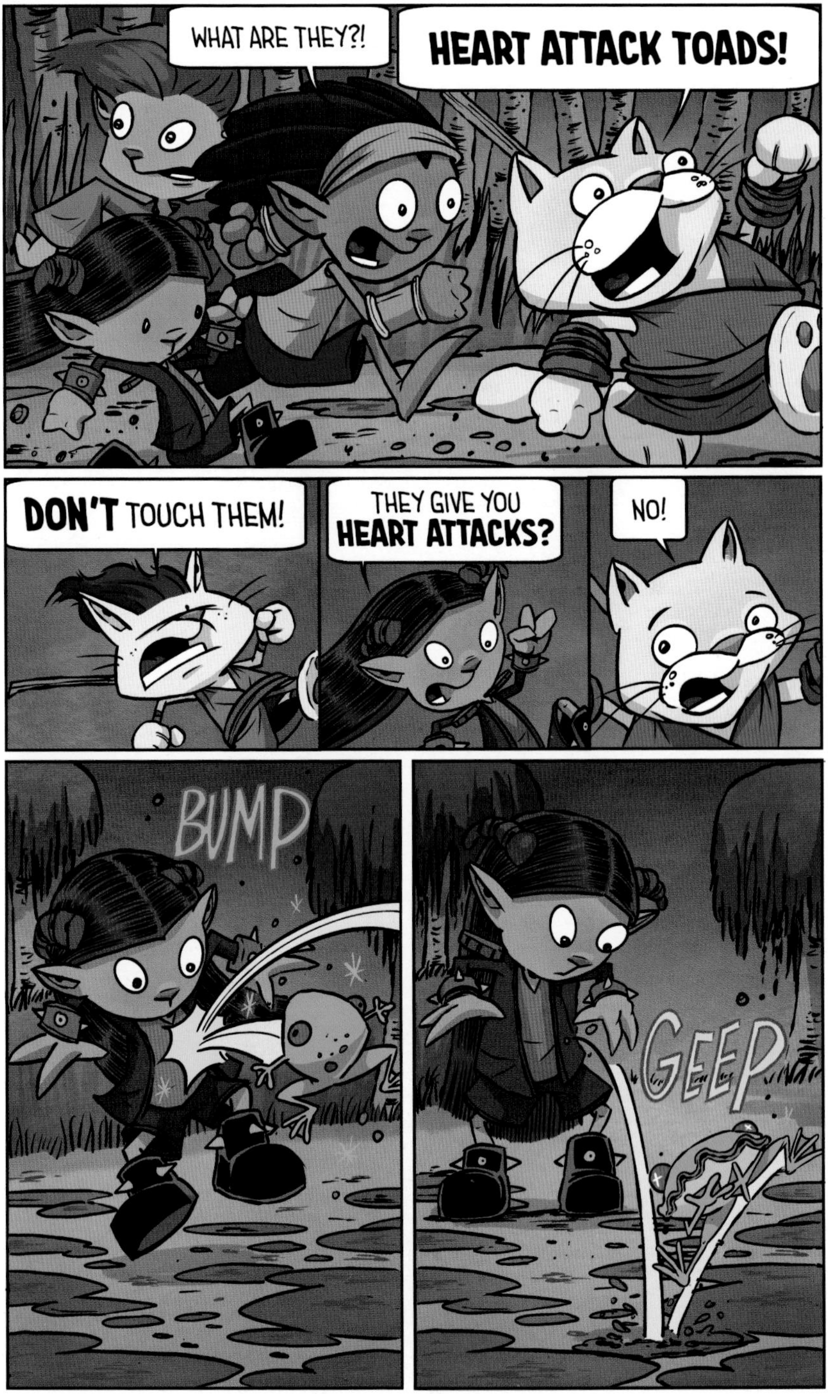
WHAT ARE THEY?!
HEART ATTACK TOADS!
DON'T TOUCH THEM!
THEY GIVE YOU HEART ATTACKS?
NO!
BUMP
GEEP

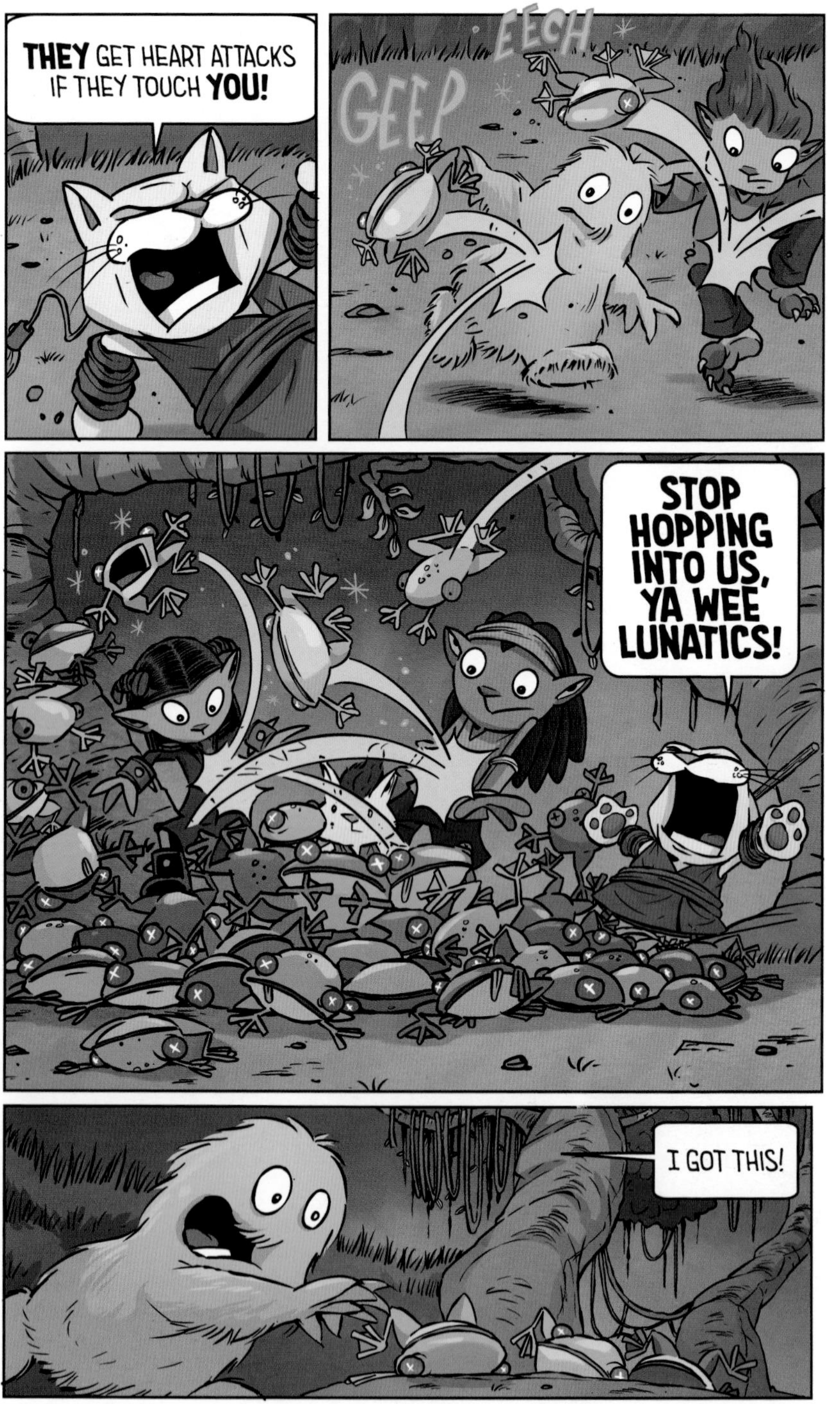
THEY GET HEART ATTACKS IF THEY TOUCH YOU!
GEEP
EECH
STOP HOPPING INTO US, YA WEE LUNATICS!
I GOT THIS!

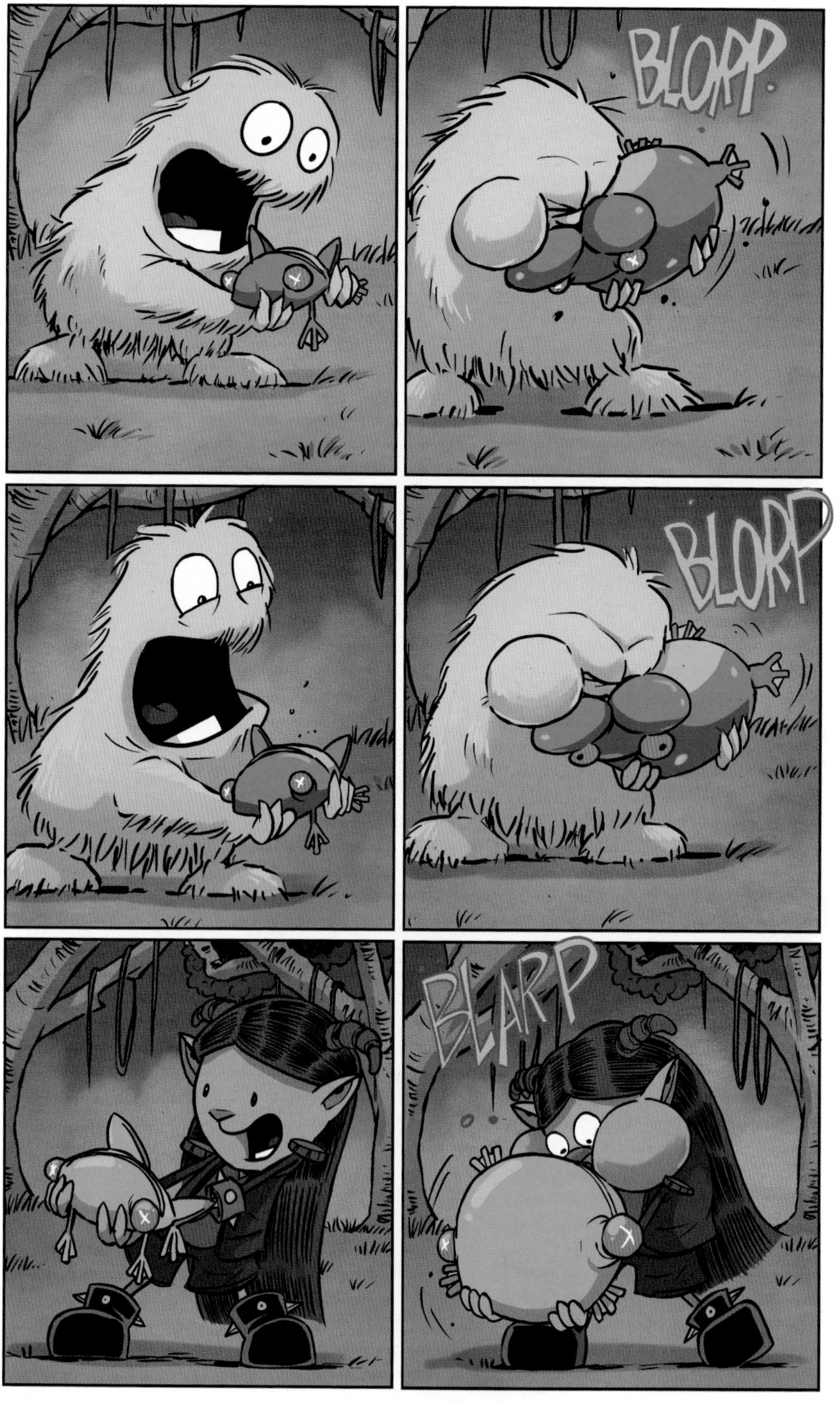
BLORP
BLORP
BLARP

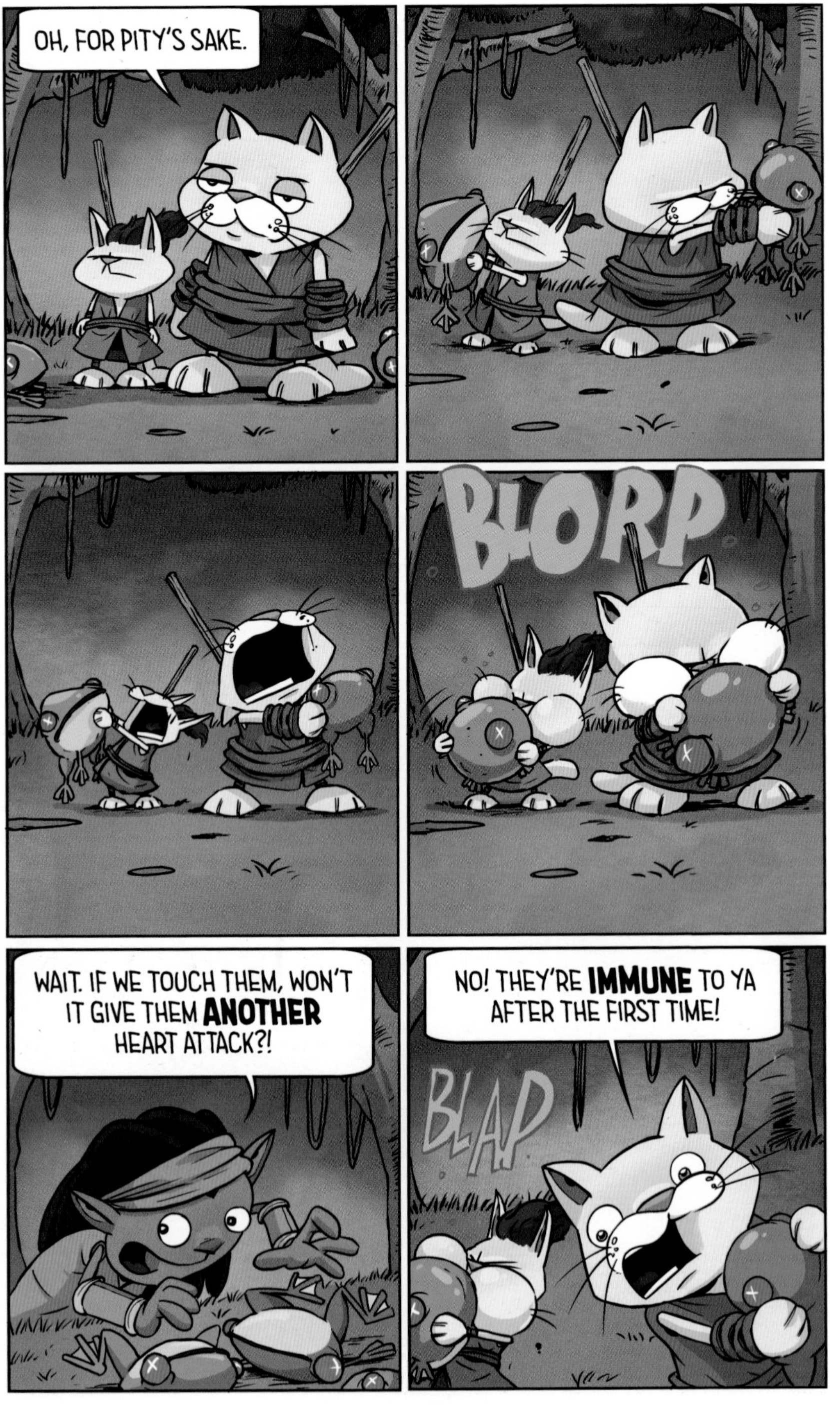
OH, FOR PITY'S SAKE.
BLORP
WAIT. IF WE TOUCH THEM, WON'T IT GIVE THEM **ANOTHER** HEART ATTACK?!
NO! THEY'RE **IMMUNE** TO YA AFTER THE FIRST TIME!
BLAP

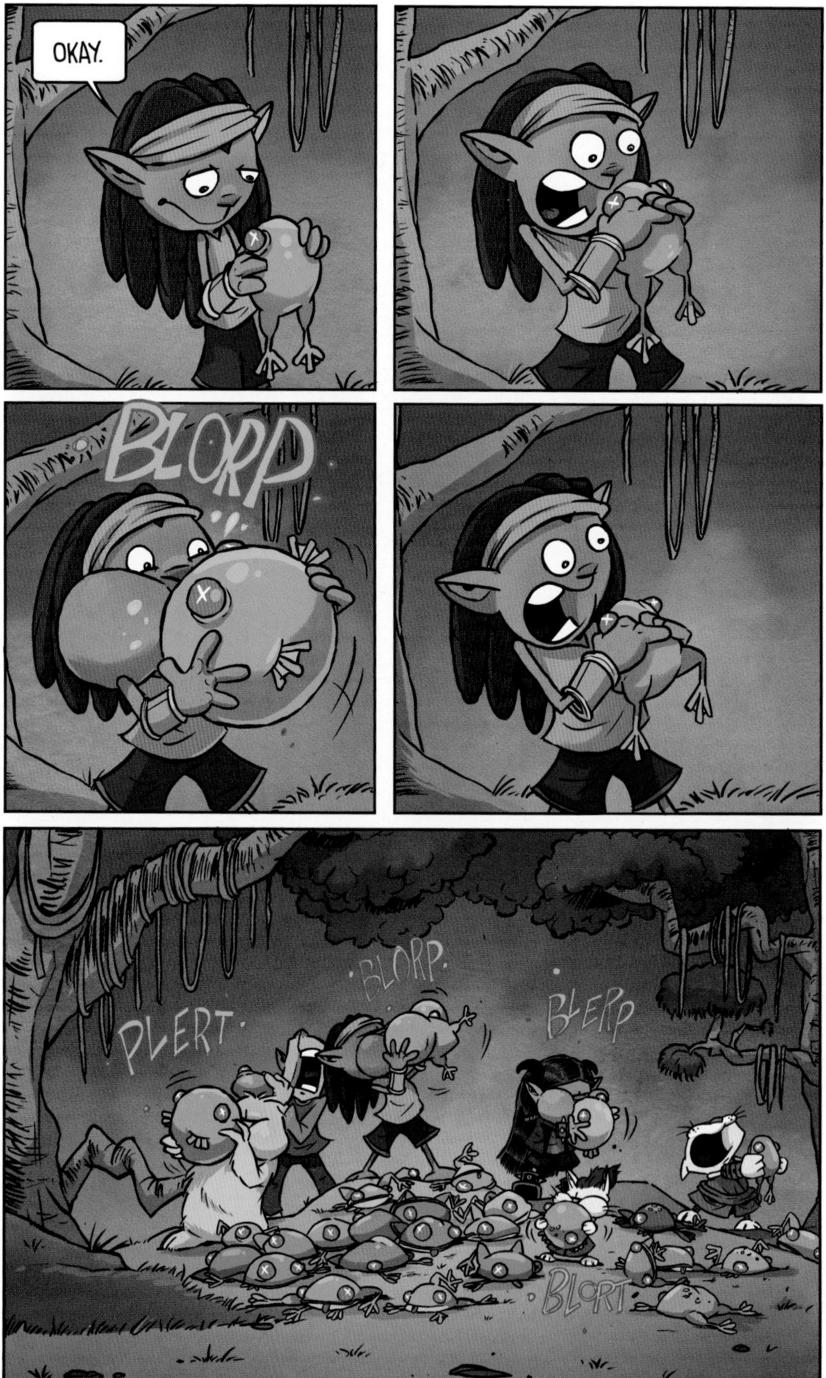
OKAY.
BLORP
PLERT
BLORP
BLERP
BLORT

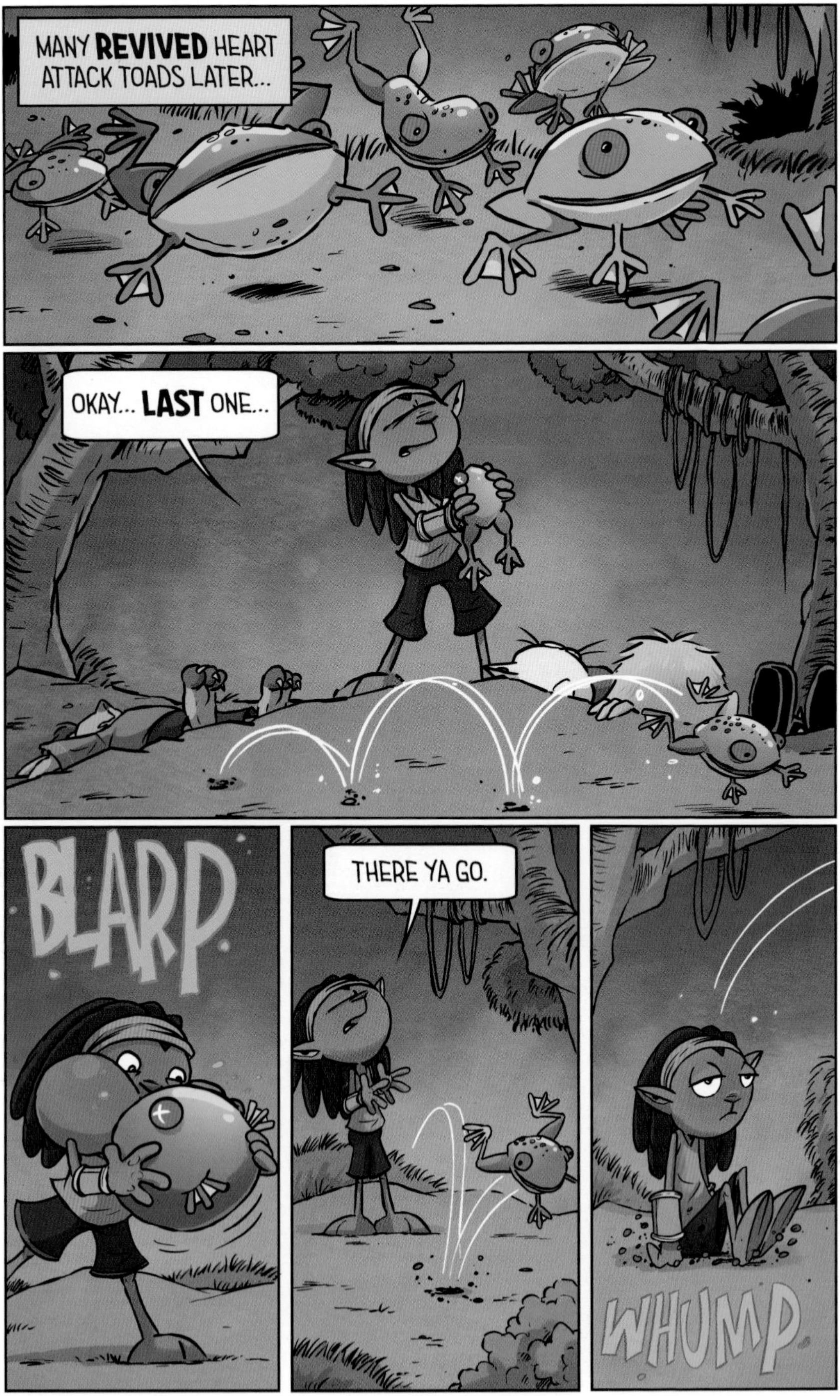
MANY **REVIVED** HEART ATTACK TOADS LATER...
OKAY... **LAST** ONE...
BLARP
THERE YA GO.
WHUMP

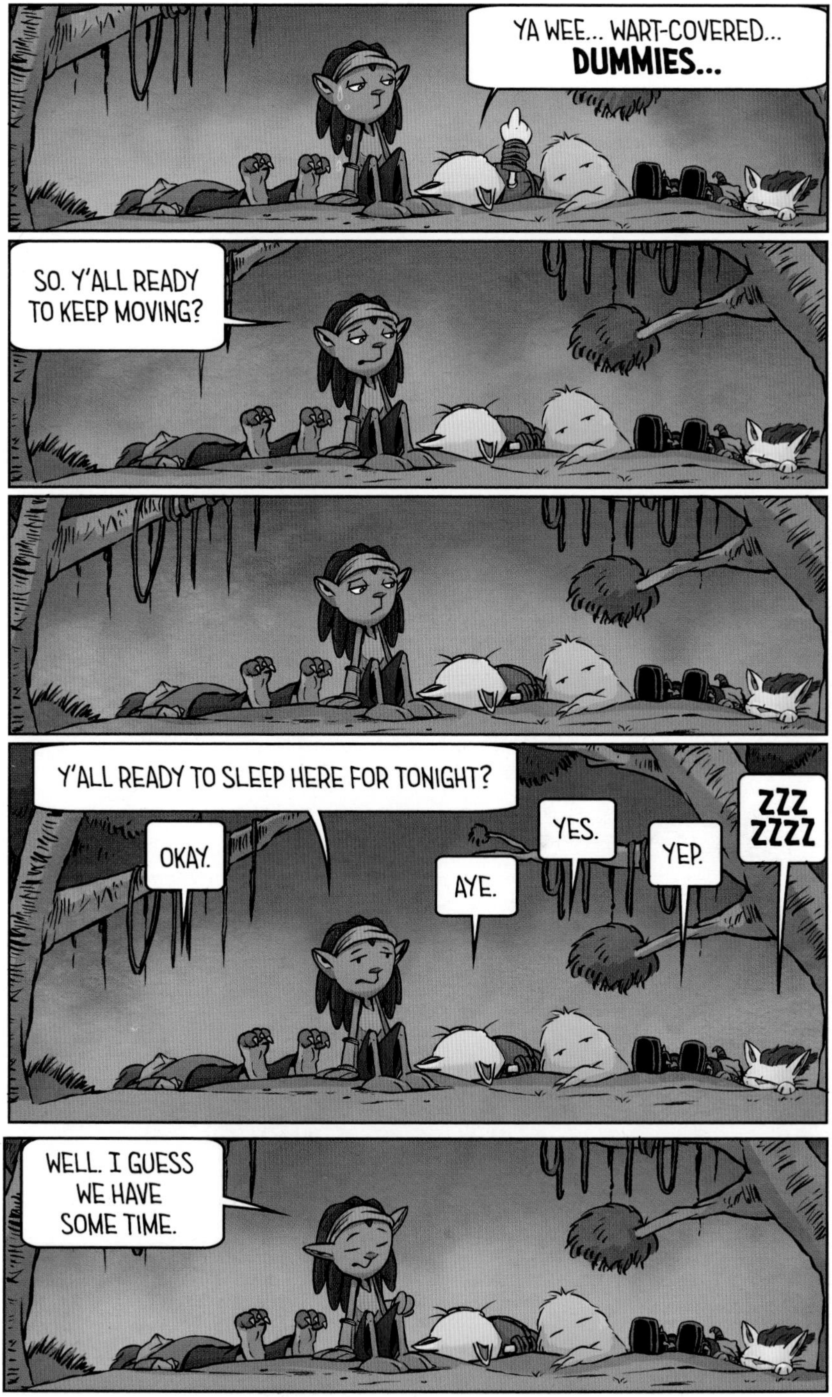
YA WEE... WART-COVERED... **DUMMIES...**
SO. Y'ALL READY TO KEEP MOVING?
Y'ALL READY TO SLEEP HERE FOR TONIGHT?
OKAY.
AYE.
YES.
YEP.
ZZZ ZZZZ
WELL. I GUESS WE HAVE SOME TIME.

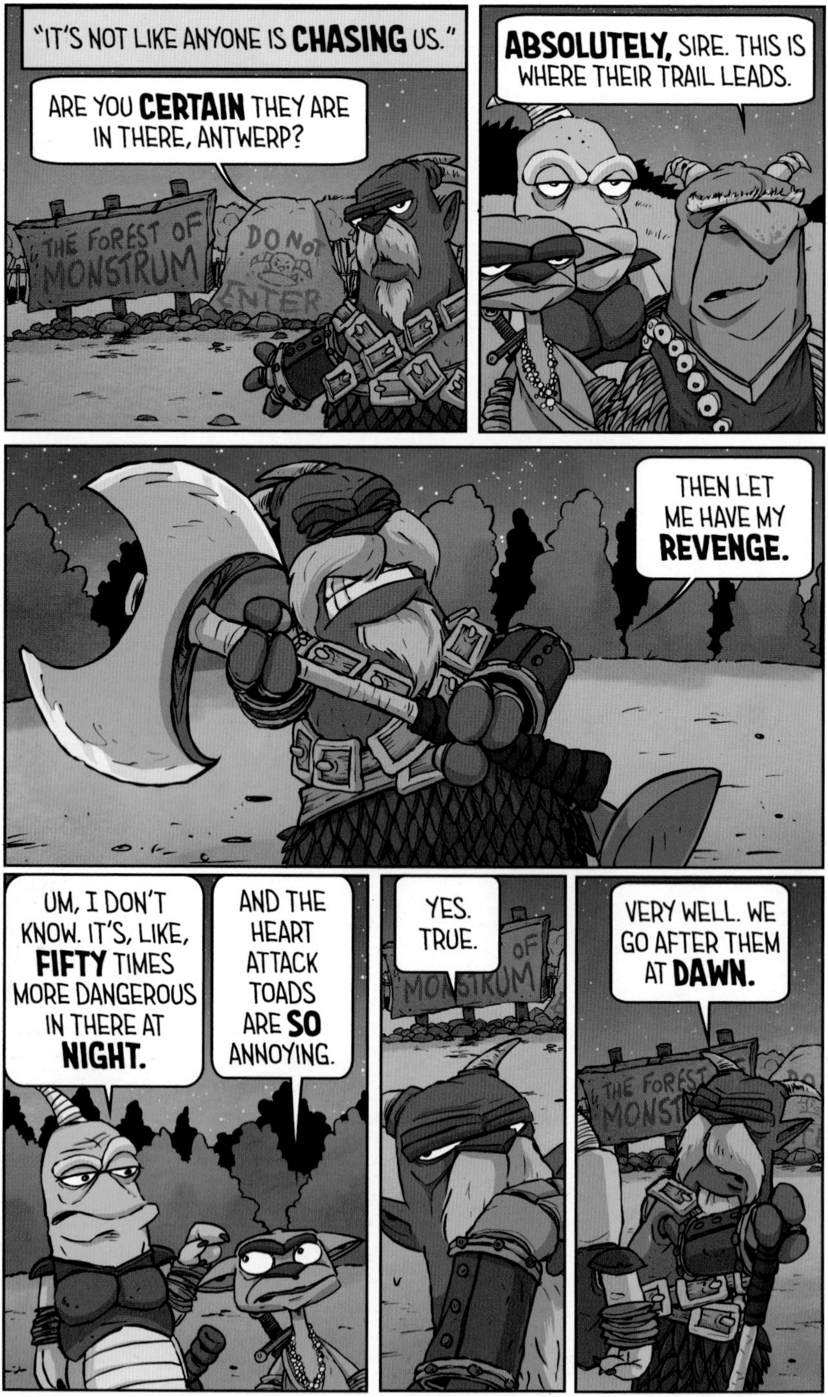
"IT'S NOT LIKE ANYONE IS **CHASING** US."
ARE YOU **CERTAIN** THEY ARE IN THERE, ANTWERP?
THE FOREST OF MONSTRUM
DO NOT ENTER
ABSOLUTELY, SIRE. THIS IS WHERE THEIR TRAIL LEADS.
THEN LET ME HAVE MY **REVENGE.**
UM, I DON'T KNOW. IT'S, LIKE, **FIFTY** TIMES MORE DANGEROUS IN THERE AT **NIGHT.**
AND THE HEART ATTACK TOADS ARE **SO** ANNOYING.
YES. TRUE.
VERY WELL. WE GO AFTER THEM AT **DAWN.**

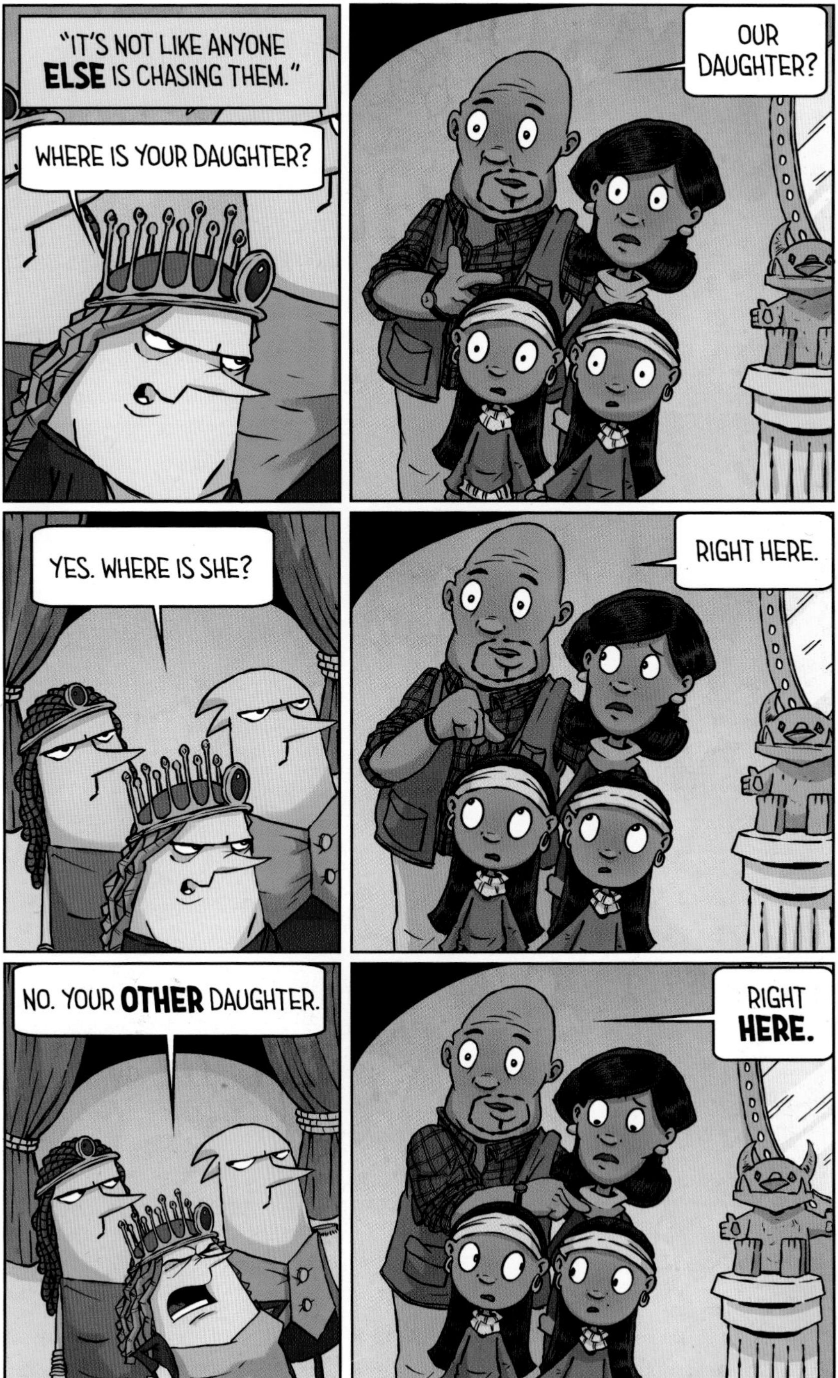
"IT'S NOT LIKE ANYONE **ELSE** IS CHASING THEM."
WHERE IS YOUR DAUGHTER?
OUR DAUGHTER?
YES. WHERE IS SHE?
RIGHT HERE.
NO. YOUR **OTHER** DAUGHTER.
RIGHT **HERE.**

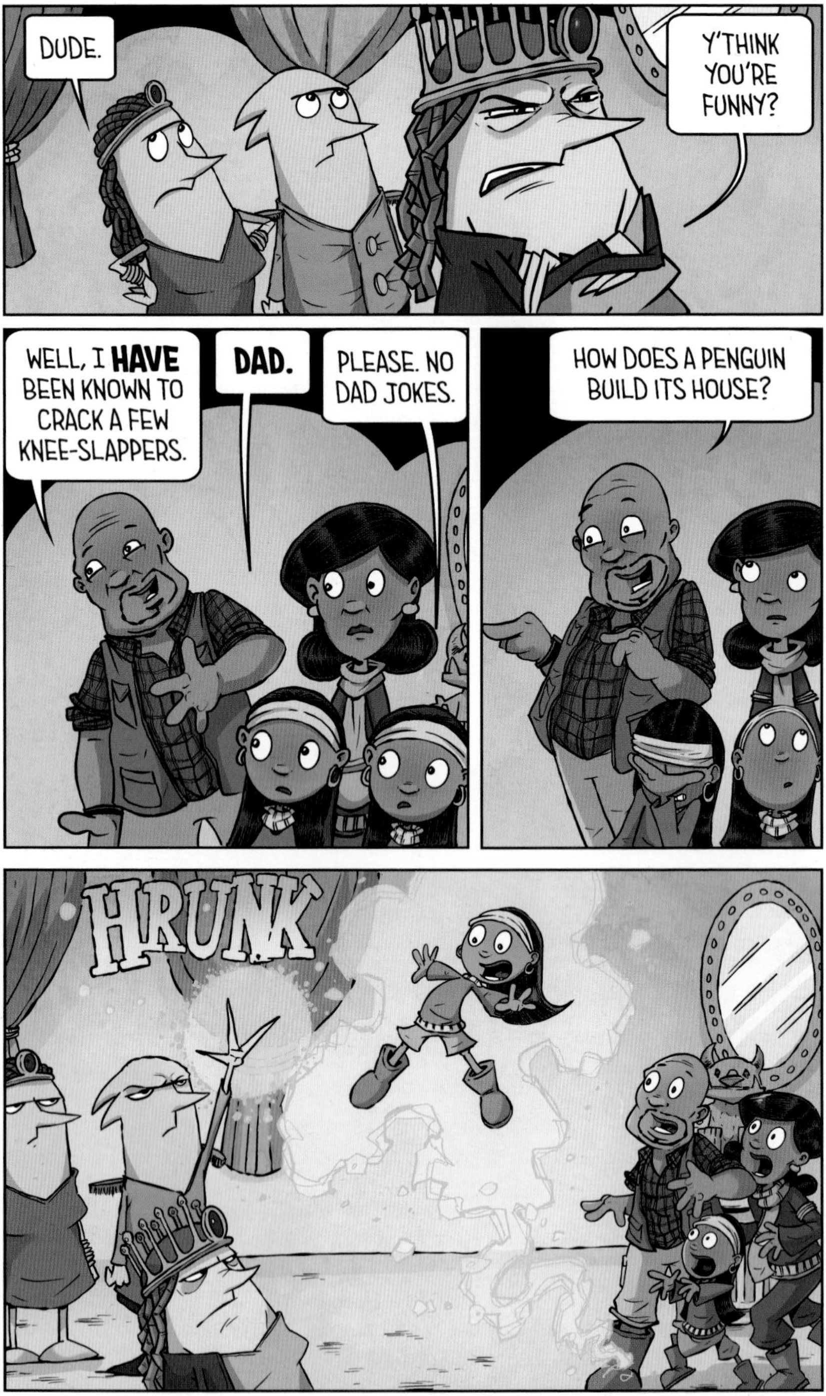
DUDE.
Y'THINK YOU'RE FUNNY?
WELL, I **HAVE** BEEN KNOWN TO CRACK A FEW KNEE-SLAPPERS.
DAD.
PLEASE. NO DAD JOKES.
HOW DOES A PENGUIN BUILD ITS HOUSE?
HRUNK

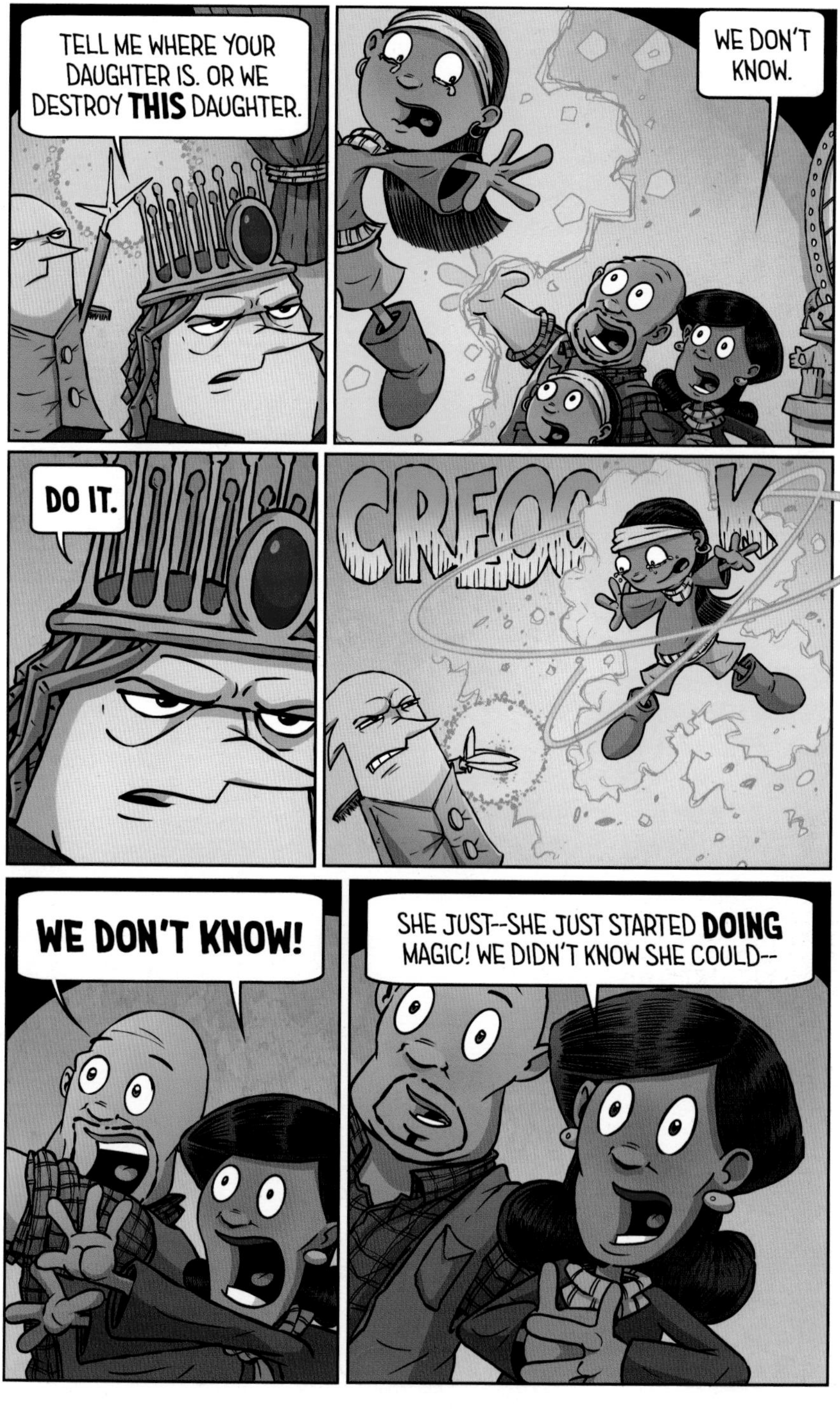

TELL ME WHERE YOUR DAUGHTER IS. OR WE DESTROY **THIS** DAUGHTER.
WE DON'T KNOW.
DO IT.
CREOO K
WE DON'T KNOW!
SHE JUST--SHE JUST STARTED **DOING** MAGIC! WE DIDN'T KNOW SHE COULD--

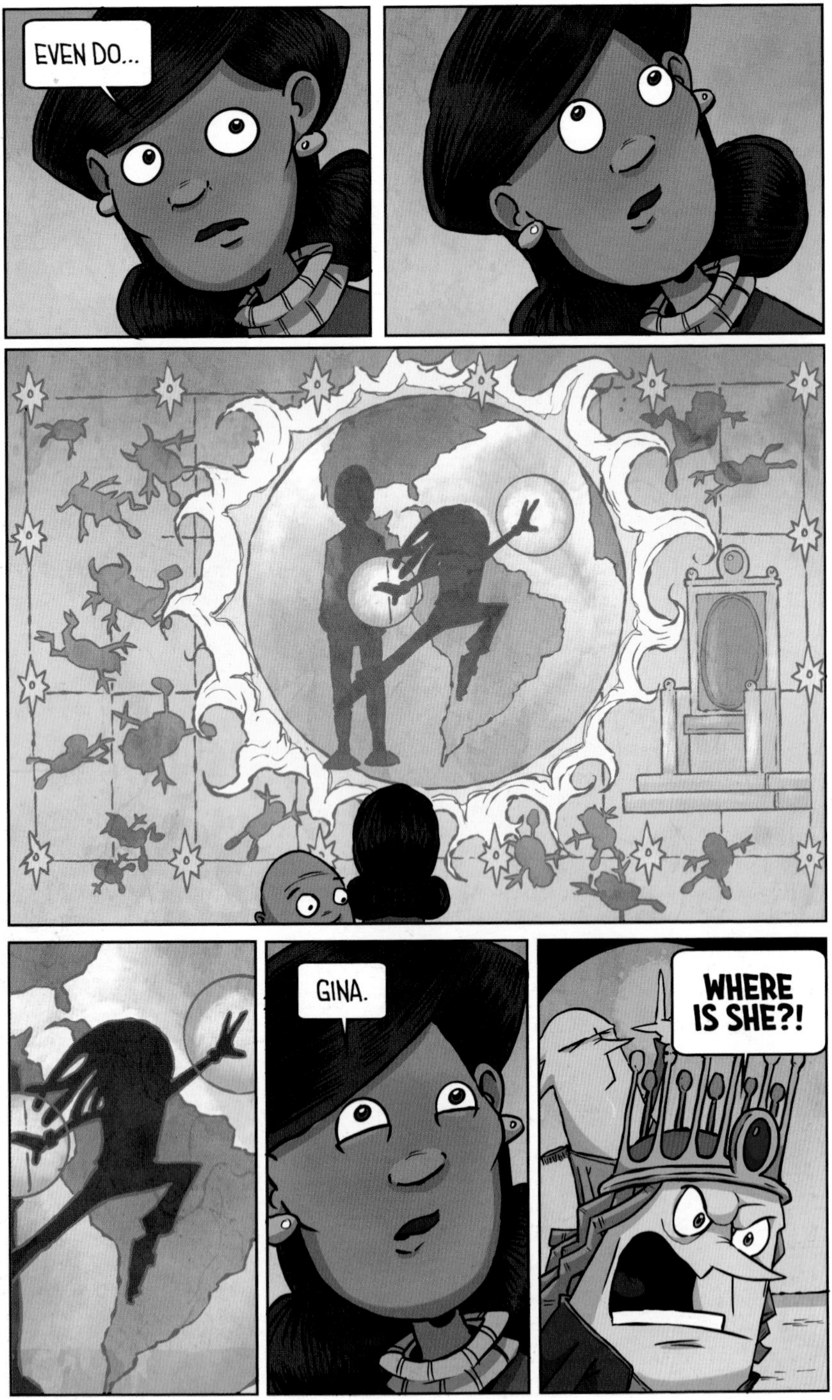
EVEN DO...
GINA.
WHERE IS SHE?!

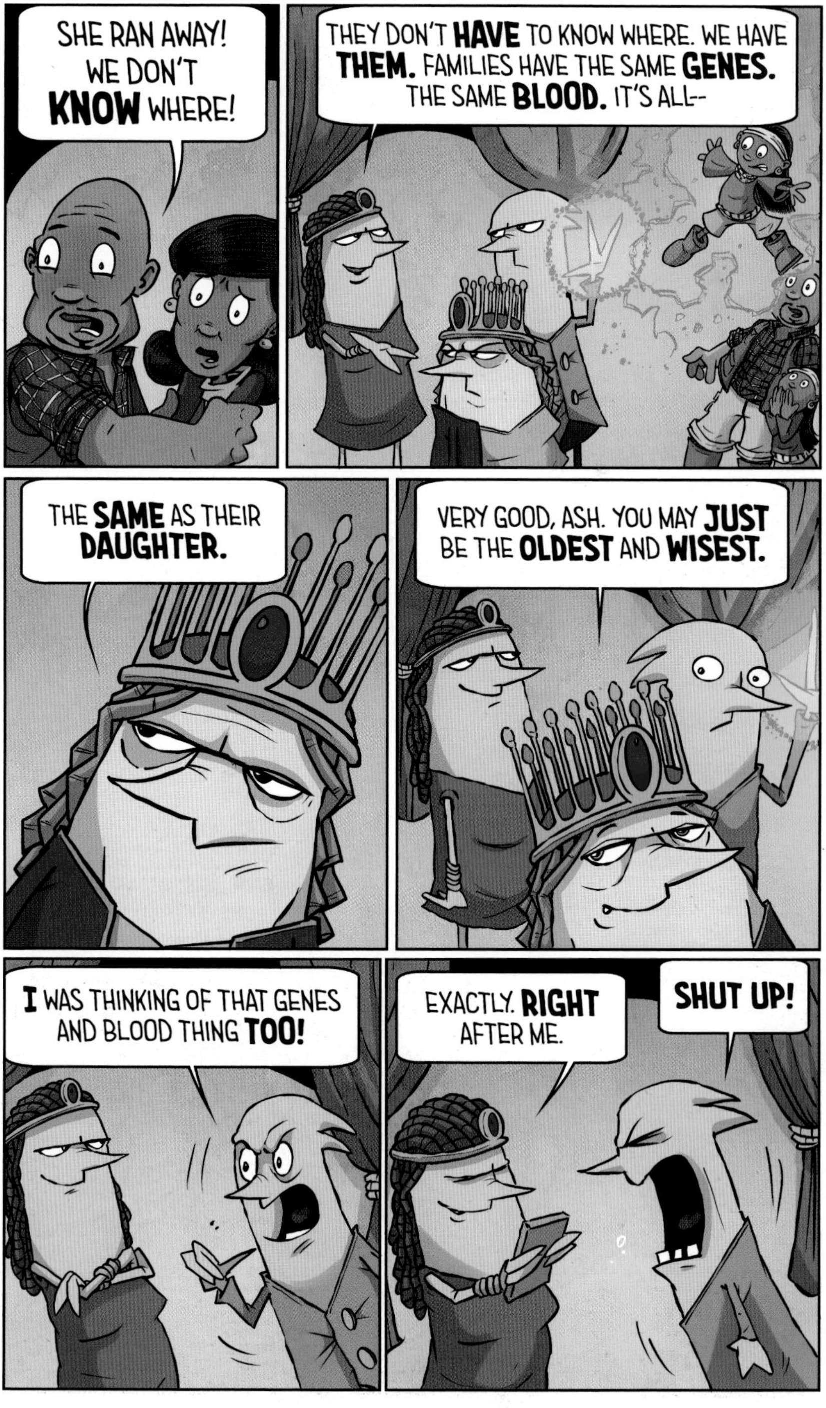
SHE RAN AWAY! WE DON'T KNOW WHERE!
THEY DON'T HAVE TO KNOW WHERE. WE HAVE THEM. FAMILIES HAVE THE SAME GENES. THE SAME BLOOD. IT'S ALL--
THE SAME AS THEIR DAUGHTER.
VERY GOOD, ASH. YOU MAY JUST BE THE OLDEST AND WISEST.
I WAS THINKING OF THAT GENES AND BLOOD THING TOO!
EXACTLY. RIGHT AFTER ME.
SHUT UP!

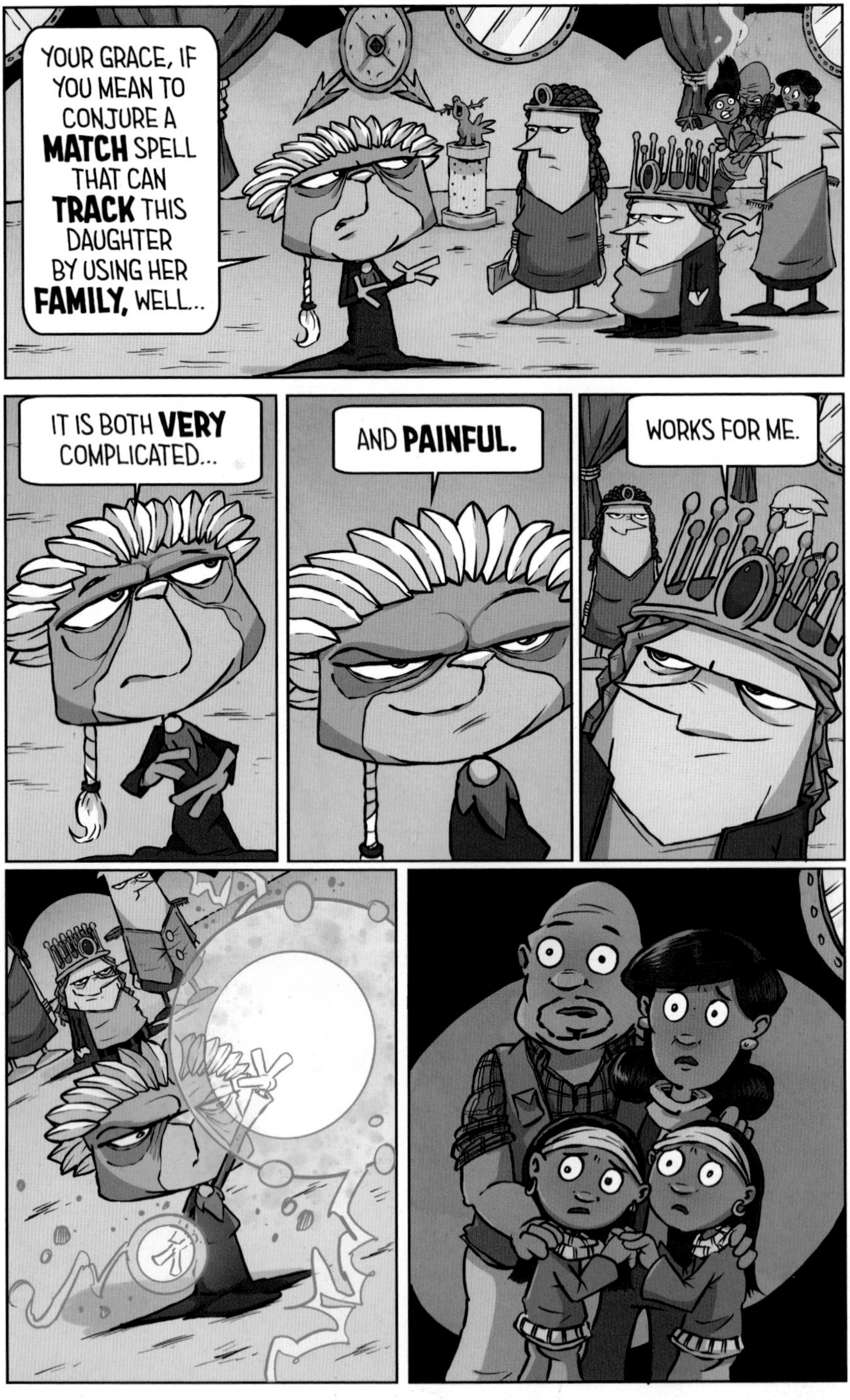
YOUR GRACE, IF YOU MEAN TO CONJURE A **MATCH** SPELL THAT CAN **TRACK** THIS DAUGHTER BY USING HER **FAMILY**, WELL...
IT IS BOTH **VERY** COMPLICATED...
AND **PAINFUL.**
WORKS FOR ME.

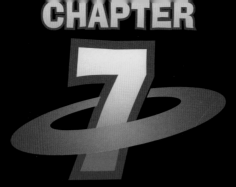

CHAPTER 7

REGINA LEE COOPER

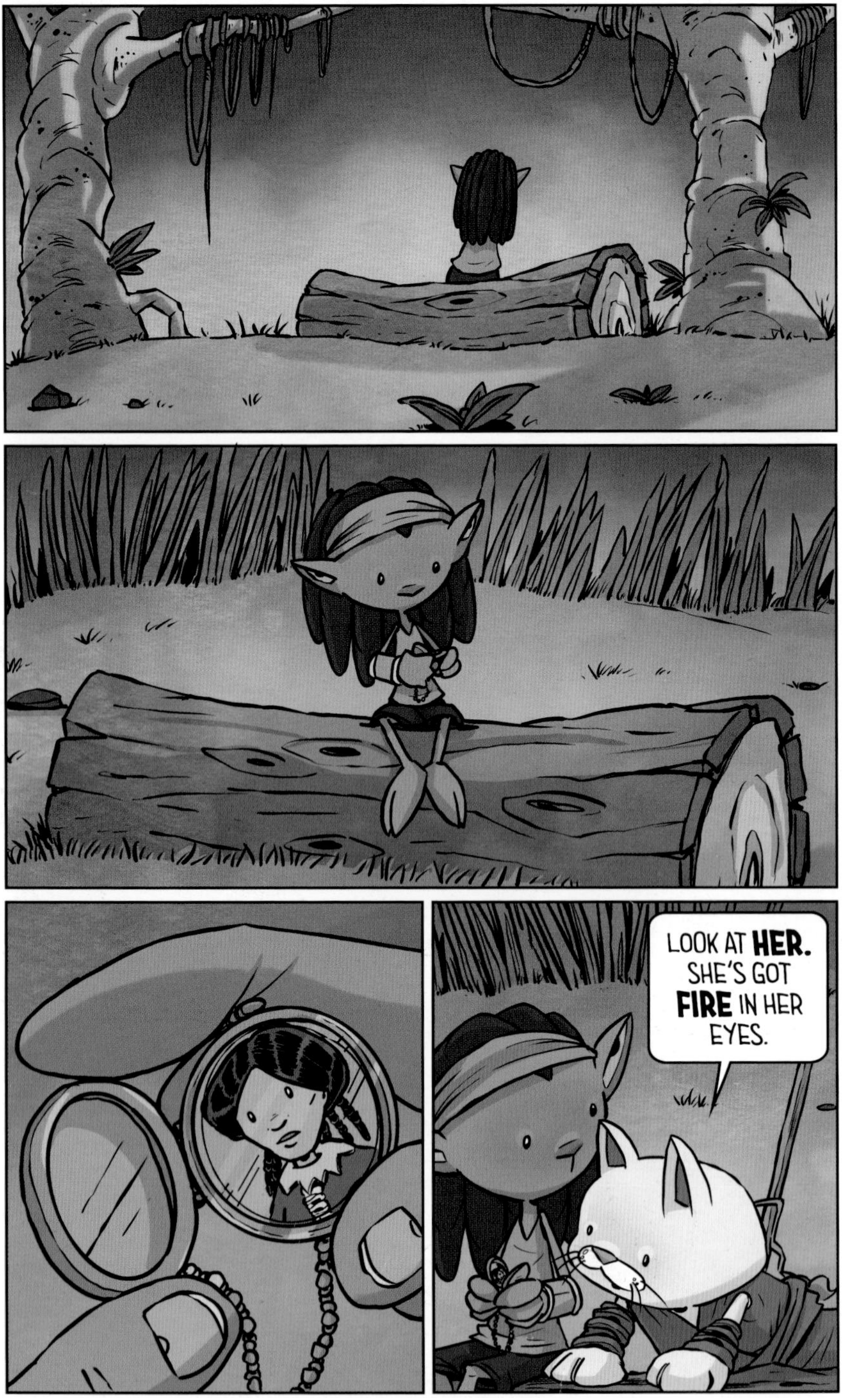
LOOK AT **HER.** SHE'S GOT **FIRE** IN HER EYES.

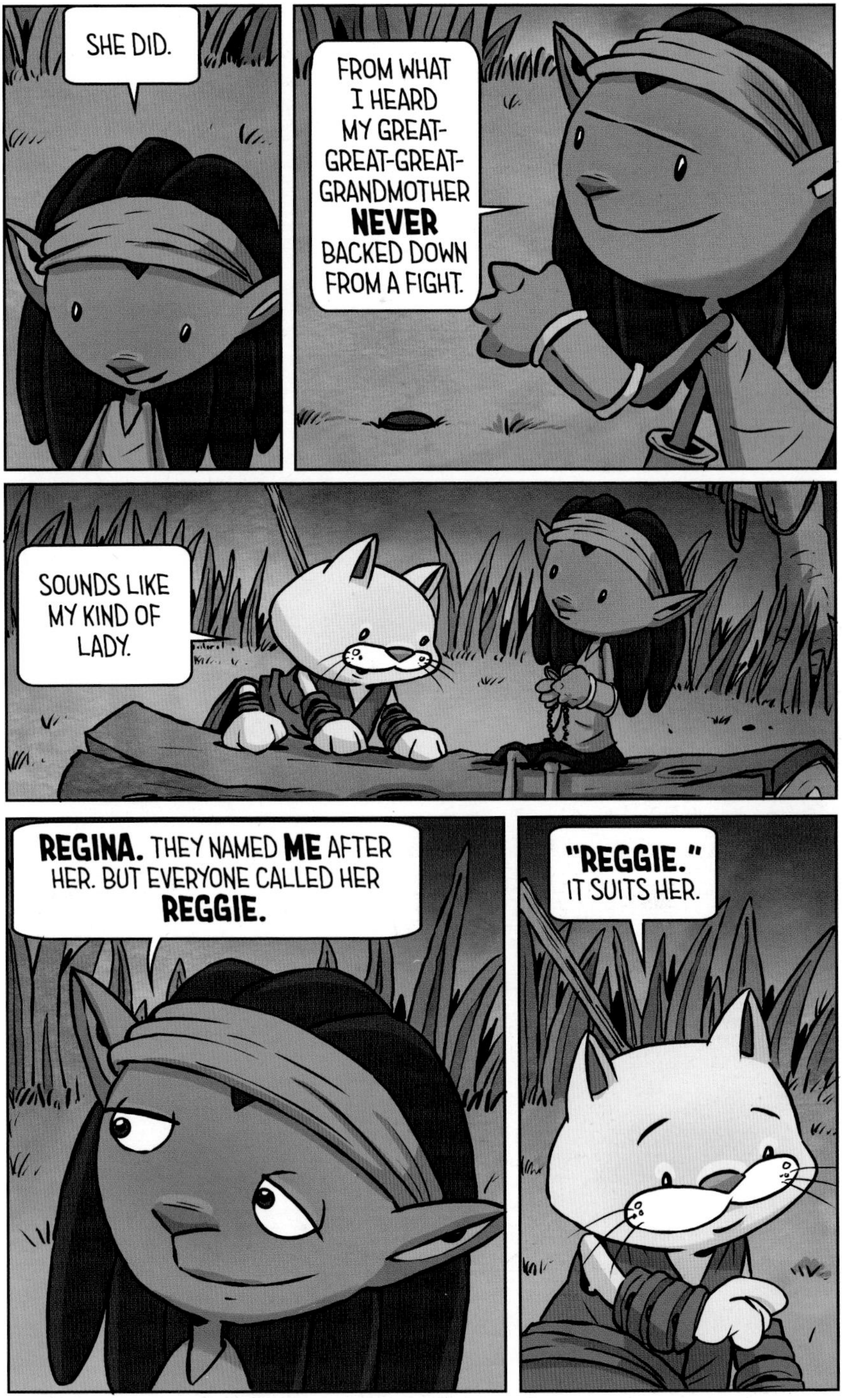
SHE DID.
FROM WHAT I HEARD MY GREAT-GREAT-GREAT-GRANDMOTHER **NEVER** BACKED DOWN FROM A FIGHT.
SOUNDS LIKE MY KIND OF LADY.
REGINA. THEY NAMED **ME** AFTER HER. BUT EVERYONE CALLED HER **REGGIE.**
"REGGIE." IT SUITS HER.

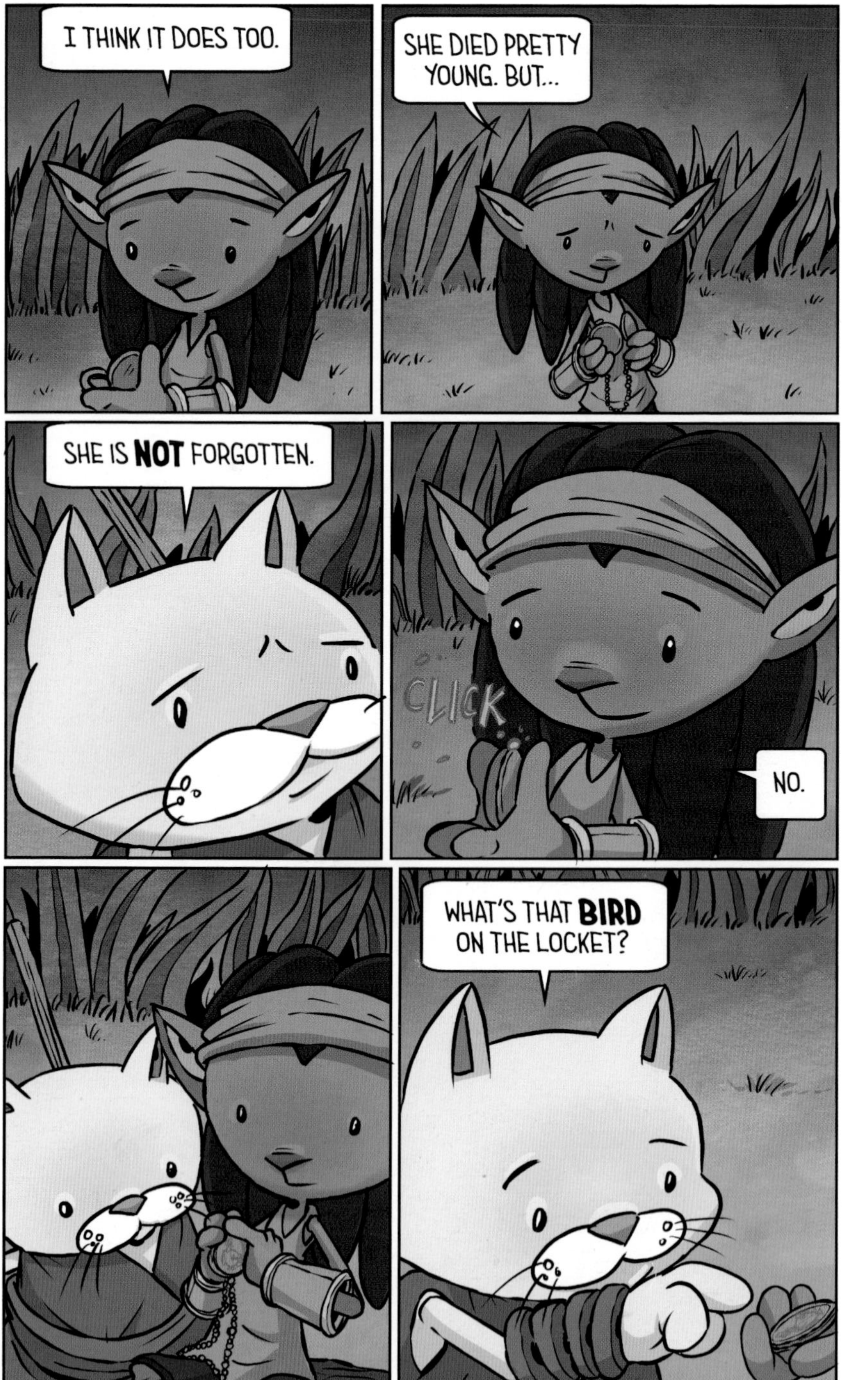
I THINK IT DOES TOO.
SHE DIED PRETTY YOUNG. BUT...
SHE IS **NOT** FORGOTTEN.
CLICK
NO.
WHAT'S THAT **BIRD** ON THE LOCKET?

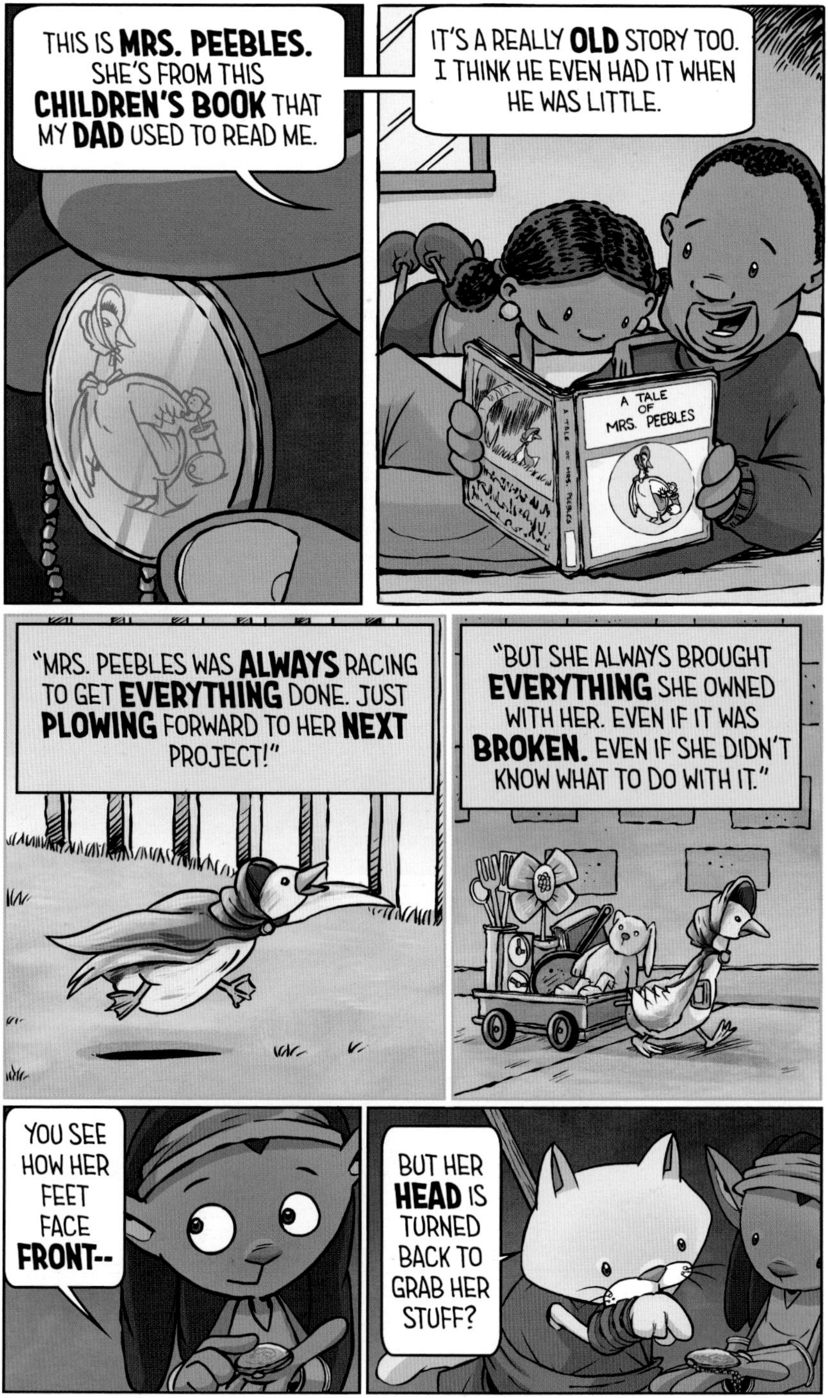
THIS IS MRS. PEEBLES. SHE'S FROM THIS CHILDREN'S BOOK THAT MY DAD USED TO READ ME.
IT'S A REALLY OLD STORY TOO. I THINK HE EVEN HAD IT WHEN HE WAS LITTLE.
A TALE OF MRS. PEEBLES
"MRS. PEEBLES WAS ALWAYS RACING TO GET EVERYTHING DONE. JUST PLOWING FORWARD TO HER NEXT PROJECT!"
"BUT SHE ALWAYS BROUGHT EVERYTHING SHE OWNED WITH HER. EVEN IF IT WAS BROKEN. EVEN IF SHE DIDN'T KNOW WHAT TO DO WITH IT."
YOU SEE HOW HER FEET FACE FRONT--
BUT HER HEAD IS TURNED BACK TO GRAB HER STUFF?

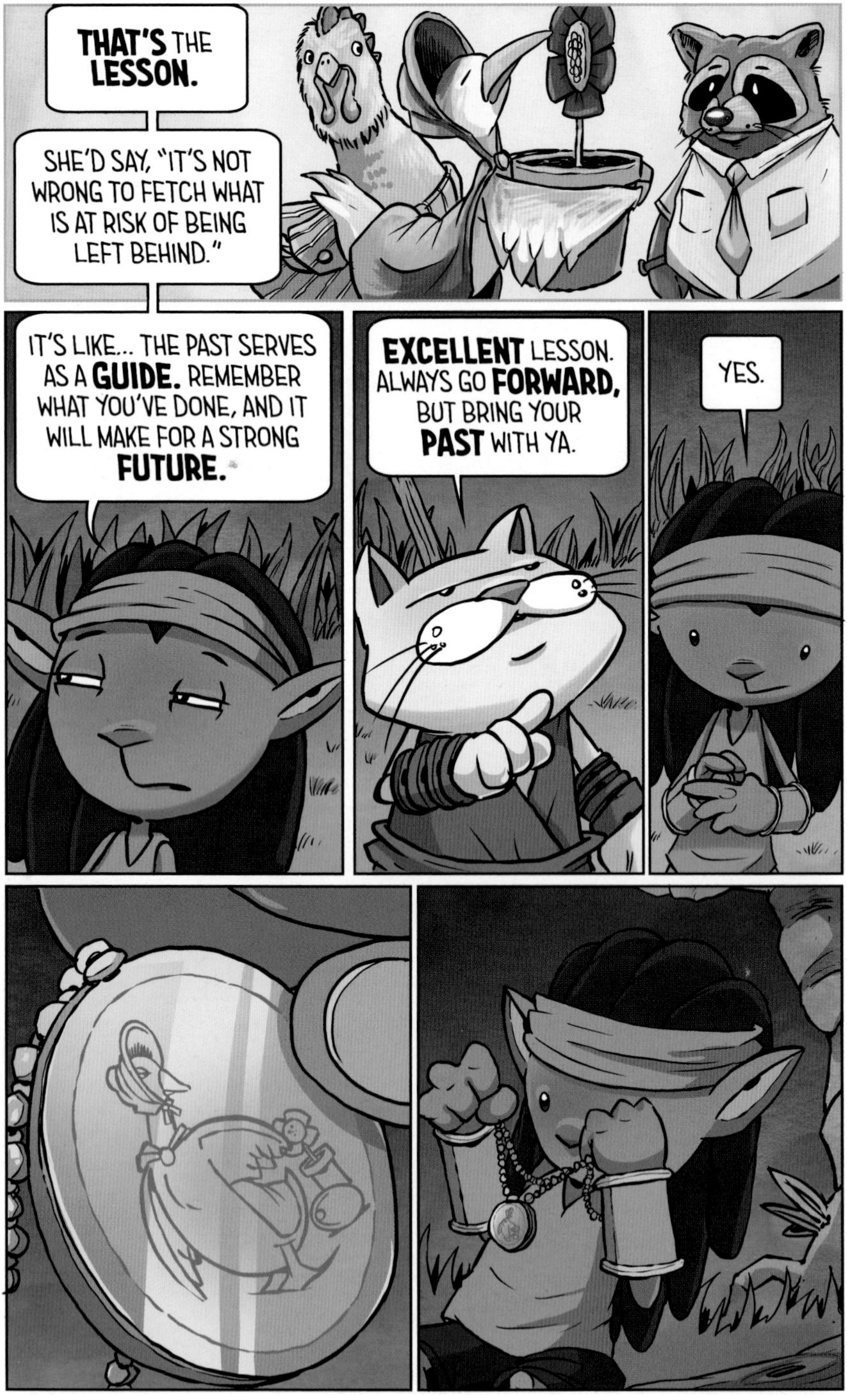
THAT'S THE LESSON.
SHE'D SAY, "IT'S NOT WRONG TO FETCH WHAT IS AT RISK OF BEING LEFT BEHIND."
IT'S LIKE... THE PAST SERVES AS A GUIDE. REMEMBER WHAT YOU'VE DONE, AND IT WILL MAKE FOR A STRONG FUTURE.
EXCELLENT LESSON. ALWAYS GO FORWARD, BUT BRING YOUR PAST WITH YA.
YES.

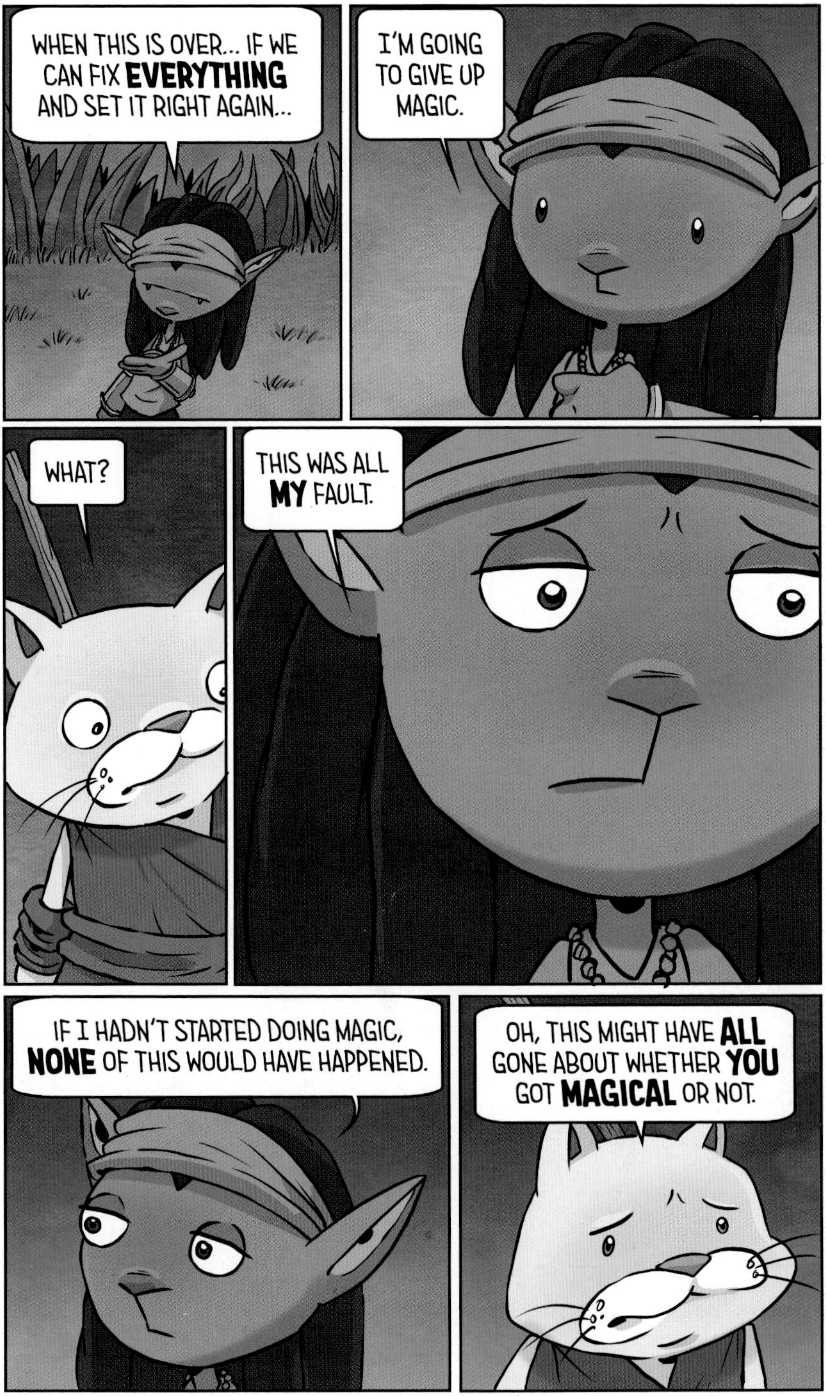
WHEN THIS IS OVER... IF WE CAN FIX EVERYTHING AND SET IT RIGHT AGAIN...
I'M GOING TO GIVE UP MAGIC.
WHAT?
THIS WAS ALL MY FAULT.
IF I HADN'T STARTED DOING MAGIC, NONE OF THIS WOULD HAVE HAPPENED.
OH, THIS MIGHT HAVE ALL GONE ABOUT WHETHER YOU GOT MAGICAL OR NOT.

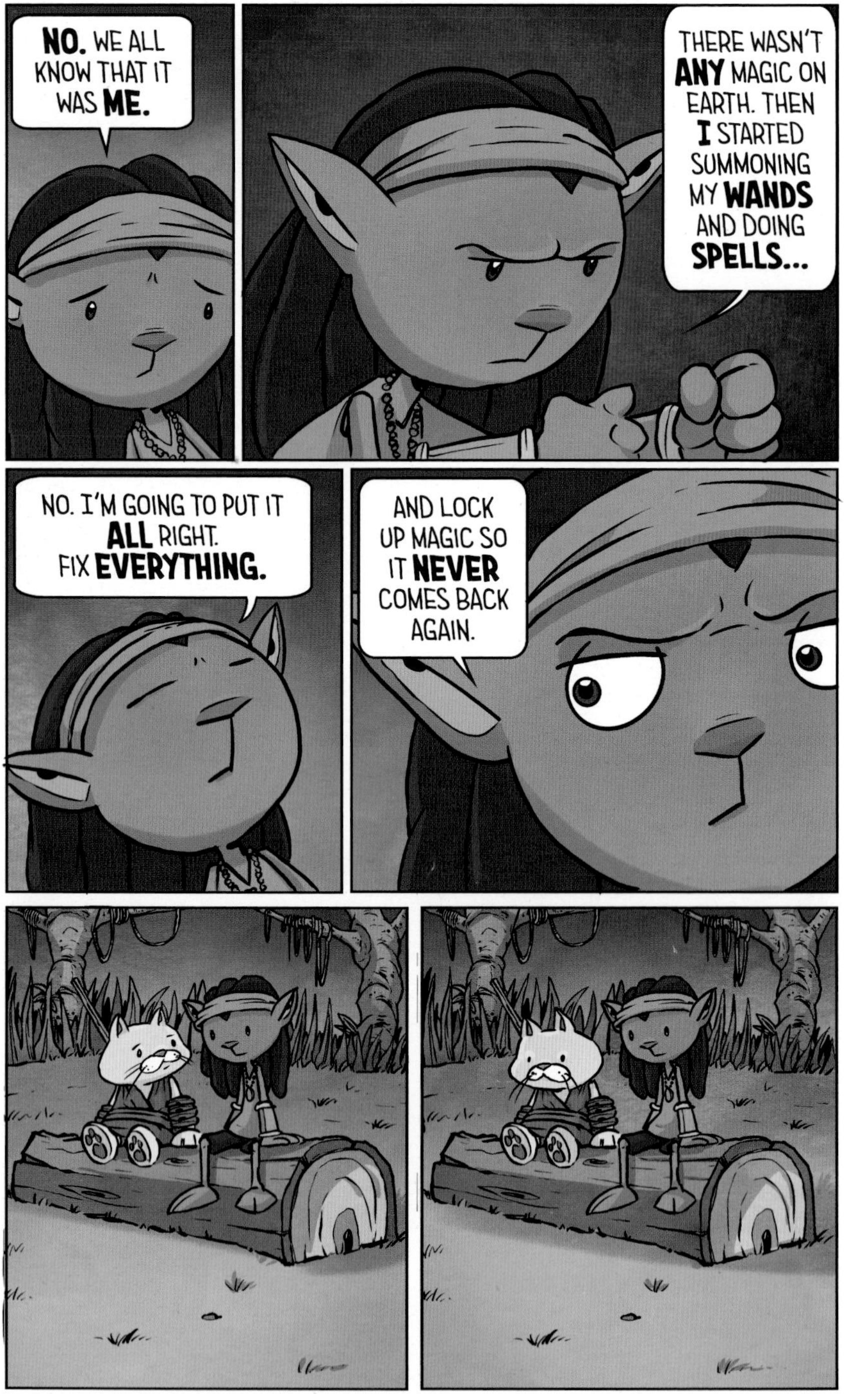
NO. WE ALL KNOW THAT IT WAS ME.
THERE WASN'T ANY MAGIC ON EARTH. THEN I STARTED SUMMONING MY WANDS AND DOING SPELLS...
NO. I'M GOING TO PUT IT ALL RIGHT. FIX EVERYTHING.
AND LOCK UP MAGIC SO IT NEVER COMES BACK AGAIN.

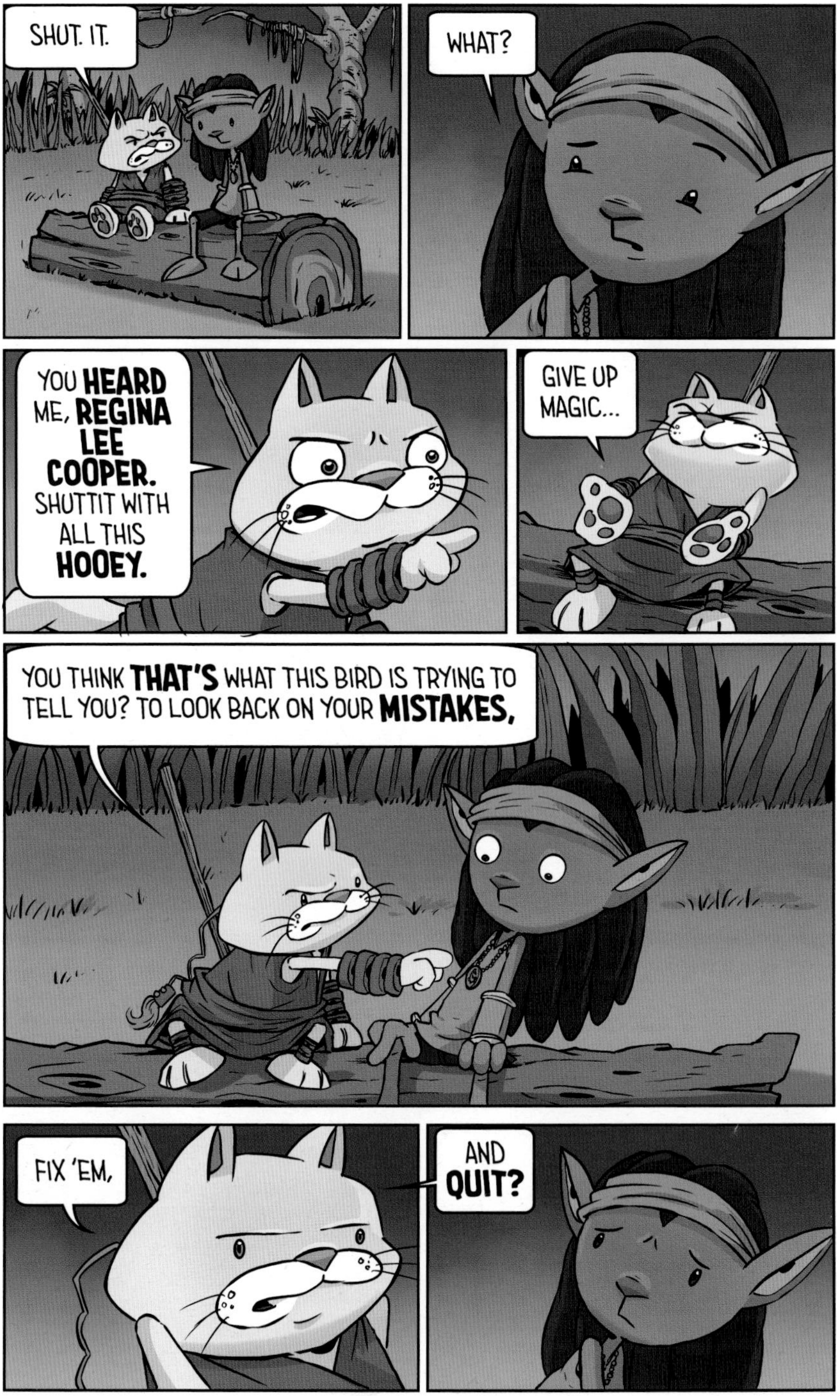
SHUT. IT.
WHAT?
YOU HEARD ME, REGINA LEE COOPER. SHUTTIT WITH ALL THIS HOOEY.
GIVE UP MAGIC...
YOU THINK THAT'S WHAT THIS BIRD IS TRYING TO TELL YOU? TO LOOK BACK ON YOUR MISTAKES,
FIX 'EM,
AND QUIT?

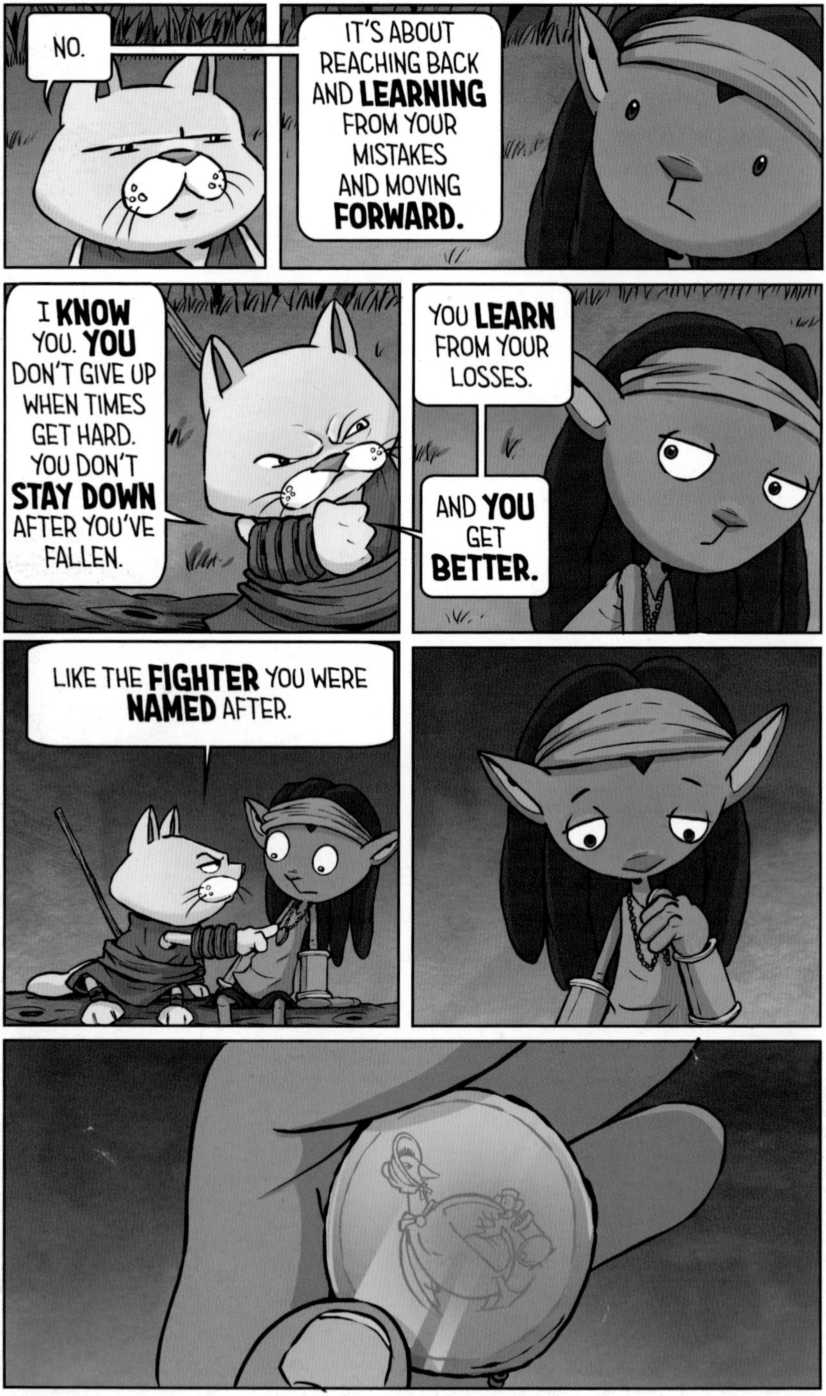
NO.
IT'S ABOUT REACHING BACK AND **LEARNING** FROM YOUR MISTAKES AND MOVING **FORWARD.**
I **KNOW** YOU. **YOU** DON'T GIVE UP WHEN TIMES GET HARD. YOU DON'T **STAY DOWN** AFTER YOU'VE FALLEN.
YOU **LEARN** FROM YOUR LOSSES.
AND **YOU** GET **BETTER.**
LIKE THE **FIGHTER** YOU WERE **NAMED** AFTER.

CHAPTER 8

OH, FOR PITY'S SAKE

SO. THIS MUST BE **THE WALL** THAT'S ON THE MAP.
IS IT **SUPPOSED** TO BE THIS...

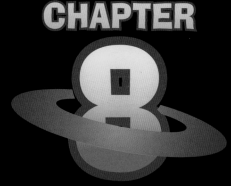

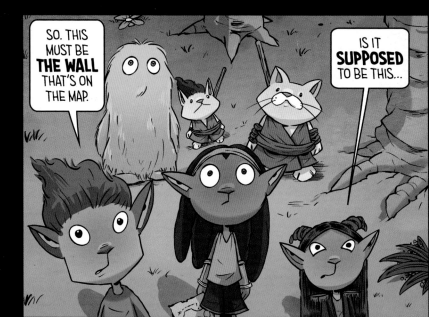

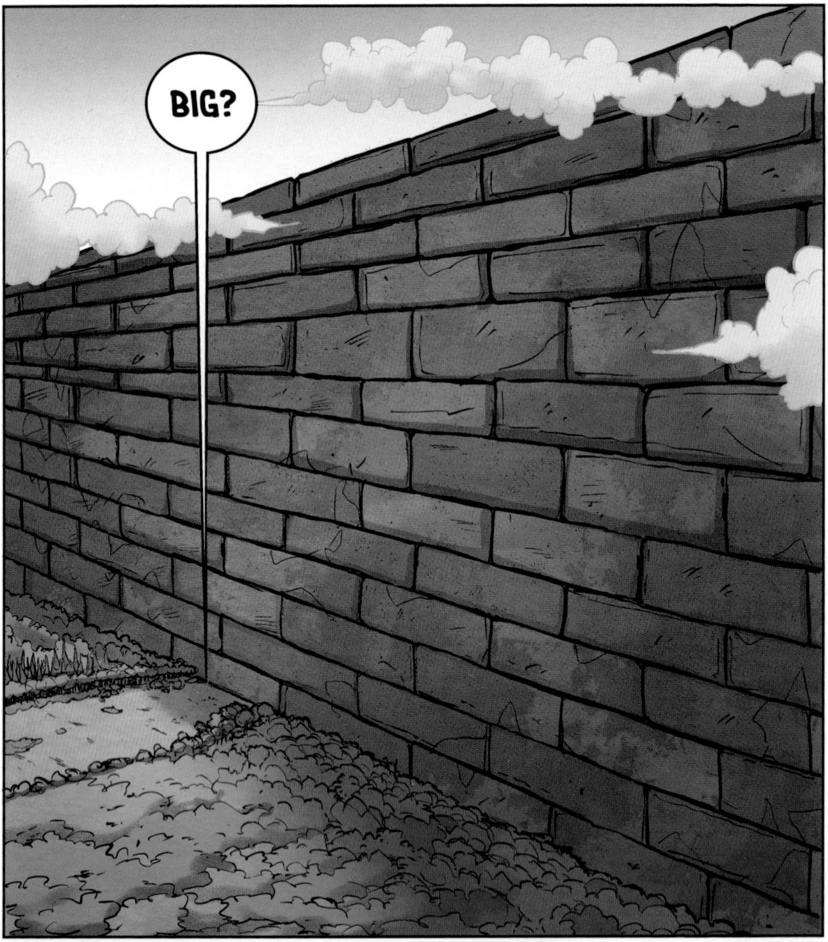
BIG?

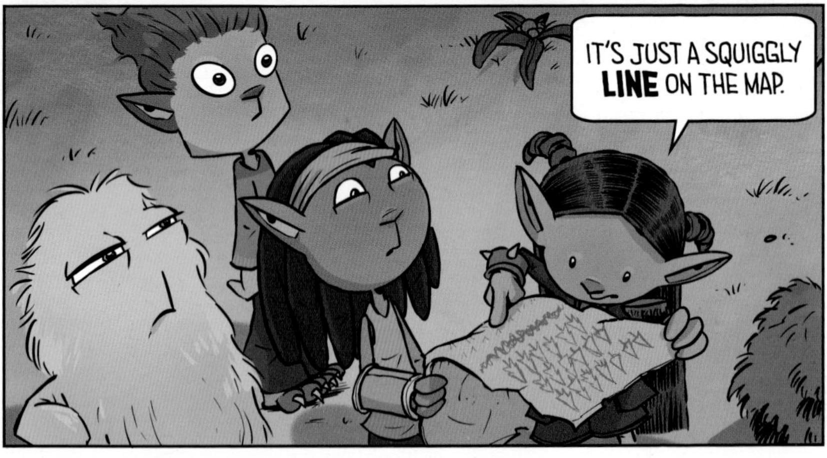
IT'S JUST A SQUIGGLY
LINE ON THE MAP.

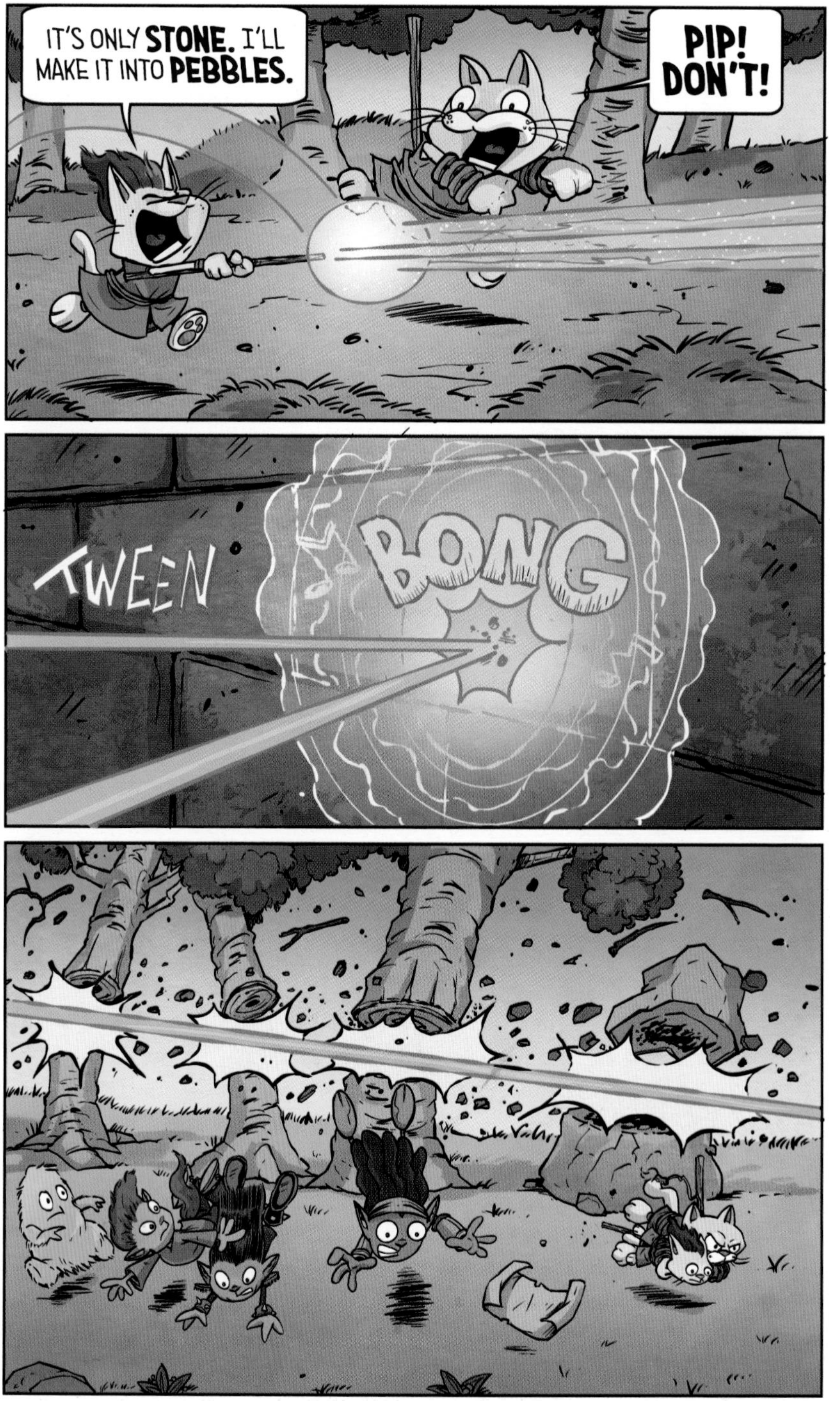

IT'S ONLY **STONE.** I'LL MAKE IT INTO **PEBBLES.**
PIP! DON'T!
TWEEN
BONG

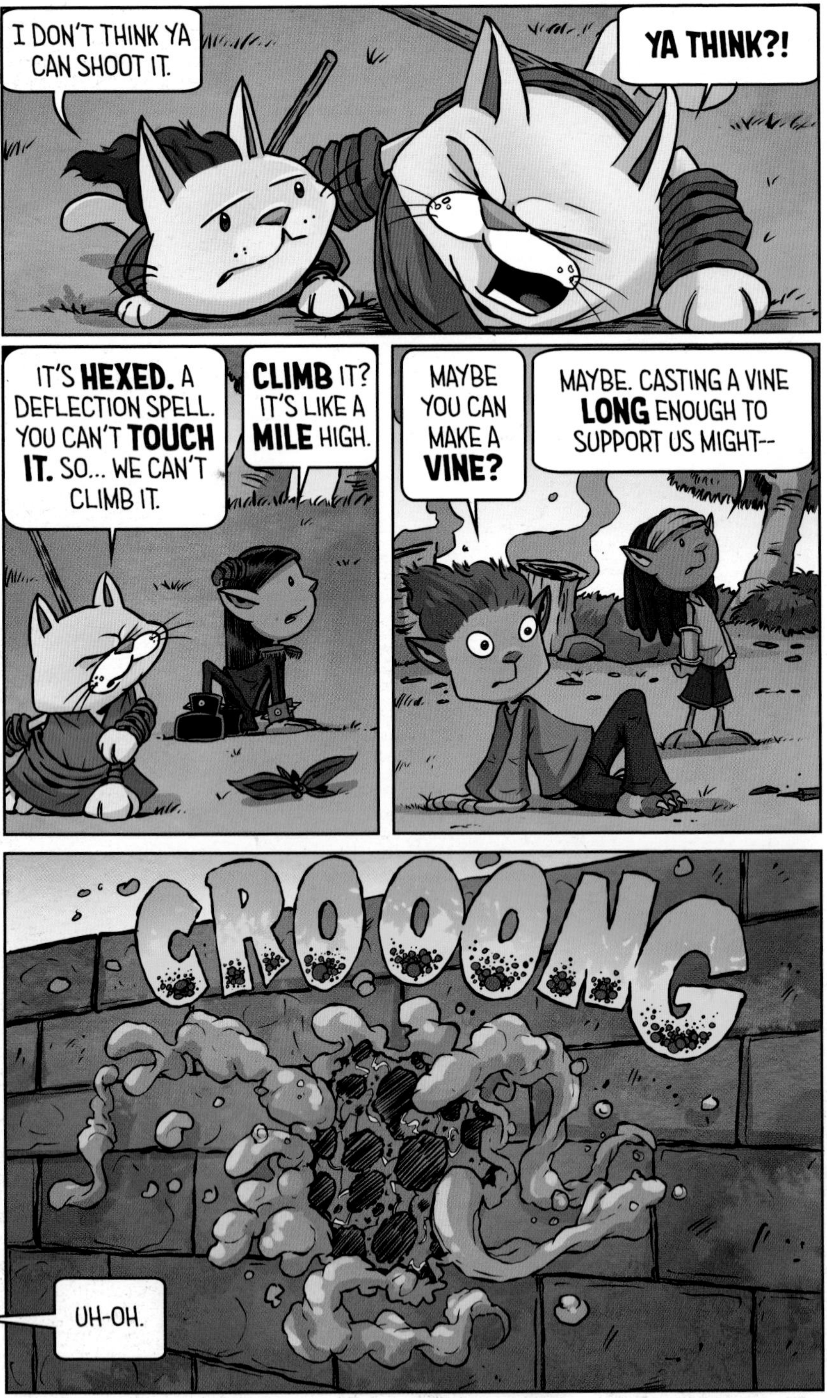
I DON'T THINK YA CAN SHOOT IT.
YA THINK?!
IT'S HEXED. A DEFLECTION SPELL. YOU CAN'T TOUCH IT. SO... WE CAN'T CLIMB IT.
CLIMB IT? IT'S LIKE A MILE HIGH.
MAYBE YOU CAN MAKE A VINE?
MAYBE. CASTING A VINE LONG ENOUGH TO SUPPORT US MIGHT--
CROOONG
UH-OH.

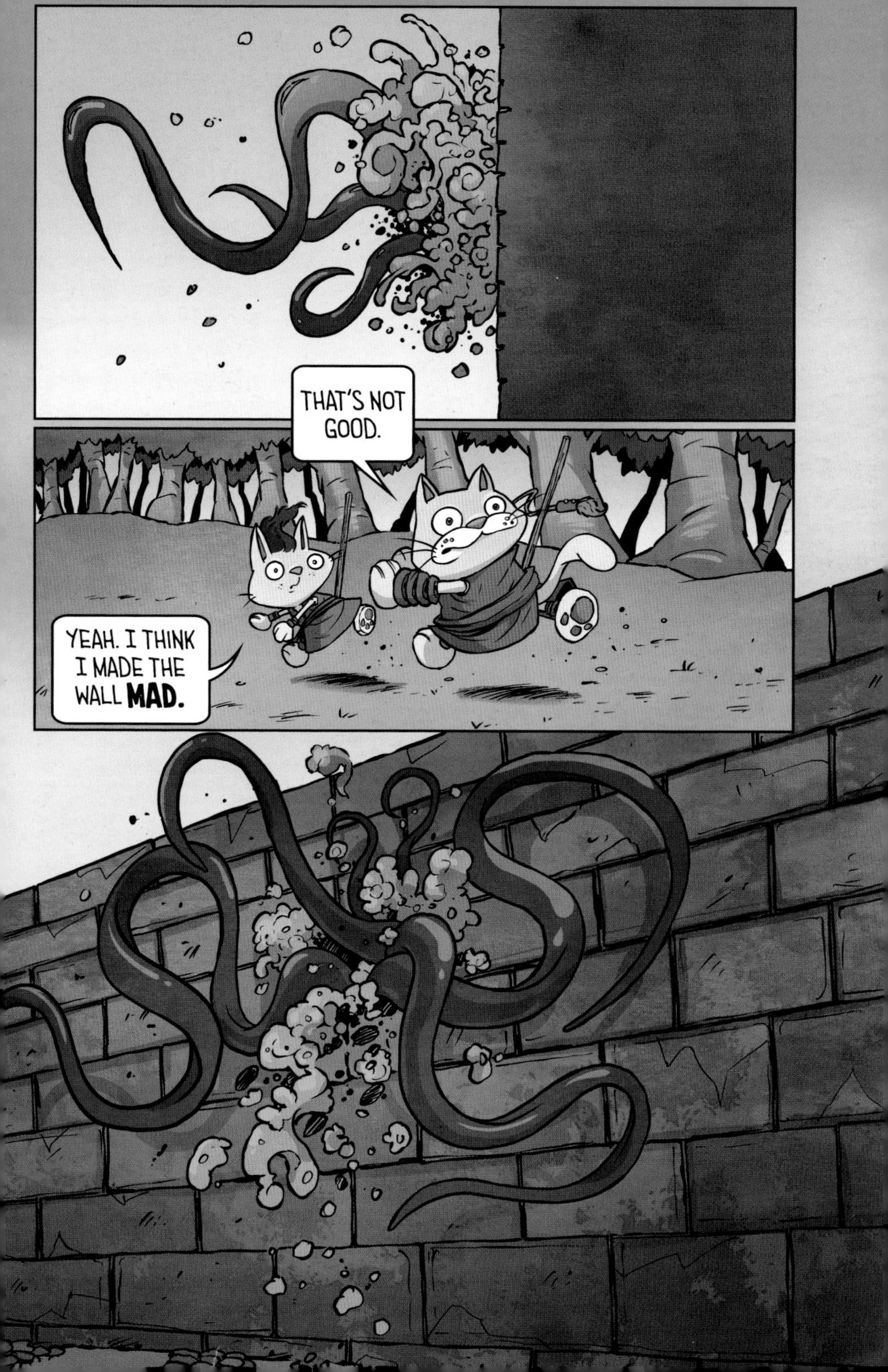
THAT'S NOT GOOD.
YEAH. I THINK I MADE THE WALL **MAD.**

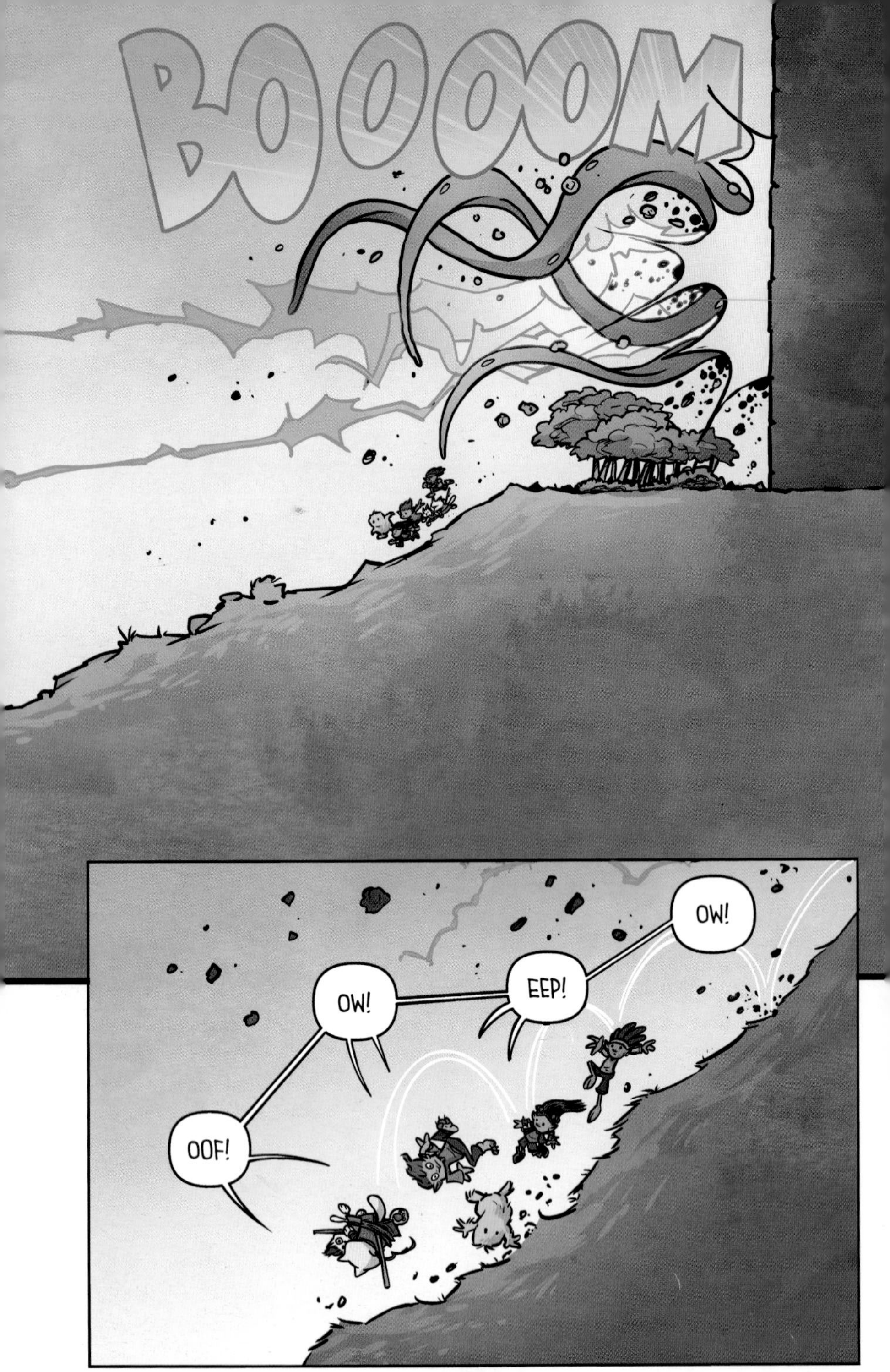
BOOOOM
OW!
EEP!
OW!
OOF!

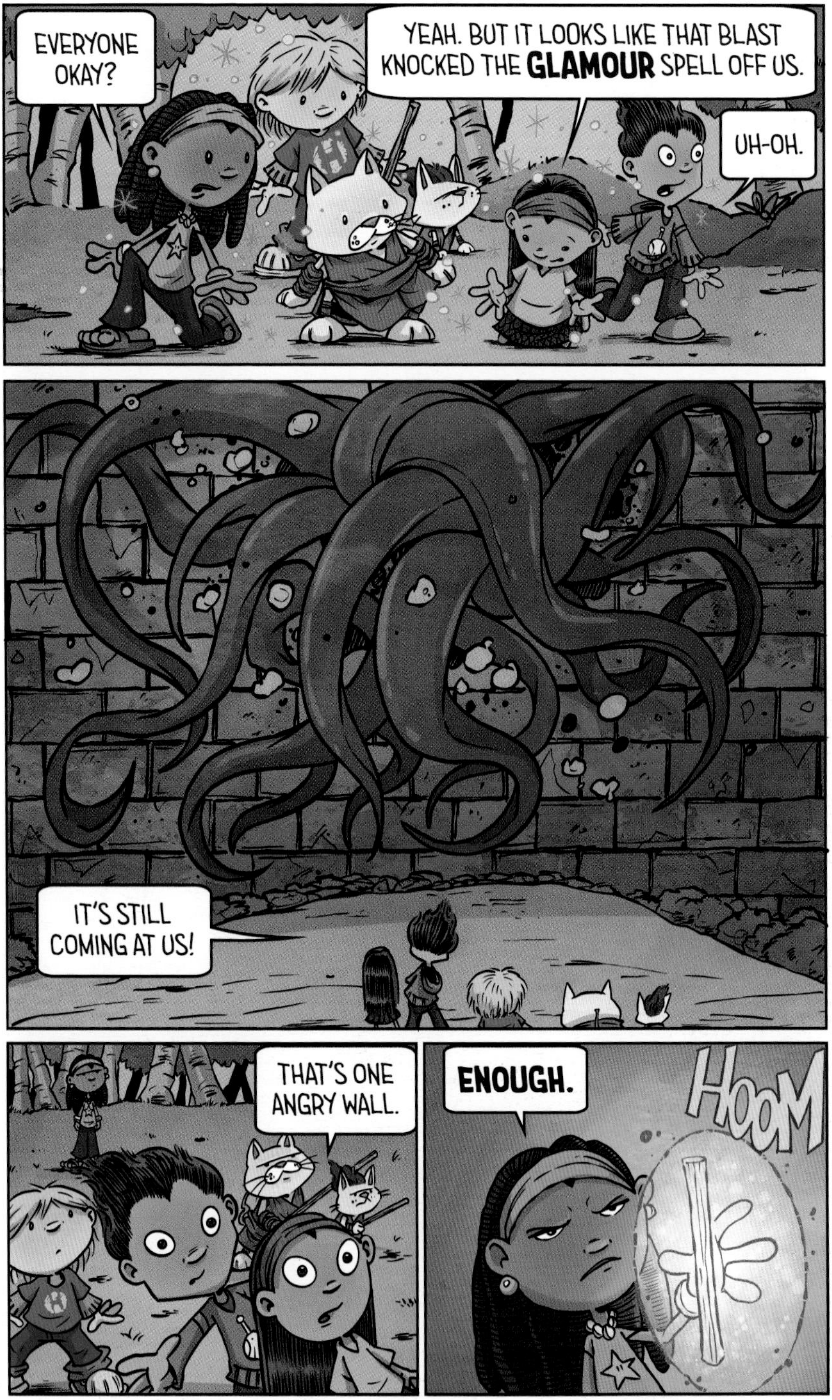
EVERYONE OKAY?
YEAH. BUT IT LOOKS LIKE THAT BLAST KNOCKED THE **GLAMOUR** SPELL OFF US.
UH-OH.
IT'S STILL COMING AT US!
THAT'S ONE ANGRY WALL.
ENOUGH.
HOOM

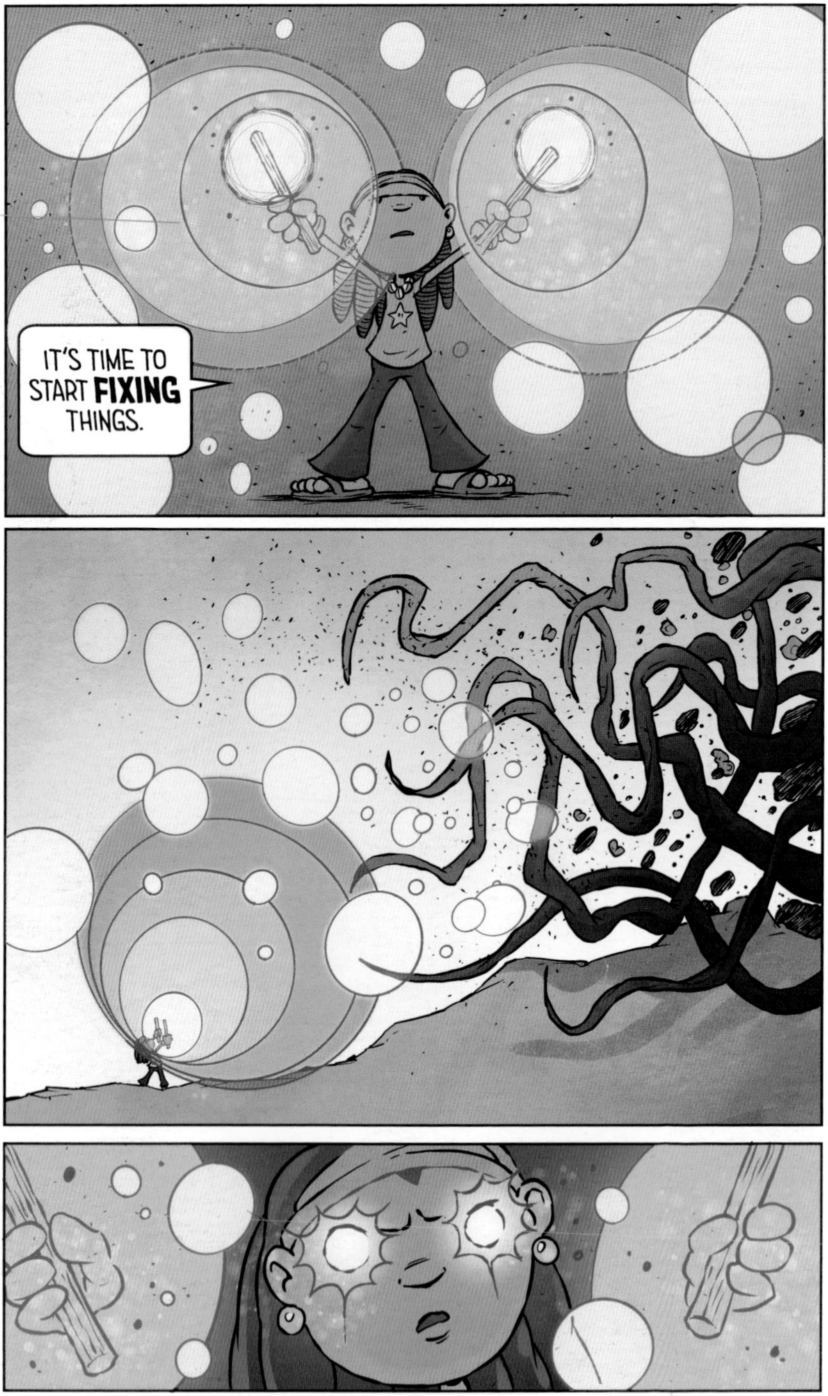
IT'S TIME TO START **FIXING** THINGS.

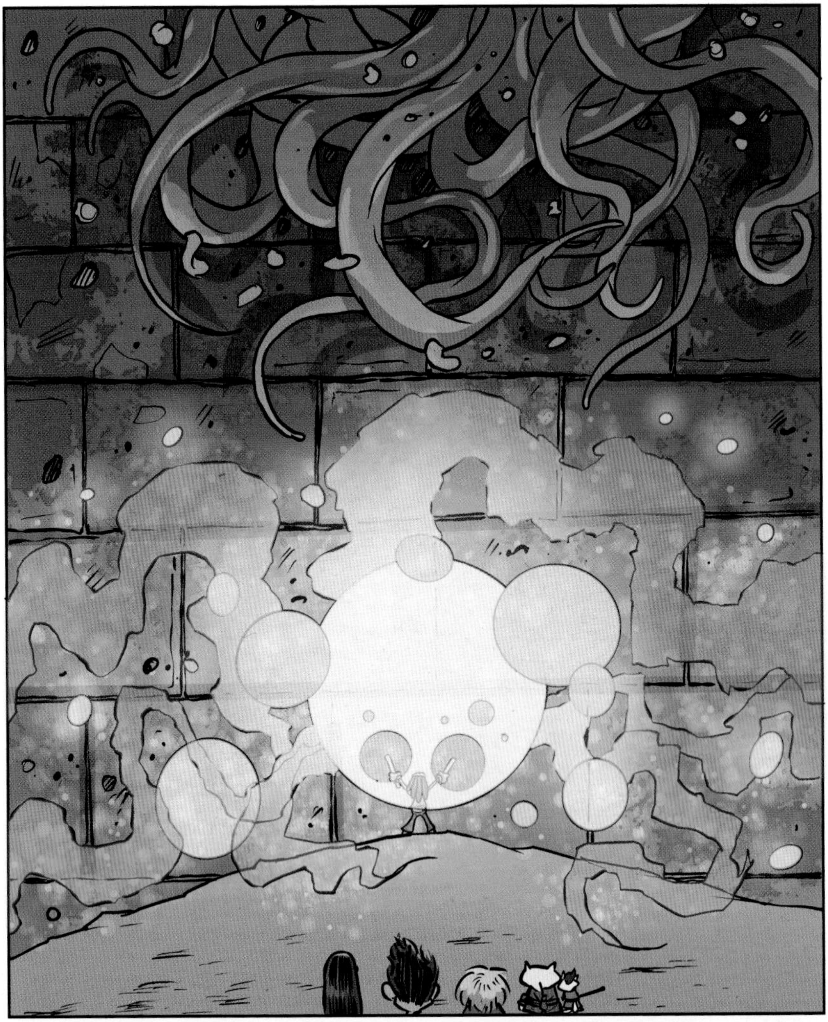

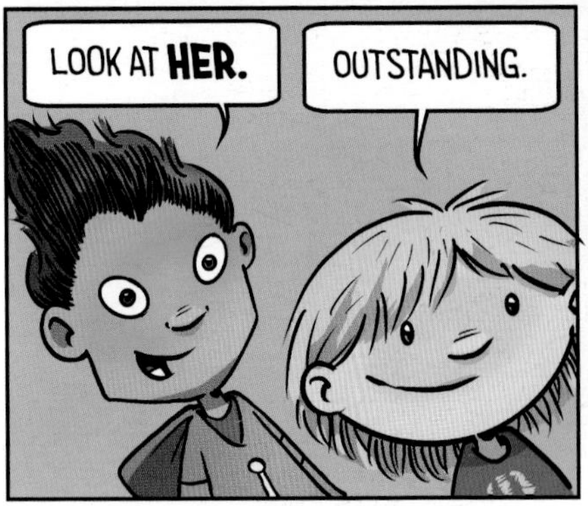
LOOK AT **HER.**
OUTSTANDING.

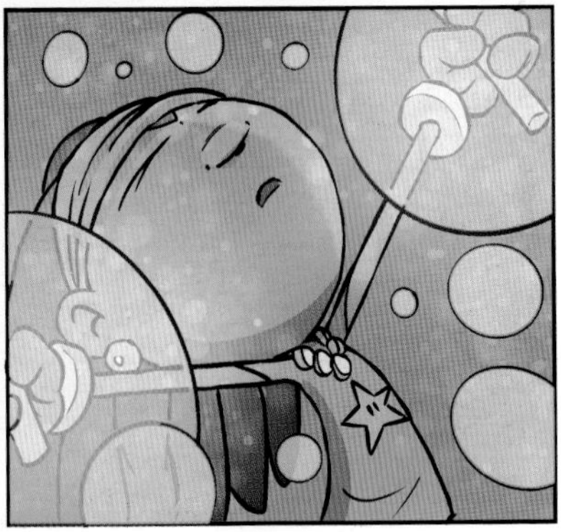

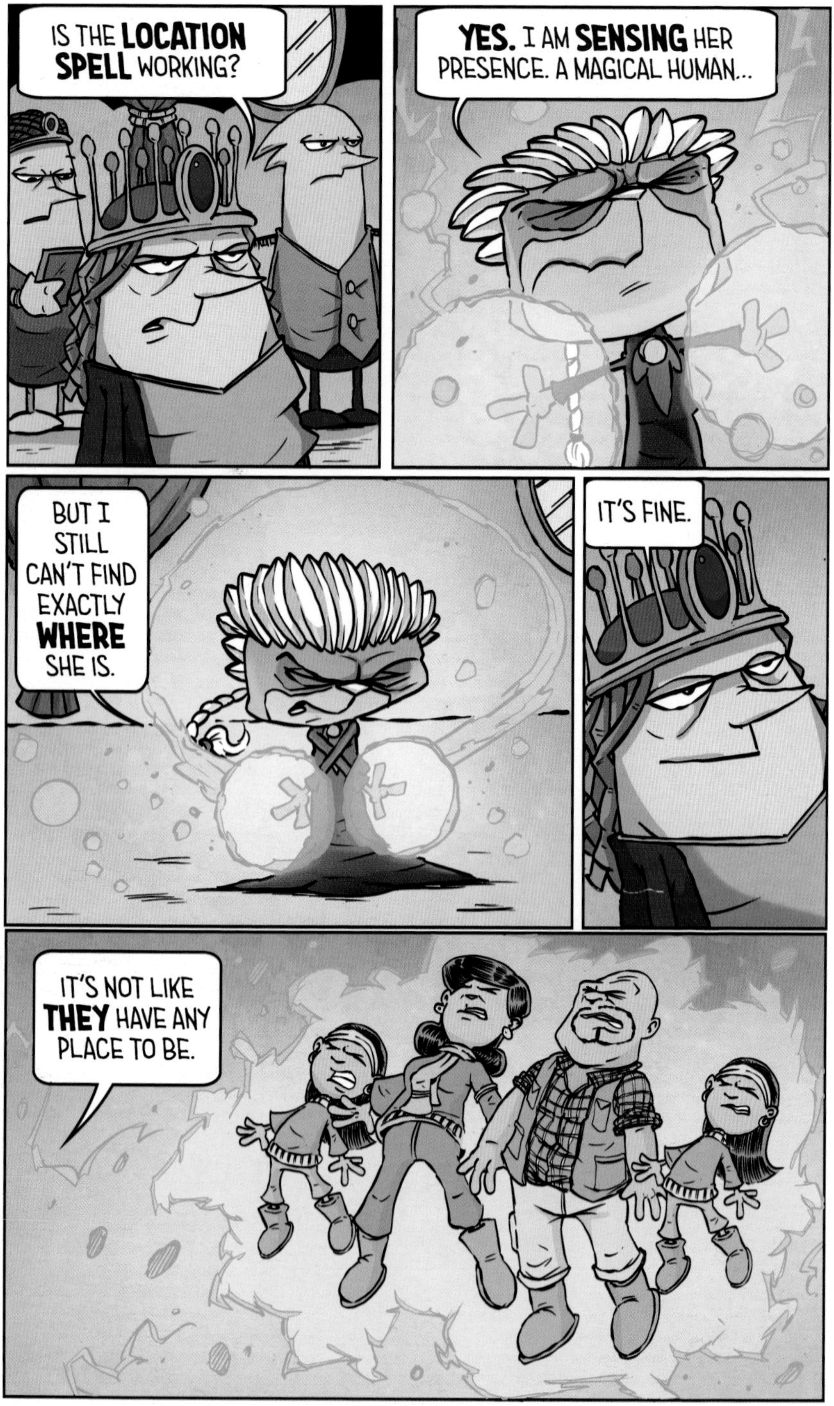
IS THE **LOCATION SPELL** WORKING?
YES. I AM **SENSING** HER PRESENCE. A MAGICAL HUMAN...
BUT I STILL CAN'T FIND EXACTLY **WHERE** SHE IS.
IT'S FINE.
IT'S NOT LIKE **THEY** HAVE ANY PLACE TO BE.

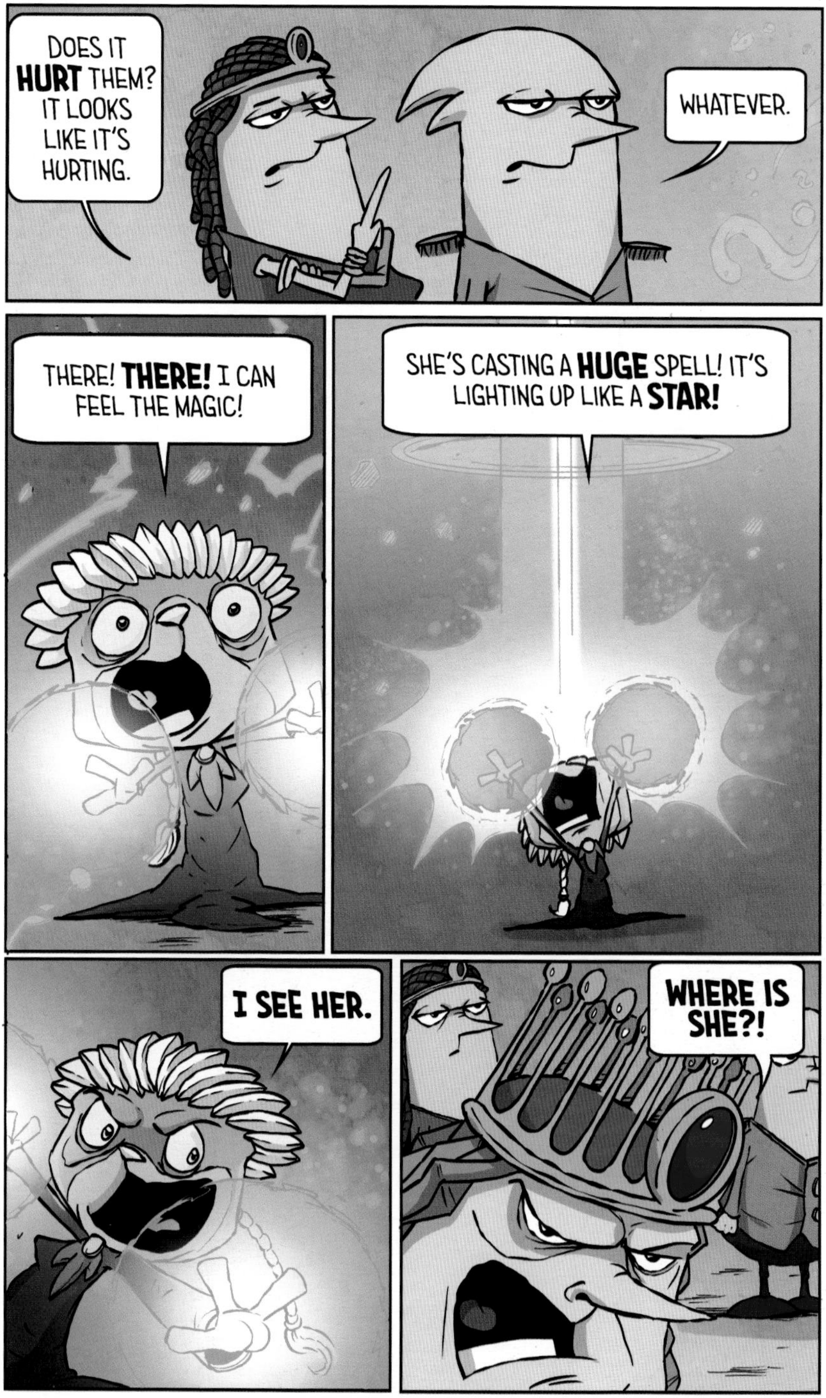
DOES IT **HURT** THEM? IT LOOKS LIKE IT'S HURTING.
WHATEVER.
THERE! **THERE!** I CAN FEEL THE MAGIC!
SHE'S CASTING A **HUGE** SPELL! IT'S LIGHTING UP LIKE A **STAR!**
I SEE HER.
WHERE IS SHE?!

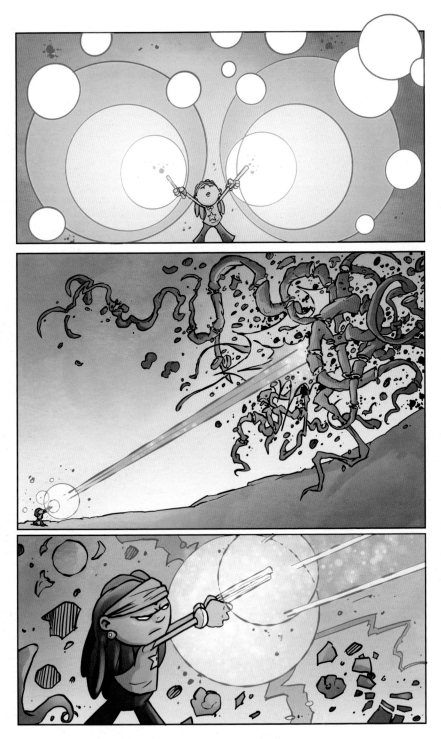

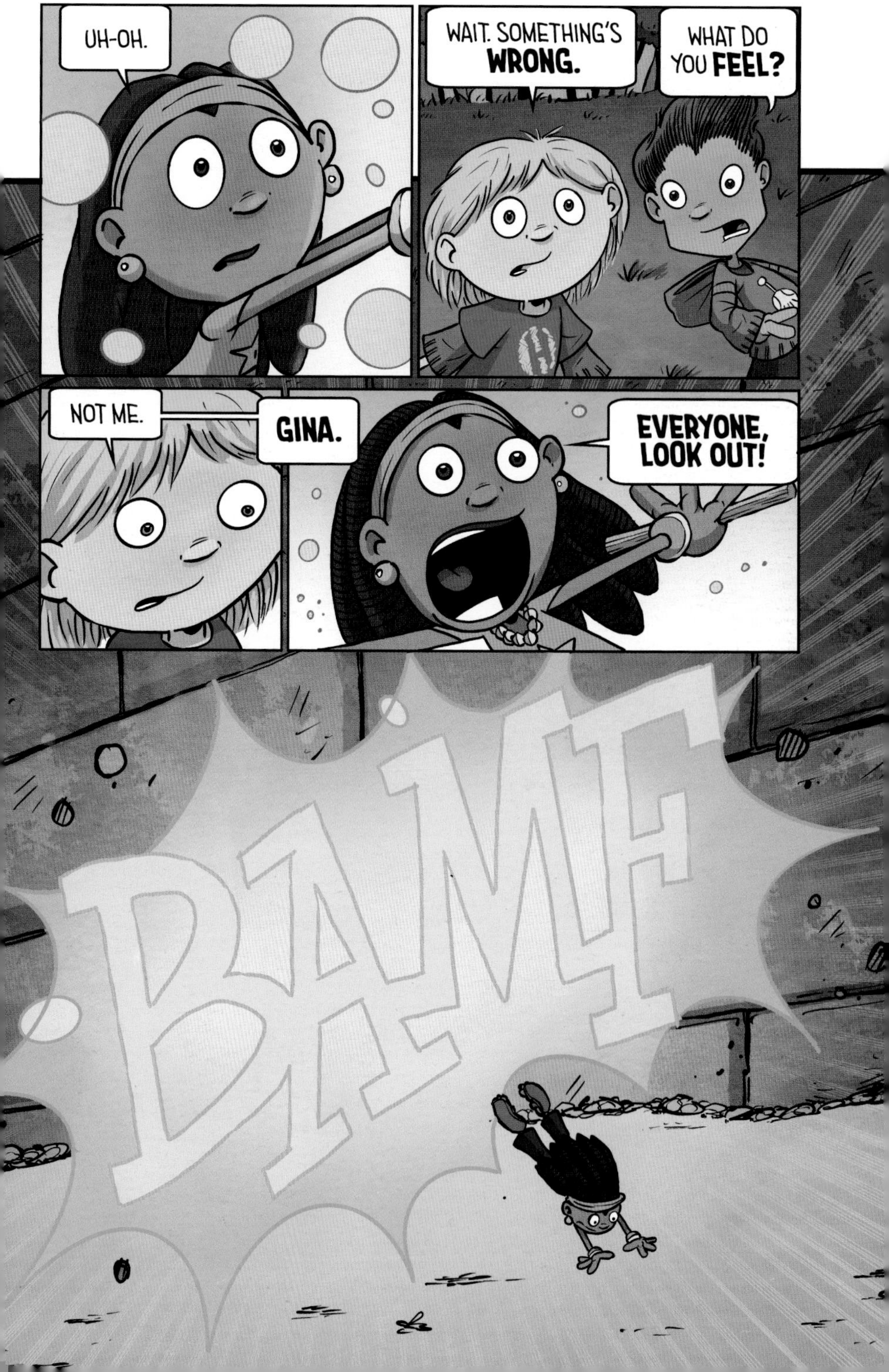
UH-OH.
WAIT. SOMETHING'S WRONG.
WHAT DO YOU FEEL?
NOT ME.
GINA.
EVERYONE, LOOK OUT!
BAMF

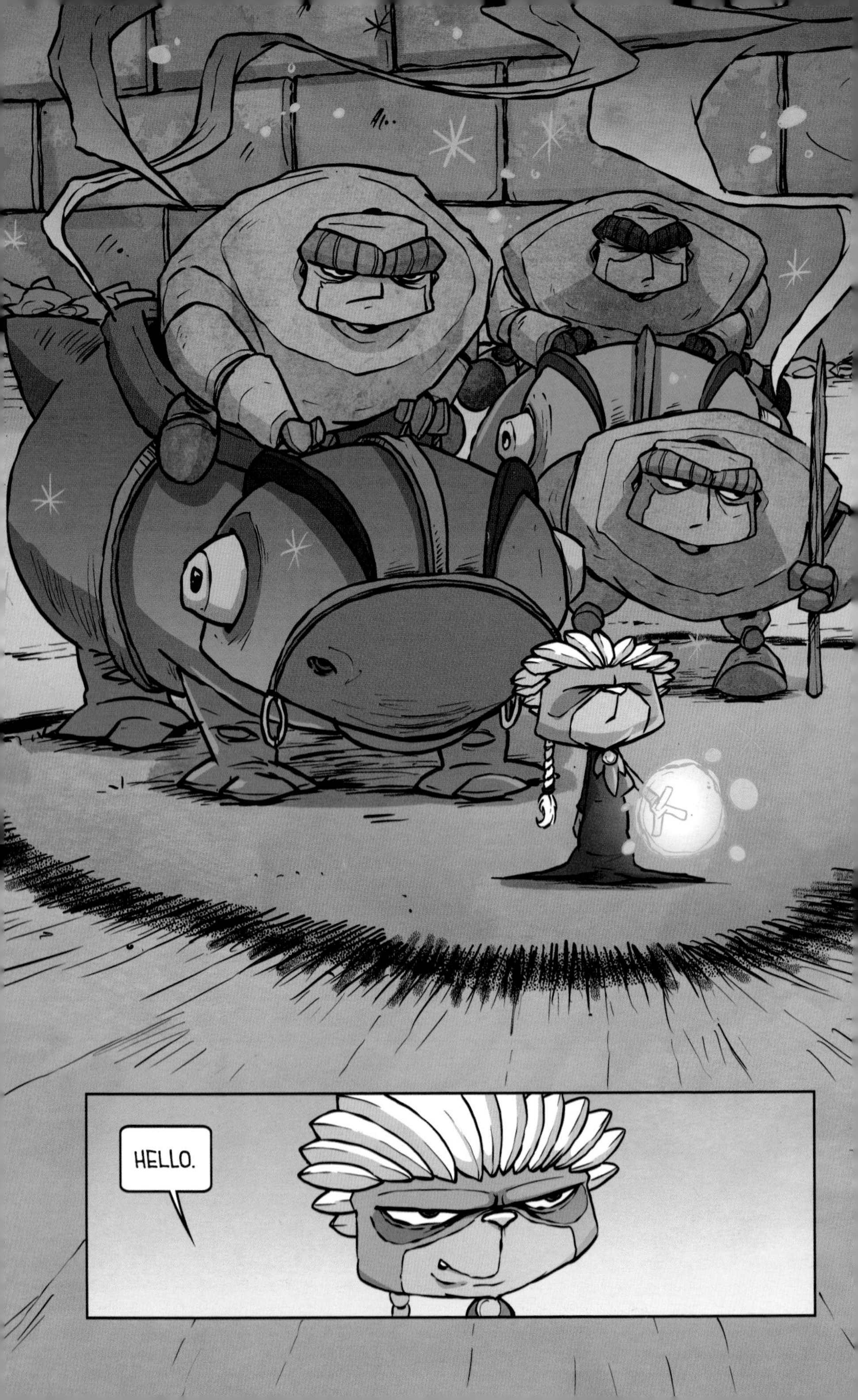
HELLO.

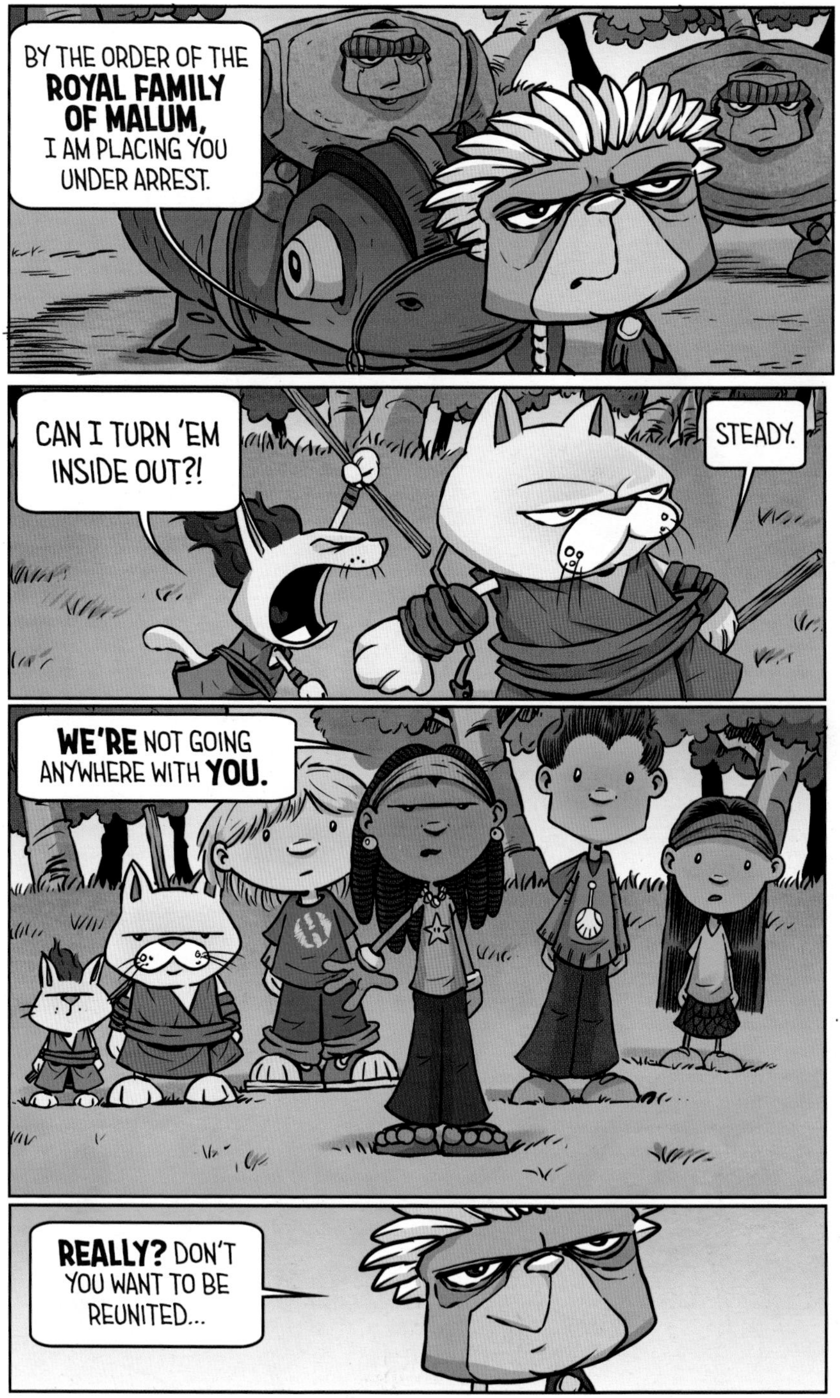
BY THE ORDER OF THE **ROYAL FAMILY OF MALUM,** I AM PLACING YOU UNDER ARREST.
CAN I TURN 'EM INSIDE OUT?!
STEADY.
WE'RE NOT GOING ANYWHERE WITH **YOU.**
REALLY? DON'T YOU WANT TO BE REUNITED...

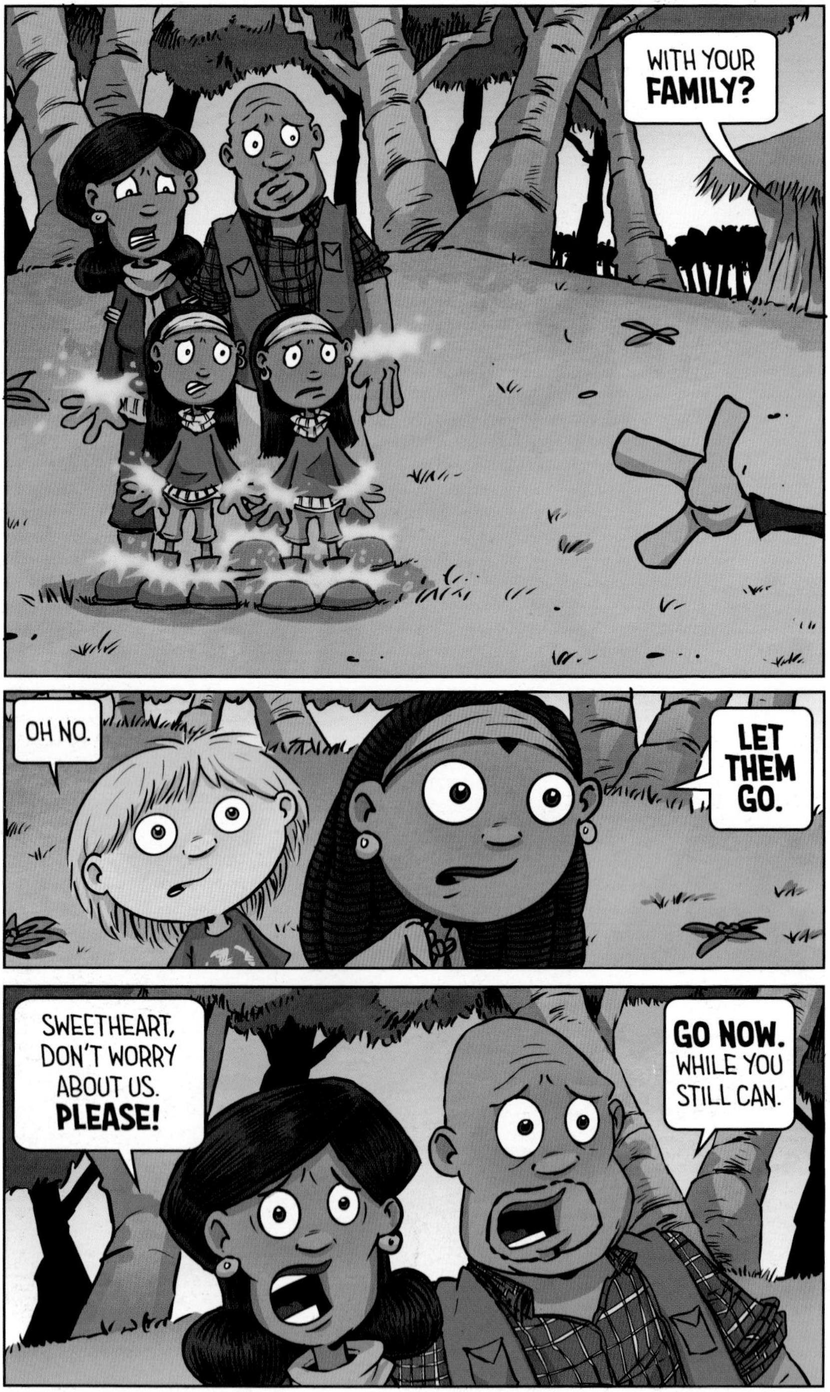
WITH YOUR FAMILY?
OH NO.
LET THEM GO.
SWEETHEART, DON'T WORRY ABOUT US. PLEASE!
GO NOW. WHILE YOU STILL CAN.

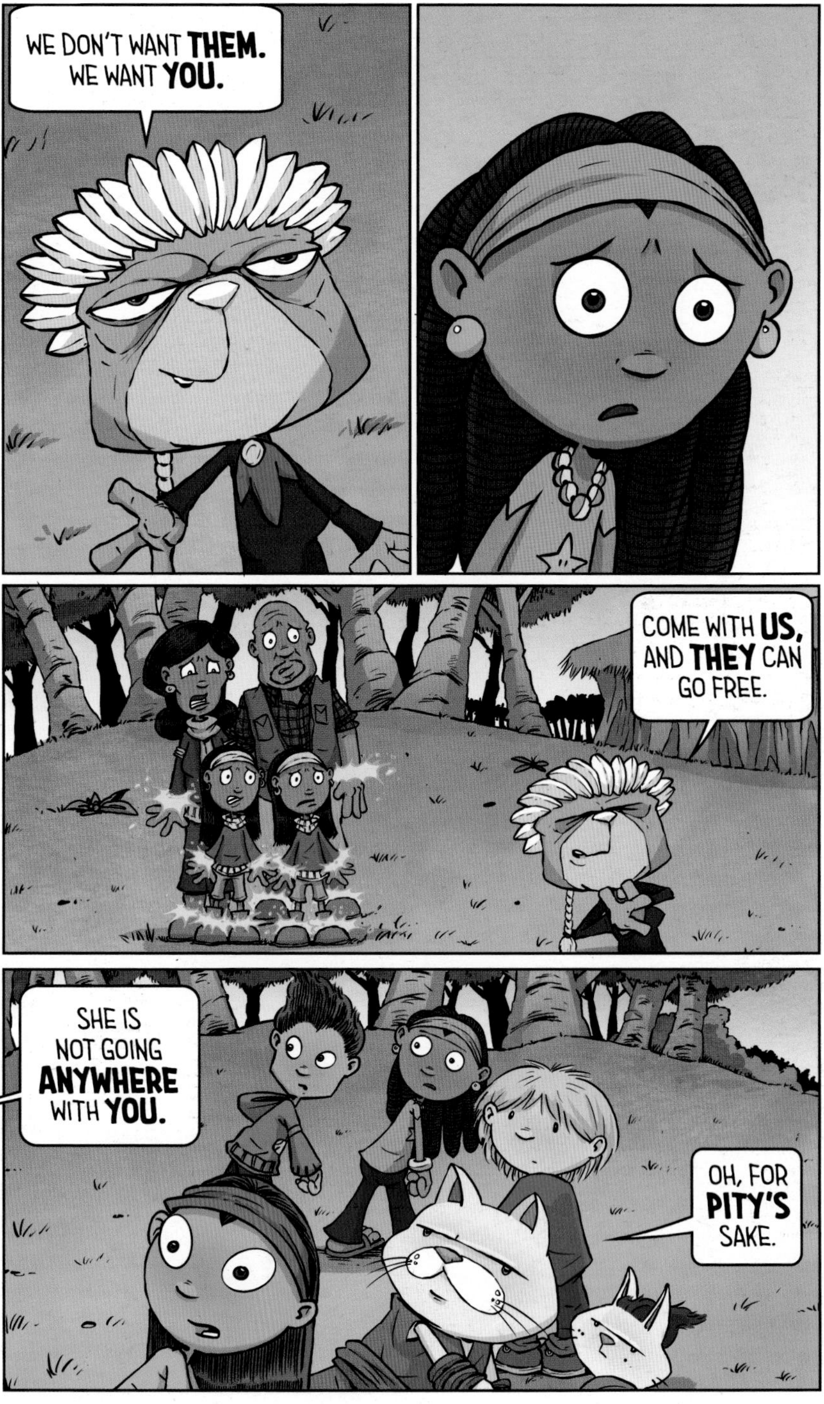
WE DON'T WANT **THEM.** WE WANT **YOU.**
COME WITH **US,** AND **THEY** CAN GO FREE.
SHE IS NOT GOING **ANYWHERE** WITH **YOU.**
OH, FOR **PITY'S** SAKE.

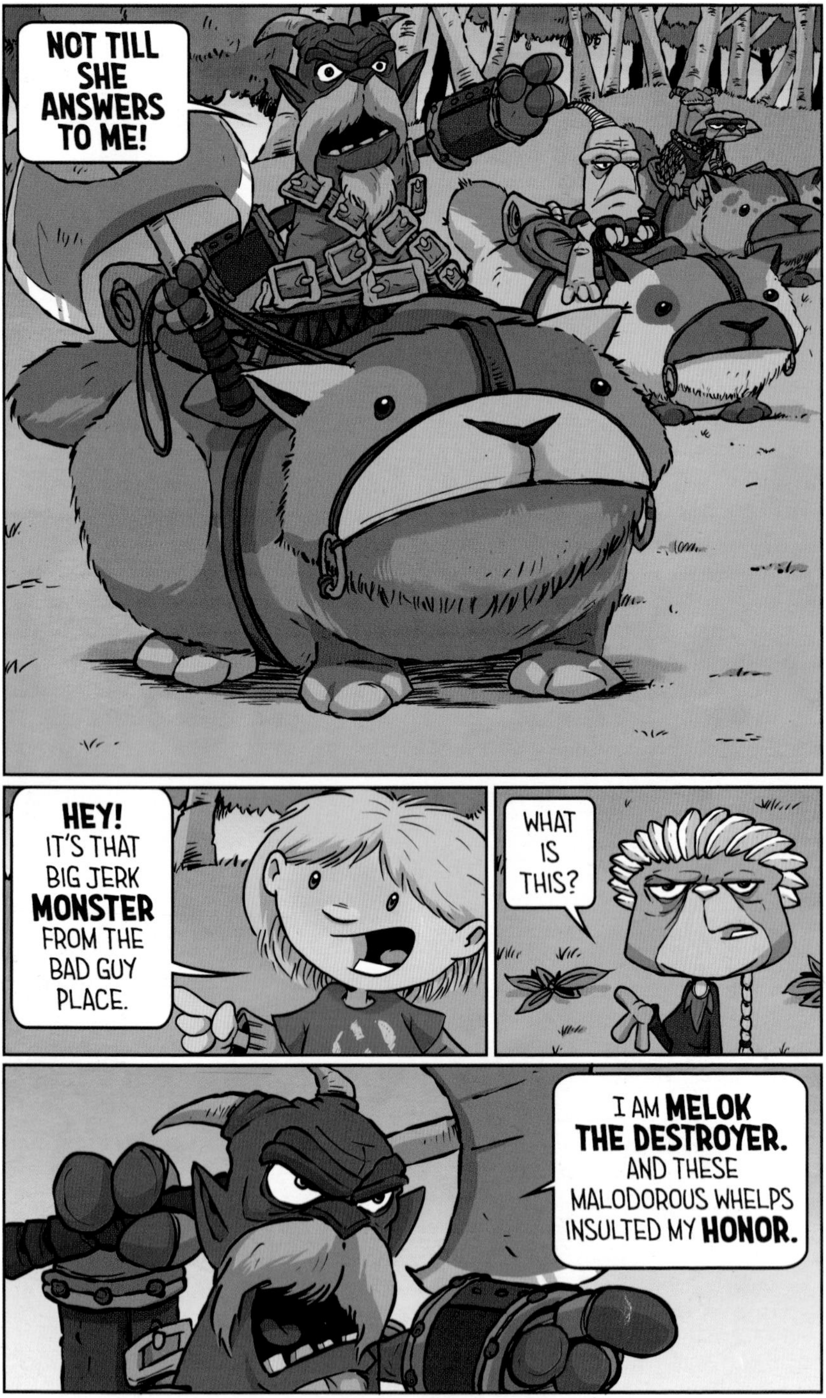
NOT TILL SHE ANSWERS TO ME!
HEY! IT'S THAT BIG JERK MONSTER FROM THE BAD GUY PLACE.
WHAT IS THIS?
I AM MELOK THE DESTROYER. AND THESE MALODOROUS WHELPS INSULTED MY HONOR.

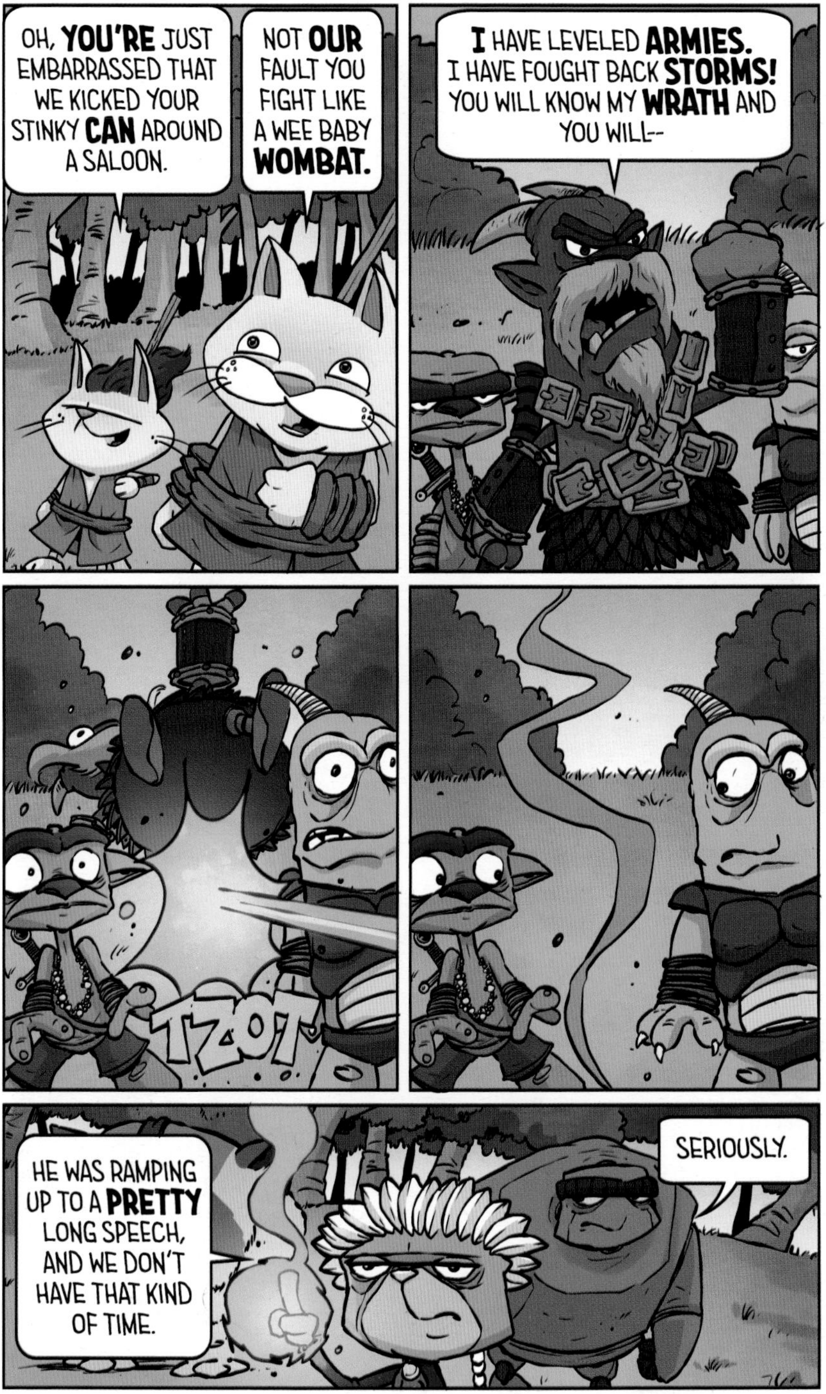
OH, **YOU'RE** JUST EMBARRASSED THAT WE KICKED YOUR STINKY **CAN** AROUND A SALOON.
NOT **OUR** FAULT YOU FIGHT LIKE A WEE BABY **WOMBAT.**
I HAVE LEVELED **ARMIES.** I HAVE FOUGHT BACK **STORMS!** YOU WILL KNOW MY **WRATH** AND YOU WILL--
TZOT
HE WAS RAMPING UP TO A **PRETTY** LONG SPEECH, AND WE DON'T HAVE THAT KIND OF TIME.
SERIOUSLY.

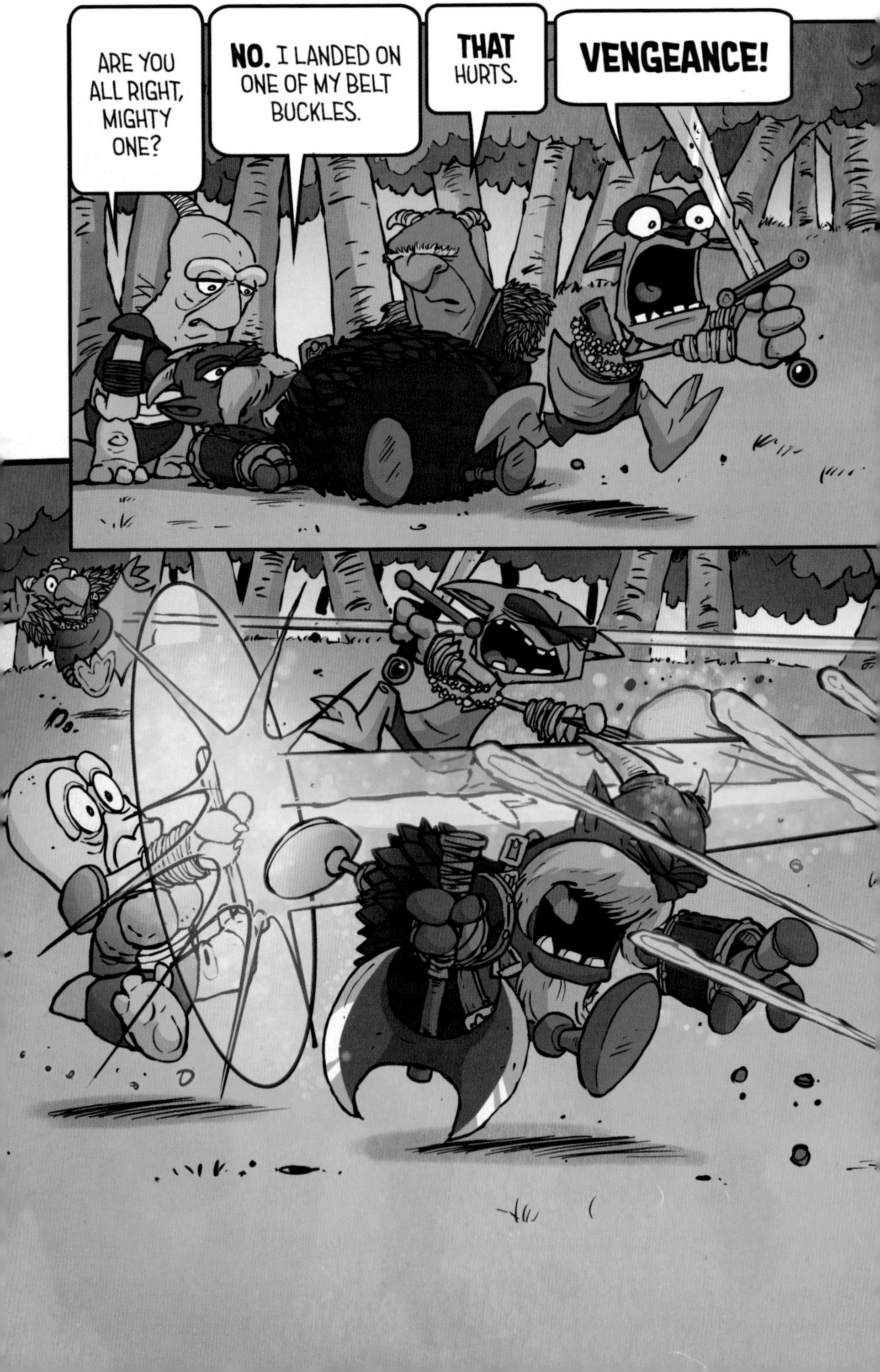
ARE YOU ALL RIGHT, MIGHTY ONE?
NO. I LANDED ON ONE OF MY BELT BUCKLES.
THAT HURTS.
VENGEANCE!

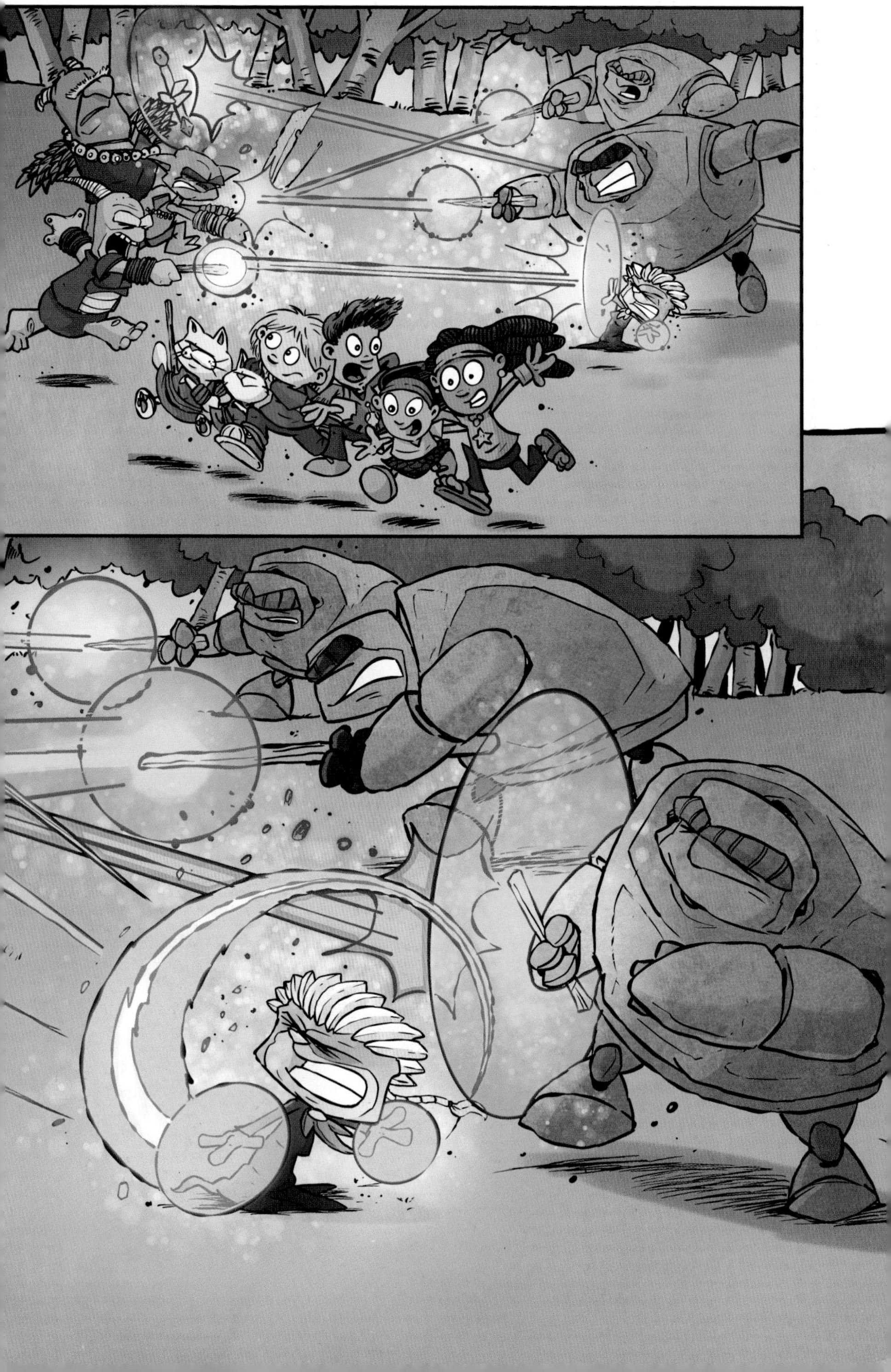

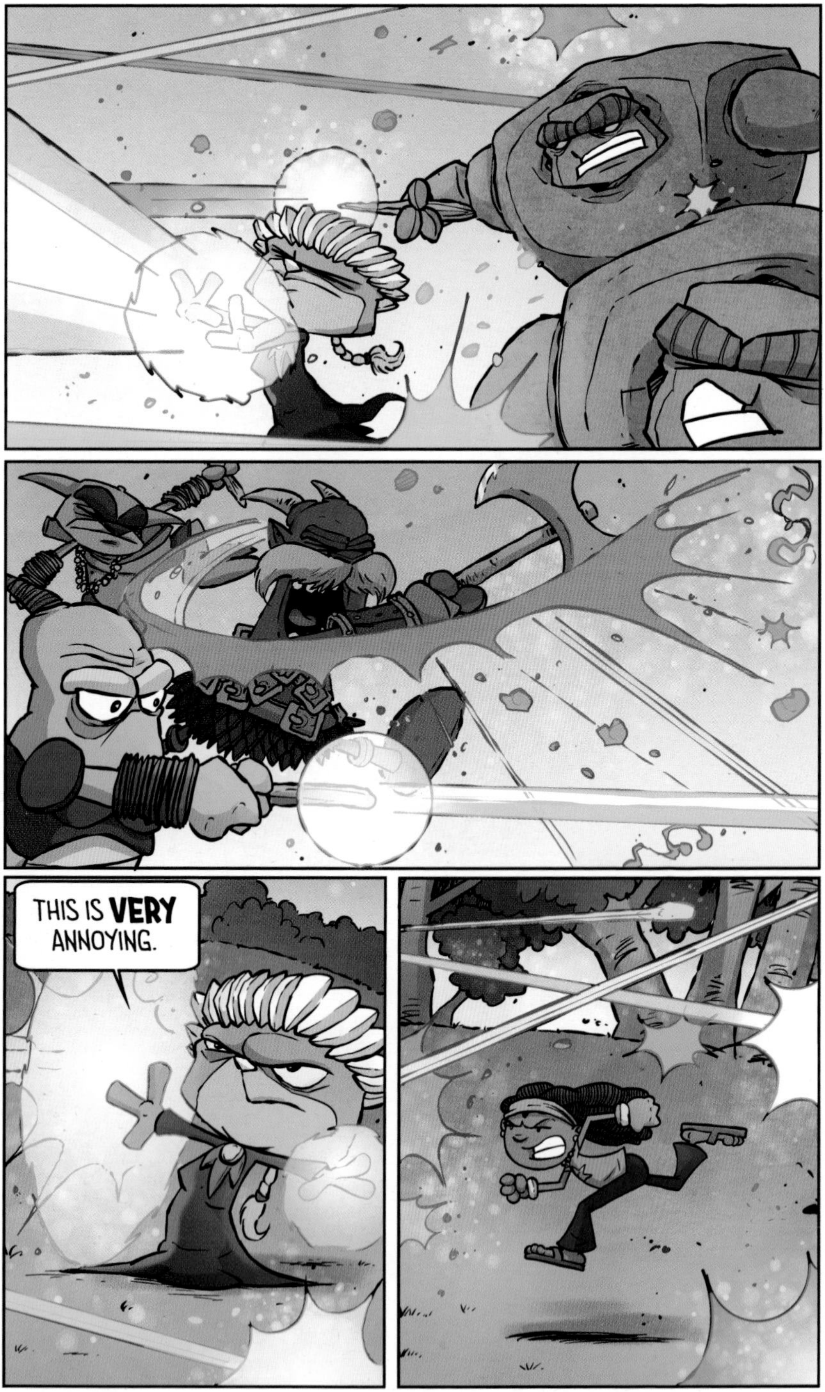
THIS IS **VERY** ANNOYING.

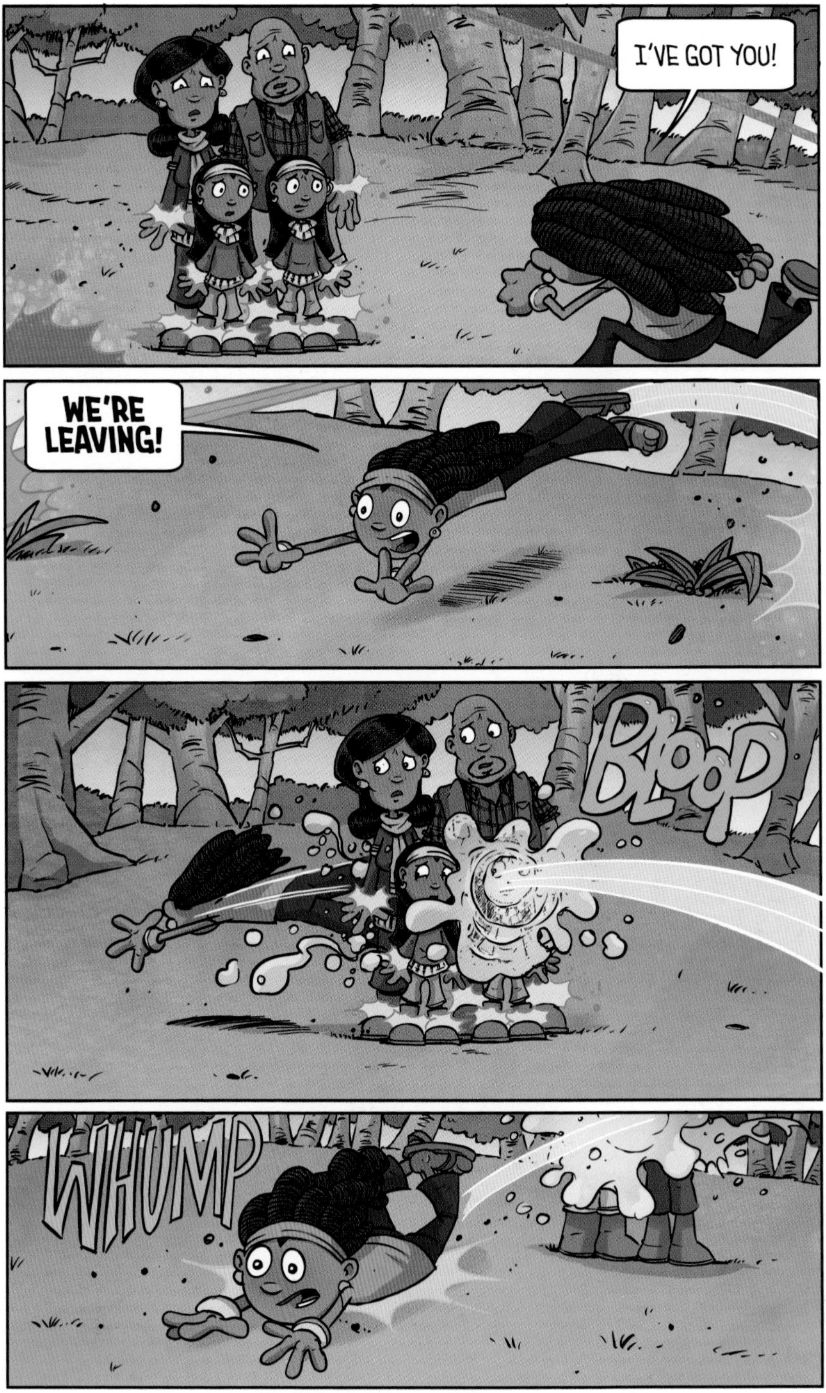
I'VE GOT YOU!
WE'RE LEAVING!
BLOOP
WHUMP

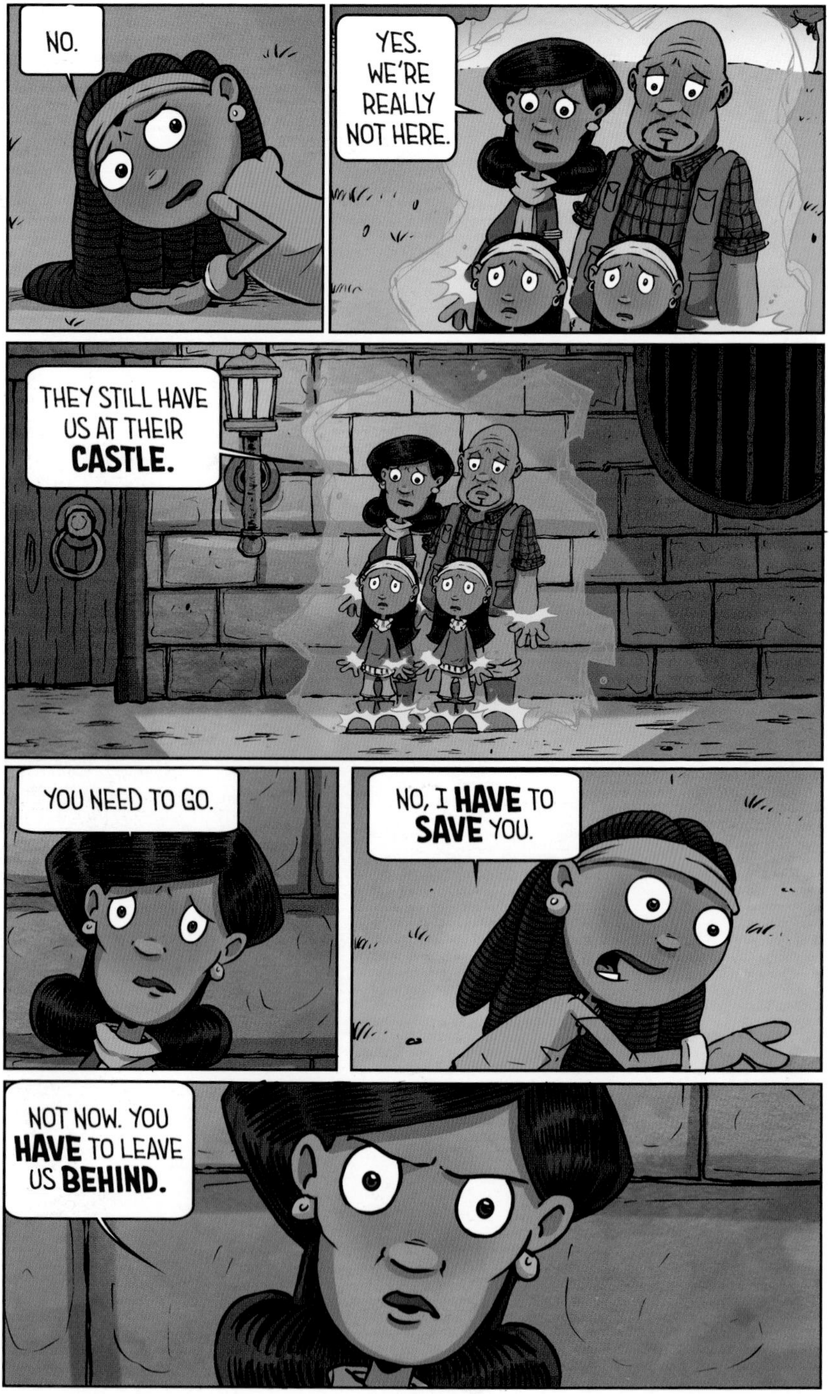
NO.
YES. WE'RE REALLY NOT HERE.
THEY STILL HAVE US AT THEIR **CASTLE.**
YOU NEED TO GO.
NO, I **HAVE** TO **SAVE** YOU.
NOT NOW. YOU **HAVE** TO LEAVE US **BEHIND.**

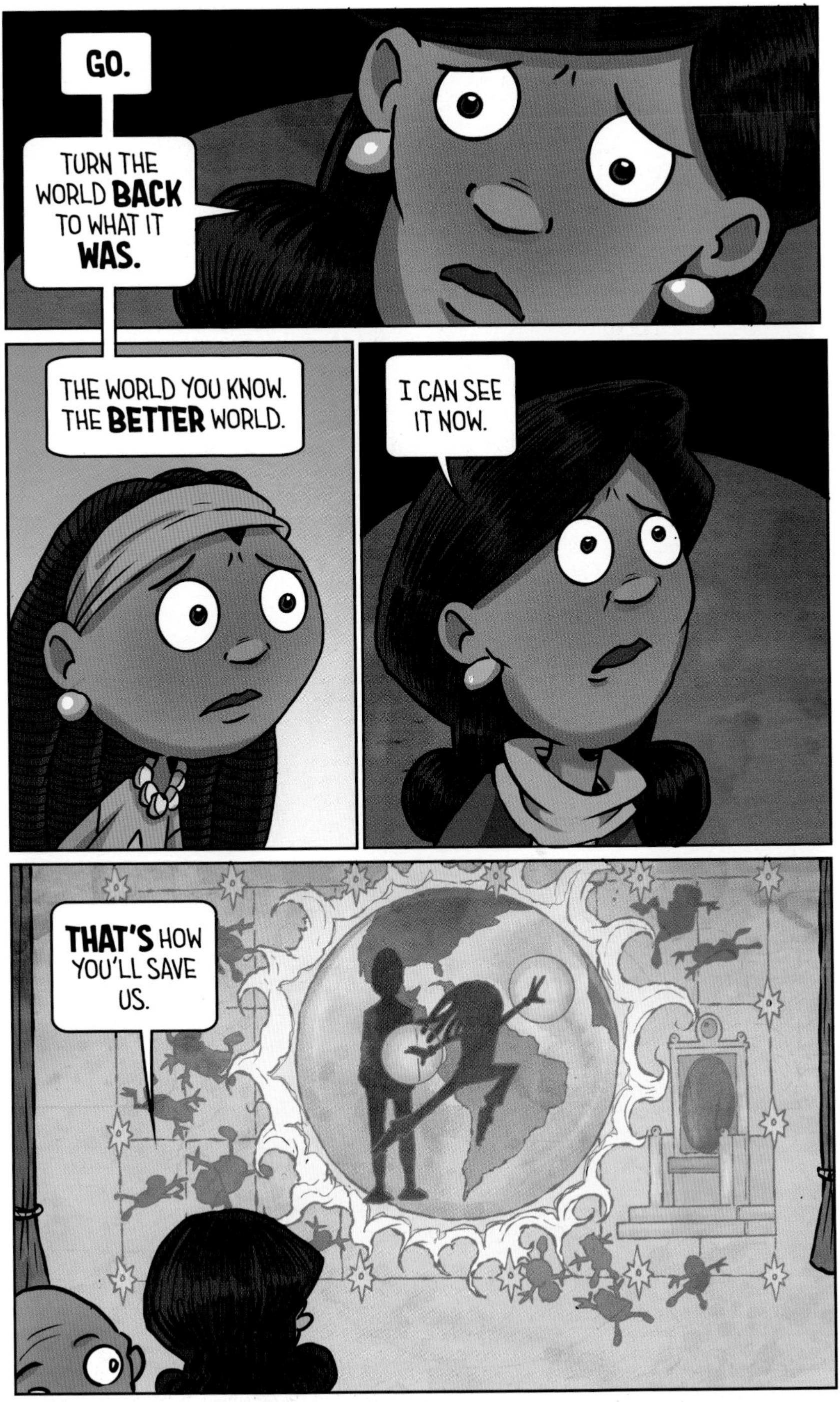
GO.
TURN THE WORLD BACK TO WHAT IT WAS.
THE WORLD YOU KNOW. THE BETTER WORLD.
I CAN SEE IT NOW.
THAT'S HOW YOU'LL SAVE US.

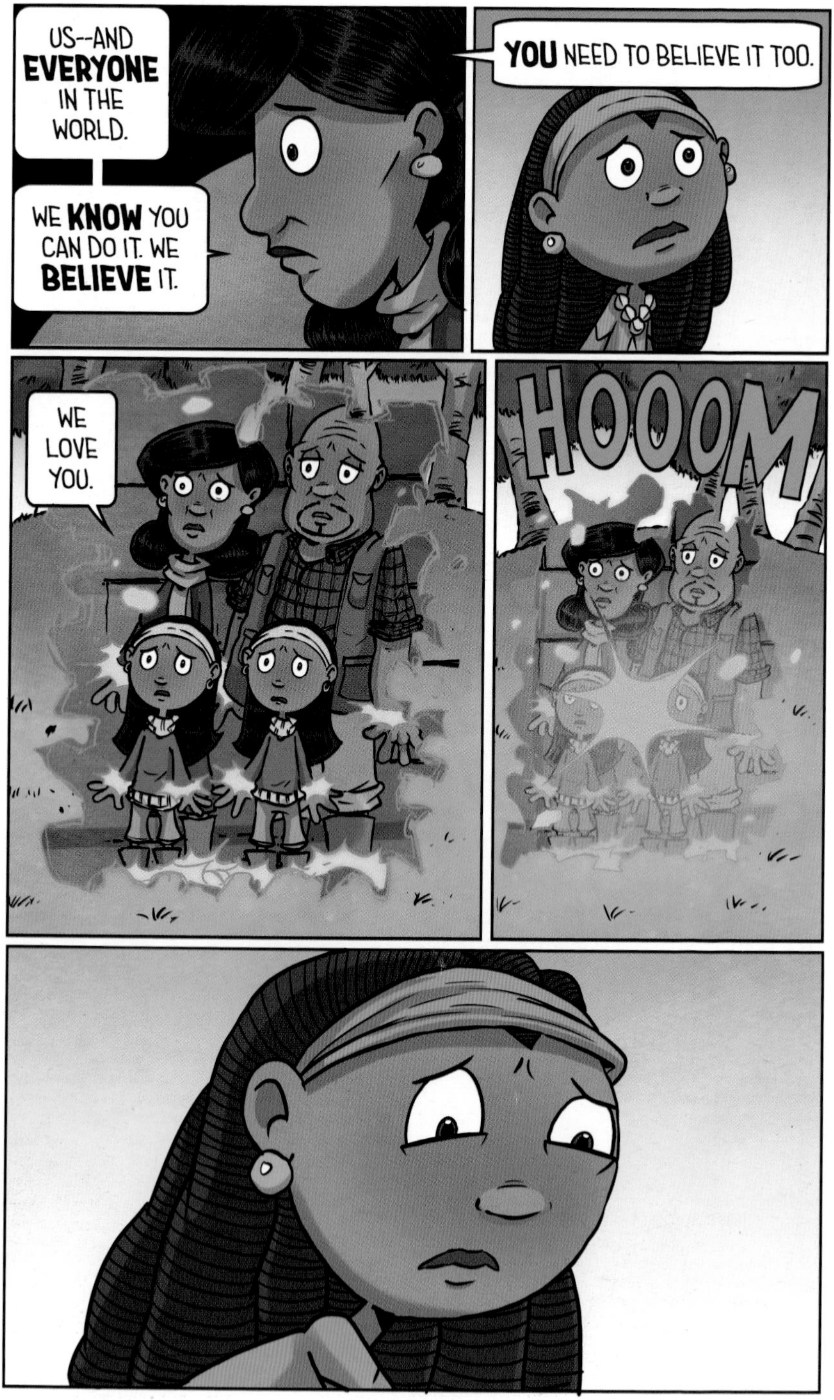
US--AND EVERYONE IN THE WORLD.
WE KNOW YOU CAN DO IT. WE BELIEVE IT.
YOU NEED TO BELIEVE IT TOO.
WE LOVE YOU.
HOOOM

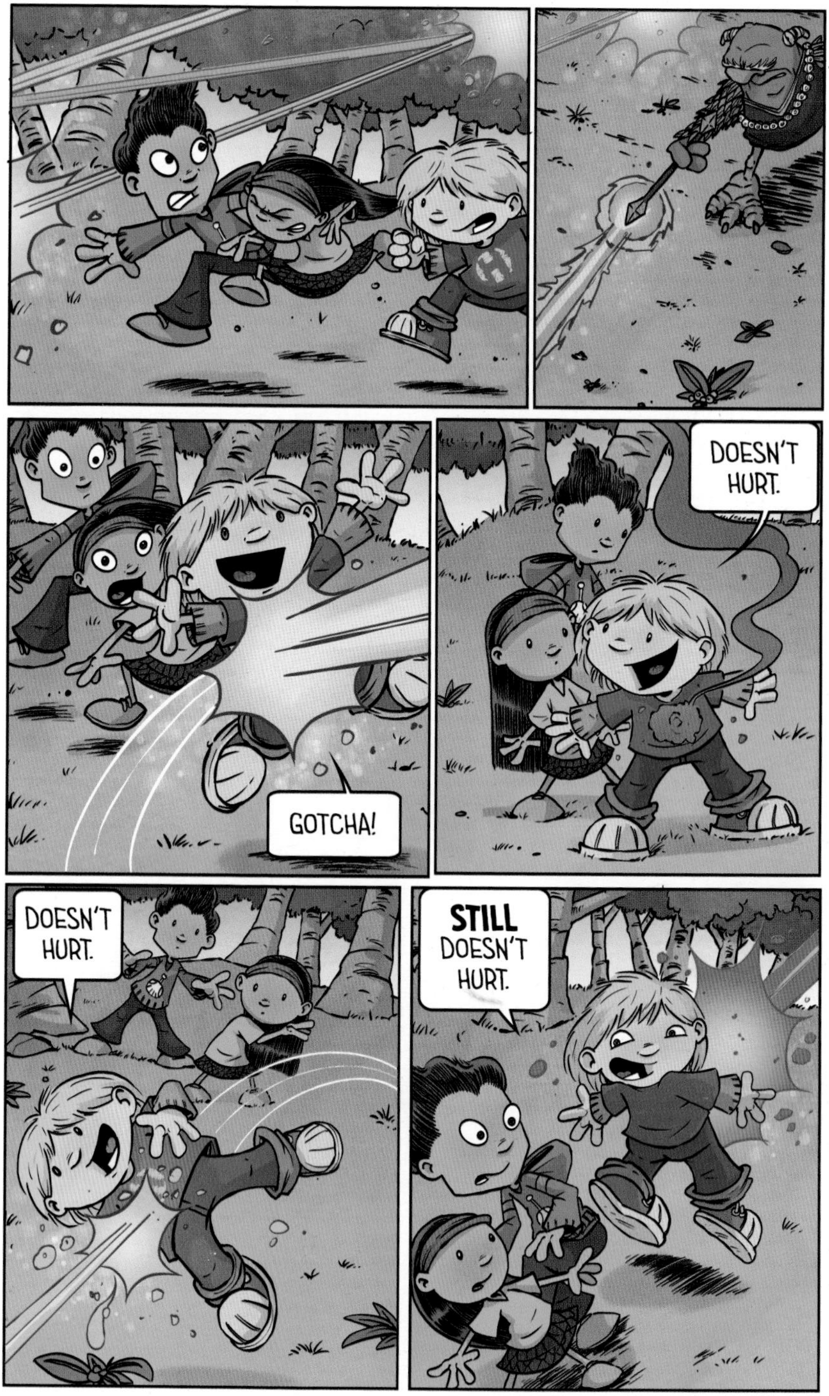
GOTCHA!
DOESN'T HURT.
DOESN'T HURT.
STILL DOESN'T HURT.

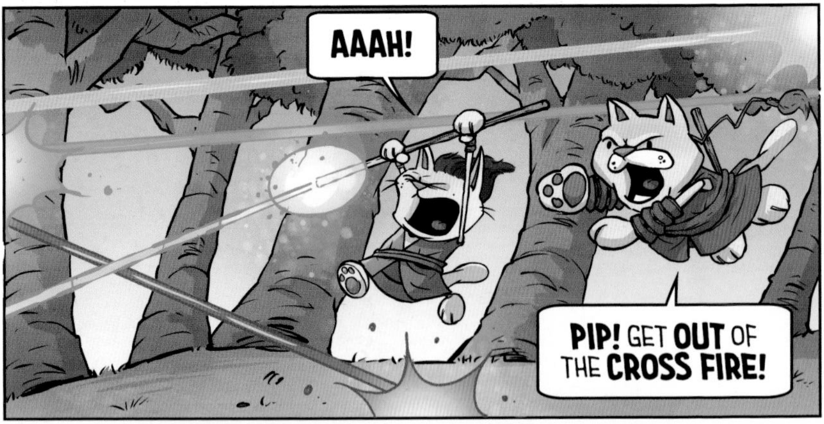
AAAH!
PIP! GET OUT OF THE CROSS FIRE!

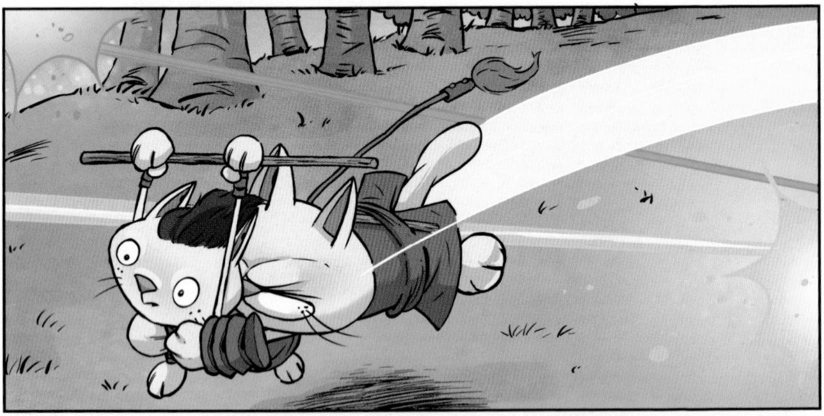

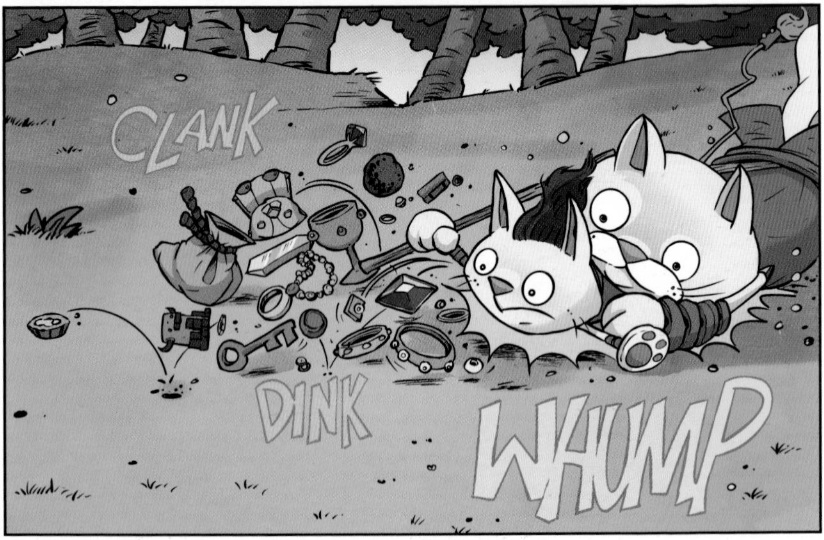
CLANK
DINK
WHUMP

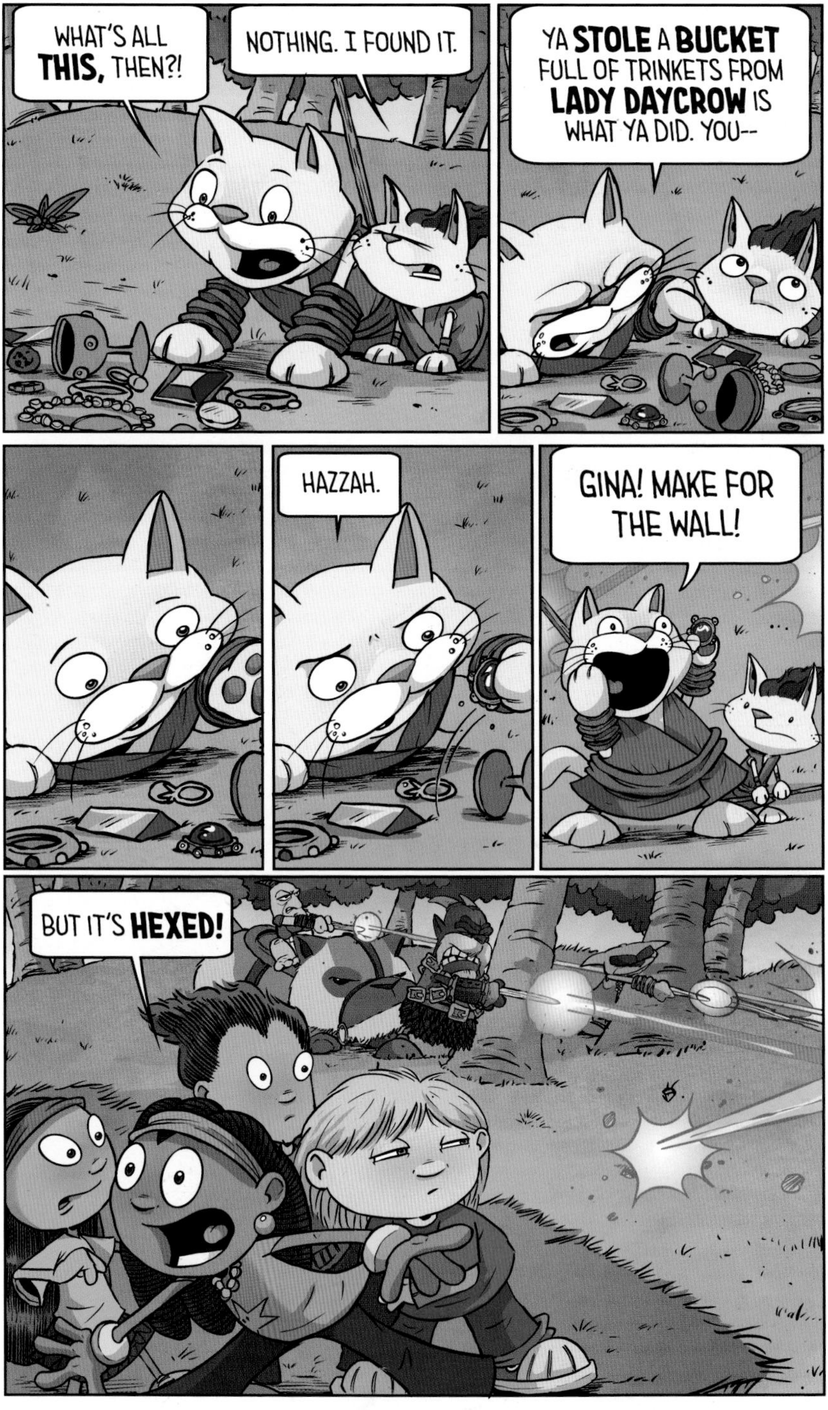
WHAT'S ALL THIS, THEN?!
NOTHING. I FOUND IT.
YA STOLE A BUCKET FULL OF TRINKETS FROM LADY DAYCROW IS WHAT YA DID. YOU--
HAZZAH.
GINA! MAKE FOR THE WALL!
BUT IT'S HEXED!

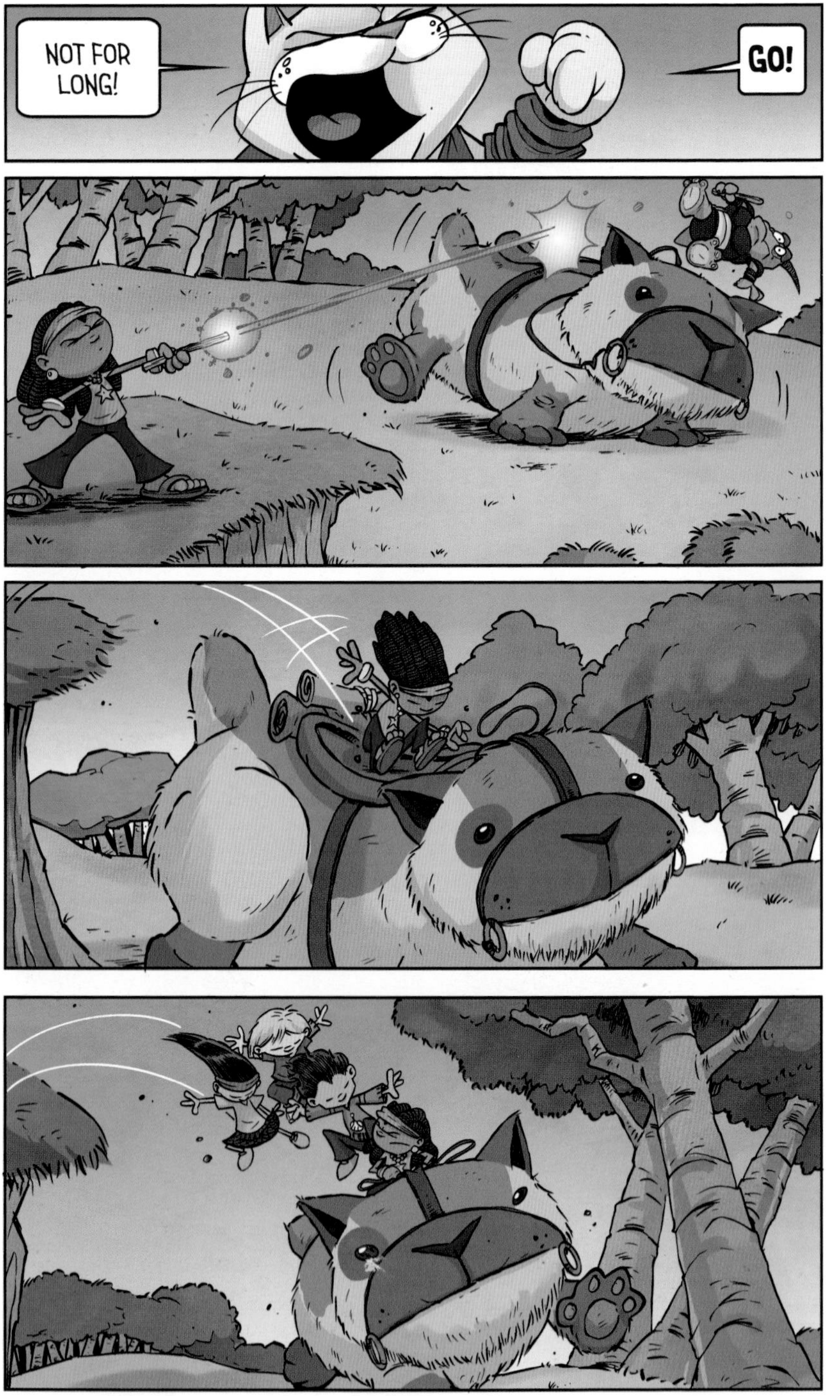
NOT FOR LONG!
GO!

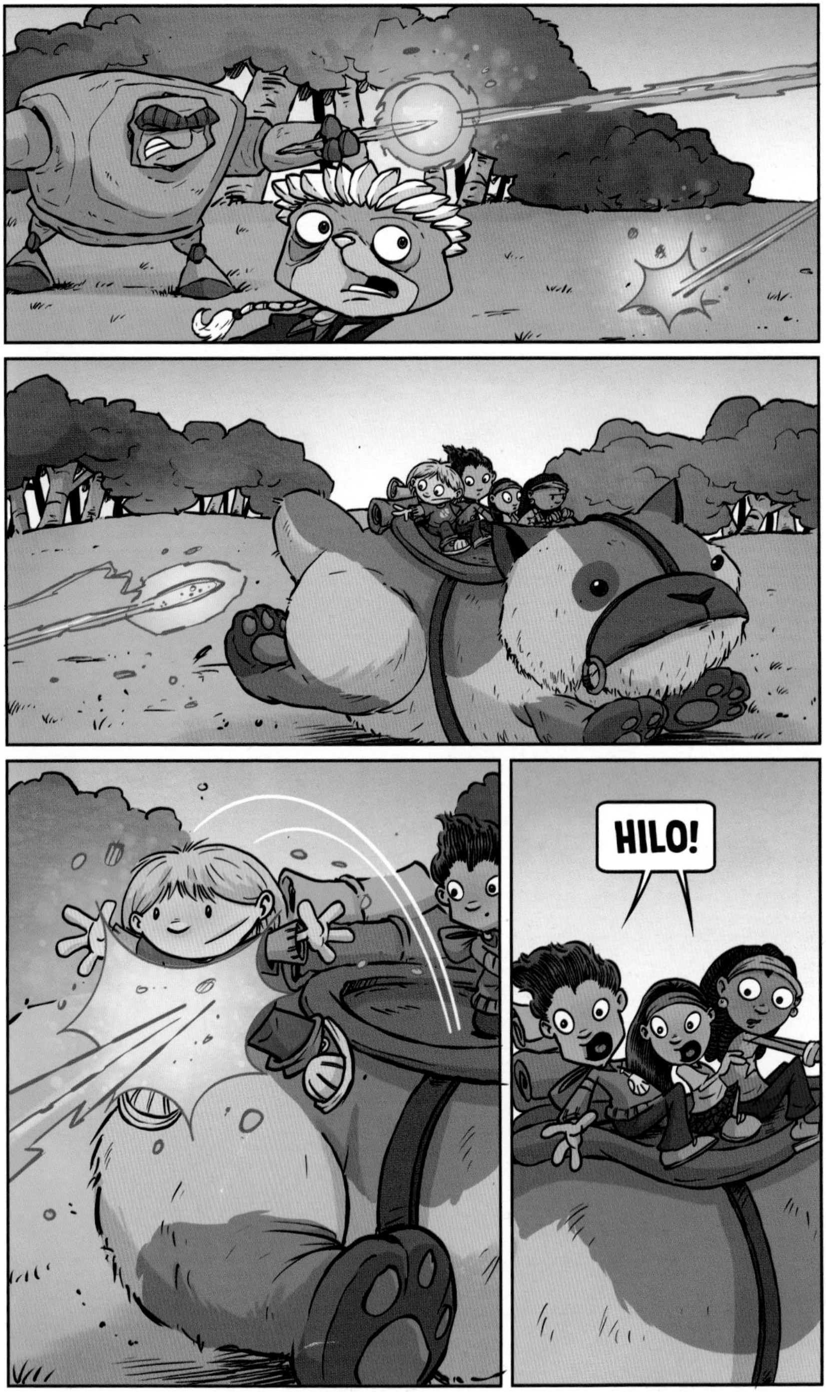
HILO!

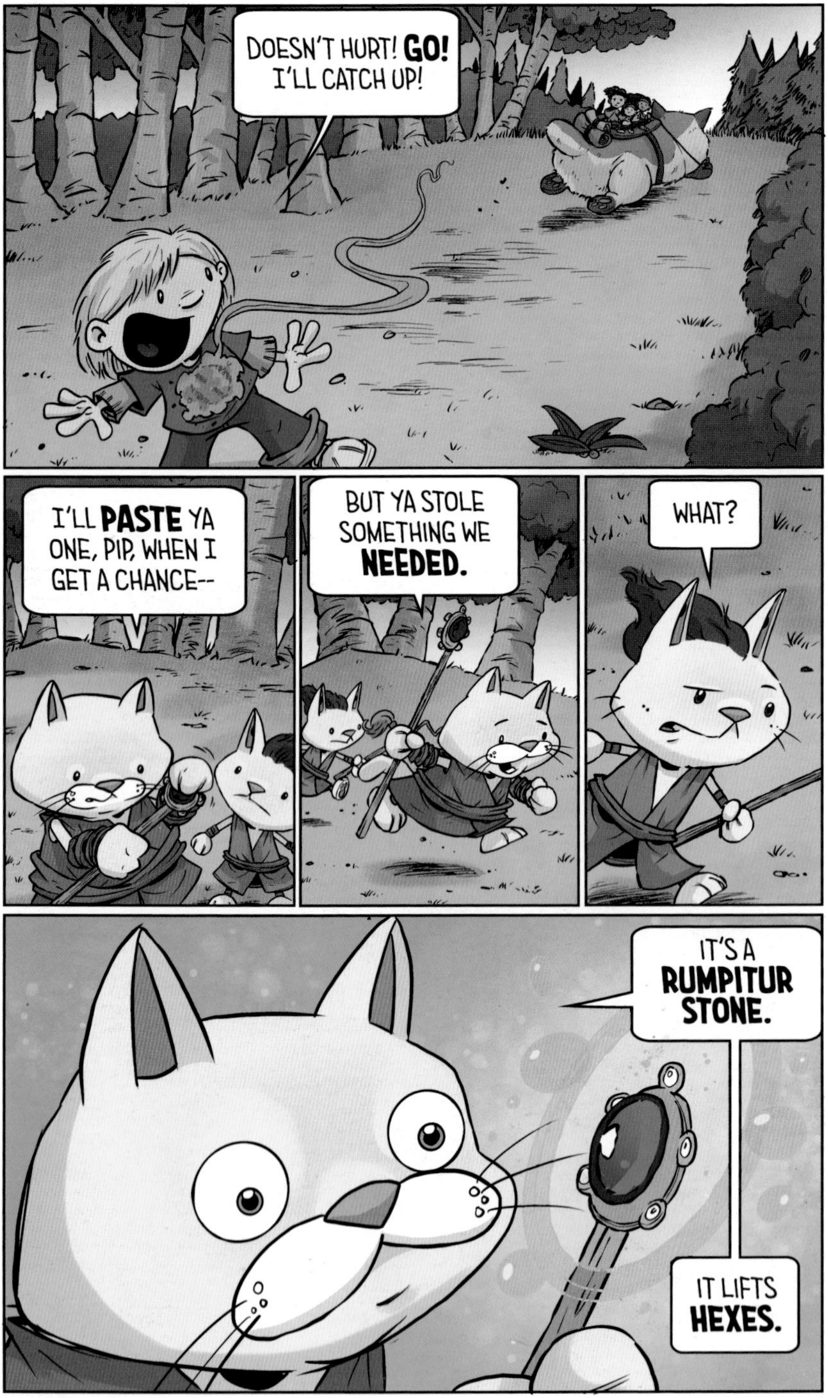
DOESN'T HURT! GO! I'LL CATCH UP!
I'LL PASTE YA ONE, PIP, WHEN I GET A CHANCE--
BUT YA STOLE SOMETHING WE NEEDED.
WHAT?
IT'S A RUMPITUR STONE.
IT LIFTS HEXES.

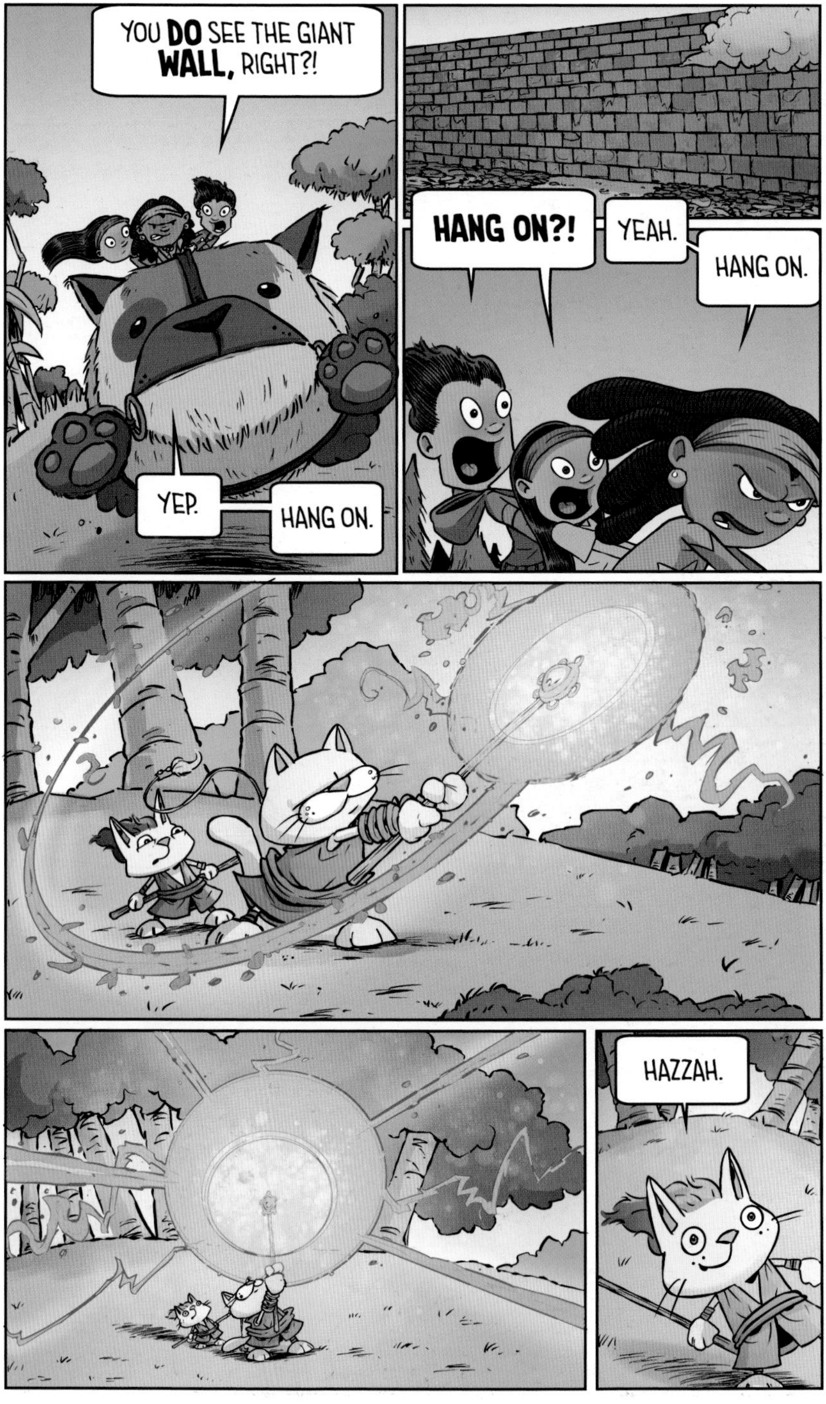
YOU DO SEE THE GIANT WALL, RIGHT?!
YEP.
HANG ON.
HANG ON?!
YEAH.
HANG ON.
HAZZAH.

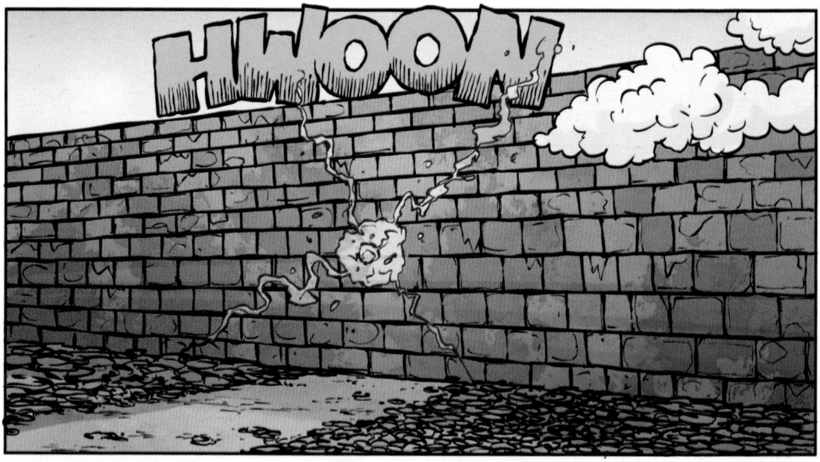
HWOOM

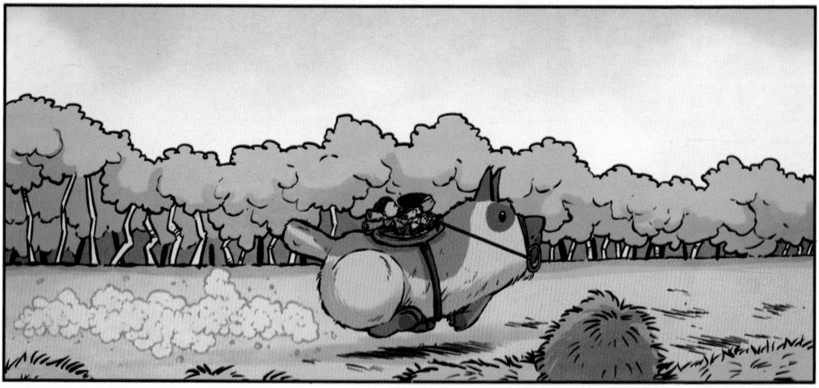

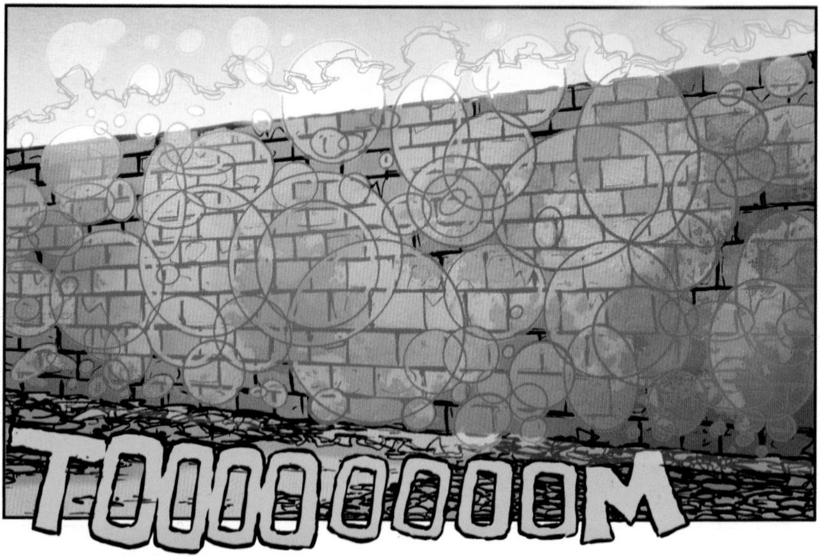
TOOOOOOOM

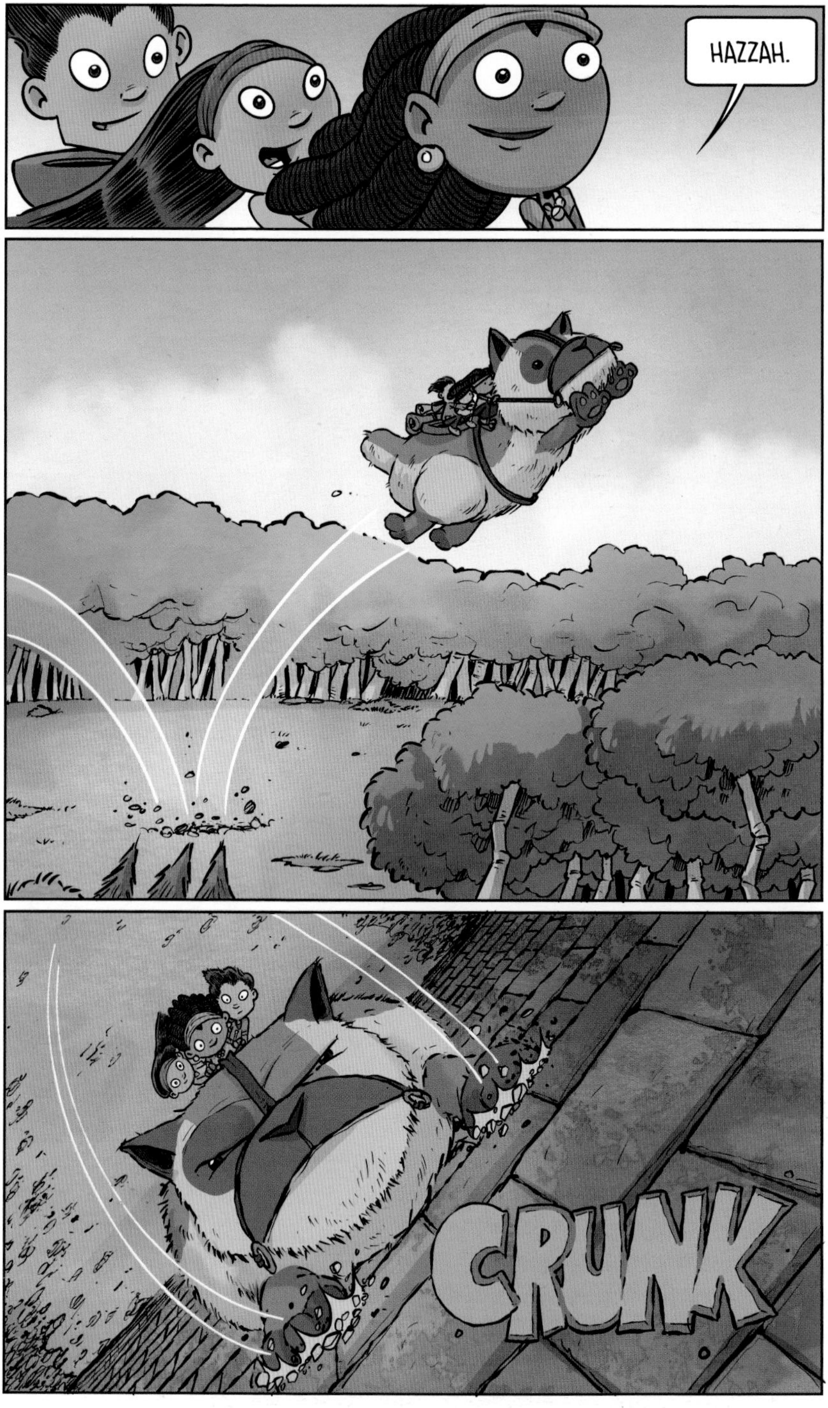
HAZZAH.
CRUNK

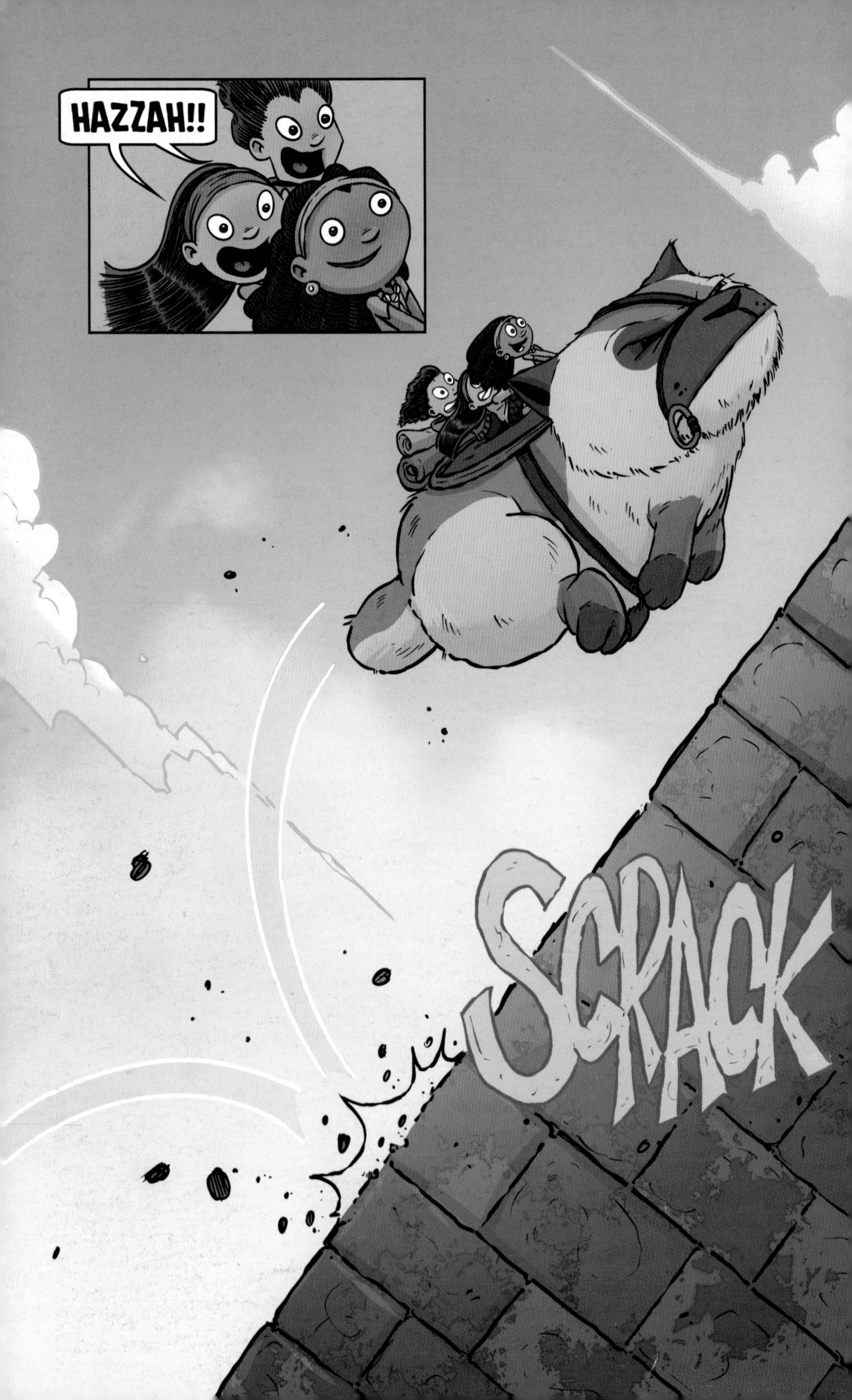
HAZZAH!!
SCRACK

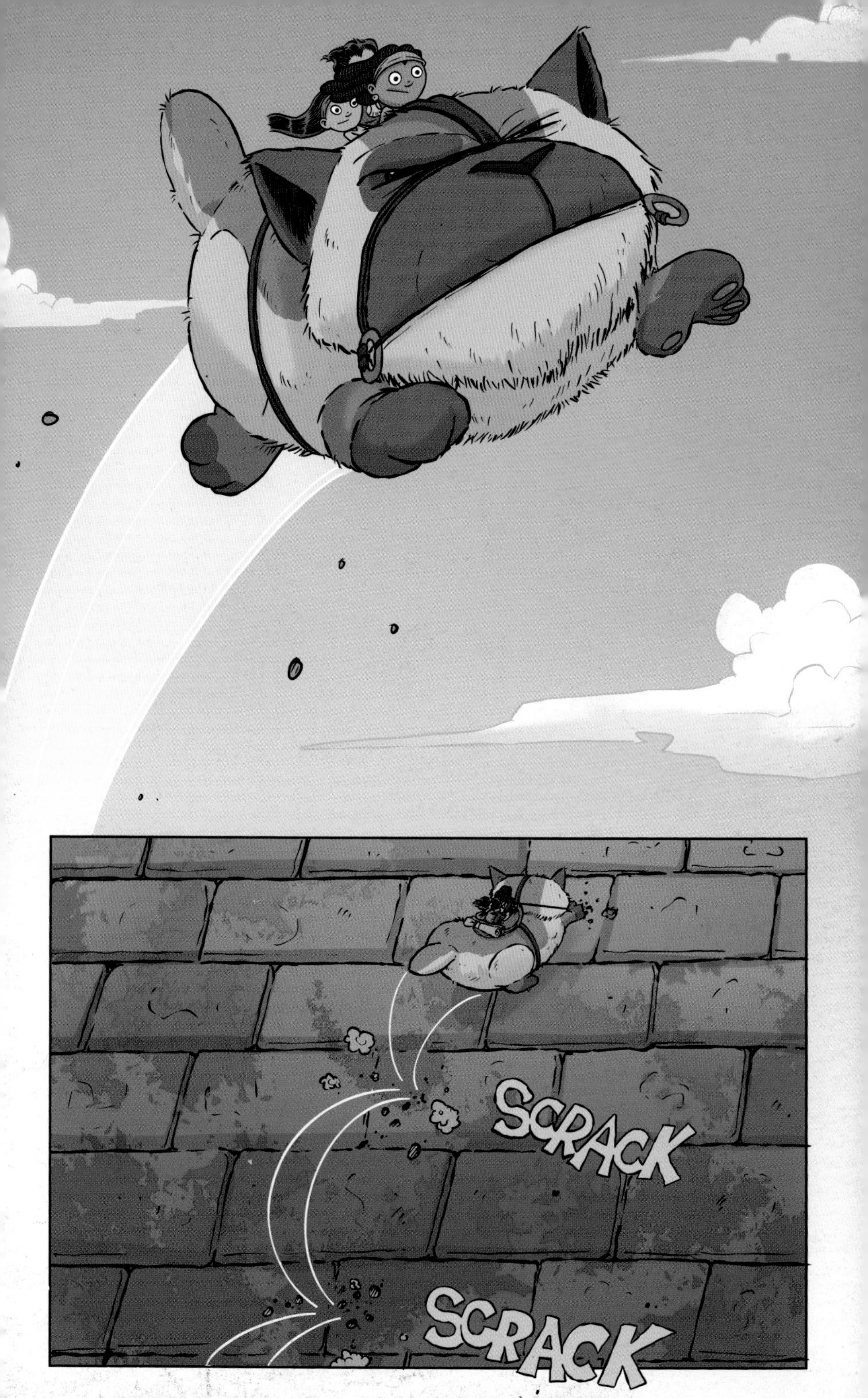
SCRACK
SCRACK

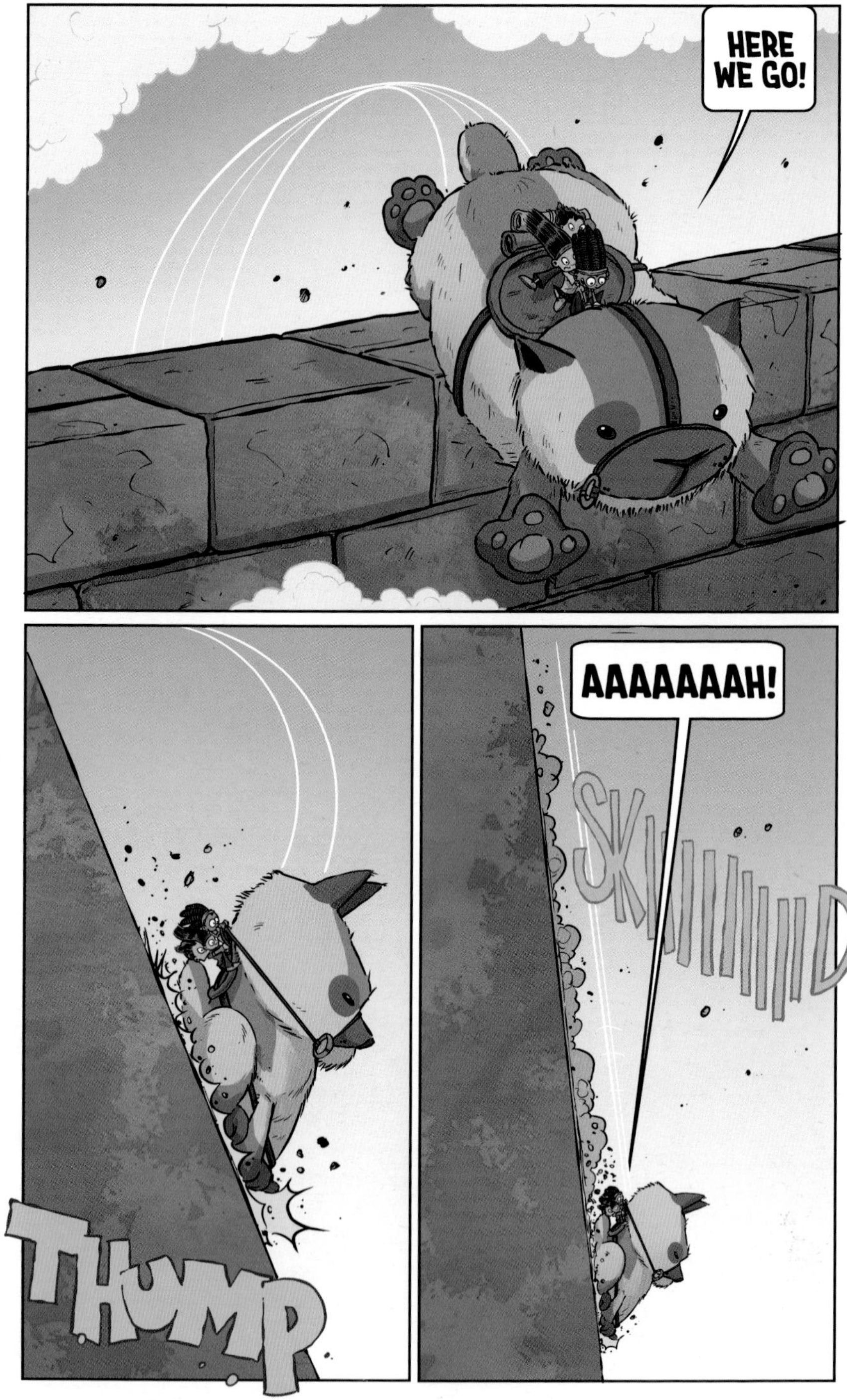
HERE WE GO!
THUMP
AAAAAAAH!
SKIIIIIIIID

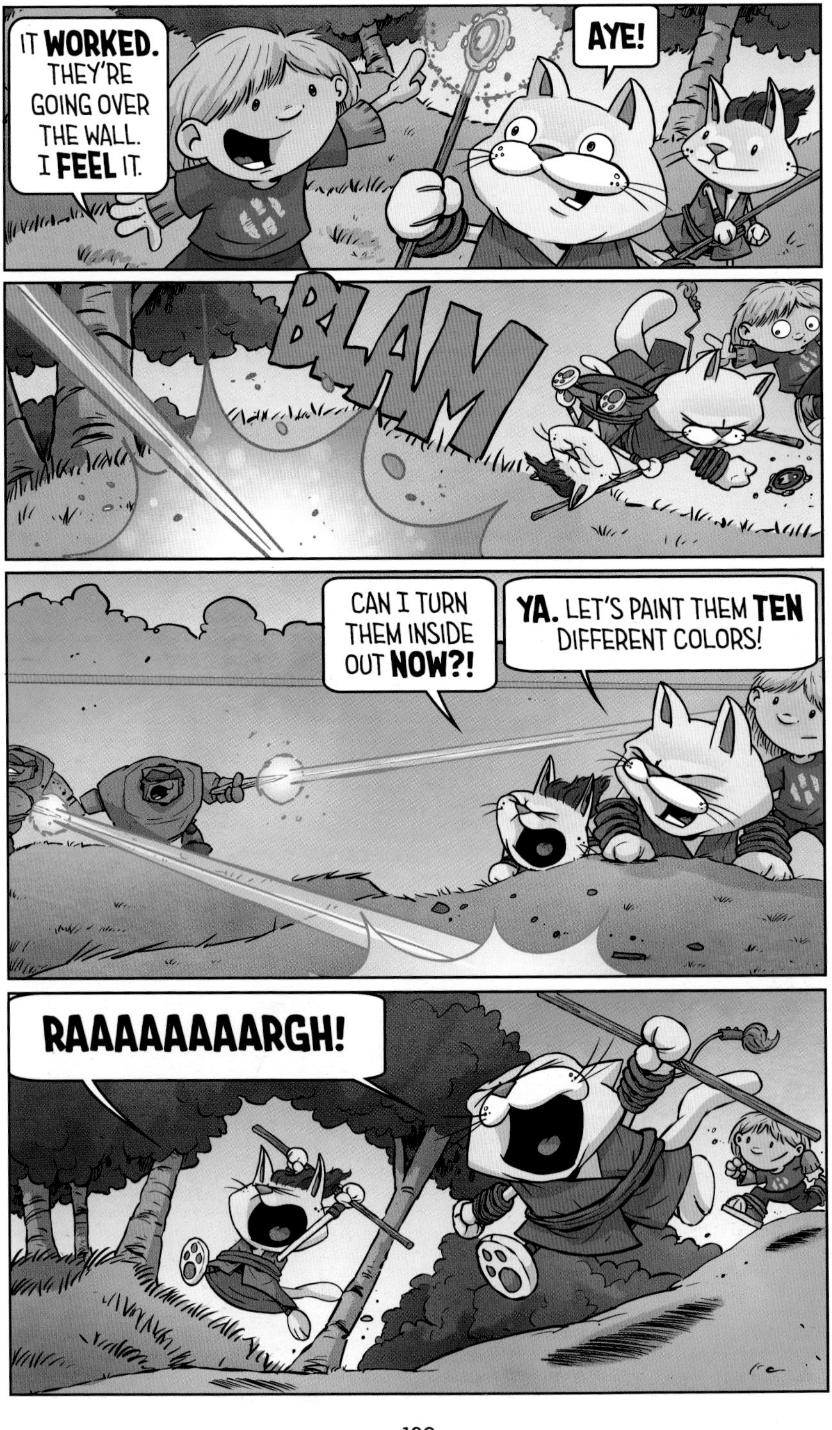
IT WORKED. THEY'RE GOING OVER THE WALL. I FEEL IT.
AYE!
BLAM
CAN I TURN THEM INSIDE OUT NOW?!
YA. LET'S PAINT THEM TEN DIFFERENT COLORS!
RAAAAAAAARGH!

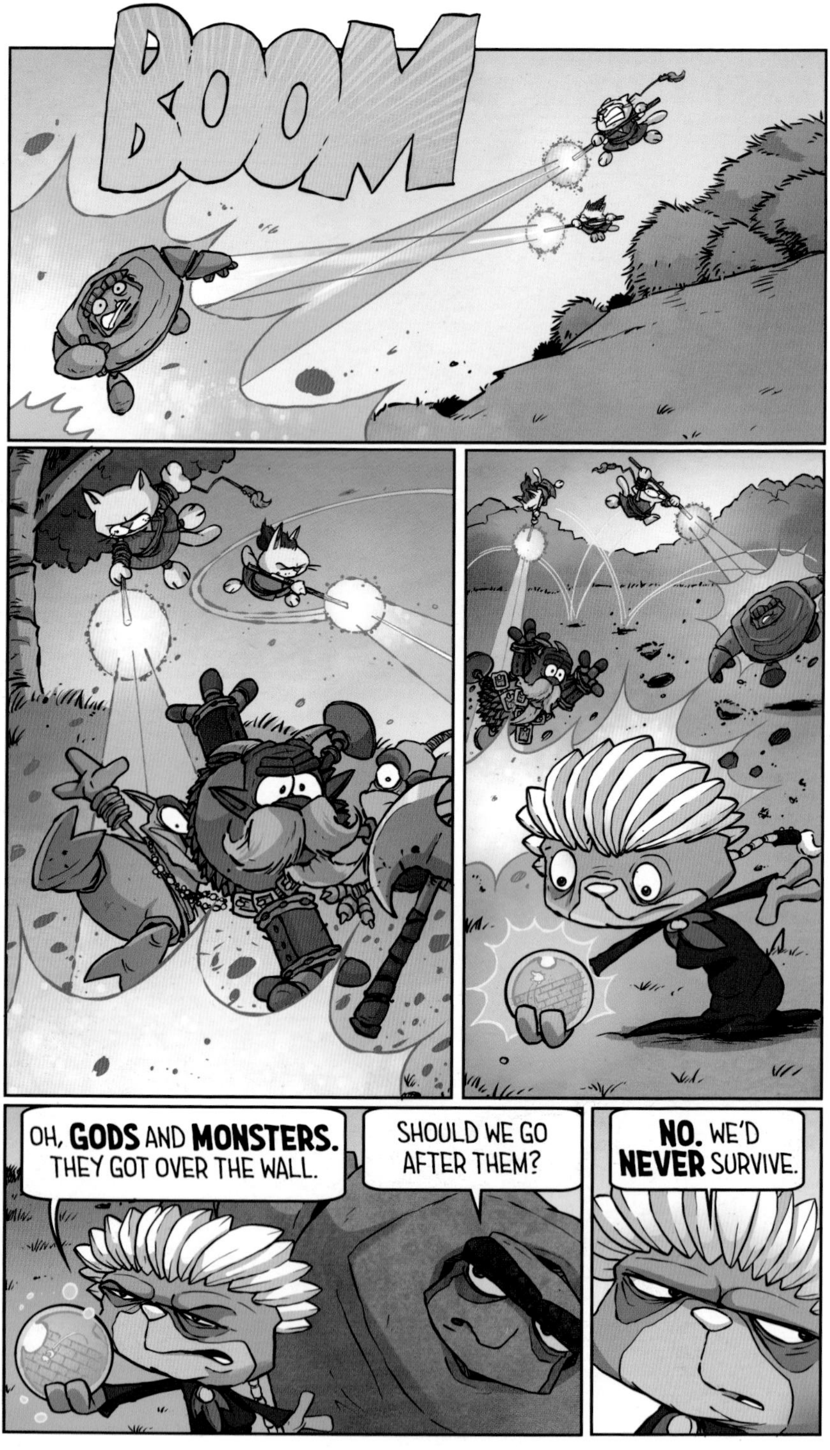
BOOM
OH, GODS AND MONSTERS. THEY GOT OVER THE WALL.
SHOULD WE GO AFTER THEM?
NO. WE'D NEVER SURVIVE.

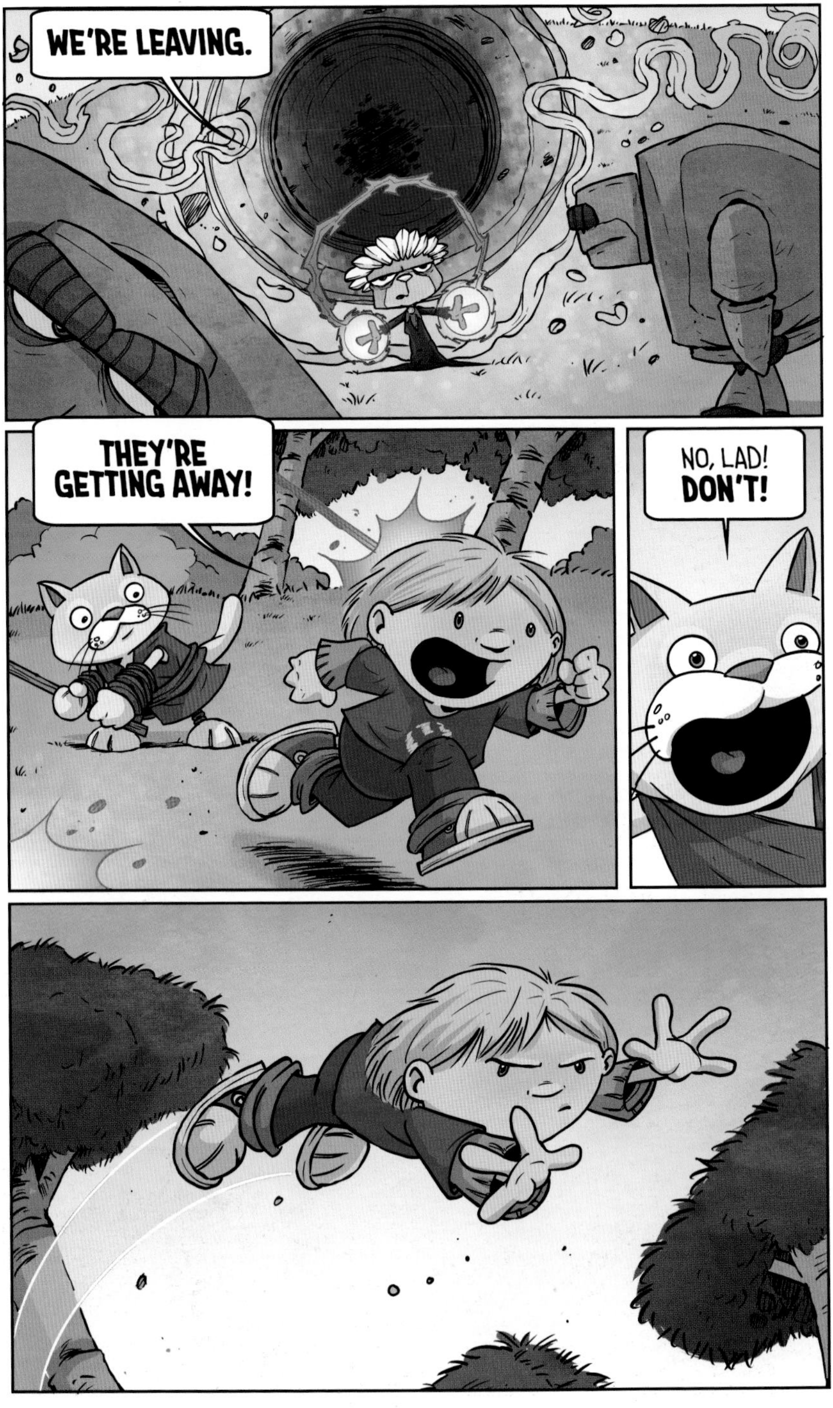
WE'RE LEAVING.
THEY'RE GETTING AWAY!
NO, LAD! DON'T!

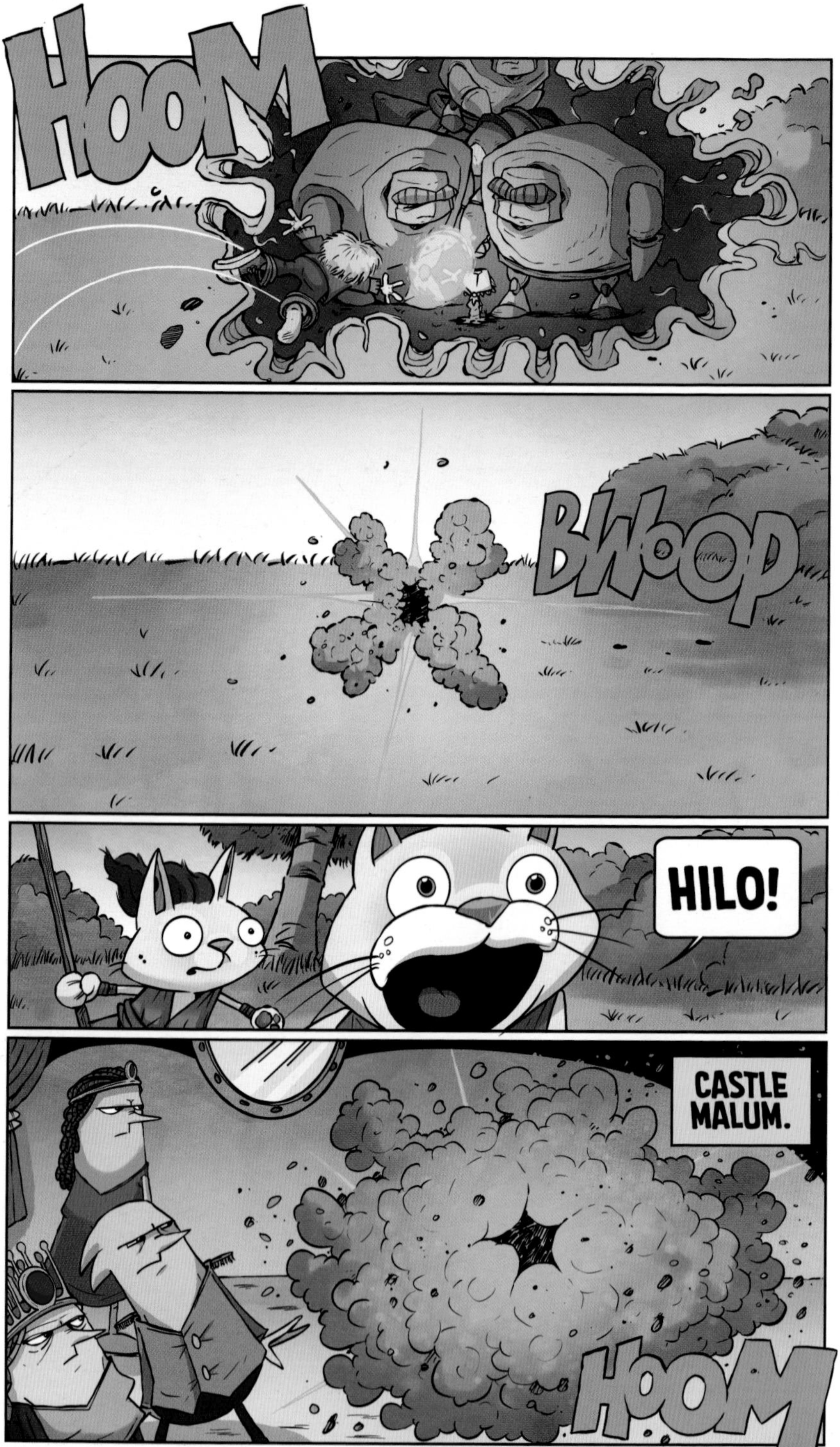
HOOM
BWOOP
HILO!
CASTLE MALUM.
HOOM

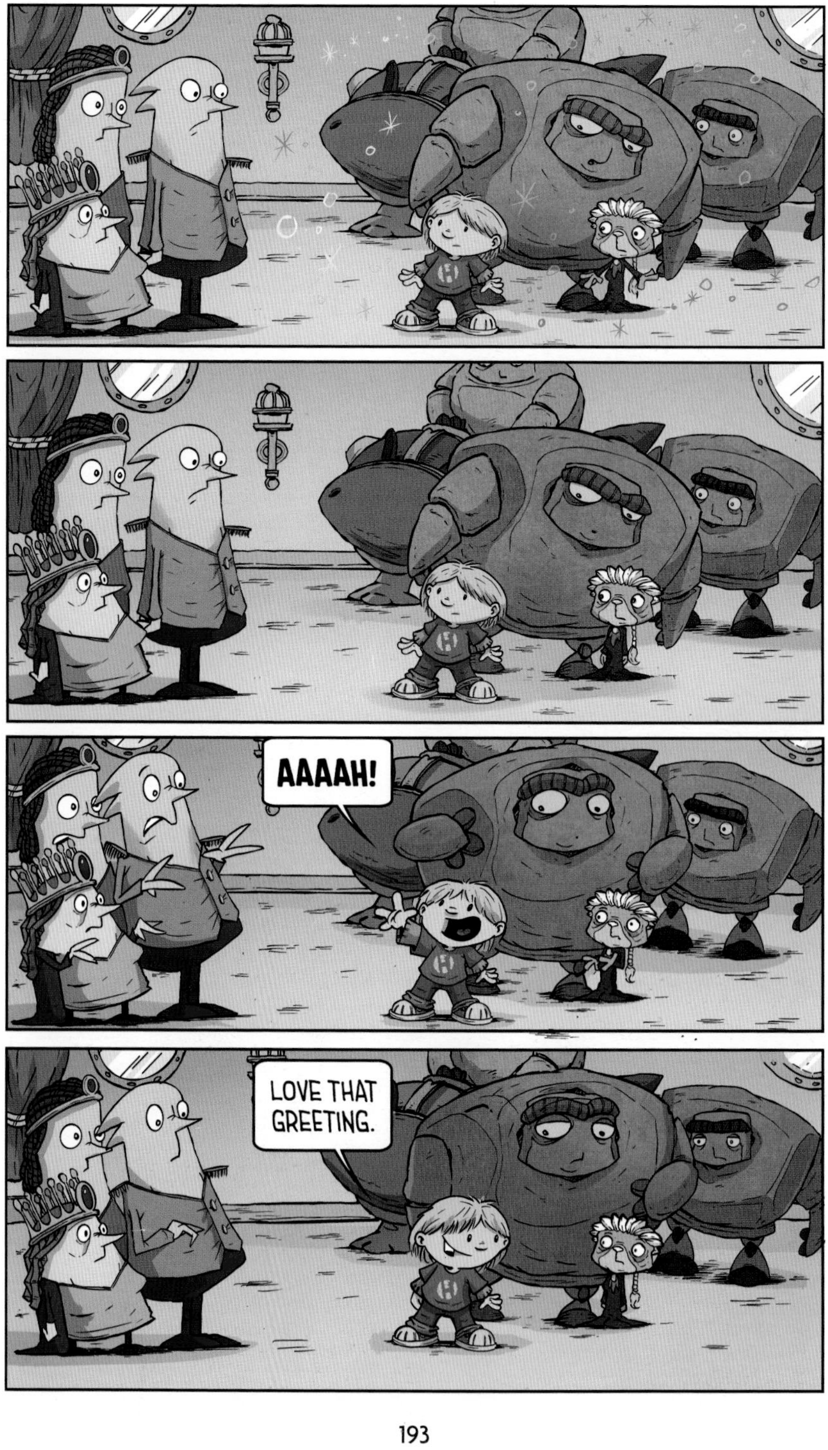
AAAAH!
LOVE THAT GREETING.

CHAPTER 9

A TALE OF MRS. PEEBLES

WHUMP

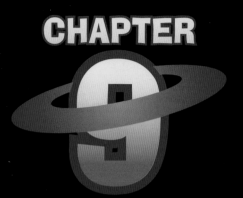

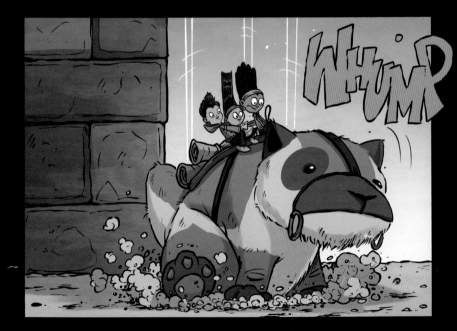

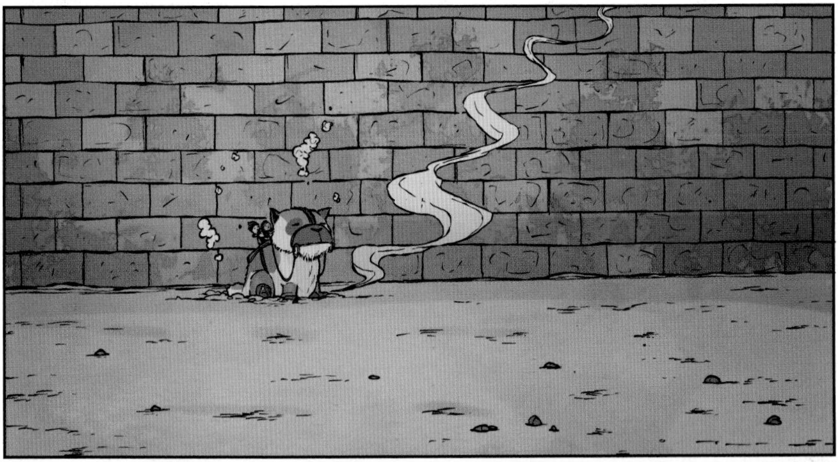

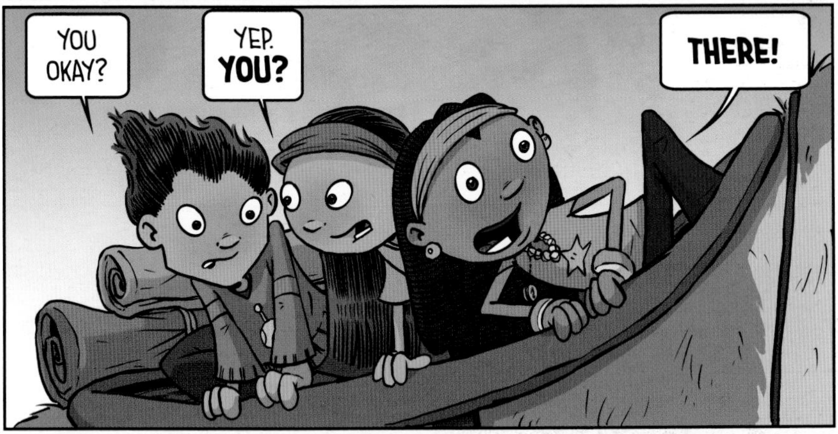
YOU OKAY?
YEP. **YOU?**
THERE!

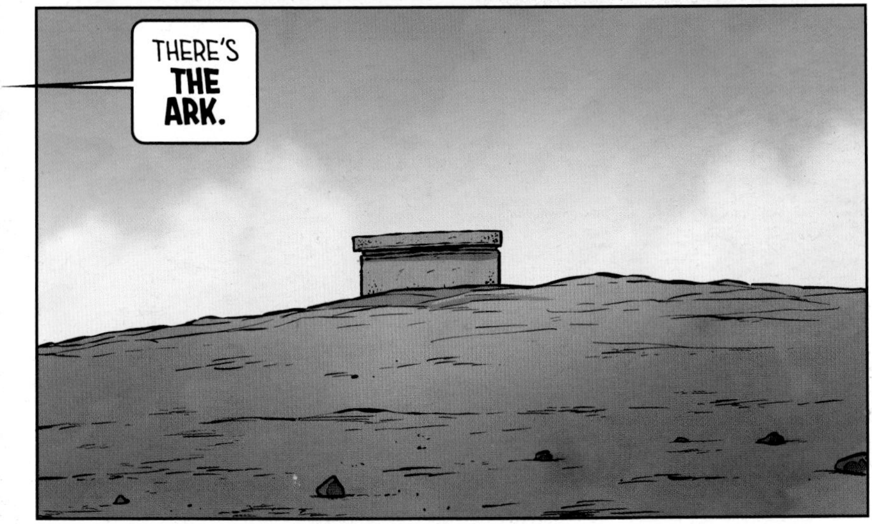
THERE'S **THE ARK.**

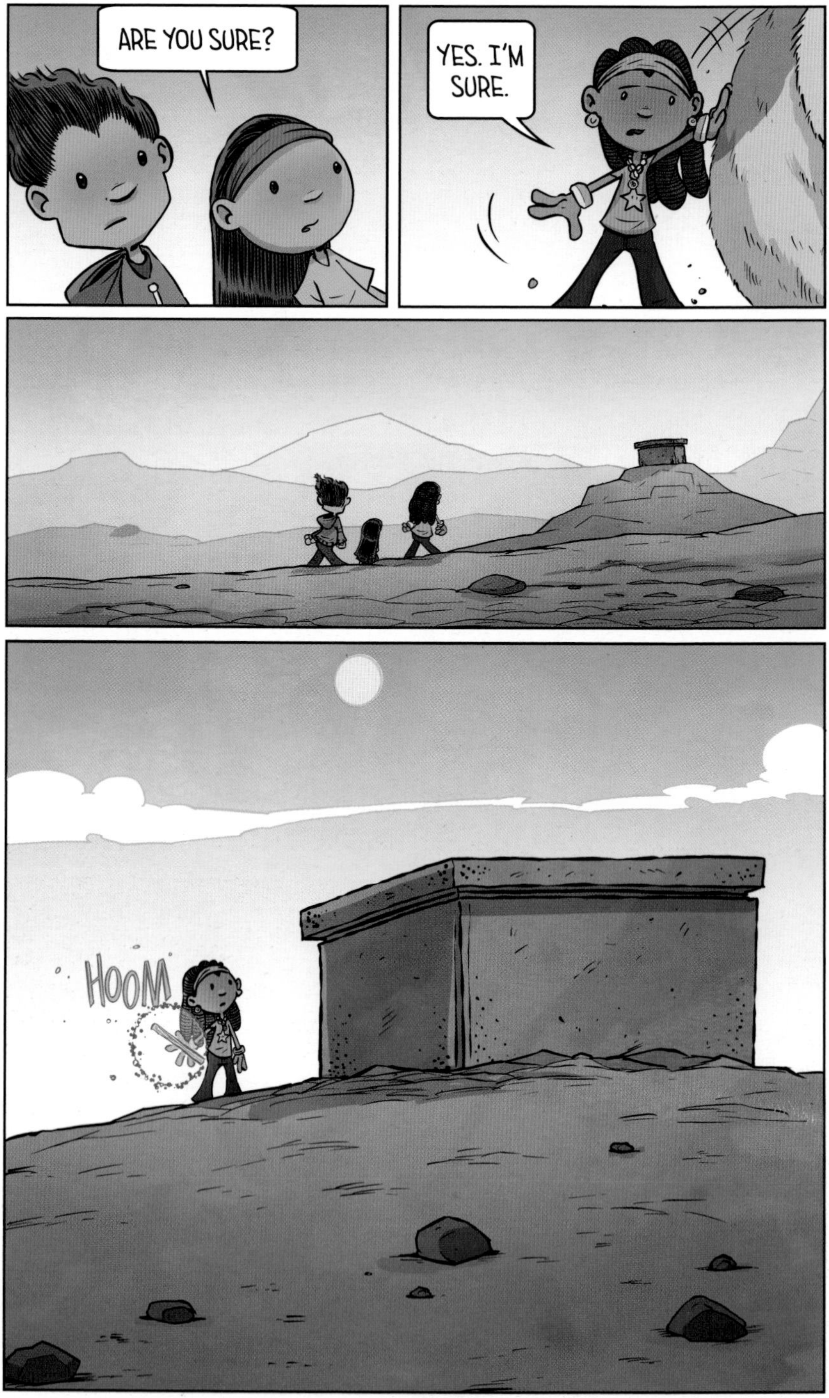
ARE YOU SURE?
YES. I'M SURE.
HOOM

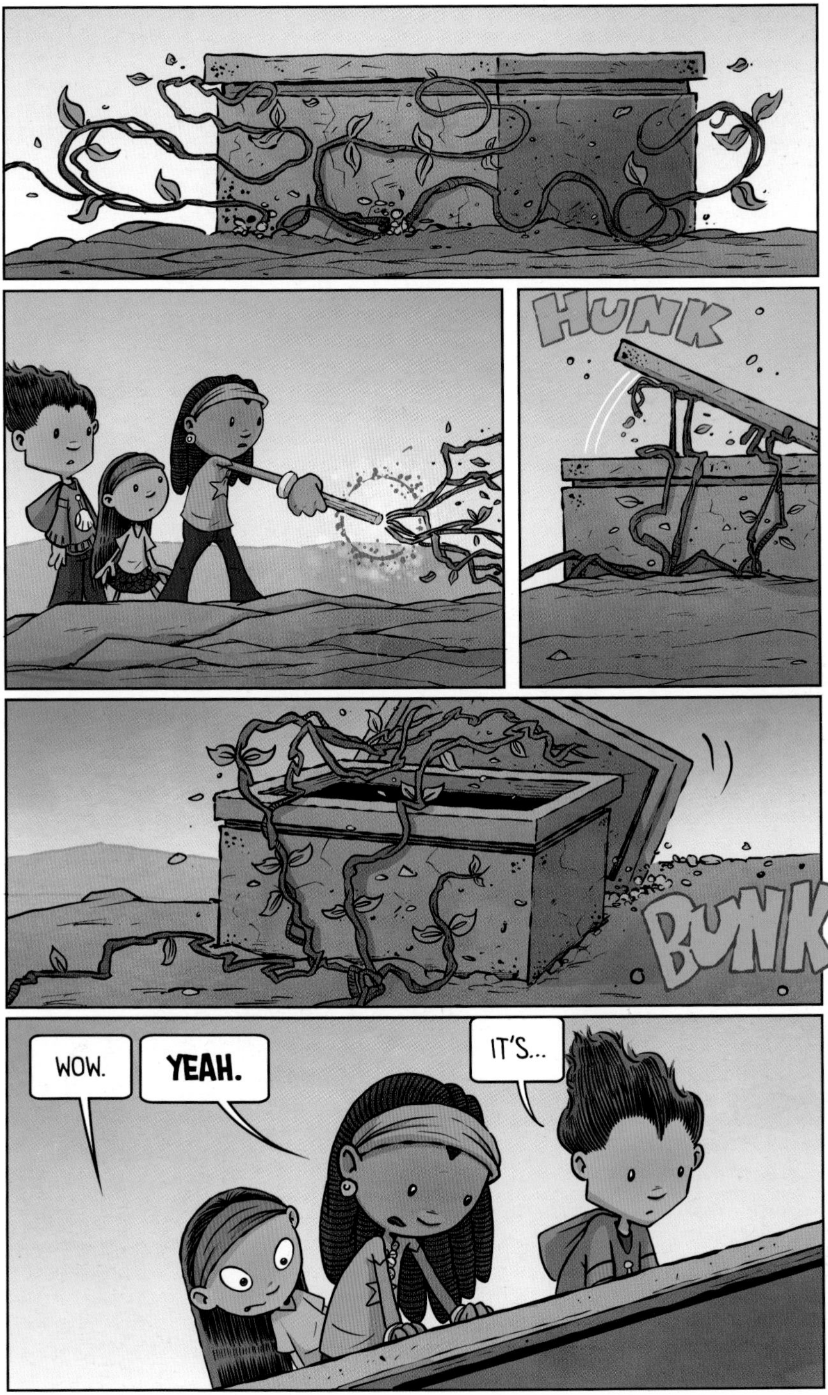
HUNK
BUNK
WOW.
YEAH.
IT'S...

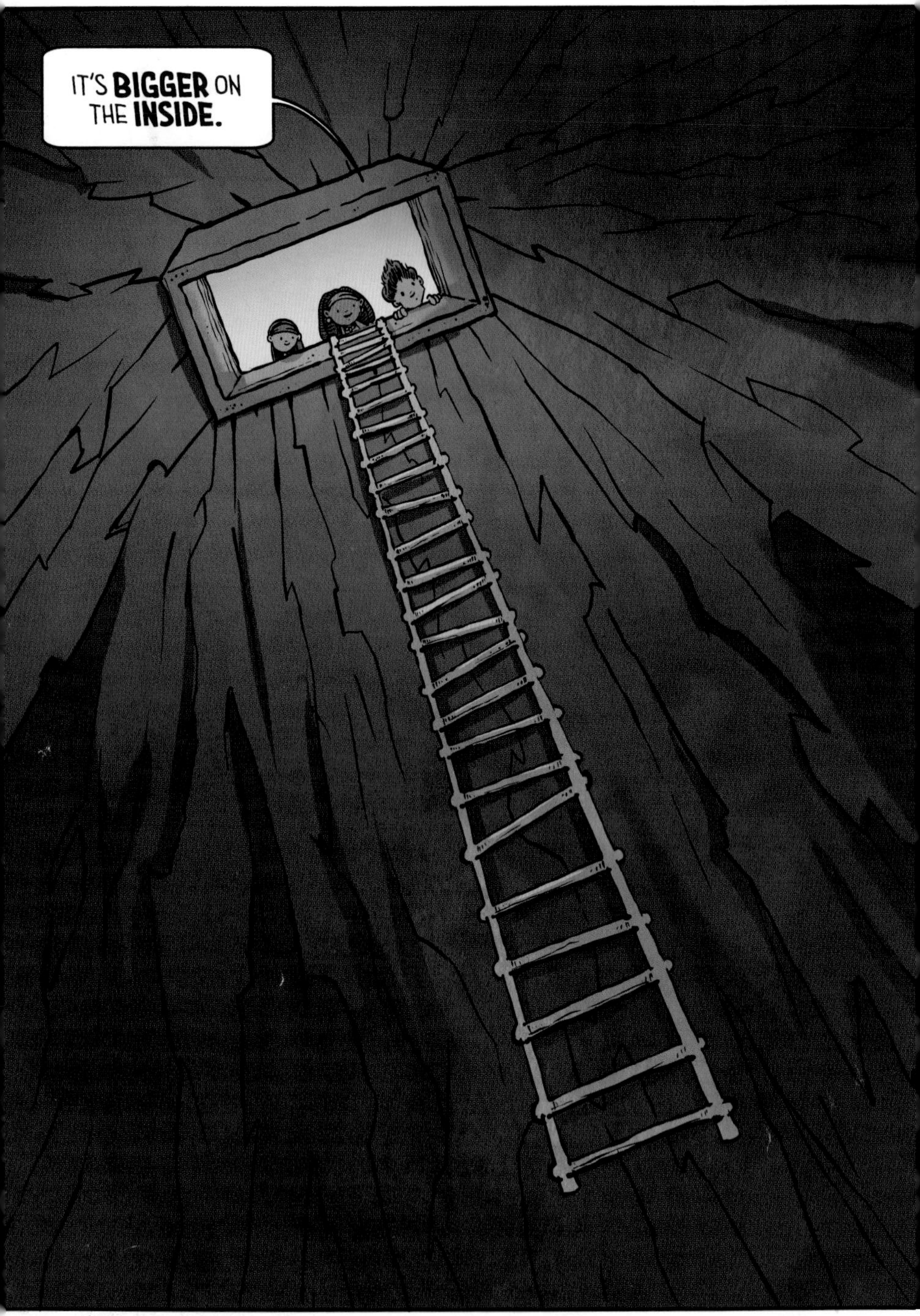
IT'S **BIGGER** ON THE **INSIDE.**

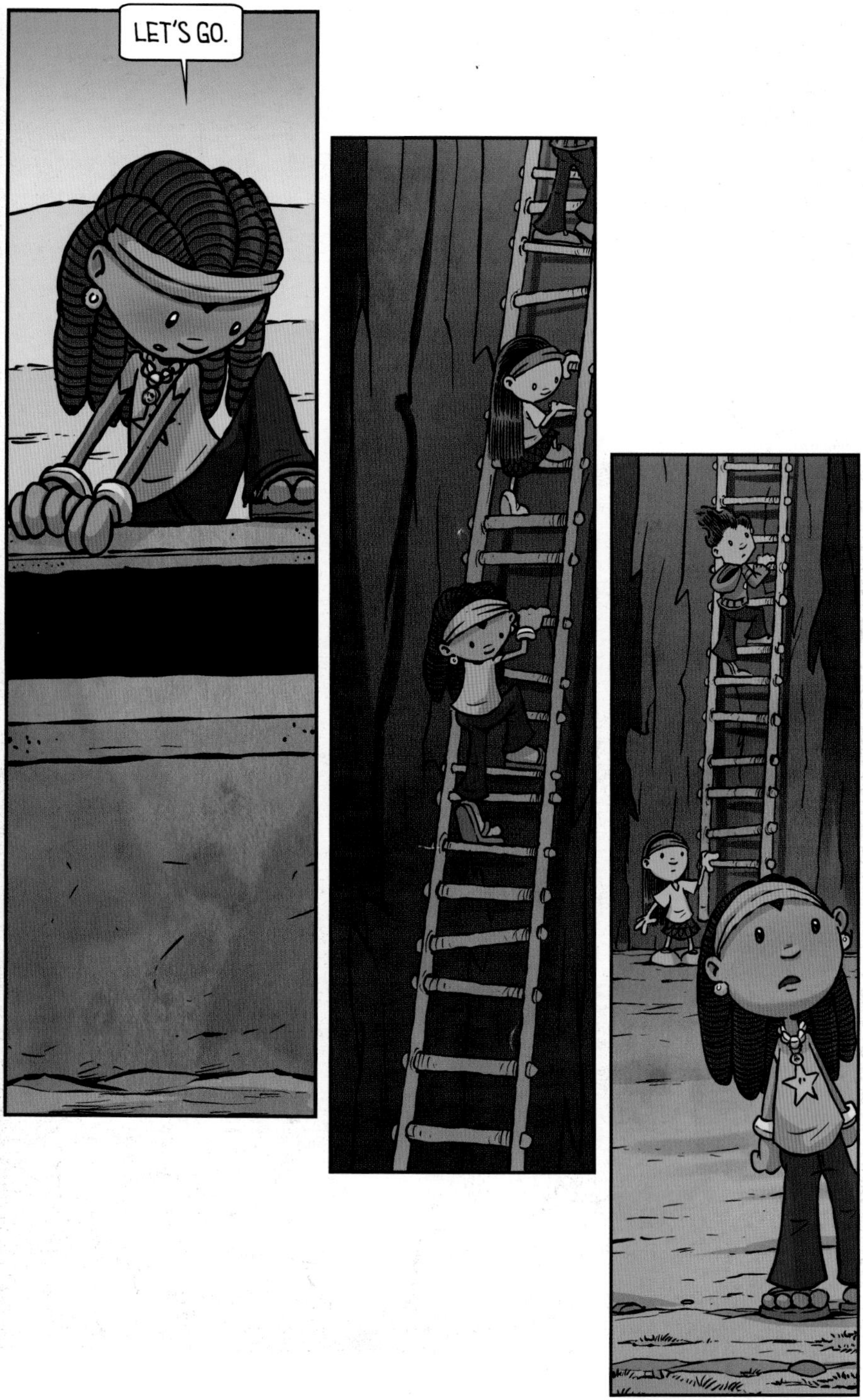
LET'S GO.

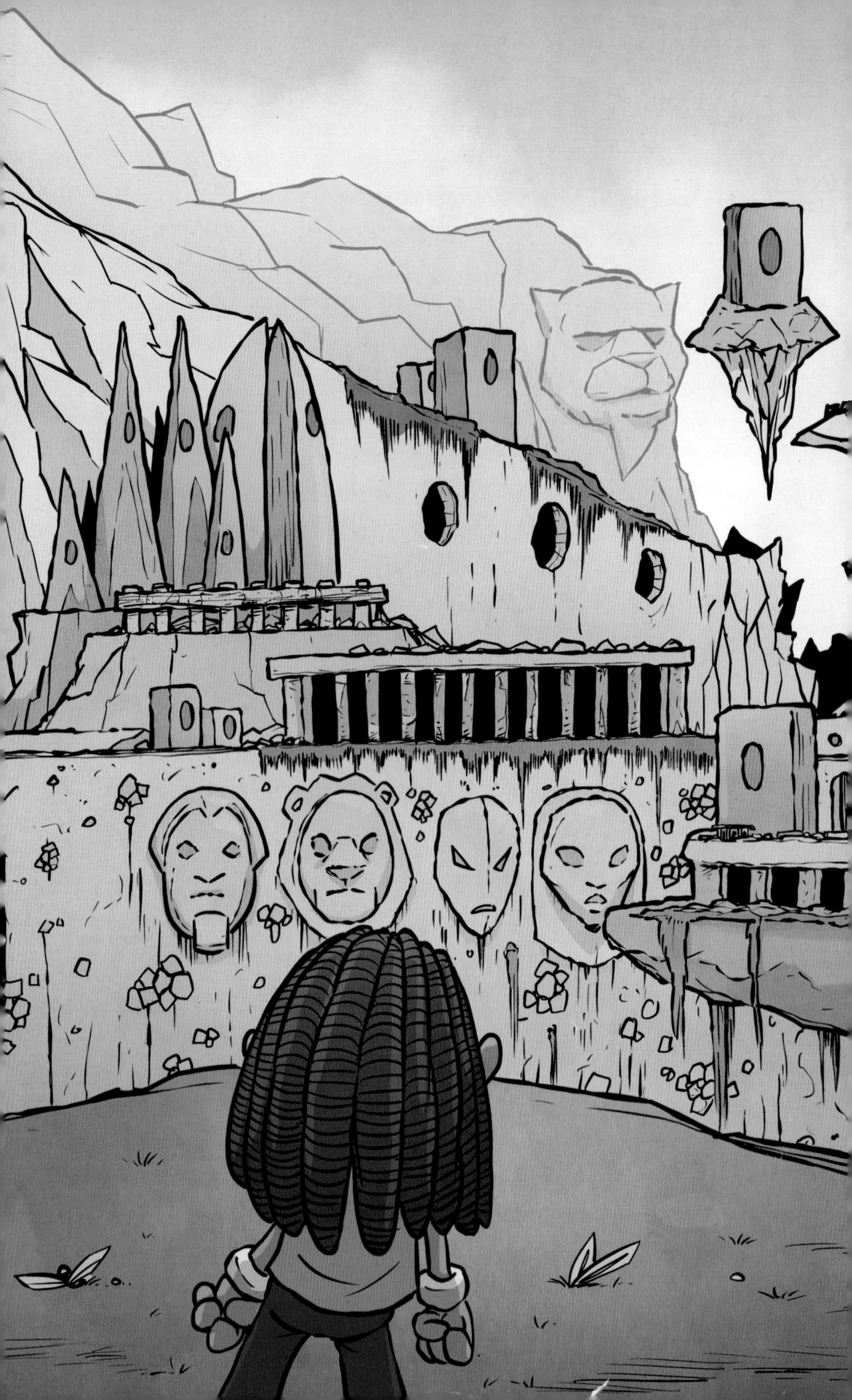

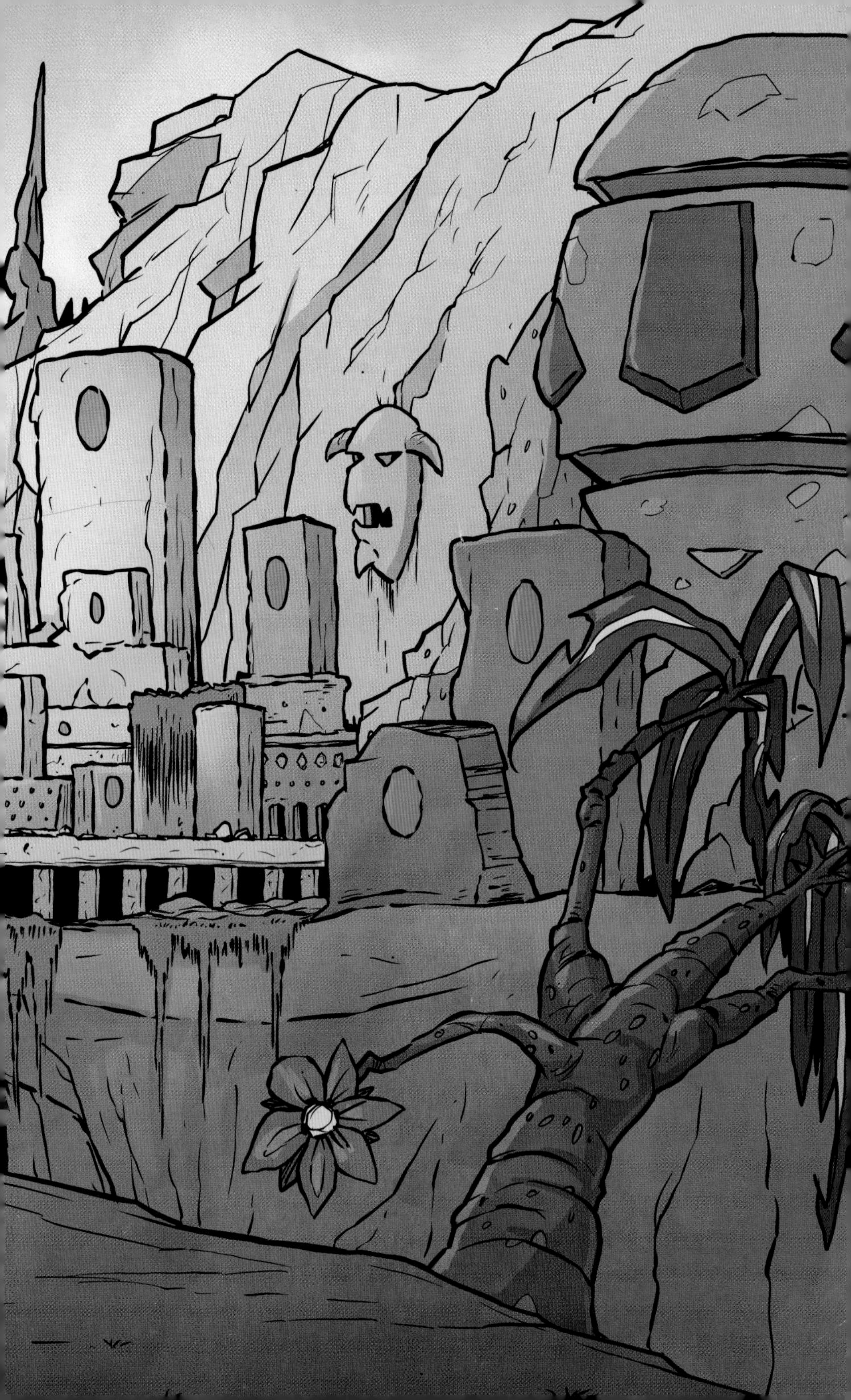

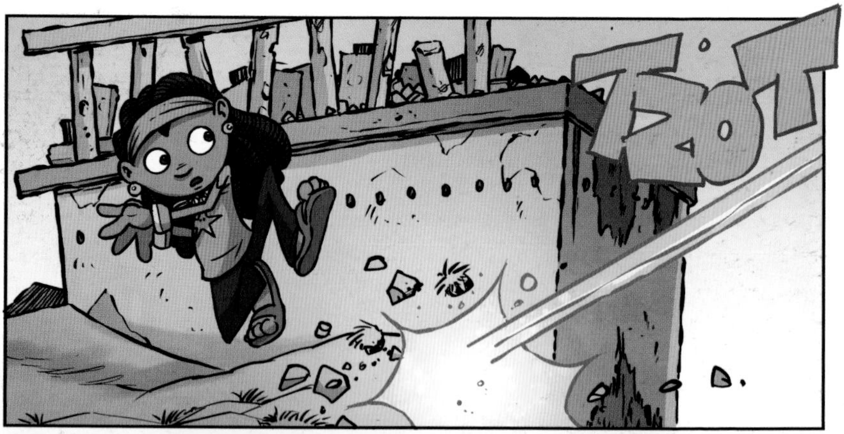
TZOT

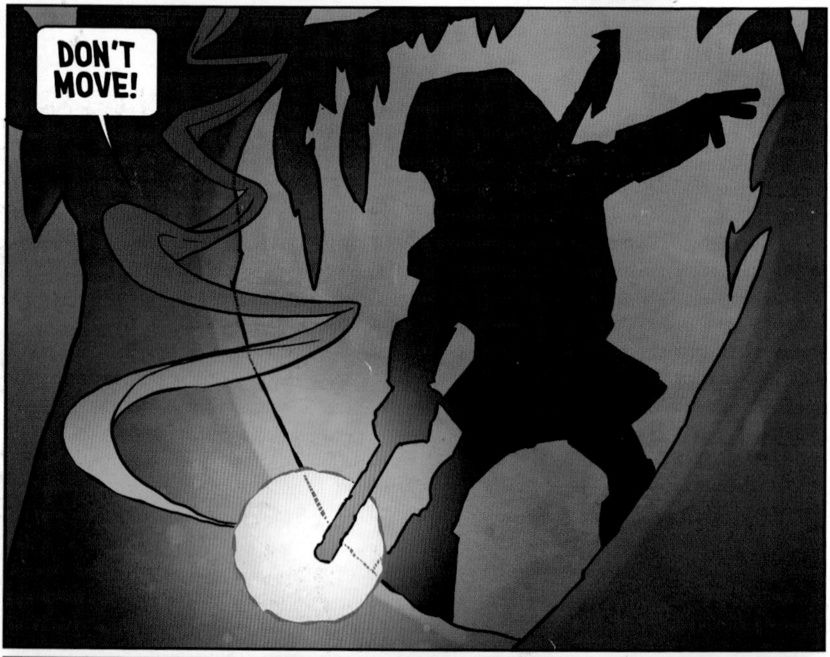
DON'T MOVE!

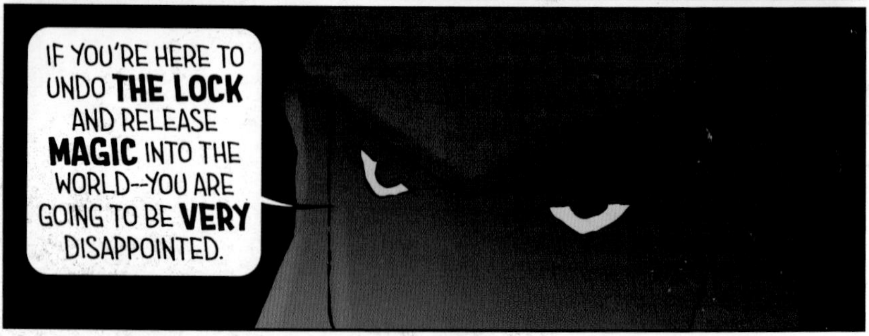
IF YOU'RE HERE TO UNDO **THE LOCK** AND RELEASE **MAGIC** INTO THE WORLD--YOU ARE GOING TO BE **VERY** DISAPPOINTED.

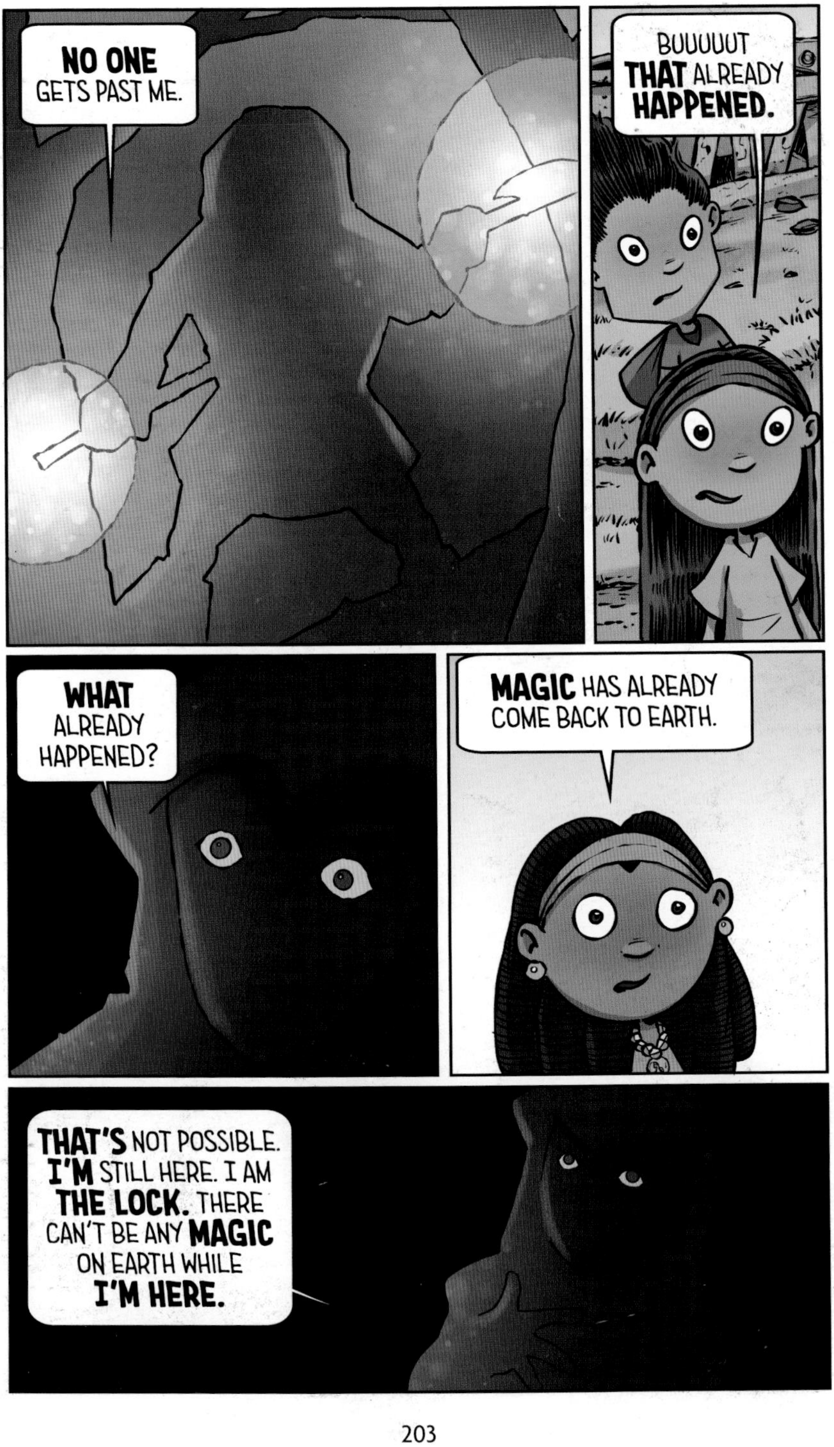
NO ONE GETS PAST ME.
BUUUUUT THAT ALREADY HAPPENED.
WHAT ALREADY HAPPENED?
MAGIC HAS ALREADY COME BACK TO EARTH.
THAT'S NOT POSSIBLE. I'M STILL HERE. I AM THE LOCK. THERE CAN'T BE ANY MAGIC ON EARTH WHILE I'M HERE.

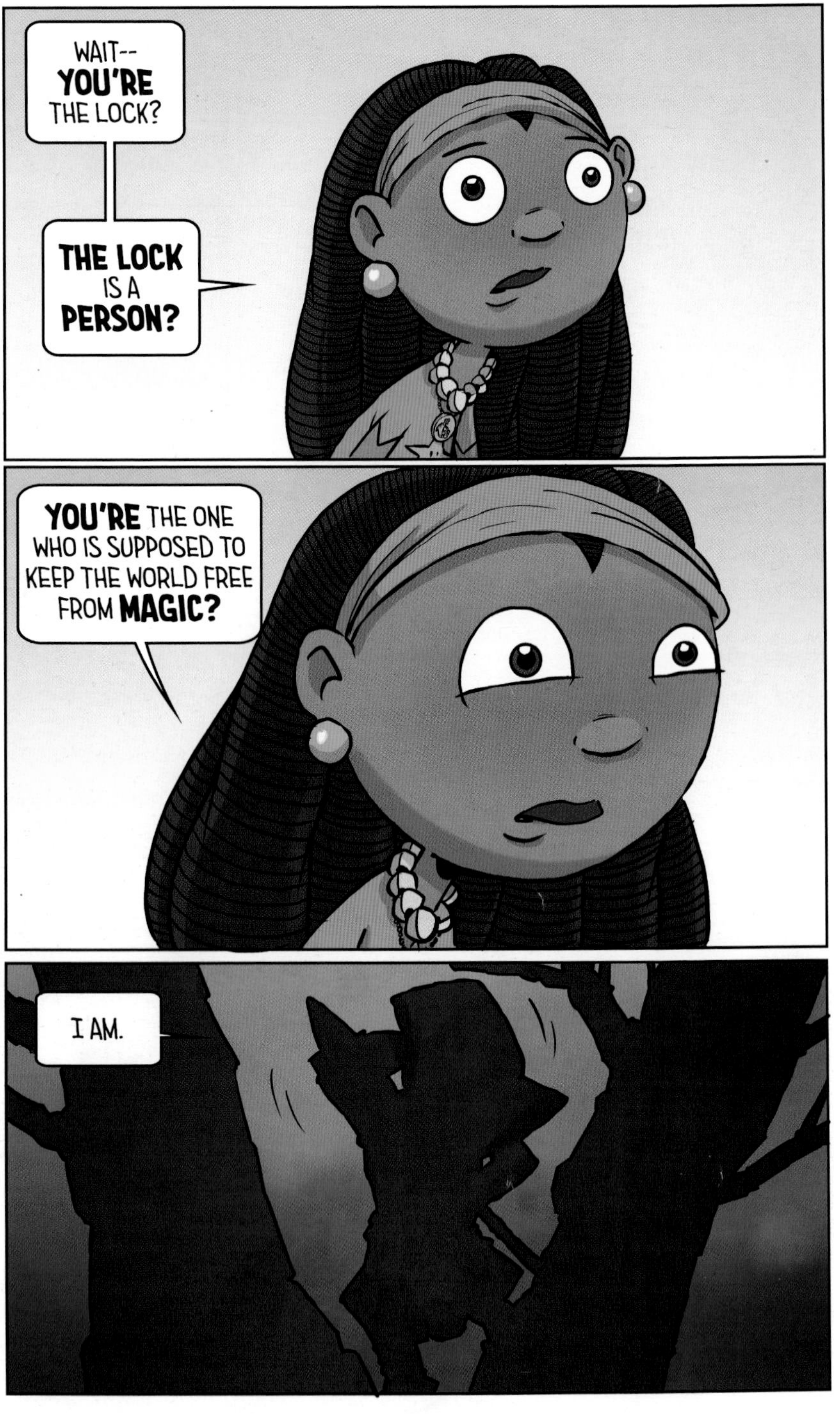
WAIT--
YOU'RE THE LOCK?
THE LOCK IS A PERSON?
YOU'RE THE ONE WHO IS SUPPOSED TO KEEP THE WORLD FREE FROM MAGIC?
I AM.

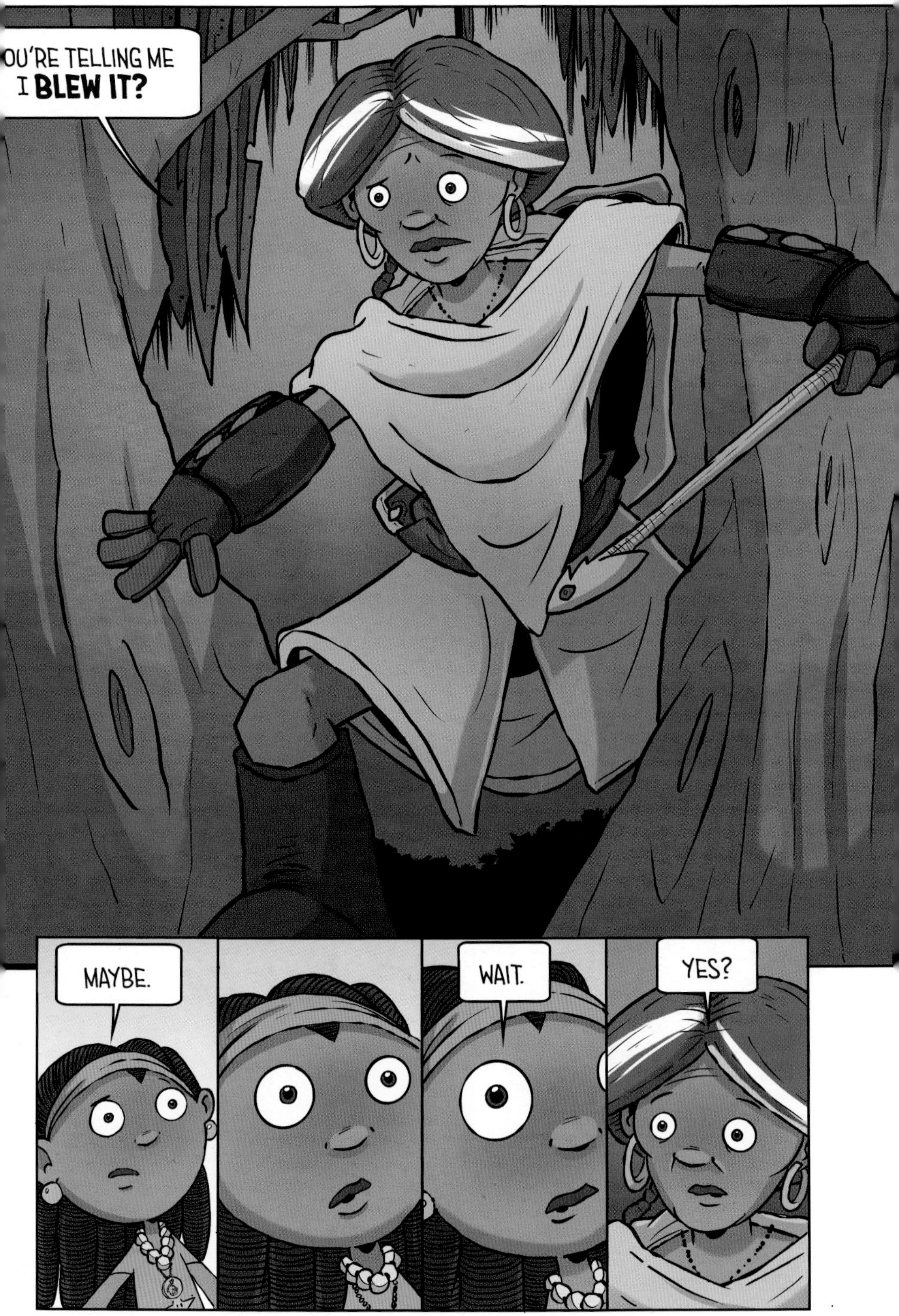
OU'RE TELLING ME I **BLEW IT?**
MAYBE.
WAIT.
YES?

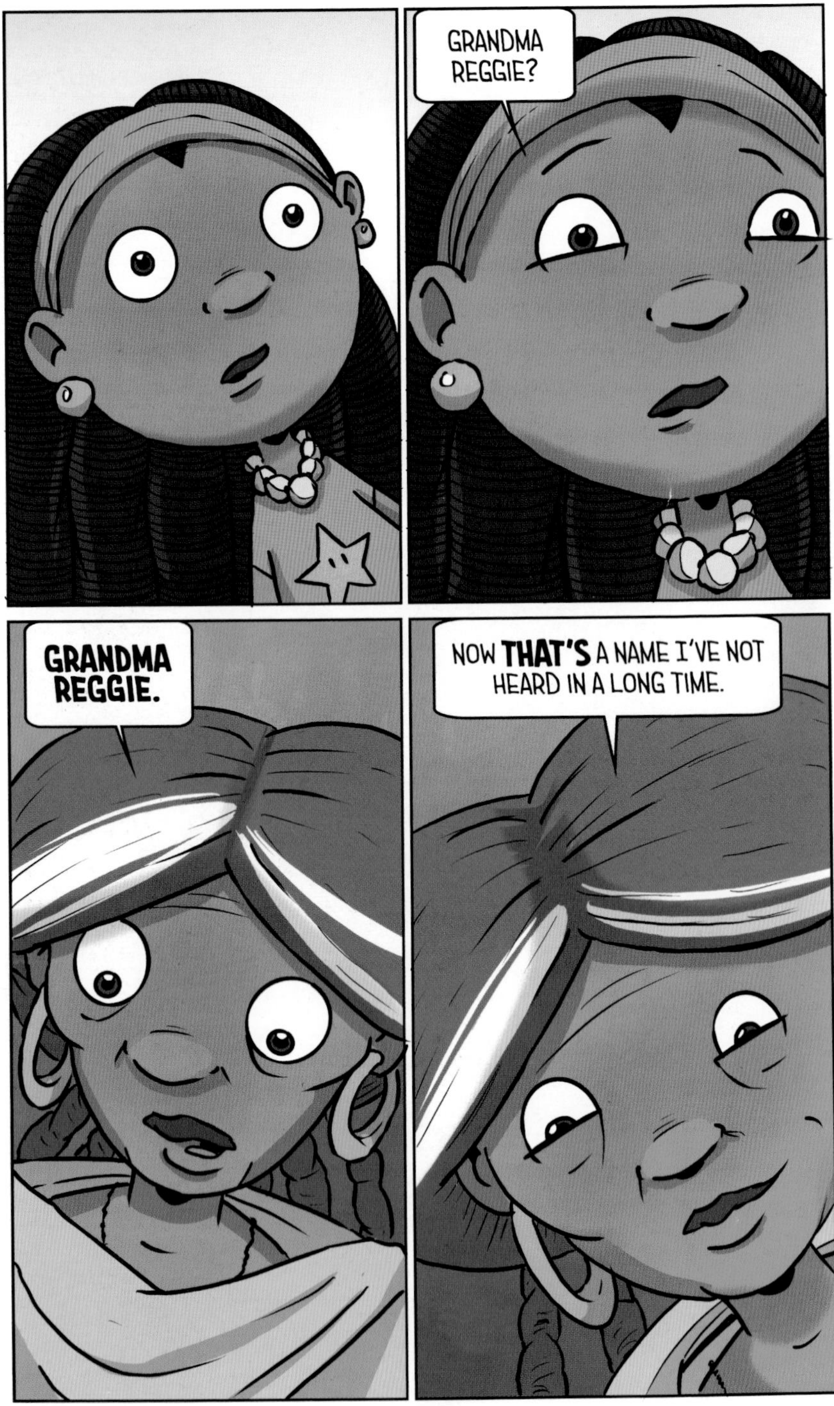
GRANDMA REGGIE?
GRANDMA REGGIE.
NOW THAT'S A NAME I'VE NOT HEARD IN A LONG TIME.

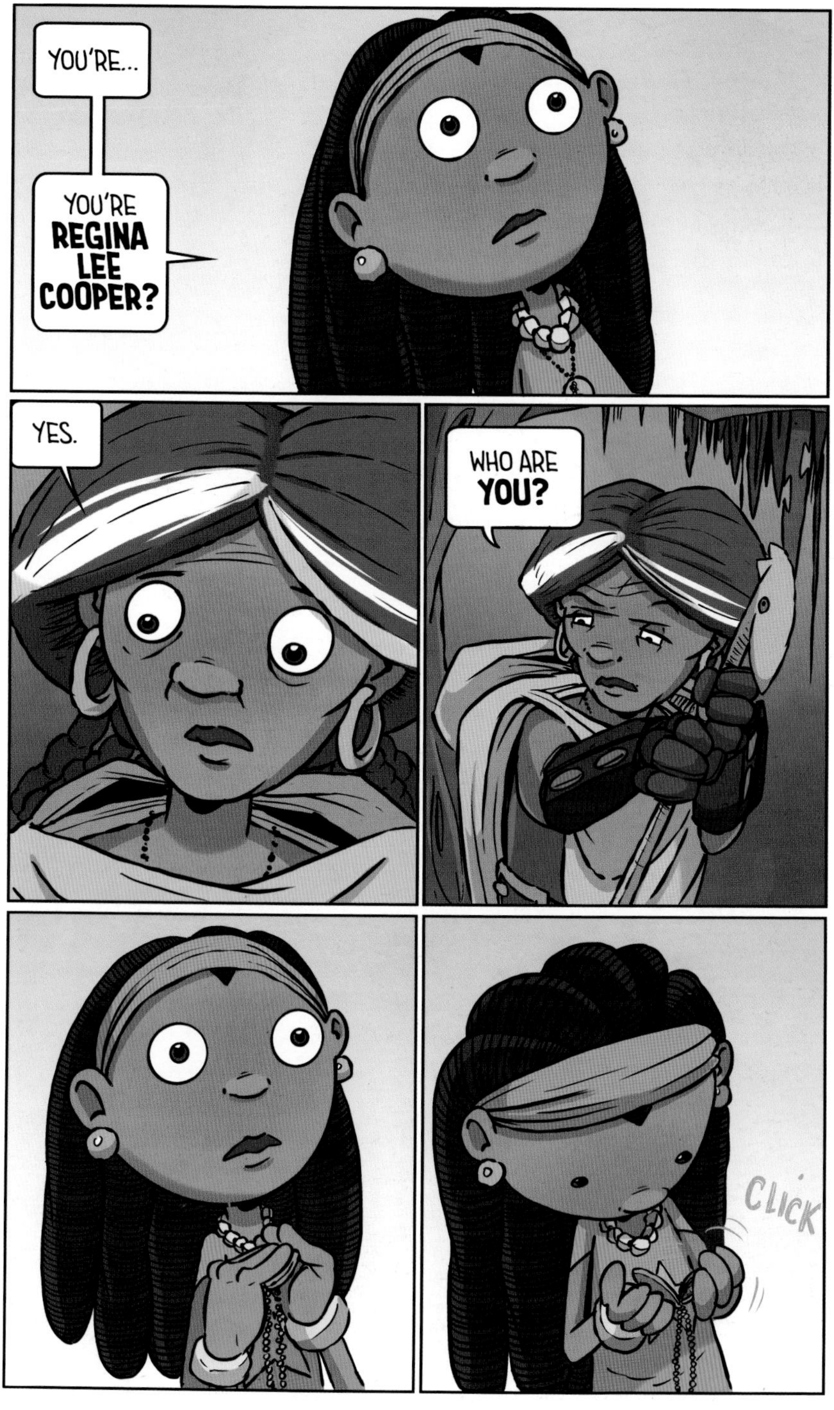
YOU'RE...
YOU'RE **REGINA LEE COOPER?**
YES.
WHO ARE **YOU?**
CLICK

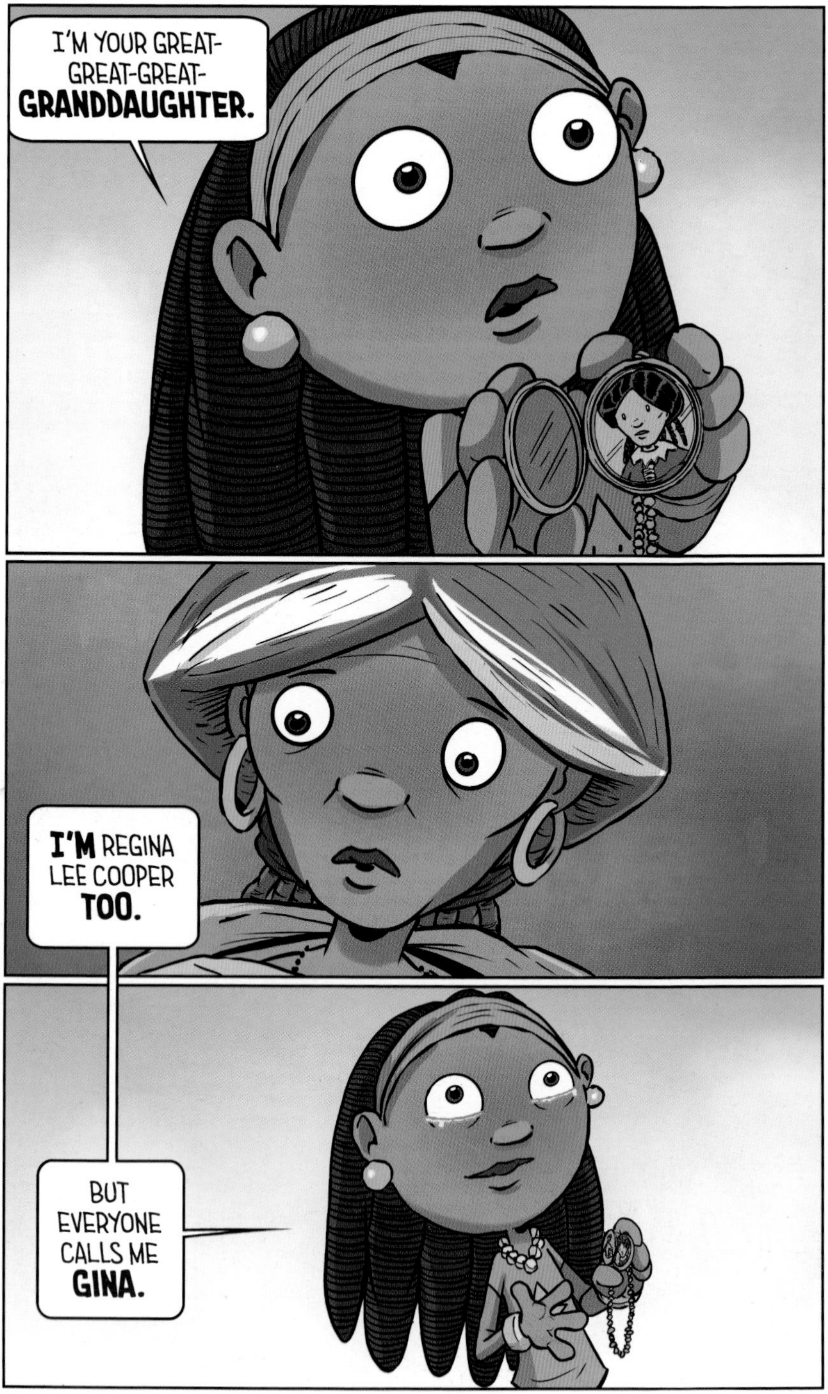
I'M YOUR GREAT-GREAT-GREAT-GRANDDAUGHTER.
I'M REGINA LEE COOPER TOO.
BUT EVERYONE CALLS ME GINA.

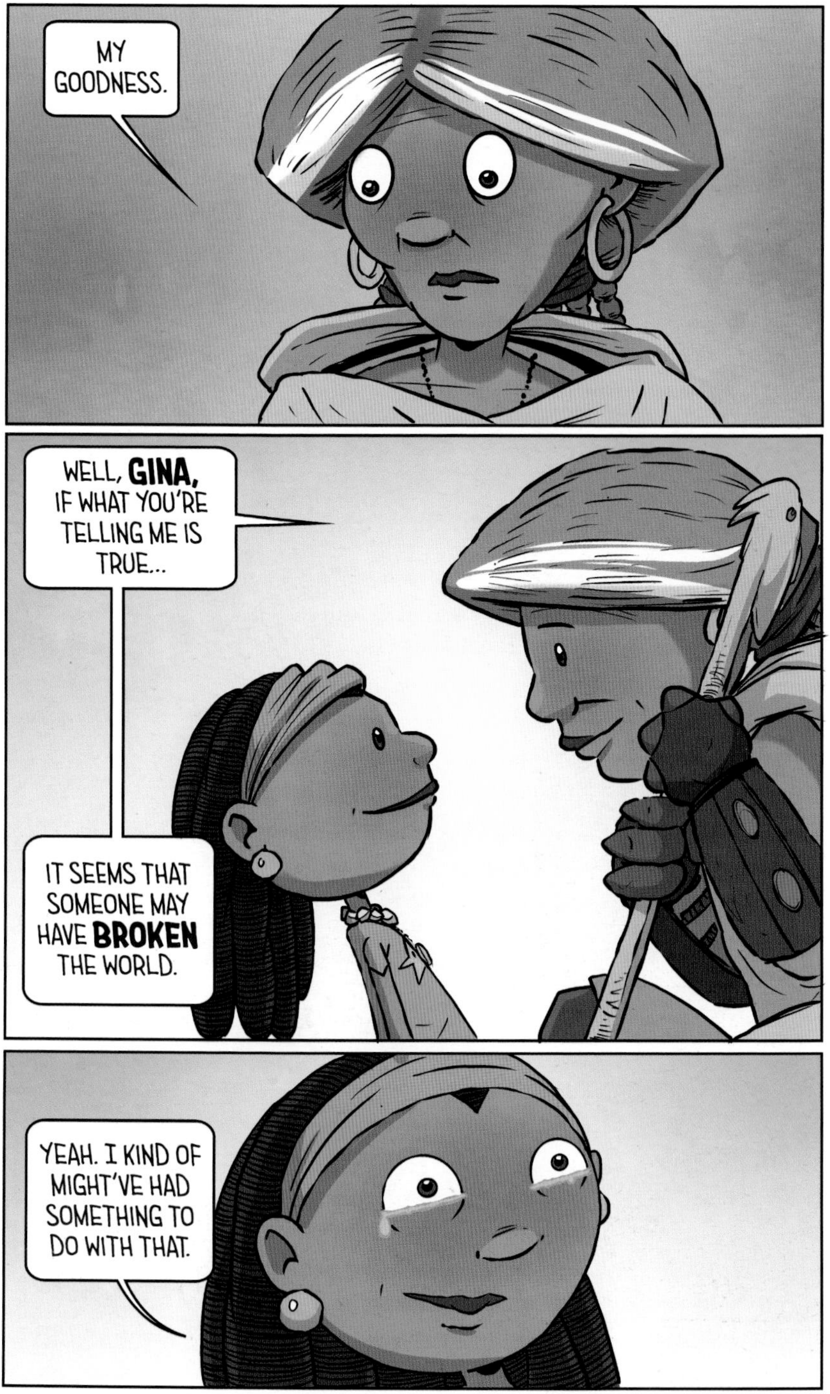
MY GOODNESS.
WELL, **GINA,** IF WHAT YOU'RE TELLING ME IS TRUE...
IT SEEMS THAT SOMEONE MAY HAVE **BROKEN** THE WORLD.
YEAH. I KIND OF MIGHT'VE HAD SOMETHING TO DO WITH THAT.

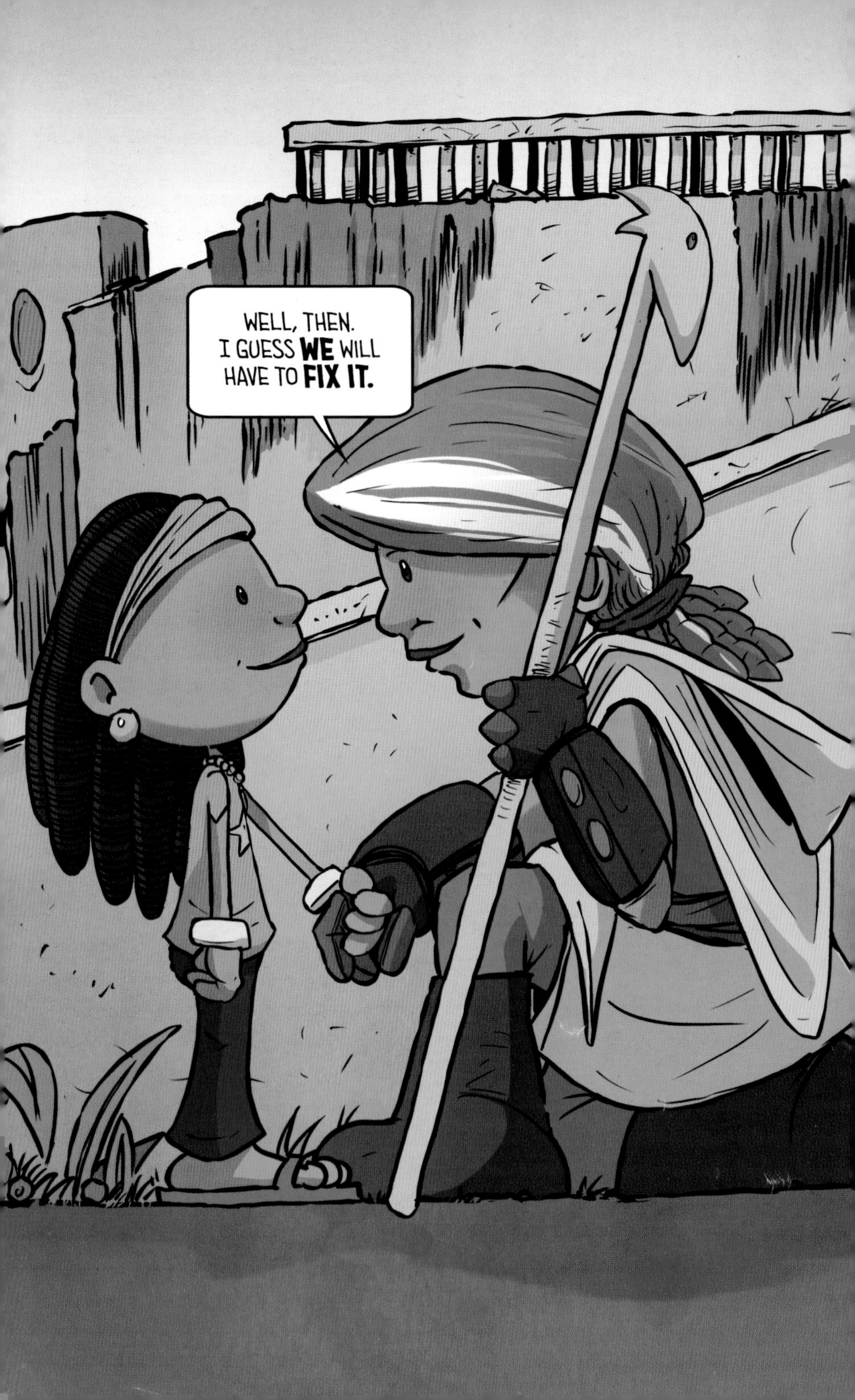
WELL, THEN. I GUESS **WE** WILL HAVE TO **FIX IT.**

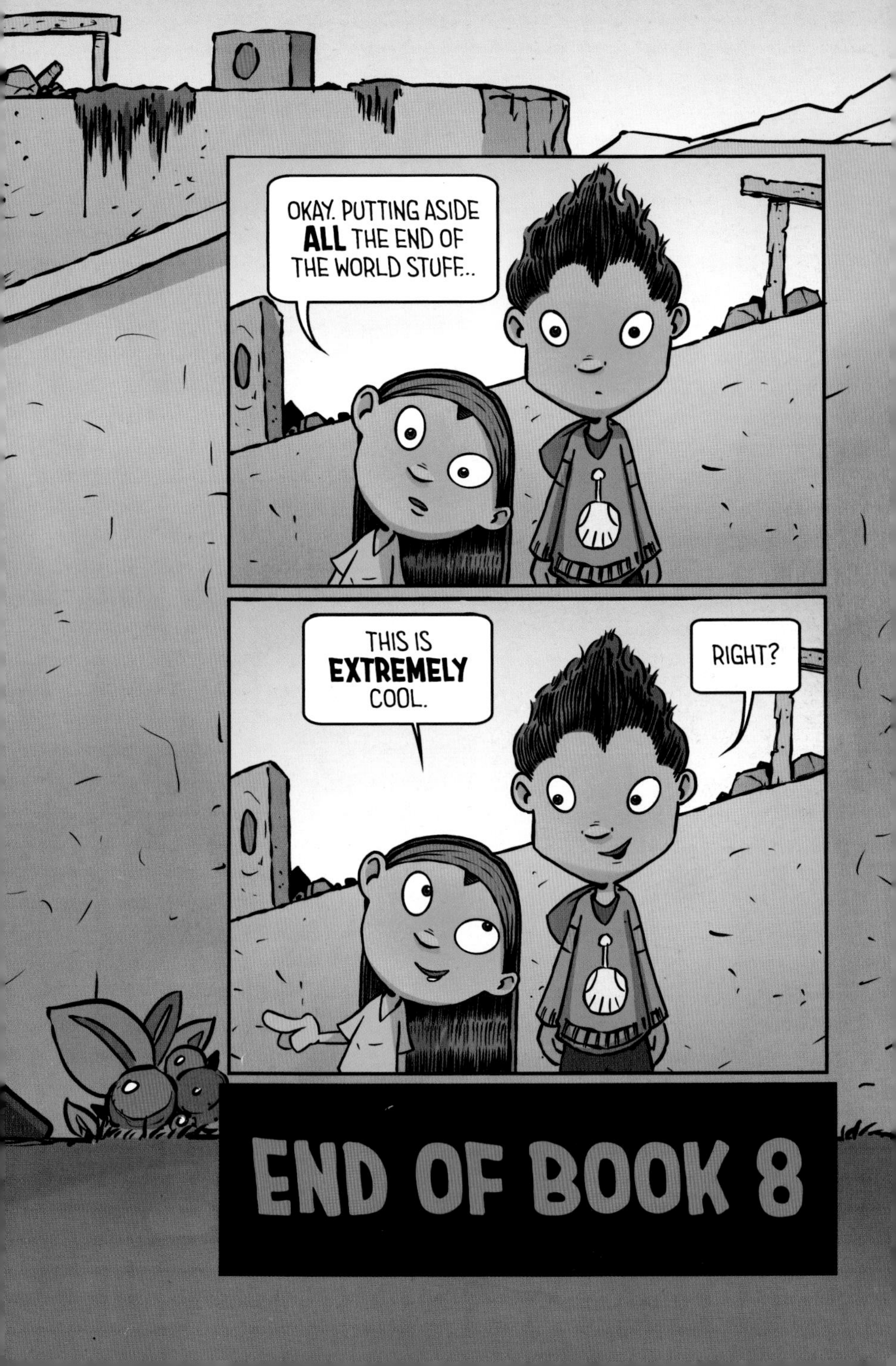
OKAY. PUTTING ASIDE **ALL** THE END OF THE WORLD STUFF...
THIS IS **EXTREMELY** COOL.
RIGHT?
END OF BOOK 8

Find out what happens next in—

HiLo

GiNA AND THE LAST CITY ON EARTH

BOOK 9 coming in spring 2023!

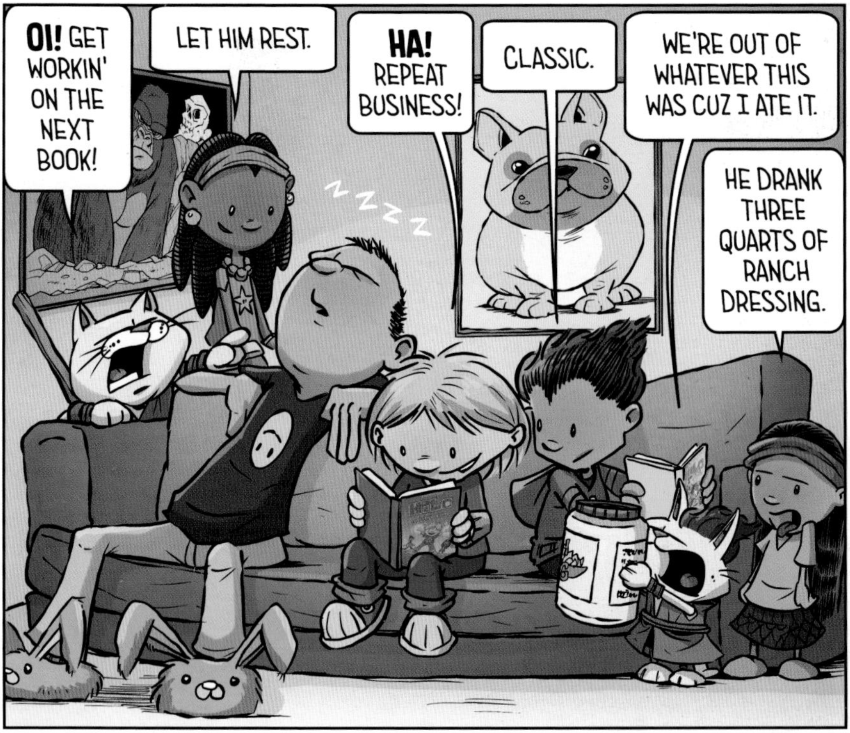
OI! GET WORKIN' ON THE NEXT BOOK!
LET HIM REST.
HA! REPEAT BUSINESS!
CLASSIC.
WE'RE OUT OF WHATEVER THIS WAS CUZ I ATE IT.
HE DRANK THREE QUARTS OF RANCH DRESSING.
ZZZZ

JUDD WINICK is the creator of the award-winning, **New York Times** bestselling Hilo series. Judd grew up on Long Island with a healthy diet of doodling, **X-Men** comics, the newspaper strip **Bloom County,** and **Looney Tunes.** Today, he lives in San Francisco with his wife, Pam Ling; their two kids; their cats, Troy and Abed; and far too many action figures and vinyl toys for a normal adult. Judd created the Cartoon Network series **Juniper Lee;** has written superhero comics, including Batman, Green Lantern, and Green Arrow; and was a cast member of MTV's **The Real World: San Francisco.** Judd is also the author of the highly acclaimed graphic novel **Pedro and Me,** about his **Real World** roommate and friend, AIDS activist Pedro Zamora. Visit Judd and Hilo online at juddspillowfort.com or find him on Twitter at @JuddWinick.

SOMETIMES THE UNIVERSE

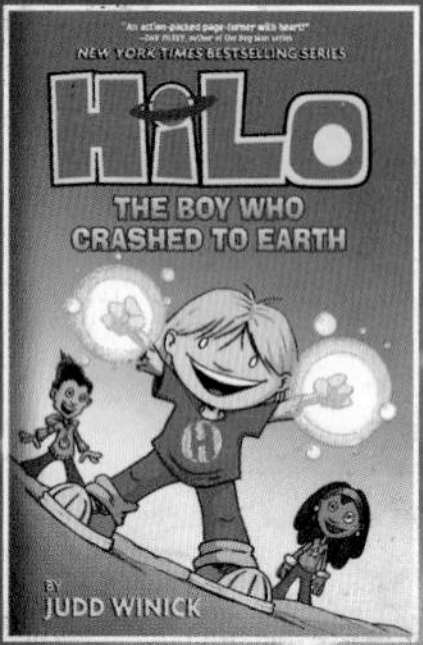
HiLo
THE BOY WHO CRASHED TO EARTH
BY JUDD WINICK

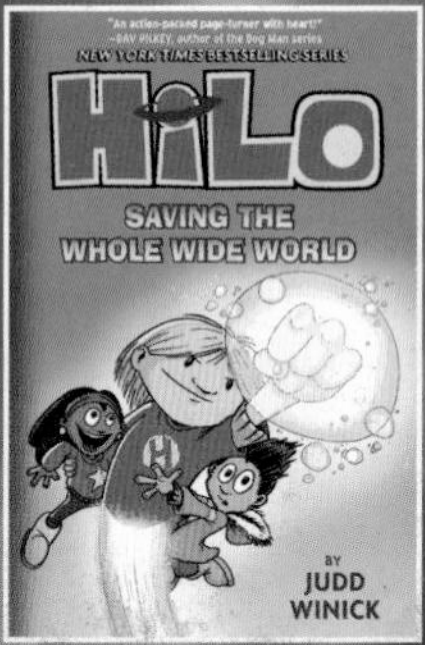
HiLo
SAVING THE WHOLE WIDE WORLD
BY JUDD WINICK

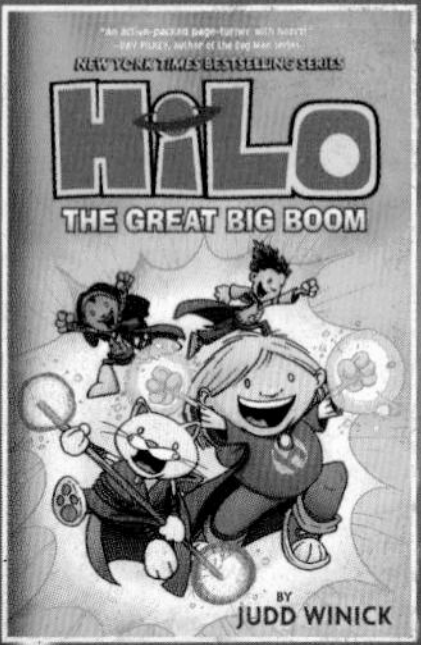
HiLo
THE GREAT BIG BOOM
BY JUDD WINICK

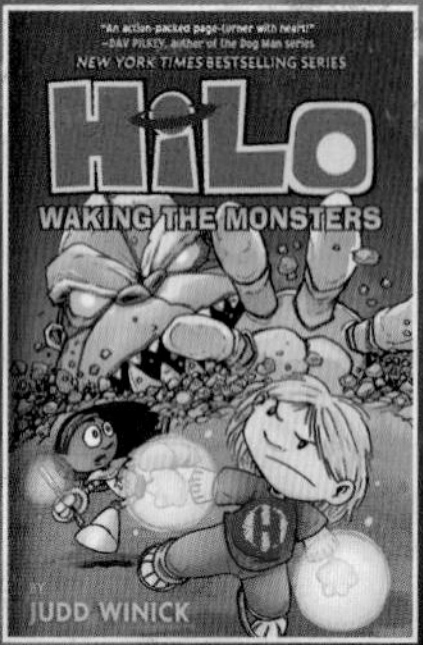
HiLo
WAKING THE MONSTERS
BY JUDD WINICK

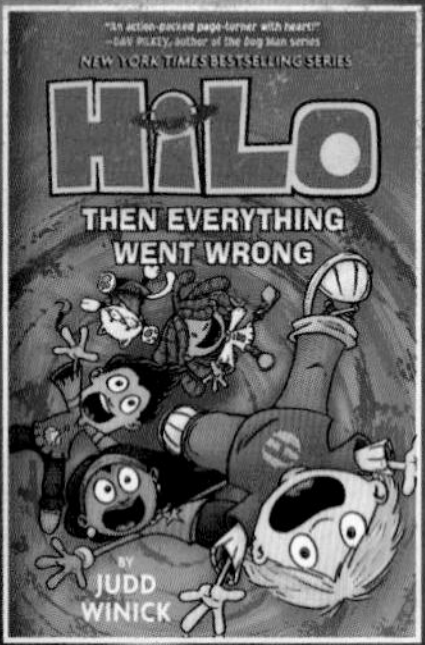
HiLo
THEN EVERYTHING WENT WRONG
BY JUDD WINICK

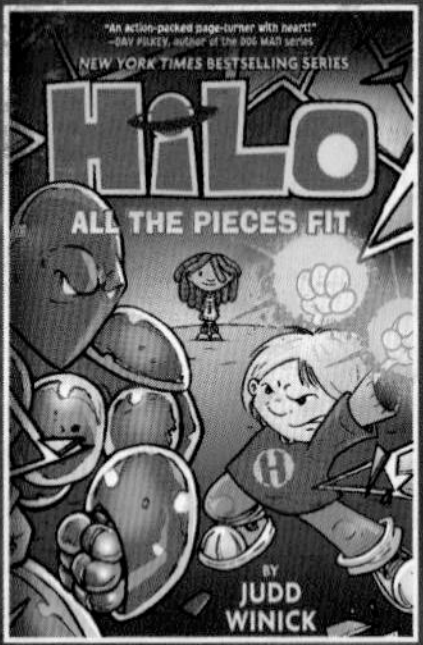
HiLo
ALL THE PIECES FIT
BY JUDD WINICK

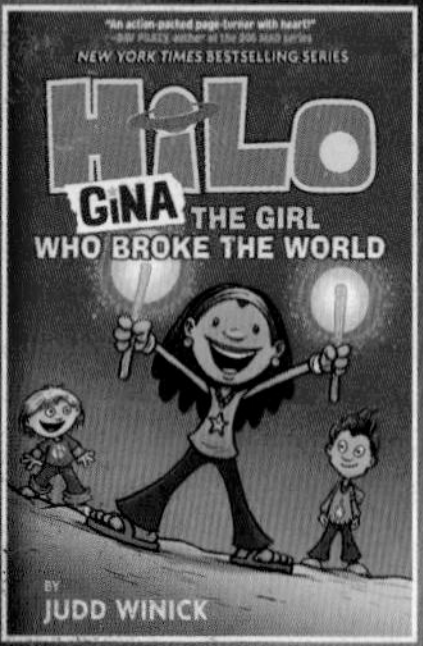
HiLo
GINA THE GIRL WHO BROKE THE WORLD
BY JUDD WINICK

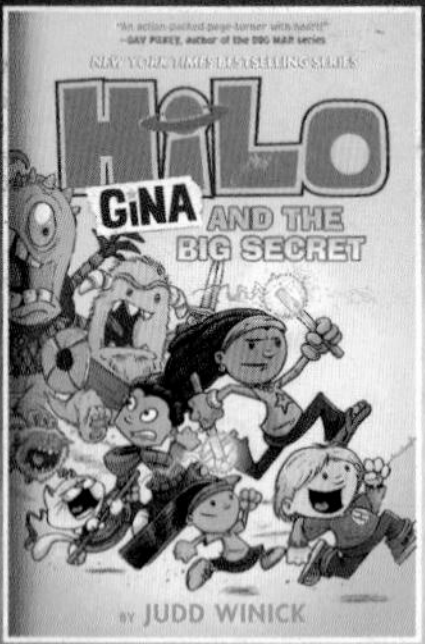
HiLo
GINA AND THE BIG SECRET
BY JUDD WINICK

Collect them all!